The Conflict Unending

A Lost Fleet Novel

(*The Originator Wars*, Book 3)

By
Raymond L. Weil

USA Today Best Selling Author

Raymond L. Weil

Books in The Originator Wars Series

The Originator Wars: Universe in Danger (Book 1)
The Originator Wars: Search for the Lost (Book 2)
The Originator Wars: Conflict Unending (Book 3)

Website: http://raymondlweil.com/

Copyright © January 2018 by Raymond L. Weil
All Rights Reserved
Cover Design by Humblenations.com
ISBN-13:978-1983726811
ISBN-10:1983726818

DEDICATION

To my wife Debra for all of her patience while I sat in front of my computer typing. It has always been my dream to become an author. I also want to thank my children for their support.

Raymond L. Weil

This book is a work of fiction. Names, characters, places, and incidents are either products of the author's imagination or used fictitiously. Any resemblance to actual events, locales, or persons, living or dead, is purely coincidental. All rights reserved. No part of this publication can be reproduced or transmitted in any form or by any means without permission in writing from the author.

The Originator Wars: Conflict Unending

The Originator Wars: Conflict Unending
A Lost Fleet Novel

Chapter One

The Eternal Fleet dropped out of hyperspace twelve million kilometers from the large fleet base of the Originators. Twelve thousand massive ships were in the fleet formation. Each vessel was four kilometers in length, eight hundred meters in width, and six hundred and seventy meters from the top of the hull to the bottom. The ships were armed with heavy energy cannons and antimatter missiles. Sensor arrays, communication dishes, and hundreds of hatches covered the warships. This was a fleet designed for one purpose and one purpose only; war!

"We've been detected," reported Marloo at Communications. "Eternal battlecruisers are forming up between us and the fleet base."

"They must have detected us before we dropped out of hyperspace," said Lomart from Tactical.

"This is their only base in this galaxy," reported Garald, the ship's sensor operator.

Fleet Commander Tarsal nodded. "That is why we chose this galaxy to attack. It has only the one base. Once we destroy it the Originator presence in this galaxy will be terminated."

Tarsal had direct orders from First Leader Clondax to eliminate as many of these Originator fleet bases as possible. The Originators controlled six hundred and fourteen galaxies. However, there were Dyson Spheres in only two hundred and twelve of them. The rest were protected by the large fleet bases. This galaxy was on the far side of Originator space away from Galaxy X-938, which was the closest Originator galaxy to Eternal space. The Originators would not be expecting an attack here. Also, after the stinging defeat by the Originators and the Humans in that star cluster the Originators were experimenting in, Tarsal wanted revenge.

Torun, the military AI assigned to the fleet base gazed in sadness at the tactical display showing the Eternal fleet rapidly approaching his base. It had been detected in hyperspace earlier and the defending fleet ordered to prepare to protect the base. "Inform Fleet Admiral Strong we will not be able to hold. The Eternal fleet preparing to attack us is too strong. We will try to cause as much damage as possible but we are heavily outnumbered."

Just outside the fleet base a small intergalactic communications vortex formed. It allowed almost instantaneous communication between the fleet base and the Communications and Transport hub.

Torun gazed at the viewscreens showing the advancing Eternals. Just a few more weeks and stronger weapons would have been added to the fleet base. Dark energy cannons were planned for all fleet bases as well as the Shrieels, weapons that might have kept the Eternals at bay. "Activate the energy shield and prepare all weapons to fire." Around Torun, the other AIs followed his orders without hesitation. There were no living beings in the fleet base; a few hundred AIs and those AIs assigned to the battlecruisers were the only intelligent beings. The Originators considered their AIs to be life forms and treated them accordingly. There were several thousand of the small repair robots as well as a full company of combat robots on board the base as well.

In space between the Eternal fleet and the fleet base two hundred Originator battlecruisers formed up. Each battlecruiser was two thousand meters in length and heavily armed. These were not the new more heavily armed battlecruisers being produced at the Shrieels but the older ones responsible for protecting the two thousand and eighteen fleet bases scattered throughout the six hundred and fourteen Originator controlled galaxies. The battlecruisers had been updated as much as possible, and new more powerful battlecruisers were being built in the fleet base's four construction bays. Unfortunately none were ready.

The two fleets closed with neither showing any signs of backing off. The Originator ships moved closer together with their energy shields nearly overlapping, adjusting their formation into a wedge aimed directly at the heart of the approaching Eternal vessels. The shields and weapons had been strengthened as much as possible, and it was hoped they would be able to stand up at least briefly to the Eternal energy weapons.

-

Fleet Commander Tarsal studied his tactical display. There were none of the larger ships of the race allied with the Originators or the larger Originator battlecruisers. It had been a shock to learn that actual living Originators still existed. One of them had spoken to First Leader Clondax at the battle in the Originator star cluster. How many Originators were still living was open conjecture in the Council of Eternals; it might be just a few hundred or several thousand. It was still unknown what had been occurring at the mysterious base in that star cluster. The Council of Eternals were convinced it was some type of advanced research facility. As to what type of research would probably never be known as the entire facility, both in orbit and on the planet had been destroyed.

"We're nearly in engagement range," reported Garald from the Sensors.

Tarsal had spread the fleet out into a half globe formation with the inside of the globe empty of ships. This would allow his fleet to partially englobe the Originator fleet and destroy it. "Remember, we want to capture this base intact to study its technology and see what we can learn about Originator space." His fleet heavily outnumbered the defenders and he expected few if any losses to his fleet. This should be a swift and easy victory.

"Weapons locked on," reported Lomart from Tactical.

"Fire!" ordered Tarsal. He still felt anger from the stinging defeat at the Originator star cluster. It was time to show the Originators the real power of the Eternals.

Energy weapons fire erupted from each side within just a few seconds of one another. Both began firing antimatter missiles in overwhelming numbers. Space lit up with the fury of thousands of explosions.

Energy beam fire from the Eternal battlecruisers slammed into the main part of an Originator warship, setting off massive explosions and hurling glowing debris into space. The ship seemed to shudder as secondary explosions began tearing it apart. In a final explosion the ship disintegrated, sending flaming debris in every direction.

In the Eternal fleet, one of their massive battlecruisers was under heavy attack from twelve Originator battlecruisers. The energy shield fluctuated and flared up brightly as gravitonic cannon fire and antimatter missiles pummeled it. Suddenly a gravitonic beam penetrated, blowing out a huge section of the hull. Then an antimatter missile detonated, nearly splitting the ship in two. The weakening shield wavered and then failed completely. Dozens of gravitonic beams and antimatter missiles struck the damaged vessel. In moments it ceased to exist. In its place, a small star was born as antimatter explosions annihilated the four-kilometer long warship.

Fleet Commander Tarsal watched the tactical displays and the viewscreens as the defending Originator fleet was slowly pushed back toward their fleet base. Ship after ship was dying as screens were overloaded and Eternal energy beams tore the defending battlecruisers apart. Occasionally an Eternal antimatter missile would send a ship to oblivion.

"One hundred and seventeen Originator battlecruisers have been eliminated," reported Garald.

"Our own losses?"

"Fourteen vessels so far."

In all the years Tarsal had been in the Eternal military, only the Originators and their allied race had been able to destroy an Eternal vessel. The Eternal Council was still reeling from the defeat at the Originator star cluster. "Continue the attack. Our losses are inconsequential." Tarsal flexed his hand, feeling the strength from his nanites. He was strong enough that he could crush a normal organic being. The nanites the Eternals fused with their bodies made them the most powerful race in the known universe. He was determined to bring victories to the Eternals no matter what the cost.

-

In space, the battle intensified as the weapons from the fleet base opened up. Antimatter beams, gravitonic cannons, and hundreds of antimatter missiles were directed at the inbound Eternal fleet. Several more Eternal vessels vanished as weapons fire knocked down their screens, leaving the ships vulnerable to attack. However, the Originator fleet was nearly destroyed and losing ships at an ever-increasing rate even with the tremendous firepower from the fleet base. The battle would not last much longer.

-

"We cannot stop them," reported Sheree, a female AI operating the sensor console in the fleet base's Command Center. "There are simply too many of them. Our gravitonic cannons are causing considerable damage as well as our antimatter beams. We just need more of them."

Torun accepted his forces would be defeated. He just needed to make this as costly as possible to the Eternals. "Have the self-destruct charges been set?" These were antimatter warheads, which had been hastily placed throughout the fleet base. The Eternals could not be allowed access to the fleet base's core computer and database.

"Yes," replied Mannart from his tactical post. "We can detonate them at your command. Combat robots have also been deployed at strategic locations throughout the base in case the Eternals try to board."

Torun gazed at a viewscreen. Only a handful of Originator battlecruisers were still fighting; the rest had been destroyed. He had only recently been created as the Originators and the Humans felt more military AIs were needed to command the many fleet bases and ships of the Originators. His life was going to be extremely short compared to the average lifespan of an AI, which was in the tens of thousands of years. "We will let them come in close and then detonate all the warheads simultaneously." While Torun regretted his life would be so short, he knew his duty as a military AI and had no problem fulfilling it.

On the viewscreens, the few surviving Originator ships were lit up by increasing fire from the inbound Eternal fleet. Ships were dying rapidly as defensive fire lessened. Even the fleet base was beginning to shake occasionally as antimatter missiles and Eternal energy beams struck its powerful shield. The fleet base was protected by the new triplex energy shield as well as more powerful energy weapons. It would not be as easy to destroy as the Eternals believed.

-

Fleet Commander Tarsal watched as the last Originator battlecruiser died in a pyre of energy as hundreds of antimatter missiles blew it into oblivion.

"Originator fleet has been destroyed," confirmed Garald.

"Focus our weapons fire on the fleet base. I want its weapons disabled and then prepare our warrior robots to board and eliminate all opposition."

The *Conqueror* suddenly shook violently as a gravitonic beam from the fleet base penetrated its screen, striking the hull. Warning alarms sounded, and several red lights flared to life on the damage control console.

"Major damage to the stern," reported the Eternal at damage control. "We have a hole in our hull forty meters wide and seventy deep. That gravitonic beam went right through our energy screen."

"All ships are to focus their energy weapons fire on that base," ordered Tarsal. It was evident to him the weapons on the base were far more powerful than those used by the Originator ships. This might pose a problem with his plans to board the base and take it intact.

"Are we still transmitting data?" asked Torun as he kept abreast of the ongoing battle. He had watched as the Eternals destroyed the last defending Originator battlecruiser, sending it into oblivion.

"Yes, the intergalactic communications vortex is still open," answered the AI at Communications. "We're transmitting all of our data on the battle as well as live video."

Torun hoped this information would be useful to Fleet Admiral Strong and the others back at the Communications and Transport Hub.

The fleet base was shaking more often now. On the damage control console red lights were steadily flaring into existence. The base was beginning to take damage as Eternal energy beams occasionally managed to penetrate the triplex energy shield. Explosions could be heard through the thick battle armor of the Command Center. Across the base repair robots were scurrying about trying to repair the growing damage.

On one of the viewscreens, an Eternal battlecruiser exploded as the base's powerful gravitonic beams ripped it in two. Others were being damaged but due to their size continued to fight.

"We've managed to take out six more of their battlecruisers," reported Mannart. "Strength of the energy shield is down to 42 percent. It will fail within ten minutes."

Torun looked around the Command Center. None of the AIs showed any fear of their immediate demise. "Send a final message to Fleet Admiral Strong. We will activate the self-destructs upon failure of the energy shield. The Eternals will glean no information from the ruins of this base."

The fleet base shook more violently and for a moment the lights dimmed but then returned to full brightness. The damage control console was now covered with more red lights than green. Torun knew the end was near.

Fleet Commander Tarsal nodded in satisfaction as more energy beams were now penetrating the steadily weakening energy shield of the Originator fleet base. The warrior robots were inside their assault shuttles ready to breach the hull. No doubt there would be Originator combat robots inside but Tarsal had no doubt the Eternal warrior robots would prevail. On the screen, a massive explosion occurred on the fleet base, hurling huge pieces of debris into space. Antimatter projectors and gravitonic cannons were being annihilated, reducing the firepower focused on the Eternal fleet. Even so, he watched as another Eternal battlecruiser was obliterated by massed antimatter missile fire from the base.

"Fleet base's energy field has failed," reported Garald. "That last explosion must have damaged their power system."

"Hold fire and launch the assault shuttles," ordered Tarsal. The Council of Eternals would be pleased with the information gathered from the Originator base.

On the tactical display, twenty shuttles departed the fleet and headed toward the fleet base. Soon they would breach the hull and release their loads of warrior robots. The robots would sweep through the base, securing it and its valuable computers.

Torun watched in silence as the Eternal assault shuttles neared the base. He would initiate the self-destruct sequence once they were in range. He planned on taking them out when the antimatter warheads detonated. It was quiet in the Command Center as the AIs waited for their end. It was gratifying to know they now served living Originators.

The shuttles reached the base and explosives were set off, penetrating the hull. Reports came in from several areas of the fleet base that Eternal warrior robots were inside. Without hesitation Torun reached forward and touched the icon on his command console, which would activate the warheads. He could have done it with a simple command from his neural implant but he preferred this time to touch the icon, which would kill them all as well as the enemy.

In a flash of brilliant light, the fleet base turned into a miniature nova, destroying all twenty of the Eternal assault shuttles. A few moments later the light died down revealing a mass of twisted wreckage. The fleet base was no more.

Fleet Commander Tarsal stared coldly at the ship's viewscreen. He had not been expecting the military AI in charge of the fleet base to take such a drastic step. He strongly suspected this strategy was the result of the mysterious Humans who were aligned with the Originators. Future battle strategies would have to be modified to take this into account.

"Set a course for our next target," Tarsal ordered. There was another galaxy nearby that only held four fleet bases. He intended to destroy all of them before returning to Eternal space.

At the Communications and Transport Hub Fleet Admiral Jeremy Strong, Councilor Bartoll, Commander Belson, and Ariel were watching and listening to the reports coming in from Torun and his besieged fleet base. They continued to watch until the incoming video turned to static, indicating the destruction of the base. They were in the large Communications Center in the Tower.

"That's it," said Angela as she turned to face Jeremy. "All data being broadcast from the fleet base has stopped."

"Destroyed," said Bartoll, shaking his head. "I was not expecting the Eternals to strike so far away and so swiftly."

"You must remember," answered Jeremy. "The Eternals have been conquering galaxies for over a thousand years. They are used to fighting battles and have no doubt developed strategies for quick conquests. They chose Galaxy X-257 since it had only one fleet base protecting it and there is no Dyson Sphere there." He turned toward Ariel. She was a Human built AI with dark hair and looked like a young woman in her early twenties. "What is the nearest galaxy with only a few fleet bases? That may be their next target. That fleet is too large to have been sent against only one galaxy."

"Galaxy X-268," replied Ariel promptly. "There are only four Originator fleet bases in that particular galaxy."

Jeremy let out a deep breath. "We need to rush our deployment of the dark energy cannons. These bases are too vulnerable." The dark energy cannons were a development of the Originators from the Lost Originator star cluster and extremely deadly to Eternal warships.

"I will put it before the council," replied Bartol. "But I agree; we need those cannons to protect the fleet bases."

"I would recommend increasing the size of the fleets protecting those fleet bases in Galaxy X-268," suggested Commander Belson. "It may cause the Eternals to think twice before attacking them. We cannot allow them to pick off the galaxies in our space which don't have Shrieels."

"Those ships would have to come from the nearest Dyson Sphere," said Ariel as she scanned the database for the nearest one. "Galaxy X-243 has the necessary ships. However, I would suggest sending some of the new battlecruisers as well to reinforce the bases. We could send four fleets of twelve hundred ships each, one thousand regular Originator battlecruisers and two hundred of the newer ones. The latter with their triplex energy shields and more powerful energy weapons will be a greater threat to the Eternals."

"We should send a few dreadnaughts along as well," suggested Jeremy. "Ariel, contact that Dyson Sphere and arrange for those fleets to be sent to the fleet bases in Galaxy X-268. Add ten dreadnaughts to each fleet." Jeremy hoped the addition of the larger ships might deter the Eternals from attacking. "Also send a warning to all four of the fleet bases in Galaxy X-268 that an Eternal fleet is in the neighborhood and might be dropping by. Make sure the four bases know to expect the reinforcing fleets."

For months since the battle at the Lost Originator star cluster, it had been quiet. It seemed now that was about to change.

Later, after the others had left, Jeremy stood talking to Angela. She was nearly seven months pregnant and could not wait to have her next child. The girls had been planning for months what they were going to do when they had their children. Kelsey and Katie were also pregnant with Katie expecting twins. Jeremy didn't think Kevin was ever going to get over Katie telling him she was having two babies.

"Any word from Rear Admiral Barnes?" Kathryn had left over a month ago to speak to the Federation about furnishing fleet personnel for the Originator fleets. Even though there were a large number of Humans, Altons, and Carethians on the Dyson Sphere where they had their new homes, it was not enough to fight an all out war against the Eternals. After speaking with the Originator Council, they had agreed to allow the Federation to send help.

Angela shook her head. "No, they should have arrived there days ago. I don't understand why we haven't heard anything."

Jeremy didn't either. They needed the Federation and its resources to fight this war against the Eternals. Without the Federation's aid, they would be sending ships into combat with just AI crews. It had already been demonstrated while the AIs, particularly the military AIs, were well qualified to command a ship their losses were considerably higher than those of crewed vessels.

"I'm sure there's nothing to be worried about," said Ariel, standing there with her hands on her shapely hips. "Rear Admiral Barnes and her father can handle the Federation."

The Originators had made Ariel an android body similar to their own AIs. In almost every way, it functioned like a normal Human body. It was warm, she could feel, breathe, experience emotions, and even eat. She could easily pass for a young Human woman if she wanted to.

"Politics," said Angela in frustration. "I guarantee you the Federation Council is tied up in politics trying to decide what to do."

Jeremy looked over at Ariel. "Have you sent the messages to the Dyson Sphere about sending the support fleets?"

Ariel nodded. "Yes, the fleets should be leaving within the next few hours. They should easily arrive at the four fleet bases before the Eternals do."

"Let me know if you hear anything from Rear Admiral Barns," Jeremy said as he and Ariel turned to leave. The silence from Kathryn was worrisome. Jeremy hoped nothing had gone wrong.

—

Later, Jeremy was standing at the large open window, which looked out over the city the Originators had built for their Human friends. The city was large and impressive with over four million Humans occupying it. It was full of tall towers with ribbon-like walkways connecting them. It was like no other Human city ever built. It was unique and contained everything the Human race could ever want. Looking down at the street below, he could see vehicles traveling along the wide thoroughfares. Large green parks were visible where families could go to enjoy themselves. The city was pollution free and unusually quiet for containing so many people.

"It is a beautiful city," Jontel said. Jontel was an Originator and had been the military leader in charge of the large space station in the Lost Originators' star cluster.

Jeremy turned around to face Jontel. Over the months since they had returned from the star cluster Jontel and Jeremy had become good friends. "Have all of your people been awakened from stasis?"

Jontel nodded. "The last only a few days ago."

"What have they decided?" Jeremy was concerned many of them would want to return to their old homes in the other Dyson Spheres and not remain at the Communications and Transport Hub.

Jontel smiled. He knew why Jeremy was concerned. "Most have elected to stay and live in the Shrieels here at the hub. Only a few hundred thousand have elected to return to their own Shrieels. Even most of those have agreed to aid us in the war effort."

This was a relief to Jeremy. That meant nearly twelve million Originators would be remaining. "How do they feel about Humans, Altons, and Carethians being here at the hub?"

"At first many were shocked," Jontel admitted. "But when they learned of the new war against the Eternals and the role your people have played in helping Bartoll and even in finding us, nearly all agree it's best to have your people here aiding us. We cannot fight this war on our own; we are too few."

Jeremy and Jontel spoke for a while longer until it was time for Jeremy to head home. Grayseth and his mate, Marille, were coming over for a cookout. As a matter of fact all of the Special Five would be there. For months now Jeremy had remained at the Communications and Transport Hub. Kelsey and Katie had made it very plain they expected their husbands to be present at the birth of their children. Even Ariel was making big plans for the coming event. She and Clarissa were already calling them the new Special Children. Jeremy was uncomfortable with that name but knew there was nothing he could do to prevent it.

Chapter Two

Two weeks previously…

Rear Admiral Kathryn Barnes breathed out a long sigh of relief as the *Distant Horizon* and her accompanying fleet exited intergalactic hyperspace just inside the Milky Way Galaxy near the Human Federation of Worlds. She had the *Distant Horizon*, two dreadnaughts and ten of the new enhanced Originator battlecruisers with her. They wanted to make an impression on the Federation Council with their arrival.

"We're here," said Clarissa as she quickly checked the stellar coordinates. "We can be at Ceres in four more hours."

"What will your people say when they see our ships?" asked Camlin. Camlin was an Originator AI. She had dark brown hair with a slight bluish tint to her skin. She was very tall as were most Originator AIs at a little over seven feet.

Kathryn leaned back in her command chair. She had wondered about this as well. "We'll enter the solar system under stealth and drop our stealth fields when we reach Ceres." This should produce the maximum effect for their entrance into the solar system.

"It will feel strange to be back home," her father said. "I wonder how much it's changed."

"Ceres will still be there," said Clarissa, brushing her blonde hair back from her eyes. "It's just that most of the people are at the Communications and Transport Hub."

"Not all," Governor Barnes reminded Clarissa. "A few thousand remained behind."

"Andram, we're in range of your people. I want you to send a message to Ambassador Tureen asking him to meet us at Earth."

The Altons would no doubt play a big role in what was to come. The Federation Council could be swayed more easily if the Altons decided to support the war against the Eternals. When

Kathryn was here last that had not been a problem as Ambassador Tureen arranged for two million Altons to come to the Communications and Transport Hub.

"I have no doubt he will come, particularly if we offer some Originator technology as an inducement," replied Andram from his science console.

"Only a limited amount," cautioned Kathryn. "We're prepared to offer a better power system and increased sensor range as well as a few medical advances. More than that has to be approved by the new Originator Council. Captain Travers, send a message to Malrez on Careth telling him we've returned and would like to meet with him at Earth if he can come." Malrez was the chief clan leader of Careth. There was no doubt in Kathryn's mind he would support the war against the Eternals. The Carethians were intensely loyal to Grayseth and Fleet Admiral Strong.

Commander Grissim looked away from her command console, gazing at the viewscreen, which was full of familiar stars. "It feels good to be back home again."

Kathryn agreed. What concerned her most was last time they were here they had pretty much kidnapped millions of Federation citizens. Well, it wasn't really kidnapping as they had agreed to come voluntarily but the Federation hadn't been told. The first they knew was when they found Ceres and the ships around it empty of life. Nearly everyone had vanished. Kathryn left a message behind with former Fleet Admiral Hedon Streth. She wasn't sure how Fleet Admiral Nagumo and the Federation Council had felt when they were given the message. It was one of the things she was soon to find out.

"Set a course for the solar system," Kathryn ordered. "Let's go home."

-

Fleet Admiral Nagumo was in the large orbiting shipyard above Earth, which served as his command base. The shipyard was the largest in the Federation and heavily armed. Not only that, there were twelve huge battlestations around Earth that added to the firepower available in Earth orbit. Only the New Tellus System with its asteroid fortresses was more heavily defended.

He was speaking to Admiral Race Tolsen about the Ralift and reports of them still causing trouble on the outskirts of Shari space.

"The Ralift have been driven back to their prewar boundaries," Nagumo said as he gazed at a large star map showing the borders of Shari and Ralift space. "The Shari have not crossed the old border under pressure from our government. The Shari have too much to lose by angering us and risk some of the new trade deals being canceled. However, the Ralift have large fleets of their warships at the border and there's still sporadic fighting occurring."

"What about the AIs? Any signs of any of their vessels?"

Nagumo shook his head. "No, we're hoping you got the last of them though there are rumors there are still a few in Borzon space."

Race was about to respond when alarms began sounding and the Condition One alert was broadcast over the station's comm system.

"What the hell?" said Nagumo, his eyes widening in surprise. They were in the second most secure system in the Federation. How could there be a threat here?

"What is it?" asked Race as Nagumo spoke quickly to the station's Command Center. He put his comm device back down, his face pale as if he had just seen a ghost.

"Rear Admiral Barnes is back and she's brought some very large warships with her. Hell, the *Distant Horizon* is barely recognizable. If not for the ID codes they're broadcasting we would never have recognized the ship."

"Where are they? How soon before they arrive in the solar system?" Race's own flagship, the *WarHawk*, was docked to the shipyard.

Nagumo let out a deep breath of frustration. "They're already here in orbit around Ceres. They must have used some type of advanced stealth field. We didn't detect them until they dropped the field at Ceres. Governor Barnes is with her and requesting to speak with me and President Malle."

"What are you going to do?"

"Prep my flagship, the *Luna*, and fly out there. Want to come along?"

Race nodded. "I wouldn't miss this for anything."

Since returning from Shari space, Race had managed to pay a quick visit to Fleet Admiral Hedon Streth. He had been both amazed and frightened at what Hedon had confided to him in that brief meeting about where Rear Admiral Barnes had come from and what Fleet Admiral Strong was facing. He had not revealed to anyone what the former fleet admiral had told him. The return of Rear Admiral Barnes was not a surprise.

-

Several hours later the *Luna* and her escorts neared Ceres and upon the viewscreen, massive warships became visible. The first was the *Distant Horizon* at three thousand meters. Scans of the vessel indicated power readings totally off the scale. The next were the two dreadnaughts, each was 3,200 meters in length and then the ten battlecruisers at 2,200 meters.

"If the power readings from those ships are correct we don't have a weapon that can touch them," reported the sensor operator. "The *Distant Horizon* by herself could probably take out all the defenses in the solar system."

Fleet Admiral Nagumo nodded. "So I'd better not make them mad. See if you can raise either Rear Admiral Barnes or her father on the comm. We're close enough to see each other now. Helm, bring the fleet to a stop one thousand kilometers from the *Distant Horizon*." On the main viewscreen, the huge exploration dreadnaught became visible.

"I have Rear Admiral Barnes on the comm," reported the communications officer. "She is requesting you take a shuttle and come over to her ship to talk. She believes you will be very interested in what she has to offer."

Fleet Admiral Nagumo nodded. "Tell her I'm on my way and Admiral Race Tolsen will be accompanying me." When Rear Admiral Barnes had taken the people from Ceres, she had left some technology behind on a computer disk with Fleet Admiral Streth. Nagumo was curious as to what she was up to this time that she felt the need to offer further inducements. "Let's go, Race. I have a feeling this is going to be mind-boggling as she has had contact with the builders of the Dyson Sphere."

Race looked at the viewscreen. It was obvious neither Humans nor Altons had been involved in the redesign of the *Distant Horizon*. In many ways, it now looked like an alien vessel of war.

-

On the *Distant Horizon*, Kathryn watched as a shuttle left the *Luna* and began heading toward the exploration dreadnaught. It was escorted by four Talon fighters.

"The communications officer on the *Luna* is reporting Fleet Admiral Nagumo and Admiral Tolsen are on the shuttle," reported Captain Travers.

"Admiral Tolsen," said Governor Barnes, smiling approvingly. "He must have gotten a promotion. It will be good to see him. He's one of the better admirals in the Federation."

"He may be the best admiral in the Federation," replied Kathryn. She wondered what the odds were she could talk Fleet Admiral Nagumo into allowing Admiral Tolsen to return with them. They could certainly use some qualified admirals in the war against the Eternals. Jeremy was certainly going to need additional admirals as the fleet was expanded.

-

As they neared the *Distant Horizon*, Race could see the influence of Alton technology in its basic design. The Altons, along with Clarissa, Kelsey, and Katie had helped design the original *Distant Horizon*. While this ship was similar, it was considerably larger and obviously much heavier armed. The ship now looked deadly and almost sinister.

A large hatch slid open, revealing a brightly lighted flight bay. Race watched with interest as the shuttle entered and then landed without a jar. Looking out a nearby viewport, he saw a full platoon of Marines lined up waiting for them to disembark. "Looks like we have a welcoming committee," Race said as he stood up.

Fleet Admiral Nagumo glanced through the viewport at the waiting Marines who were standing at attention. Through a hatch he saw several of the *Distant Horizon's* officers enter and walk over to the Marines. "Let's go find out what's going on. After Rear Admiral Barnes last visit I didn't expect to ever see her again."

Opening the hatch the two walked down the ramp and halted in front of the Marines and the two ship officers.

Race's eyes opened wide at recognizing Clarissa. The other officer was Commander Anne Grissim. Race knew her from her days on the *StarStrike*.

"Fleet Admiral," Commander Grissim said saluting. "If the two of you will follow me, Rear Admiral Barnes and her father are in briefing room two near the Command Center."

Race reached out, touching Clarissa's arm. He was stunned when his hand brushed what felt like actual human flesh.

"Surprise," said Clarissa with a pleasant smile. "This is an android body the Originators built for me. It is very similar to a human body in most of its functions."

"I'm impressed," Race said. "I wasn't expecting this." As the four of them walked through the flight bay toward the hatch to enter the ship Race couldn't help but wonder what other surprises were ahead. Looking around the bay he saw a few Anlon bombers and Talon fighters lined up near the walls. If he remembered correctly, Major Carl Arcles was the CAG on the ship.

As they made their way to the briefing room Race felt overwhelmed by all the automation and the small repair robots which were everywhere. He realized the crew was much smaller than what he was accustomed to. It was obvious while there had been major changes to the outside of the ship the inside had been redesigned as well. It was almost as if the ship had been taken apart and put back together again.

Kathryn was waiting nervously for Fleet Admiral Nagumo to arrive in the briefing room. She wasn't sure how she would be received after her last visit and leaving with so many Federation citizens.

"I can handle Fleet Admiral Nagumo," her father said with a gentle smile. "I've had to deal with military people all of my life, even back when I was a senator."

The door opened and the two Federation officers entered. Kathryn wasn't sure if she should stand up and salute or what. Technically, she was part of the Originator military forces under the command of Fleet Admiral Jeremy Strong. Taking a deep breath, she decided it was best not to offend Nagumo. Kathryn stood and gave a brief salute.

"Rear Admiral Barnes," said Nagumo, returning the salute. "I wasn't expecting to see you again. Not after the stunt you pulled last time."

"Have a seat," said Governor Barnes, indicating for the two Federation officers to sit down. "We have a lot to talk about. The very future of this galaxy and the Federation is at risk. I need to tell you about a new and extremely dangerous enemy, one which could be at your doorstep any day. This enemy possesses ships as powerful as the ones Rear Admiral Barnes has under her command and maybe some even more powerful. I think it would be wise if you listen."

Fleet Admiral Nagumo shook his head and smiled. "I knew there was a reason why I missed you being around. You've never had a problem telling the military how things are even if it makes them angry." Nagumo sat down with Admiral Tolsen taking a seat next to him. "Well, I'm listening."

Taking a deep breath, Governor Barnes began speaking of the Originators and the Eternals. For nearly two hours he spoke, leaving nothing out. Several times either Fleet Admiral Nagumo or Admiral Tolsen stopped him, asking detailed questions.

Sometimes Kathryn had to answer from her experience in combat against the Eternals.

"And that's a brief rundown on where we're at now," said Governor Barnes, leaning back in his chair and gazing at the two Federation officers.

Fleet Admiral Nagumo felt overwhelmed by what he had just heard. The computer disk Rear Admiral Barnes had left with Fleet Admiral Streth had covered some of this but not in such detail. "How soon can these Eternals, as you call them, show up here?"

Governor Barnes looked over at Kathryn, indicating for her to answer.

"We don't know," Kathryn replied. "After their defeat at the Lost Originator star cluster they pulled back to their own galaxies. Fleet Admiral Strong and Councilor Bartoll believe the Eternals could have a fleet numbering in the millions as they currently control over ten thousand galaxies. However, a large number of those ships are tied down in patrol duty keeping those galaxies pacified and under Eternal rule."

"This is an Eternal warship," said Clarissa. On the large viewscreen in the briefing room an Eternal battlecruiser appeared. Next to it was one of the Originator dreadnaughts for size comparisons. "As you can see, the average Eternal ship is larger and more heavily armed than anything we currently have."

Admiral Tolsen spent a moment examining the Eternal warship and then he looked over at Rear Admiral Barnes. "What do you want of us? I suspect this isn't just a friendly visit."

Kathryn took a deep breath and then replied. "With the construction capacity of the Originator Dyson Spheres and their fleet bases, we have the ability to build warships at a very fast rate. Unfortunately we don't have crews for so many vessels. We're having to depend on Originator AIs and their military AIs to operate and command many of the vessels. As a result our ship losses are much higher than they need to be. Some estimates indicate 30 to nearly 80 percent higher depending on the class of the ship and the experience of the military AI."

"You need crews," said Fleet Admiral Nagumo in sudden realization. "That's why you've come back. The Humans, Altons, and Carethians who went with you originally aren't enough."

Governor Barnes nodded. "No, they're not and many of the people who came back with us are not fleet personnel but civilians and scientists."

"Our new ships only need small crews," explained Kathryn, "a command crew and maybe a few engineers. Everything else in our ships can be done by the Originator AIs and their repair robots. We also have combat robots in place of Marines for ship security though a few Marines are still on board for command purposes."

"You're asking the Federation to commit to an intergalactic war against an enemy that outnumbers us by possibly millions to one," said Nagumo frowning. "You can't say for sure if these Eternals will ever even come here. By becoming involved we could be alerting them to our presence. I can't see the Federation Council agreeing."

Kathryn looked Nagumo directly in the eyes. "It's only the threat posed by the Originators that's kept the Eternals at bay all of these years. I can promise you if the Originators fall you will see Eternal warships in the skies above Earth very shortly afterward."

Fleet Admiral Nagumo was quiet for several long moments. "Do you have any video files of your battles against these Eternals?" He wanted to see more evidence of the power of these beings before making any type of commitment.

Kathryn looked over at Clarissa. "Show the videos."

For the next two hours Fleet Admiral Nagumo and Admiral Tolsen watched the horrid battles on the large viewscreen. They saw Eternal warships blowing Originator battlecruisers out of space and causing dreadful damage. Occasionally they saw the Originator fleets victorious after suffering heavy losses. The battle at the Lost Originators' star cluster held them enthralled for the longest. Several times Admiral Tolsen asked Clarissa to replay a section or magnify a view. When the video presentation ended, the two admirals looked at each other with pale faces. Never had they witnessed such firepower as the Eternals and Originators possessed. It made the AIs, Hocklyns, Shari, Borzon, and Ralift look like minor players in the grand scheme of things. Even the Federation would be overwhelmed if faced with such firepower.

"How many crews do you need?" asked Fleet Admiral Nagumo in a subdued voice.

"We have a Dyson Sphere at the Communications and Transport Hub the Originators are allowing us to settle. We would like to take as many volunteers as possible to colonize it. For the time being we would like to limit that to Humans, Altons, and Carethians."

"What about access to Originator technology?"

Kathryn looked at her father.

"That is open to discussion. You must realize it is very advanced, far more so than even the Altons. This technology could be very dangerous if it falls into the wrong hands or if used incorrectly."

"Do you have some technology you're willing to share with us now?" asked Race.

"Some," replied Governor Barnes, his brow lifting slightly. "It may be best to form a committee of scientists to determine what technology would be safe to introduce. Not only is some of this technology extremely dangerous it could tear apart the economic foundation of the Federation as well."

"What about the Dyson Sphere in this galaxy?" asked Fleet Admiral Nagumo, his eyes narrowing. "Will we be allowed access to it?"

"Access to the Dyson Sphere is not necessary or wise at this point," Kathryn said. "However, we can build what's called an Accelerator Ring which will allow faster hyperspace travel between the Milky Way and the Originators' Communications and Transport Hub. At the Hub some access will be granted to Originator technology under close supervision."

Governor Barnes leaned forward. "We need to move on this as quickly as possible. Fleet Admiral Strong is expecting more attacks by the Eternals at any time. We need those crews!"

"I have a lot more questions to ask, and I would like time to study some of those videos we just watched in more detail," said Nagumo, refusing to be rushed. "If I agree to take your cause to the Federation Council, we won't be able to keep the secret of the Originators' existence any longer. Only a few members of the council have seen the message you left with Fleet Admiral Streth. This time the entire council will have to be told in full what happened to the people here at Ceres as well as the others who went missing at New Tellus. I can tell you already there are some senators who will never agree to sending the people you need."

"I believe we could still get many volunteers from New Tellus, the Altons, and the Carethians," countered Governor Barnes in a calculating voice. "I would hate to see those worlds be the only ones which benefit from advanced Originator technology."

Admiral Tolsen began laughing. "You play a mean game of poker. I would hate to sit across from you in a game."

Fleet Admiral Nagumo stared at Governor Barnes for a long moment. "This is almost like the old days. Let's go over some more of this information and then see what we can come up with to convince the council."

—

A week passed and the *Distant Horizon* was being allowed to go into orbit above Earth. A number of the council members wanted to come aboard and tour the exploration dreadnaught. It had been a busy week with Governor Barnes spending most of it talking to individual members on the council. Many of the council members had been stunned when told about the Originators and the Eternals. President Malle had also requested Kathryn not attempt to contact Fleet Admiral Strong until the negotiations were over. He was concerned about the Eternals managing to trace the communications back to the solar system. Kathryn had assured him that wasn't possible but had agreed not to send a message. Kathryn wasn't pleased about this as contacting Jeremy was long overdue.

"We're in Earth orbit at twenty thousand kilometers," reported Sible from the Helm and Navigation. Sible was an Originator AI and very well versed in hyperspace travel and navigation.

"I'm concerned about moving the *Distant Horizon* here and leaving the rest of our fleet at Ceres," said Camlin. "What if this is a trick of some kind?"

"They have nothing that can harm our ship," stated Clarissa, folding her arms across her chest. "Besides, the council will feel safer visiting the ship with it so close to Earth."

"I'm keeping the ship at Condition Three just in case," Kathryn said. "There are a few members of the council I don't trust and I wouldn't put it past them to try some trickery. Lieutenant Barkley has also deployed his Marines throughout the ship to ensure our visitors don't wander into restricted areas." The *Distant Horizon* no longer had the huge Marine complement it once did. However, there were still enough on board to handle security. The combat robots had been placed in a cargo hold so as not to frighten the councilors.

"I've spoken to Ambassador Tureen," said Andram. "He's currently on Earth and is speaking to a few senators as well. I fully expect him to support sending more Altons to the Communications and Transport Hub. He seems quite interested in acquiring more Originator technology."

Kathryn nodded. She had been counting on the support of the Altons.

-

A few days later Kathryn, Commander Grissim, and Governor Barnes were each taking a group of Federation Senators on tours of the *Distant Horizon*.

"I can't believe the technology on this ship," said Senator Amy Karnes from New Tellus as several of the small and versatile repair robots moved past them in the corridor. They stopped, took a panel off the wall with their manipulator arms, used another instrument to take some readings, made a couple of adjustments, put the cover back on and then went on down the corridor.

"Do they always stop and take the ship apart like that?" asked Senator Karl Davis from Bliss, which was in the Epsilon Eridani System. "Who's watching to make sure they're not sabotaging the ship's systems?"

Kathryn laughed. "The repair robots are programmed to initiate basic repairs and maintenance on their own. They're supervised by the ship's main computer which in turn is watched over by Mikow Lall who is an Alton and by our own AI, Clarissa."

"I don't trust AIs," muttered Davis with a deep frown. "I'm against creating any more in the Federation."

"Don't forget the spider robots we use for construction," countered Senator Karnes. "They're used all over the Federation."

Senator Davis ignored her, refusing to reply.

They continued on the tour meeting several of the crew including Major Karl Arcles who took time to show them the main flight bay containing more of the Talon fighters and Anlon bombers as well as a number of shuttles.

"How effective are these against the Eternals?" asked Senator Karnes as she stood near one of the Talons. She reached out, placing her hand against the smooth metal hull.

Major Arcles shook his head. "They're not. None of the weapons we can place on a fighter or a bomber can penetrate an Eternal vessel's energy screen. In our battles so far the Eternals have not deployed any small attack craft."

"Just as I thought," said Davis emphatically. "It's a waste of Federation credits to be building more of these worthless space fighters."

Senator Karnes ignored Senator Davis as she continued to examine the Talon. "How big a threat do you think the Eternals are, Major?"

Major Arcles let out a deep breath. "The biggest threat we've ever faced. They've added mechanical nanites to their bodies, and they are no longer true organic beings. They believe themselves superior to every other life form."

"We've heard this before," said Senator Davis in disgust. "Every time the military wants something the threat is bigger and more dangerous than the one before. I've seen enough. My vote to involve the Federation in this foolish war is a big no!"

"Mine will be a yes," replied Senator Karnes, staring at Davis. "Keep your head buried in the sand. Someday you'll regret your foolishness."

Senator Davis whirled around and headed toward the open hatch. "I'm going back to the shuttle. I've seen and heard enough of this rubbish!"

Senator Karnes turned toward Kathryn. "Ignore him. He was always going to be a no vote."

Kathryn nodded. She knew what they were telling and showing the Federation Senators was hard for some of them to swallow. Some of them had shown fear when explained the danger the Eternals represented.

"Would you like to see the Command Center?" asked Kathryn. She liked Senator Karnes. Of course she was from New Tellus, which had been settled by the old Human Federation of Worlds survivors. New Tellus had always stood with Ceres and Governor Barnes. It felt good to know they still did.

-

Two days later Governor Barnes, Rear Admiral Barnes, Clarissa, Andram Muce, and Camlin stepped into the Federation Council chambers. The presence of Camlin created an instant stir as the Originator AIs on board the *Distant Horizon* had been kept out of sight from all the visitors.

With surprise Kathryn noticed the presence of Malrez, the leader of Careth. She had not expected him to arrive so quickly. Malrez must have already been in the Federation as Careth was thousands of light years away.

"Rear Admiral Barnes," roared Malrez, stepping forward and embracing her in a huge bear hug. "It is wonderful to see you again. When you have the time we must speak of Grayseth and the clans that have gone to this mysterious Dyson Sphere. My people are anxious to hear what hunts they have gone on."

Kathryn felt the air go from her lungs in one sudden whoosh.

Malrez stepped back in apology. "I am sorry. I forget at times how fragile you Humans are. I am pleased to inform you Careth will fully support this war against the Eternals. I have asked for two million volunteers from my world to go with you. There will be no problems finding enough volunteers from the clans. It will be an honor to join Grayseth and Fleet Admiral Strong as well as the others of the Special Five in this war."

The entire council chamber became quiet upon hearing this. There was a stunned look on several senators' faces. The mention of the Special Five still held a lot of sway in the Federation. It was a reminder to many of them who they were dealing with. If the council was to refuse the request for aid and the civilian public were to find out it could be bad news for many of the senators next time they came up for reelection.

"I would also like to travel with you to speak to Grayseth if possible."

Kathryn nodded. "I think that can be arranged." She was pleased with Malrez's announcement. It would help to put pressure on the Federation to follow suit. It was also good he had mentioned the Special Five as she had hesitated to play that card.

"The Altons pledge another six million volunteers," said Ambassador Tureen, stepping forward. "Many of them are fleet officers and recognize the threat posed by these Eternals. There are also a large number of scientists who would like to go and study Originator technology."

A number of senators began speaking to one another at this announcement. Some looked concerned and others excited.

President Malle stood up and gazed at his fellow council members. "Can we do no less? All of us have seen the videos of the battles against the Eternals. Is it not better to fight them in their own galaxies than in ours?"

"If we send our fleet personnel to Fleet Admiral Strong, who will protect us?" demanded Senator Davis. "I say we're better off keeping our people here at home and out of this foolish and dangerous war. It seems as if we constantly go from one war to the next. I say it's time to end these wars. Just think of what we could do if the credits spent on our military were spent on our worlds instead." Several other senators nodded their heads in agreement.

"I say we support Fleet Admiral Strong in this war," countered Senator Karnes. "He would not be calling for aid unless he felt it was necessary. Don't forget all the Special Five have done for our galaxy."

More senators began talking. Several were standing up, arguing with one another.

Kathryn was about to interrupt when she felt a hand touch her shoulder.

"May I speak?" asked Camlin. "I'm an Originator AI."

The senators all shifted their attention to her. Some looked surprised she could speak. Silence held the Council Chamber.

"This robot has no rights within these chambers," bellowed Senator Davis.

"Let her speak," said Senator Karnes, staring down Senator Davis. "She's no robot; she is an AI. What are you afraid of?"

"You may speak," said President Malle in a decisive voice. "I for one would like to hear what you have to say."

Camlin looked from one senator to the next and then began speaking. "As you are aware, in this galaxy there is an Originator Dyson Sphere."

"Yes, we are," answered President Malle. "Our military has already fought several battles protecting it."

"We thank you for your assistance," Camlin replied. "The Dyson Sphere is only one of two hundred and twelve in numerous galaxies within this section of the universe. At some point in the future, the Eternals will come to this galaxy because of the presence of the Dyson Sphere. You must realize due to its massive size it cannot be moved."

"You have said the Dyson Sphere is off limits to us," said Fleet Admiral Nagumo, sounding disappointed.

Camlin nodded. "Yes, due to the amount of Originator science and technology. However, what you are not aware of is the Originators also have massive fleet bases in all of the galaxies they control. For many years these bases have been inactive. Since the advent of the Eternals all have been reactivated. There are six such bases here in your galaxy."

"What!" bellowed Senator Davis, standing up, his face livid with rage. "You mean to tell me your people have six secret bases here in our galaxy we are not aware of? Are you spying on us?"

Camlin looked coldly at Senator Davis. "You forget yourself, Senator. Our Dyson Sphere is here as well, and we were exploring this galaxy far before even the Altons. This galaxy is as much ours as it is yours."

Davis sat back down, still fuming.

"Continue," said President Malle, his eyes focused on Camlin. "Where are these bases located and why haven't we detected them?"

"There are two bases in what you call Federation space which includes the former Hocklyn Empire. There is one in Shari space, two in Borzon space, and one in Ralift space. All are now fully activated and protected by fleets of no less than two hundred Originator battlecruisers. As to why none of your ships or the other races have detected our bases it is quite simple; they are located in interstellar space and not in star systems. They are also protected by Originator stealth fields which your sensors cannot penetrate."

The council chamber was deathly silent as everyone weighed the thought there were over four hundred Originator warships in Federation space, ships which could easily conquer the Federation if the Originators were so inclined. Uneasy looks began to pass between senators.

"Why are you telling us this?" asked President Malle.

"The Originators are willing to make some of these ships available to finish pacifying this galaxy. The Originators abhor slavery which the Borzon and the Ralift practice. We will allow qualified Federation admirals to command these ships and free those worlds held in slavery by your adversaries. It is not necessary with the Shari as they are already moving in that direction."

"Are you saying you will allow Federation crews on those ships?" asked Fleet Admiral Nagumo, his eyes lighting up with excitement.

Camlin shook her head. "Not at first. We will allow you to furnish the command ship and our vessels will follow your orders as long as they follow certain parameters. There will be military AIs on board some of our ships which will know if the vessels are being used for anything other than freeing the slave worlds of the Borzon and the Ralift."

"We could end the last threats of the former AI Empire," said Senator Karnes. "Our galaxy could finally know peace."

"The Altons will fully support such a move," spoke up Ambassador Tureen.

"Will we ever be allowed on the ships?" asked Fleet Admiral Nagumo.

"In time," replied Camlin. "Once some of your crews have been trained at the Communications and Transport Hub we may be willing to allow some of them to crew a few of the battlecruisers. At the Communications and Transport Hub there are many Humans, Altons, and Carethians who have nearly full access to Originator technology and our warships. You have seen the *Distant Horizon*. It is full of Originator technology and has a mixed crew of Originator AIs, Humans, and Altons."

President Malle was silent as he mulled over the offer. "I would ask that the five of you step out while we discuss this. If we have questions you will be called back in."

-

Stepping outside the Council Chambers, Kathryn looked over at Camlin. "Why did you not mention this before about the bases?" Kathryn knew after thinking about it she should have known some fleet bases were in the galaxy. She had been in the briefing where Councilor Bartoll had revealed to Jeremy how many there were and that they were in every galaxy in Originator space.

"Fleet Admiral Strong asked me not to," Camlin replied. "He didn't want that knowledge to affect the negotiations. I was only to make the offer if I felt the negotiations were going to fail. In the Council Chamber I was studying the reactions to your comments on the faces of the senators. It was my opinion the vote was going to fail by a small margin. I computed that by making the offer the vote will pass."

Kathryn nodded. Leave it to Jeremy to have an ace up his sleeve. "I hope you're right. The people from Careth and the Altons will help immensely but the crews we really need have to come from the Federation."

"Be patient," her father said. "We knew this was never going to be easy. I expect over the next few hours we will all be called in to answer questions."

-

Governor Barnes proved to be right. Over the next four hours each one of them was called in and asked more detailed questions about the Eternals, the Originators, access to certain technologies and the fleet bases. Finally they were summoned to come back inside the Council Chamber.

-

Stepping back inside Kathryn noticed a thoroughly disgusted look on the face of Senator Davis. She hoped that indicated how the vote had gone.

"Governor Barnes and Rear Admiral Barnes," began President Malle. "We have voted to allow up to twenty million of our citizens to volunteer to travel to this Communications and Transport Hub. In addition, we will make arrangements at the Fleet Academy on the Moon for half of their future graduates to be assigned to warships of the Originators under the command of Fleet Admiral Strong. However, we have several requests. The first is anyone who wishes to return from the Originators' Communications and Transport Hub will be allowed to do so. The second is we want more access to Originator technology." President Malle raised his hand before Kathryn or her father could object. "Ambassador Tureen has volunteered to form a committee of Alton scientists under the guidance of Originator AIs to determine what technologies will be acceptable which will not endanger the Federation or its economy."

"I think we can live with that," said Governor Barnes, looking over at Kathryn who nodded. "However, there may be an Originator involved with this committee to help determine suitable technologies."

President Malle nodded. "I would like to meet one of these Originators."

"With your permission, I will summon the construction ships to begin building an Accelerator Ring to facilitate travel between the Federation and the Communications and Transport Hub," said Kathryn. "Have you decided where it needs to be located?"

"New Tellus," answered President Malle. "It has the necessary defenses with the asteroid fortresses to protect it as well as ensuring nothing hostile ever comes out of it."

"A wise decision," said Governor Barnes. New Tellus had originally been settled by survivors from the old Human Federation of Worlds, the same as Ceres. It would be a good place for the Accelerator Ring.

"I will inform Admiral Hazelton to expect your vessels," said Senator Karnes. If you need anything from New Tellus, all you have to do is ask."

"Thank you, Senator," replied Governor Barnes. "If anything is needed we will inform either you or the admiral immediately."

"If the five of you will remain we have a few more details to iron out and then I think we can sign an agreement," said President Malle with a satisfied look on his face.

Kathryn allowed herself to smile. She could hardly wait to send Jeremy a message telling him her mission was a success. The crews to fight the Eternals would shortly be on their way.

Chapter Three

On the planet Gardell, the Council of Eternals was meeting. There had been much discussion and blame cast for the debacle at the Originator star cluster. There was still disbelief living Originators had put in an appearance.

"Are you certain the being who spoke to you was a living Originator and not a facsimile created by their AIs or this race of proxies?" asked Second Leader Fehnral who was responsible for scientific development.

"Our latest information calls them Humans," replied First Leader Clondax. "And everything we know points to the Originator who spoke to me as being real."

Second Leader Fehnral shook his head. "This is not good. All of our plans are based on the Originators being extinct and our being able to take over their Shrieels. In time, their AIs would have capitulated and recognized us as the rightful heirs of their creators."

"Those Shrieels have a tremendous industrial capacity," said Second Leader Barrant who was responsible for raw resources and procurement. "Not only that, the Originators have other fleet bases scattered throughout all the galaxies they control. Those bases are capable of repairing ships as well as building new ones. This threat could grow rapidly and imperil the expansion of our empire."

"We are working on neutralizing those fleet bases," replied Clondax. "Fleet Commander Tarsal has a fleet of twelve thousand battlecruisers currently clearing those bases from the galaxies where there are no Shrieels to send reinforcements."

"Twelve thousand ships are not enough," said Second Leader Queexel who was responsible for warship production. "In time, he will suffer sufficient losses to make his fleet too weak to accomplish its mission."

"That's why I'm deploying more fleets," Clondax answered. "By attacking in multiple galaxies, we will be able to spread the ships of the Originators thin enough to allow attacks upon stronger bases, perhaps even a few of their Shrieels. It will also prevent them from being able to attack us."

"I have ramped up ship construction," said Queexel. "More resources will be needed and I highly recommend we suspend expansion of our empire until the Originators are dealt with. Too many of our battlecruisers are tied down patrolling the galaxies we've conquered."

"No," replied Clondax, his cold eyes focusing on Queexel. "We will continue to expand, adding new galaxies to our empire. Nothing will be allowed to interfere with that. We must expand our fleet as rapidly as possible to deal with this new threat posed by the Originators."

"How many Originators still survive?" asked Second Leader Tallard who was in charge of military research. "Is it possible a few were in stasis and their AIs woke them after learning of our existence and empire?"

Clondax had already considered this possibility. "It's possible but we must not assume that is the case. We could be dealing with a few hundred Originators or a few thousand. There is no way to know without conquering a Shrieel and gaining access to its computer database."

"What about the Humans?" asked Tallard. "From what we saw at the Originator star cluster they are taking a big part in the battles we've had thus far. I am surprised the Originators and their AIs have allowed another race access to their ships and technology."

"We are operating on the assumption this is a race which may have developed inside one of the Shrieels. That would explain why the Originators trust them with their technology. It is one of the reasons we are attacking the fleet bases. If we can access the primary computer system on one of the bases, we may be able to learn which Shrieel the Humans come from. Once we know that we can make it a priority target."

Tallard shook his head. "Conquering a Shrieel will result in massive fleet losses, something we can't afford at this time."

Clondax knew Tallard was right. If they discovered which Shrieel the Humans came from they would need a way to conquer it from the inside.

"This war against the Originators may be a mistake," said Second Leader Fehnral. "It is going to require the commitment of too many resources."

"They will be defeated," reiterated Clondax, staring at Fehnral. "We cannot let them to continue to exist."

Fehnral did not respond. He merely bowed his head, his eyes showing he was deep in thought.

-

After the meeting First Leader Clondax met with Fleet Commander Parnon who was responsible for doing a complete survey of Originator space.

"We have completed the survey," Parnon reported. "There are currently 211 surviving Shrieels. The one in the dark matter nebula has been destroyed. It appears the Shrieel's sun went supernova."

"What about the fleet bases?" Clondax knew there were several thousand of these.

Parnon shook his head. "The news is not good. All have been reactivated and are building new warships. We must assume the same construction is occurring on the Shrieels. The Originators are greatly increasing the size of their fleet."

Clondax was not pleased to hear of this. "Do we have the forces to destroy all of the fleet bases?" This would help to isolate the Shrieels.

"No, not without taking substantial ship losses. We believe the fleet bases are updating their battlecruisers and building larger ones. We have also noticed construction at some of the shipyards indicating they are upgrading their defensive weapons."

"These bases were inactive a short time ago. I wonder what has changed?"

"We believe the bases could only be reactivated by the direct orders of a senior military AI or by an Originator."

To Clondax this was all confusing. Why had the Originators waited so long to interfere? He was starting to wonder if Second Leader Tallard was correct when he suggested a few Originators might have been in stasis. It would explain much of what had happened. Of course if these Originators were still infected with the pathogen, there was a good chance they would soon die.

"There are also two galaxies controlled by a militaristic race called the Simulins. We captured one of their ships and downloaded its computer files. It seems they have managed to gain access to one of the Shrieels."

Clondax's eyes widened. "Make arrangements to further study that galaxy. If we can gain access to the Shrieel, it might solve many of our problems." This might be a way into the Shrieel where the Humans lived. If he could destroy them, the Originators might be willing to capitulate. Clondax would be willing to allow them to continue to live in one Shrieel if they would turn all of the others over to the Eternals.

"There are eight Originator fleet bases in that galaxy," added Parnon. "Keep in mind the Simulins only have access to one small part of the Shrieel and only one intergalactic vortex station."

"It doesn't matter," Clondax said as a plan formed in his mind. "Prepare a fleet of twenty thousand of our warships. At some time in the future we will be paying this Simulin galaxy a visit." That single vortex Control Center would allow the Eternals access to all of the Shrieels. He may have just found an easier way to win this war.

-

Jeremy was in the backyard of his home standing over the barbeque grill. His home was on the outskirts of the city and there was actually an underground tunnel, which led from his home to the Tower. Its high-speed car could get him there in less than five minutes in case of an emergency.

"Those hamburgers sure smell good," said Kevin who was standing at Jeremy's side supervising the cooking.

"So do the steaks," said Brace, Angela's husband. He looked over at Kevin. "How can you turn down a good steak for a hamburger?"

Kevin grinned. "I'm having both."

Jeremy smiled. The last few months had been extremely enjoyable. None of them had left the Communications and Transport Hub except for Clarissa who was with Rear Admiral Barnes. He looked over toward the two large picnic tables crammed full of food. The three girls were all chattering away with Ariel listening. Clair was playing with some puzzles Kelsey had bought for her. Since all three were pregnant, he could well imagine what their conversation was like. He was glad he was over here at the grill.

-

"I think four antimatter chambers will furnish enough power," said Katie. "Ariel and I ran some simulations and that should provide plenty of power for all the systems on the new super exploration dreadnaught as well as for emergencies."

"The increase in power alone will allow for a 22 percent increase in the strength of the ship's energy weapons," added Ariel.

"Are we going to be able to make it safe enough for our children?" asked Angela with a little concern in her voice.

Ariel nodded. "No problem. All of you are aware of how Grayseth and his command crew survived. The central section of all Originator dreadnaughts is designed to survive the destruction of the vessel. The one we're designing for the new ship will be even stronger and have its own space drive and weapons. If the ship is destroyed, it will survive and be able to make it back home. Not only that I've added extra armor around the section where the nursery and the living quarters will be located."

"Just so the children are safe," said Angela, looking over at Clair who was playing with a puzzle. The puzzle had large pieces and she was struggling with the last two. Ariel stepped over and patiently showed her where they went.

"We won't be going alone," Kelsey said. "We'll have other exploration dreadnaughts with us as well as a full warfleet of dreadnaughts. We should be able to handle anything we come across."

Kelsey looked over at Jeremy who was talking with Kevin and Brace. He looked so relaxed. It had been good for him to stay away from the war these last few months. Unfortunately Kelsey knew that would not last much longer. "We're going to start actual construction in another few weeks."

"Just how big is this ship going to be?" asked Angela. "I have the communication system designed. Several of the Originators who specialize in subspace and hyperspace communications have been helping me."

Kelsey had to grin. "Fifty-two hundred meters," she replied. "Slightly larger than the *Dominator* and more heavily armed."

Ariel stepped away from Clair who was starting another puzzle. "The ship will have the blue energy spheres of the Originators as well as dark energy cannons. As far as the Originators know, there is nothing that can stand up to such weapons. The ship will have a double triplex energy shield and the most advanced stealth technologies known. Her intergalactic hyperspace speed will be nearly 42 percent faster than what we have now."

"What about the crew?" asked Katie. "Who will be the commanding officer? Are you going to do it, Kelsey?"

Kelsey shook her head. She'd had enough of command the months she had been in charge of the *Dominator*. "No, I've spoken about it to Jeremy and he's suggested offering it to Rear Admiral Barnes with us as an advisory council. There will be a few Originators on board, a number of their AIs and others we've worked with in the past."

"Clarissa and I will both be on the ship," added Ariel. "I can assure you we will make certain no harm ever comes to the new special children."

Angela walked over to Clair who was trying to smash a round puzzle piece into a square hole. She took the puzzle piece out of Clair's hands and showed her where it was supposed to go. "How long will it take to build the ship?"

"With Originator construction technology and everything we want in it, about six months," answered Kelsey. "We still need to finish designing some of the labs and a few other facilities. I have a team of Altons along with several Originators who are working on that."

Katie looked over at Kevin who was eyeing a hamburger Jeremy was turning over on the grill. She let out a deep sigh. She had long since given up on changing Kevin's eating habits. "I talked to Mikow before she left on the *Distant Horizon* and she's interested in transferring to our new ship."

Kelsey laughed. "If we can talk Rear Admiral Barnes into taking command I suspect a lot of the crew will be requesting a transfer." Kelsey had no problem with that. The crew on the *Distant Horizon* was the best one in the fleet.

—

"They're probably discussing baby names," muttered Kevin, looking over at the girls.

"You need two names," Brace reminded Kevin as he held out a platter so Jeremy could load it up with hamburgers and steaks.

Kevin turned slightly pale. "I still can't believe we're having twins and Katie's already talking about more later on."

"I could have told you that," replied Jeremy as he put the hamburgers and steaks on the large platter. "Even when she was young she was always talking about having a big family. Five or six wouldn't surprise me."

Kevin's eyes bulged. "Five or six!"

Brace laughed. "Angela wants a large family as well."

"Look, there are Grayseth and Marille," said Jeremy as the two Bears came through the back gate carrying several large trays of food. "I'm sure they will be having a large number of cubs someday."

Kevin only shook his head. "Let's eat. I'm starving."

Jeremy watched as Kelsey took the two trays from Grayseth and Marille. Marille joined the girls and was excitedly telling them something. Grayseth walked over to Jeremy. "Any word from the *Distant Horizon?*"

"Not yet," Jeremy replied. Jeremy knew Grayseth was excited about the prospect of more Carethians coming to the Dyson Sphere. Already he was enlarging the city the Bears inhabited.

"I heard the Eternals attacked one of the Originator fleet bases earlier."

Jeremy nodded. "Yes; they managed to destroy it. I've ordered some of the fleet bases reinforced. We're pretty certain we know which galaxy they're going to hit next. Unfortunately, due to the distance and time it takes to get a major fleet there, I don't see much more we can do for now."

"I was concerned about these fleet bases being vulnerable," said Grayseth. "As soon as the Federation begins furnishing more crews for our ships, we can begin sending out fleets of powerful warships to stop these attacks by the Eternals."

"Soon," promised Jeremy. "All the Dyson Spheres, the shipyards here, and the fleet bases are building new battlecruisers. We also have a number of shipyards building more dreadnaughts. When the time comes we'll be ready and will go back on the offensive."

This seemed to please Grayseth. "My people are ready to go out on the hunt. We train daily for future battles."

"What is Marille so excited about?" asked Kevin. Even the girls seemed thrilled over what Marille was telling them.

Grayseth grinned, showing his incisors. "Today is a day to celebrate as she just learned in a few months we will be having our first cubs."

"Little Grayseths," said Kevin in shock. He could already see his house overrun with little Bears eating all the food in the pantry. The Bears were known for voracious appetites. It was one reason Jeremy had fixed a number of very large steaks.

"Congratulations," said Jeremy, knowing Grayseth must be thrilled about having future heirs. The Bears took family responsibilities extremely seriously.

"Clair will be excited," said Brace. "I can't wait to see her and the cubs playing together."

"They will make fine playmates and will learn the way of the hunt together," proclaimed Grayseth.

Jeremy looked over at Ariel. She didn't look surprised. Somehow, Jeremy suspected Ariel already knew. She made it a habit to keep track of all of them, and it was evident she had now added Grayseth to her list. He wondered what type of training she would set up for Grayseth's cubs.

"It's time to eat," announced Jeremy as he set the platter of hamburgers and steaks on one of the picnic tables.

Everyone gathered around the tables and began filling their plates. Kevin grabbed two hamburgers and placed them on a bun, adding all the fixings. He added potato salad and baked beans until his plate was nearly overflowing.

"I see your appetite is still there," said Brace as he picked up a medium rare steak.

Kevin nodded. "I have to keep up my strength."

"You're going to get fat if you keep eating like that," said Katie, shaking her head.

"He won't," replied Ariel, smiling broadly. "I've already set up an appointment at the gym in the morning. I'll make sure he burns off all the extra calories he's having tonight."

Kevin groaned and then took a healthy bite of his hamburger. "It's worth it."

"How are the Originators doing since all of them have been awakened?" asked Brace as he cut into his steak.

"Fine," Jeremy answered. "They seem to be accepting this new reality with us living in this Dyson Sphere and aiding them in the war against the Eternals. Many of them have already gone to work in the labs, the Tower, and the shipyards. Our first dreadnaughts with dark energy cannons should be coming out of the construction bays in another few days."

"What about the blue energy spheres?"

Jeremy shook his head. "No, that's one area where the Originators are not budging. The only ships allowed to have the blue energy spheres are the *Dominator* and the girls' new super exploration dreadnaught, probably because both of them are larger than Eternal battlecruisers and nearly indestructible."

Kelsey grinned at Jeremy's reference to the new ship. "It will be the most powerful ship the Originators have ever built. Even more powerful than the *Dominator*."

"The *Dominator* does have dark energy cannons," pointed out Kevin. They had been installed at the space station in the Lost Originators' star cluster. "I wonder how Commander Zafron and Kazak will feel about your ship being more powerful."

"I suspect as soon as they get back and see the latest specs on the new super exploration dreadnaught they will want the *Dominator* updated to the most recent specifications as well," said Jeremy as he buttered a roll. "Once that's been done there won't be much difference in the firepower of both ships."

Grayseth took a large bite out of his steak and smiled. "This is excellent. I truly enjoy the taste of your beef. We have nothing like it on Careth. I stopped by the shipyard building my new dreadnaught yesterday. It will be finished shortly, and I'll be taking it out on its first hunt."

'Nowhere dangerous," interrupted Kelsey with concern in her voice.

"No," replied Grayseth. "I'm taking the ship to one of the galaxies without a Dyson Sphere to inspect several of the fleet bases. I'll have other ships with me, and it is doubtful we will encounter any Eternal vessels. It will be a good opportunity to test the ship's weapons and train the new crew."

Marille looked over at Kelsey. "He's restless. It has been too long since the last hunt. It will do Grayseth good to get away from the Dyson Sphere and lead a fleet once more. The hunt is our way of life and the way our cubs will be brought up. There will be many stories of Grayseth to share around the fire pit in our den."

"To the hunt," said Grayseth, his eyes lighting up at the thought.

"To the hunt," replied Jeremy. He knew Grayseth was anxious to get back out into space after spending so long on the planet they had been stranded on and where they had nearly died. A number of his crew had met their deaths on that harrowing planet. Jeremy was glad Grayseth and part of his crew had managed to survive. Jeremy wasn't sure if the situation were reversed if he could have done so. It was the Bears' belief in the hunt which allowed them to survive in that harsh environment.

-

For the rest of the evening the group talked and laughed, even sharing stories of past adventures. For this evening there were no concerns or worries about the future.

Later, after everyone left, Jeremy and Kelsey were cleaning up the last of the dishes.

"I wish we could do this more often," said Kelsey. "I really enjoyed tonight."

"So did I," replied Jeremy. "Did you see the look on Kevin's face when he found out about Marille?"

Kelsey laughed. "Yes, it was hilarious."

Jeremy smiled. Kelsey looked so radiate and alluring when she laughed. "I promise we will do this again real soon." Jeremy walked over and put his arms around Kelsey, kissing her gently on the lips.

It was at that moment Ariel suddenly appeared in front of them. She still had the ability to use her holographic image when she felt the need. "We just received a message from Rear Admiral Barnes. The Federation has agreed to send aid. Two million Carethians, six million Altons, and twenty million Humans. In addition, half the graduating class from the Fleet Academy on the Moon will be assigned to the Communications and Transport Hub as well beginning immediately and in the future."

"She did it!" said Kelsey with relief appearing on her face.

Jeremy nodded. "Yes, she did." Now Jeremy could begin planning the real war against the Eternals. With crewed ships he could now commit fleets without fearing unnecessary losses from overzealous military AIs. Tomorrow he would speak to Bartoll and the rest of the new Originator Council. It was time for the Eternals to learn what real war was like.

Chapter Four

Commander Zafron watched the tactical display intently as the *Dominator* with its fleet of dreadnaughts and new battlecruisers moved through the outer regions of the Median Galaxy. The fleet was operating under stealth and had been following a number of Eternal ship convoys.

"We've extrapolated their destination," reported Kazak, a military AI. Kazak was easily eight feet tall and dressed in a high-collared dark red military uniform. He was very Human in form except his skin had a more bluish tone to it than did the Altons. His hair was a dark black and his facial features seemed very normal. "There's a K-Class star up ahead the convoys are heading toward."

"This may be the main base we're seeking," said Commander Zafron, who was dressed very similar to Kazak. Zafron was an Originator and the commander of the *Dominator*.

The fleet had been sent out to attack the Eternals in this galaxy. Fleet Admiral Strong and Councilor Bartoll hoped such an attack would force the Eternals to deploy more of their warships to defending their galaxies. Since there were over ten thousand of them, it could result in a vast reduction in ships the Eternals had available to attack galaxies controlled by the Originators.

The *Dominator* was five thousand meters in length and nearly six hundred in diameter. It was armed with the most powerful weapons known to Originator science and protected by a triplex energy shield.

On the tactical display, numerous friendly green icons surrounded the *Dominator*. There were one hundred and twenty dreadnaughts, all with Human and Alton command crews and eight hundred of the new and larger battlecruisers each commanded by a military AI. It was a very powerful fleet with one primary purpose; cause as much damage to the Eternals in the Median Galaxy as possible.

"We will approach the system assuming the Eternals will detect us," said Zafron. "Their sensors may be able to penetrate our stealth fields."

Kazak stepped over closer. "We will scan the system as we approach to choose our targets. We should drop out of hyperspace in combat range of any Eternal facilities in the system."

"Agreed," replied Zafron. "Prepare the fleet to attack. This needs to be a swift surgical strike. I don't want to give the Eternals time to respond."

Kazak quickly passed the orders on to the rest of the fleet. Then he took his position at the tactical station ready to use the *Dominator's* weapons to annihilate any and all opposition.

"Captain Franklyn, I want all outgoing Eternal communications jammed upon our emergence from hyperspace."

"Yes, sir," Franklyn replied. Franklyn was a Human fleet officer assigned to the *Dominator*.

-

The fleet rapidly approached the system and at thirty light years the *Dominator's* sensors began scanning the target. The sensors instantly located several convoys as well as a number of large space stations. There were also three hundred Eternal battlecruisers in the system, most around or near the space stations with a few patrolling the outer regions of the system.

-

"No signs of detection," reported Captain Grayson from his sensor console. Grayson was also a Human fleet officer. "Our new stealth fields may be fooling their sensors for now." The fields had been set to a different frequency in the hopes the Eternals were still scanning for the old one. "I believe we may be able to slip into the system undetected."

"I concur," added Kazak. "We should get in our first weapons strike before the Eternals realize we're in the system."

Commander Zafron spent a moment studying the sensor readings. "There are twelve large space stations. I want ten dreadnaughts assigned to attack each one using dark matter missiles. The *Dominator* will attack the largest station, which should be their primary shipyard. All the battlecruisers will strike the largest Eternal fleet formation."

"Ships will be timed to emerge from hyperspace simultaneously at all targets," Kazak replied as he prepared the *Dominator's* weapons and communicated the attack plan to the other AIs in the fleet.

"Take us in," ordered Commander Zafron as he leaned forward in his command chair.

-

Fleet Commander Caleeb was in the Command Center of the largest shipyard in the Alonng System. There had once been a vibrant colony world of the Malorre in the system but it had been destroyed when it refused to surrender to the Eternals. Now the largest shipyard in this galaxy orbited the dead planet. Twelve construction bays built new Eternal battlecruisers to be used in the conquest of other galaxies. Convoys were constantly bringing in raw materials and specialized parts for the construction of the warships.

Caleeb gazed at the tactical display showing the other large space stations orbiting the planet. There were two other shipyards and nine stations responsible for receiving and refining metals the convoys were bringing in. Caleeb relished the power he wielded. Much of this part of this galaxy was under his control. Thousands of worlds owed allegiance to the growing Eternal Empire. Eternal warships paid periodic visits to these worlds, escorting convoys of raw materials and vital supplies back to the various systems in the galaxy where the Eternals built new warships. There was no doubt in Caleeb's mind the Eternals would someday control all or most of this universe. It was the right of the Eternals as they were the most powerful and intelligent race.

"Convoy from the Stralon Star Cluster is entering the system," reported Dakar, the Eternal at the Sensors. "The ships will be docking at stations seven and eight for unloading. They're carrying ores of heavy metals."

"Get them unloaded and out of the system as soon as possible," ordered Caleeb. "Warship production has been increased by the Council of Eternals, and we need more raw materials." The raw materials were brought to the processing plants in the nine stations and then converted or manufactured into armor and other parts for the warships. Cargoes from inhabited worlds brought computer parts and other specialized equipment.

Caleeb turned to leave the Command Center. He normally did a complete inspection of the shipyard every day which took nearly two hours. As he neared the hatch alarms suddenly began sounding. As he turned back around the station shook violently, nearly throwing him to the deck. More alarms began sounding and red lights began flashing.

"Originator warships have exited hyperspace and are attacking all of the shipyards and stations," reported Dakar, his eyes widening in alarm. "They were not picked up on our sensors."

"Raise our energy shield!" ordered Caleeb, hurrying back to his command station. "Instruct our warships to engage immediately."

"Shield is coming up," reported Belton from Tactical.

The shipyard shook again even more violently. "Raise the shield!" commanded Caleeb, glaring in anger at Belton. What was taking so long?

"Shield is up; whatever they're hitting us with is going right through the shield."

"Activate weapons; return fire." Caleeb looked over at the damage control console. It was covered in red lights. "Send a message to the Council of Eternals, we are under attack. Send out a general broadcast ordering all warships within range to get here as soon as possible."

"Communications are being jammed," reported the officer at Communications. "All we have is short-range."

Caleeb let out a deep breath. They were the Eternals. This was not supposed to be happening.

In space, the Originator fleet emerged within engagement range of the twelve orbiting space stations. Missile hatches slid open and dark matter missiles launched. In four instances the stations were completely obliterated, leaving glowing debris in orbit. Six other stations were heavily damaged. The two largest shipyards survived as their shields snapped into place and the stations began returning fire.

"Target the largest shipyard with our dark energy cannons," ordered Commander Zafron. "Have all battlecruisers target the nearest fleet."

From the *Dominator* two beams of dark energy flashed out, going easily through the shipyard's energy screen and striking the hull. The beams tore the hull apart, penetrating deep inside. Secondary explosions began to wrack the shipyard, demolishing large sections.

A nearby Eternal fleet of eighty battlecruisers opened fire on the Originator battlecruisers. However, these battlecruisers were protected by the new triplex energy screens and possessed more powerful energy weapons due to an extra antimatter chamber for power.

The Eternals hit the Originator ships with their powerful energy beams and hundreds of antimatter missiles. Across the fleet of battlecruisers, energy ran rampant. Several shields failed, allowing Eternal weapons fire to strike the hulls. Almost instantly, with the loss of the energy shields, the ships were obliterated. More Eternal ships in orbit rushed to engage the Originator battlecruisers.

The Originators were firing dark matter missiles, energy beams, antimatter beams and their gravitonic cannons. In the Eternal fleet, energy shields began to waver and go down. Gravitonic cannons tore one Eternal battlecruiser apart. Four others died when their shields failed and dark matter missiles detonated against their hulls, releasing four hundred megatons of destructive force. In their places, small novas appeared which rapidly died away, leaving wisps of glowing gas and melted metal.

The Originator dreadnaughts quickly finished destroying the other space stations leaving only the two large shipyards still fighting back. The dreadnaughts moved to assist the battlecruisers with their heavier weapons against the attacking Eternal fleet. The battle was growing larger as more Eternal ships arrived to engage the Originator battlecruisers.

The heavier firepower of the dreadnaughts quickly shifted the battle in favor of the Originators. Across the Eternal formation, more ships lost their energy screens as the battle rapidly intensified. The Eternals were heavily outnumbered and Originator weapons began to penetrate screens more often. Eternal battlecruiser after battlecruiser was blown out of space, sending debris flying in all directions. Space seemed to be on fire from the fury of the battle.

-

Fleet Commander Caleeb could not believe the destruction caused by the attacking Originator vessels. His own flagship was docked to the station but no longer reporting.

"What of the space stations?"

"All destroyed," reported Dakar. "The other shipyard is under heavy attack and sustaining heavy damage." On one of the viewscreens, a light suddenly flared up and died back down. "Correction; the other shipyard has been destroyed."

"Our fleet?" Eternal battlecruisers were the most powerful ships in the cosmos.

"Suffering heavy damage. They are heavily outnumbered, and we're losing ships at a six to one rate compared to the Originators."

The shipyard shook again and the lights dimmed.

"There is one ship in the Originator fleet larger than one of our battlecruisers. Analysis indicates it's using some type of dark energy weapon against us which is going right through our energy screen."

"Communications?"

"Still being jammed."

The shipyard was now constantly shaking and the damage control console was covered in red lights. There was smoke in the air of the Command Center and a number of consoles had ceased functioning.

"We're having major power fluctuations," reported the damage control officer. "We won't be able to keep the energy screen up much longer."

Fleet Commander Caleeb looked at one of the still functioning viewscreens showing a massive Originator vessel. Even as he watched, missile hatches slid open and blue energy spheres were launched toward the shipyard. Almost instantly power failed and the lights went out. Fleet Commander Caleeb sat down in his command chair. He knew he was about to die and as an Eternal, he accepted his fate.

-

Commander Zafron watched in satisfaction as the last Eternal shipyard disintegrated from the influence of the blue energy spheres which were turning the shipyard into space dust.

"Move over to the fleet battle and use the blue energy spheres to destroy the rest of the Eternal battlecruisers."

Kazak quickly passed on the orders and soon began firing the deadly blue spheres at all remaining Eternal vessels. In just a few minutes the battle ended as the few surviving Eternal battlecruisers were turned into space dust. Across the system, the remaining Eternal ships began entering hyperspace and fleeing, no doubt to spread word of the presence of a powerful Originator fleet.

"All enemy ships have been destroyed," reported Kazak, folding his arms across his chest. "The dark energy beams worked as specified. The Eternals have no defense against them."

"Our own losses?"

"We lost six battlecruisers."

This was acceptable as far as Commander Zafron was concerned. The attack had been a complete surprise to the

Eternals so light ship losses were to be expected. From this battle on the Eternals would be more prepared to engage his fleet.

"Set a course for the Stralon Star Cluster. It's time we paid that cluster a visit." Zafron knew Fleet Admiral Strong had explored the cluster; he had the *Avenger's* records of that visit. He intended to go there and destroy all of the Eternals' ships and stations, effectively freeing the star cluster. In theory it should force the Eternals to commit even more of their ships to holding onto their conquered worlds.

"Course set," replied Kia, a female Originator AI.

"Engage," ordered Commander Zafron. This first battle was over and now it was time to show the Eternals the Originators were not to be taken lightly. If they wanted a war, Commander Zafron would give them one.

In the New Tellus System, Rear Admiral Kathryn Barnes watched as four Originator construction vessels assembled the large Accelerator Ring, which would allow quick transport between the Human Federation of Worlds and the Originators' Communications and Transport Hub. The ring was massive at over one hundred and ten kilometers in diameter.

All across the Federation, word of the war between the Originators and the Eternals was spreading. Volunteers were lining up to fill out paperwork to colonize the Dyson Sphere at the Hub where Fleet Admiral Strong was based. Former Fleet Admiral Hedon Streth had come out in support of the colonization effort and for the Federation joining the war against the Eternals. Even former Admiral Amanda Sheen had come out in support of the war. The fact the Special Five were at the center of the conflict also helped drive recruitment. The entire Federation considered the Five to be legends and any news of them was hungrily devoured by Federation media.

"Nearly two-thirds of the current graduating class of the Fleet Academy are prepared to travel to the Hub," reported Clarissa. "That's 3,215 recruits for our new dreadnaughts."

"We also have a number of ship crews which will be transferring as well," reported Commander Grissim. "Arrangements are being made to transfer nearly 112,000 trained crewmembers."

"The Altons and the Carethians are sending trained crewmembers in this first group as well," said Kathryn. "It should give Jeremy a quick boost in crews he can use for the new dreadnaughts."

"Where's your father?"

Kathryn gestured to one of the viewscreens showing the command asteroid fortress. The Command Fortress was twenty-two kilometers in diameter with the Command Center located in its heart. The asteroid was honeycombed with passages and power plants and had a crew of over twenty thousand. There were six of the massive asteroids in orbit around New Tellus as well as multiple huge shipyards and space stations. There were also a large number of Indomitable class battlestations, which were one thousand meters in diameter and heavily armed.

"He's visiting Senator Karnes and Admiral Hazleton on the command fortress. There are a few security precautions we want to take to ensure the safety of the Accelerator Ring. We're going to have the Altons design some new battlestations. Each will be two thousand meters in diameter and have antimatter chambers as their primary power source. The stations will be armed with antimatter projectors as well as gravitonic cannons. Their energy screen will be a triplex screen which should be able to protect them."

Commander Grissim looked surprised. "That's some pretty advanced technology. I thought we weren't going to give them anything like that, at least not yet."

"The Altons don't apply to part of that rule due to their high level of advancement. As far as the Originators know, the Altons are the most advanced race they've ever encountered. The plans are to build ten of the battlestations and place them in orbit around the Accelerator Ring. One of the stations will act as the Control Center. Each station will have a number of Originator

AIs on board to ensure the technology isn't copied or removed. The command station will have a military AI on board as well."

"What about the rest of the crew?"

"It will be a mixed crew of Humans and Altons," Kathryn replied. "All will be trained at the Hub and the commanding officer will be from the Hub as well. My father is also seeking to allow one hundred Originator battlecruisers from the Dyson Sphere in Shari space to assist in the defense of the ring. If Admiral Hazelton and Senator Karnes agree, the battlecruisers will be placed under Hazelton's command. However, they can only be used to defend the Accelerator Ring and this system. All will be the enhanced battlecruisers."

"We just received a message from Admiral Kalen," reported Captain Travers. "A number of transport ships are being dispatched from the Hub."

Clarissa turned toward Rear Admiral Barnes. "It will take them a little over two weeks to get here. To be precise the travel time will be two weeks, two days, and twenty hours."

"I suspect this ring is going to see a lot of use," said Commander Grissim, looking at the viewscreen.

Kathryn knew Anne was right. There would be fleets flying back and forth between New Tellus and the Hub almost continuously.

"There is a danger of the Eternals someday finding the Federation," stated Clarissa. "What will happen then?"

"Don't forget we have a Dyson Sphere located in Shari space plus the six fleet shipyards. I'm going to recommend Fleet Admiral Strong place a large fleet of dreadnaughts in the Dyson Sphere just in case. Two of the fleet shipyards are close enough they could send a large number of battlecruisers if needed. We need to ensure those battlecruisers are all of the newest design. The older ones can be used by the Federation to pacify the Ralift and the Borzon once the command structure is finally worked out." Kathryn knew her father still had a lot of work to do. In a few more days he would be returning to the solar system to meet with President Malle and Fleet Admiral Nagumo. Nagumo still wanted more access to Originator technology, particularly for his warships.

Commander Grissim looked over at Rear Admiral Barnes. "It's hard to believe this galaxy will finally be free of the influence of the old AI Empire."

Kathryn grinned. "It's something the Altons have been working on for generations. I suspect they will find their services needed even more across the galaxy to bring all the races together. It's going to take a lot of work to bring civilization back to many of those slave worlds. Even here in the Federation's section of space, there are many former Hocklyn Empire worlds, which are just now crawling back into space. There are Alton research vessels everywhere working with many of those planets."

"Maybe someday we'll have a galactic government of some sort here."

Clarissa shook her head. "That's highly doubtful. Many of those worlds after being dominated by the Hocklyns, Ralift, Borzon, Shari and the AIs will have no desire to join any type of galactic-wide organization. It will take generations for them to build up the trust to the point they will not fear other worlds."

"That will be for the Federation and the Altons to figure out," Kathryn said as she looked at the viewscreen showing the partially constructed Accelerator Ring. "Our concern for the foreseeable future is going to be the Eternals." Kathryn leaned back in her command chair. They were going to be here for a number of days, and she wanted to go down to New Tellus and enjoy some time off. New Tellus had some of the best resorts in the Federation. The seaside resorts were fabulous. The entire crew of the *Distant Horizon* as well as the two dreadnaughts were going to be granted some leave time. Kathryn feared once they returned to the Hub time off from fleet duty was going to be seldom and far between. There was a war that needed to be fought and she knew she would have a significant role to play.

Chapter Five

Jeremy watched from the *Avenger* as the first personnel transports entered the swirling blue vortex of the Accelerator Ring on their long journey to New Tellus. It would be a month before they returned with forty thousand fleet personnel. A second and larger group of transports would be leaving in another two days. Two dreadnaughts and ten of the new battlecruisers were escorting the two transport fleets. Jeremy didn't expect any problems but he was not taking any chances with the huge Originator vessels. Moments after the massive transport ships and their escorts entered the vortex the ring shut down, leaving only empty space.

Jeremy sat down in his command chair looking around the Command Center. Only Ariel, Commander Kyla Malen, and Lieutenant Shayla Lantz were there with him. Most of the crew was on leave and there was just a minimal crew on board. Even Aaliss, the Originator AI who had been assigned to the *Avenger*, was busy on one of the research stations.

Looking at the viewscreens, Jeremy could see the four Dyson Spheres and other structures, which made up the Communications and Transport Hub. All around the area of space where the Communications and Transport hub was located were hundreds of titanic structures. Many of them were massive ship construction yards and others giant manufacturing facilities that processed the raw material the Originators and their AIs needed to maintain the megastructures. There were also research centers where the AIs worked nonstop advancing the science of their creators. Many of those research centers now had living Originators coordinating the efforts of the AIs.

"It's impressive, isn't it?" said Commander Malen, standing next to Jeremy. "I still find it hard to believe all of this is here and it is now our home."

On one of the viewscreens, several recently completed heavy dreadnaughts exited one of the shipyards to join a large fleet waiting for living crewmembers. The new dreadnaughts were equipped with dark energy cannons, a development of the Lost Originators.

"The first of the new defense stations will be online in another few weeks," mentioned Ariel as she adjusted one of the screens to show several of the spherical structures.

At five thousand meters they seemed dwarfed by the other titanic structures around them. These were defense stations modeled after the dark energy ones around the planet the Lost Originators had hidden on. The stations had a gravity drive, dark energy cannons, antimatter projectors, gravitonic cannons, missile tubes for dark matter missiles and, more importantly, they were equipped with the blue energy spheres which there was no known defense against. The stations were powered by dual antimatter chambers and protected by the new triplex defense screen. The plans called to build nearly a thousand of the stations to protect the Hub.

"What if one of the blue energy spheres was to accidentally strike a Dyson Sphere or one of the shipyards?" asked Kyla.

"The Originator structures are so large it would cause only minor damage," Ariel replied. "However, the spheres are programmed not to strike anything of Originator origin."

This seemed to satisfy Kyla. "Do you think the Eternals will find us here at the Hub?"

"Eventually, if this war lasts long enough," replied Jeremy. "Its coordinates are programmed into all of our ships. It's general knowledge on the Dyson Spheres and all of the Originator AIs are aware of it. It's only reasonable the Eternals will discover the existence of the Hub though it may take them longer to actually find it."

"By then the defense stations will be finished," said Ariel. "Dark energy cannons are also being added to all four Dyson Spheres as well as the other Originator structures here at the Hub. We also have tens of thousands of warships which can help to repel any attack."

"Admiral, we just received a message from Commander Zafron," reported Lieutenant Lantz. "They have located and destroyed a major base of the Eternals in the Median Galaxy. He believes it was one of their primary ship construction facilities. He's on his way to the Stralon Star Cluster to continue his campaign against the Eternals."

Jeremy nodded. This was part of his plan to force the Eternals to focus more on defending their empire rather than attacking Originator space. Once the Federation crews arrived and went through training on the new heavy dreadnaughts, he would be sending several more raiding fleets into Eternal space. However, he did need to decide what to do about the Eternal fleet that had attacked and destroyed the fleet base in Galaxy X-257. Jeremy wondered it the Eternals were using the same strategy he was.

Thinking for a minute he decided it might be best to send Admiral Mann and her fleet out to handle the situation. It would take them weeks to reach that remote part of Originator space, but he couldn't allow an Eternal fleet to run rampant over the region. New fleet bases would have to be built to replace any the Eternals destroyed. He would speak to Councilor Bartoll about sending some construction ships from the nearest Dyson Sphere to begin rebuilding the fleet base in Galaxy X-257, only this time he would suggest they build four and all would have dark energy cannons. Jeremy had gone on a tour of a nearby fleet base and been pleasantly surprised at how powerful they were. The bases would be very useful in the war against the Eternals. They just needed to be updated to the most recent specifications. He also wanted the fleet bases to start sending out small patrols to search out their regions of space for any Eternal activity.

"Lieutenant Lantz, contact Admiral Mann and have her come over to the *Avenger*. I have a mission for her. Also contact Alton Admiral Lukel. I need to speak with him as well."

Jeremy leaned back in his command chair. It had been months since the battle at the Lost Originators' star cluster. During that time all the Dyson Spheres' shipyards had been operating around the clock building new warships. In hundreds of dead star systems, massive mining operations had been set up to furnish the raw materials needed by the Dyson Spheres. Jeremy had a massive fleet waiting to be deployed; he just needed the command crews for the heavy dreadnaughts and he could begin taking the war to the Eternals.

-

Kelsey and Katie were busy at the Tower working in the large office provided them by the Originators to design their new super exploration dreadnaught. There were a number of Originator AIs present as well as several Altons and even a few Originators. All were working on different sections of the ship.

Kelsey was working with Nomar Krill who was an Originator well versed in antimatter power systems as well as other Originator technology. Around the room were numerous large viewscreens showing various sections of the planned ship. There were a million items that needed to be taken care of. Kelsey knew it would have been impossible without the aid of everyone who was involved with the project. There were nearly one hundred Altons, Humans, Originator AIs, and Originators helping with the ship design.

"The planned power system should be sufficient for all of the ship's needs," Nomar said as he studied a detailed schematic of the ship's planned antimatter chambers. "However, in the central section of the ship where it's designed to survive in case of a catastrophe we have a small fusion reactor. I would recommend changing that to an antimatter chamber instead."

"Why an antimatter chamber?" asked Kelsey with a frown. "We decided on a fusion reactor because it's much smaller."

"I have spoken to several of the engineers we have recently awoken," Nomar replied. "I believe we can design a much smaller chamber which will provide three times the power output for that section than the fusion reactor. It would allow us to generate a triplex energy shield if needed."

Kelsey was pleased to hear this. Anything they could do to make the center section safer where their families were going to be sounded fine with her.

"Kelsey," said Katie with a strange look on her face. "I think we need to go to the medical center."

Kelsey glanced over at Katie with an inquiring look on her face. "Are you not feeling well?"

"She's going into labor," said Ariel suddenly appearing between the two women. "The babies are coming early."

Standing up Kelsey rushed to Katie's side. "Let's go. Ariel, notify Kevin, Angela, and Jeremy." They had all made plans to be present at the birth of their children.

Ariel let out a deep sigh. "I wish Clarissa was here."

"You can tell her all about it later," Katie said as she moaned and bent over with pain. "I think we'd better go."

Kelsey took Katie's arm and headed toward the door. "Ariel, make sure a vehicle is waiting for us."

"Already taken care of," replied Ariel.

-

On board the *Avenger*, Rear Admiral Hailey Mann was listening as Fleet Admiral Strong informed her of the mission he was sending her on.

"This Eternal fleet consists of about twelve thousand of their battlecruisers," Jeremy explained. "We believe it's going to attack more of our galaxies that don't contain a Dyson Sphere. If the fleet bases were fully updated with the new dark energy cannons, they might be able to hold with minimal losses. As it is they have their fleets and their standard weapons."

"Haven't they been updated somewhat?" asked Hailey.

Ariel nodded. "Yes, the fleet bases all have the new triplex energy screens and their battlecruisers have some updates. A few of them even have some of the new battlecruisers which have come out of their construction yards. However, we're talking about a large Eternal fleet. The firepower it can bring to bear is considerable."

Rear Admiral Mann's eyes narrowed. "How large of a fleet am I going to take?"

"Two fleets," Jeremy answered. "Admiral Lukel will be going as well."

"Will he be the senior officer?" asked Hailey.

Jeremy shook his head. "No, you have more combat experience and he has agreed to follow your command. Both fleets will have two hundred dreadnaughts and six thousand of the new battlecruisers."

This seemed to satisfy Hailey. "When do we leave?"

"As soon as your fleets are ready," replied Jeremy. "We expect the Eternals to hit the fleet bases in Galaxy X-268 shortly. There are only four in that galaxy. We have contacted the nearest Dyson Sphere and ordered them to send reinforcing fleets to all four of the fleet bases."

Rear Admiral Mann looked over at Ariel. "How long will it take us to get there?"

"Slightly less than four weeks," Ariel replied. "Galaxy X-268 is on the far end of Originator space away from the Hub."

"Will the fleet bases be able to hold out that long?"

Jeremy let out a deep breath. "We don't know. They're too far apart to really support one another and I'm hesitant to order any more ships from the nearest Dyson Sphere. This could always be a trick to get us to do just that."

Hailey frowned. "There will be no Accelerator Ring there for us to return by."

"No," Jeremy replied. "When it's time for you to return take your fleets to the nearest galaxy with a Dyson Sphere. You can use an Accelerator Ring there to return to the Hub."

"I'd better make sure all of our ships are well supplied," said Hailey.

"If you run short of anything we can send supplies from one of the fleet bases or the nearest Dyson Sphere."

Jeremy wasn't pleased to be sending Rear Admiral Mann and Admiral Lukel so far away. It meant those two fleets would be too far away if something drastic happened anywhere else. He was still concerned the Eternals might return to Galaxy X-938 and try to conquer the Dyson Sphere in that galaxy; they had already made several attempts. There was currently a large fleet at the Dyson Sphere under the command of Admiral Cross just in case the Eternals returned.

Ariel listened for a few more minutes as Jeremy and Hailey finished the necessary plans to deploy the two fleets. When both were satisfied with the arrangements, Hailey left the Command Center to go to her flagship, the heavy dreadnaught *Victory*, to get her fleet ready.

"Jeremy, we need to get down to the surface immediately."

Jeremy looked over at Ariel, his eyes narrowing. "I still have a few more things to do here yet."

"It will have to wait. Kevin's going to need your support."

Jeremy's eyes widened in understanding. "Katie's gone into labor!"

Ariel nodded. "Yes, it will still be a few hours before the babies are born. Kelsey and Angela are already there and Kevin will be in a few more minutes. I have our shuttle ready in the flight bay. I've been talking to Kelsey and Katie using one of my holograms."

"Commander Malen, if Rear Admiral Mann or Admiral Lukel needs anything let me know."

Kyla nodded. "No problem. Now you'd better get to Kevin before he passes out from the stress."

Laughing, Jeremy nodded. "Let's go, Ariel."

Ariel felt excited. More children were about to be born to the Special Five.

Kelsey was in the waiting room watching as Kevin paced back and forth.

"What's taking so long?" He stopped, looking at Kelsey expecting an answer.

"The babies will be here when they're ready," Angela said grinning.

Jeremy's on his way," announced Ariel. She was still present in her holographic form. She was not going to miss the birth of the next special children. She was recording everything for Clarissa.

Kelsey tried to relax which was difficult. She was nearly nine months pregnant and getting comfortable was next to impossible. Taking a deep breath, she looked at the door to the waiting room. She hoped Jeremy made it in time.

-

Rear Admiral Mann was busy getting her fleet lined up. Many of the ships were the same ones which had been with her at the battle in the Lost Originators' star cluster. Her fleet consisted of two hundred of the heavy dreadnaughts and six thousand of the new and larger Originator battlecruisers. All of the battlecruisers were commanded by military AIs. Unfortunately most were new with little or no battle experience.

"I have the course computed to Galaxy X-268," reported Caria. Caria was an Originator AI and the ship's helm officer.

"At least it will be more balanced this time," said Commander Erick Sutherland. "We'll be pretty evenly matched and with the new energy shields and more powerful weapons we should be able to handle this Eternal fleet."

Hailey nodded. "Do all of the dreadnaughts have full loads of the defense globes?"

"Yes," answered Sutherland. "Eighty percent are the normal defense globes and 20 percent are the larger modified ones." The modified ones had a 400-megaton dark matter warhead, a stronger defensive shield, and a more powerful gravity drive.

"How long until all ships are fully supplied? We may be gone for a few months or longer."

"In twenty hours all supplies will be on board as well as extra dark matter missiles."

"I wish all of our dreadnaughts had dark energy cannons." Unfortunately only her flagship had the new weapon. Her dreadnaughts had been scheduled for the upgrade in another few weeks.

"Admiral Lukel reports he can be ready to depart in twenty-four hours," said Lieutenant Denise Sparks from Communications.

"Then let's make it so," commanded Hailey. It looked as if they were going to be fighting the Eternals again. She just wished it wasn't going to take four weeks to get there. A lot could happen in that time.

Jeremy and Ariel reached the waiting room. Upon entering Ariel's hologram vanished. "Are we in time?"

Kelsey came over and hugged Jeremy. "Yes, Kevin just went into the delivery room."

"I guess we'll know soon if they're boys or girls," said Angela. Katie had wanted it to be a surprise.

Brace came hurrying in. "Have the babies been born yet?"

"No, silly," said Angela, indicating for him to sit down next to her. "Have a seat; this may take awhile."

"Where's Clair?"

"At the daycare in the Tower. She's fine."

For the next hour they waited and then a beaming Kevin came out of the delivery room. "A boy and a girl!" he announced excitedly. "Katie's doing fine."

Jeremy walked over and slapped Kevin on the back. "I thought you were afraid to have twins."

"I was," Kevin admitted sheepishly. "But after seeing those two helpless babies, I realized how wrong I was. I think I'm ready to be a father."

"Names!" said Ariel, striding up to Kevin. "What are the names so I can send a message to Clarissa?"

"Not yet," replied Kevin. "Katie and I are still trying to decide between a couple."

Kelsey walked up looking at Kevin. "Don't wait too long." She then looked over at Angela. "Let's go to the nursery so we can see the babies when they bring them in."

The two girls hurriedly left, talking excitedly.

Ariel was smiling broadly; the next two special children had been born. Soon Kelsey and Angela would have theirs as well. That would make five special children with possibly more on the way someday. Ariel knew she and Clarissa were going to have their work cut out for them. The children of the Special Five would be raised like no others. Their education and training would be the best possible. Ariel suspected someday the children, when they became adults, would play an important role in the war against the Eternals.

The *Dominator* and her fleet moved stealthily through the Stralon Star Cluster. They were taking care to avoid concentrations of Eternal vessels. The sensors on the *Dominator* were detecting a number of convoys under Eternal escort moving through the star cluster on their way to various destinations.

"We're nearing the inhabited planet Fleet Admiral Strong first detected," reported Captain Grayson.

On the tactical display, the fourteen planets of the star system became visible. Numerous ships moved about the system. Commander Zafron knew the system held a massive mining operation.

"There are several large mining operations ongoing," reported Grayson as he studied the data on his sensors. "The system has a significant asteroid field, and there are a number of large mining operations on several of the bigger planetoids. The same is occurring on a number of the moons of the outer planets. There are also four space stations in orbit above planet five, two large and two small. I'm also picking up about four hundred ships in the system. Most are ore carriers or mining ships."

"Just as in Fleet Admiral Strong's report," said Kazak approvingly.

On one of the viewscreens, the inhabited planet appeared. Its atmosphere was hazy and dull because of all of the pollution being generated from surface factories. Commander Zafron knew the planet held a large population though not as big as it had in the past. The Eternals had used nuclear bombardment to reduce it.

"How many Eternal warships are we detecting?"

"Twenty-three," reported Captain Grayson.

"Kazak, dispatch two dreadnaughts to each of those warships and annihilate them."

Commander Zafron leaned back in his command chair as the designated dreadnaughts accelerated toward their targets. Upon arrival, they dropped their stealth fields and blew the unsuspecting Eternal battlecruisers apart using dark matter missiles. In less than twenty seconds all twenty-three Eternal vessels were off the tactical display.

"Put the fleet into orbit around the planet," ordered Zafron. "Let's see what we can do about freeing them from the Eternals."

-

For two days the *Dominator* and her fleet orbited the planet. Attempts at communication with the planet's inhabitants were proving to be futile and aggravating. The inhabitants insisted they were better off under Eternal rule and someday the Eternals would lift them to new heights of civilization. They were also demanding Commander Zafron take his fleet and leave before the Eternals returned and took out their anger on the inhabitants of the system.

"It's useless," said Kazak, looking toward Commander Zafron. "The Eternals have brainwashed the inhabitants of this planet into nearly worshiping them. We don't dare take out the orbital stations or any of the mining operations. The inhabitants are correct; the Eternals might retaliate against the planet. Those mines and the factories on the surface are the only reason the Eternals are allowing this planet and probably many others to exist."

"A Catch-22," said Captain Grayson from Communications. "We're damned if we do and damned if we don't. There is no right decision in this situation."

Commander Zafron nodded. "I fear you're right. While it is tempting to take out all of the mining and industrial operations in this system, it will damage the Eternals little considering the vast resources at their disposal. All we would do would endanger the inhabitants of this system, and that is not why we're here."

"We're better off following the convoys and annihilating any Eternal bases or shipyards they lead us to," said Kazak. "By concentrating on military targets, we do not jeopardize any of the inhabitants of this galaxy."

"Do you suppose all the planets controlled by the Eternals worship them like this system does?" asked Captain Grayson.

"Perhaps," Commander Zafron said. If they did that posed a major problem. It indicated it would be nearly impossible to free any galaxy the Eternals controlled, particularly if sufficient time had passed to indoctrinate the civilized planets to thinking highly of the Eternals. "This is important information to take back to Fleet Admiral Strong and Councilor Bartoll. We must leave this star cluster and investigate a few more worlds. We need to discover if the entire galaxy believes as this planet does."

Kazak stared at Zafron for a long moment. "I would suggest we travel throughout this star cluster and annihilate all the Eternal battlecruisers we can locate. Then we follow the largest convoy and see where it takes us."

"I have several convoys on the long-range scanners," confirmed Captain Grayson. "It shouldn't be too hard to figure out where they're headed."

Commander Zafron nodded. "Let's check out a few more of the inhabited systems. By taking out all the Eternal battlecruisers, we will be telling the Eternals we're still here and looking for a fight."

-

For the next two days the *Dominator* and her fleet visited six inhabited systems. In each system, they destroyed every Originator battlecruiser they found. They also discovered the same attitude toward revolting against the Eternals as on the first planet.

"That makes seventy-two we've taken out," said Kazak as a dark matter missile from the *Dominator* annihilated the last Eternal battlecruiser in the latest star system they had entered. "I'm surprised they haven't rallied a major fleet to resist us."

Zafron was confused by this as well. In the six systems he had only lost one battlecruiser. "We know ships from this galaxy were used to attack Galaxy X-938. More of the ships from this galaxy may have been sent to the Lost Originators' star cluster as well. They may be having a problem with gathering sufficient ships to oppose us."

Kazak grinned at this suggestion. "Then let us attack as many Eternal bases in this galaxy as we can. An opportunity like this may not come again."

"I concur," replied Commander Zafron. "Kia, set a course for the system one of those convoy fleets was heading toward. It's time we found more substantial targets." He still wanted to investigate a few more worlds as well but he needed to hit some major Eternal bases to attract sufficient attention. The Eternals had to be made concerned enough to begin using their fleets to protect the thousands of galaxies they controlled. Just flying around hitting minor targets wasn't going to accomplish that.

Kia nodded as she began entering coordinates into the navigation system. "There is such a system seventy-four light years distant. Two of the convoys we've been tracking are heading toward it. There is another system two hundred and seventeen light years distant, which is attracting a number of convoys as well. I would suggest that system be our second target."

"Agreed," said Commander Zafron, leaning back in his command chair. "Transmit the coordinates to our other ships and we'll be on our way."

-

A few minutes later the fleet made the transition into hyperspace. On the outskirts of the system they'd just left a stealthed Eternal battlecruiser suddenly appeared. It had been following and observing the Originator fleet from the extreme range of its sensors so as to avoid detection.

"Send word the Originator fleet has fallen for the trap," ordered the ship commander. "They are heading toward the Asurian Star System."

The Eternal commander was satisfied that soon the Originator fleet would be obliterated. It had been necessary to sacrifice a number of battlecruisers in order to convince the enemy fleet commander no other ships were available to the Eternals. On the contrary, a very large fleet was waiting for the Originators at their destination. Very soon this troublesome enemy fleet would be no more.

Chapter Six

Jeremy was back in the Tower meeting with the Originator Council. Bartoll, Trallis, and Castille were listening patiently as Jeremy explained what was happening back in the Federation.

"We must be very careful about what Originator technology they have access to," said Councilor Castille with a hint of concern in her voice. "Some of it could be very dangerous and seriously affect their civilization."

"Don't forget the Altons are there as well," Jeremy reminded her. "They are a wise race and will help to determine if any of the technology is dangerous and how its introduction will impact the Federation's economy."

Councilor Trallis nodded. "Yes, I have met a number of these Altons. They are much as we were in our younger days. It is good your Federation places such trust in them. I would suggest before we release any of our technology to the Federation that a team of Altons and several of our AIs examine it beforehand."

"There is much we can offer your people," said Councilor Bartoll. "Better mining technology, more advanced medical treatments, and better alloys are just a few."

"The first personnel transports will be returning within four weeks bringing the initial Federation crews for our heavy dreadnaughts. I would also like to suggest we place stronger Marine contingents in all of the Dyson Spheres just in case the Eternals manage to gain access. We can use the combat robots and the Marines to safeguard the main Control Centers as well as the primary computer cores."

Bartoll's eyes widened at the suggestion. He looked at the other two councilors and then replied. "Our people may not feel comfortable with that. They are still getting used to the idea of three non-Originator races living upon one of the Shrieels here at the Hub with more preparing to come. While most agree with the need for help against the Eternals, it still goes against what our policy on allowing other life forms access to the Shrieels has been for millions of years. It is going to take some getting used to."

This reaction was not unexpected and Jeremy had prepared for it. "I believe Reesa Jast, Leeda, and Major Wilde are waiting outside to report on their latest findings on the escape of Commander Alvord with the aid of the Military AI Albate." Alvord had been the commander of the *Seeker* and Albate the military AI responsible for protecting the ship and its commander. Alvord was also a member of the Defenders of Zorn.

A clouded looked crossed Councilor Bartoll's face. It had been his lack of proper security, which had allowed Alvord to escape. He had never dreamed Albate would aid his former commanding officer in escaping.

"Have then come in," replied Bartoll.

Jeremy stood up and walked over to the door. Opening it he indicated for the three who were waiting outside to enter.

"Major Wilde," said Councilor Bartoll, indicating for all of them to take a seat. "How is your investigation going on the whereabouts of Commander Alvord?"

"I'll let Reesa explain where we are," Brenda replied. Reesa was a young Alton research scientist.

Reesa let out a deep breath. "We've examined all of the video footage of Commander Alvord's quarters. As you know, the video records were modified by Albate to show nothing unusual. We suspect Alvord, his four loyal crewmembers, and Albate had been gone for several days when we discovered they were missing."

"A small Originator research vessel is missing as well," Leeda added. Leeda was an Originator AI with red hair down to her shoulders. "All efforts thus far to trace its destination have failed. There are no reports from any of the Shrieels or fleet bases of the appearance of the vessel. It seems to have vanished."

"Which may indicate assistance from other AIs or even members of the Defenders of Zorn," said Reesa, her eyes narrowing.

Bartoll's eyes widened at this. "Do you think there are other stasis facilities where members of this sect may be?"

"I'm almost positive," replied Reesa, nodding her head. "It may explain while there has been no trace of Alvord."

Bartoll let out a deep and troubled sigh. "What about your research into other stasis facilities which may have been hidden and have not yet activated?"

"With the help of the computer drive Jontel furnished us we believe we have located an underground stasis facility Originators may have used during the days of the pathogen. All we need is your permission to tunnel down to it and take a look."

"If we're right about this it could lead to other stasis facilities on other Shrieels," added Leeda, her face showing excitement. "Possibly thousands of others."

Councilor Castille looked intrigued. "I say we do it." "Anything we can do to find more Originators will only aid us in our war against the Eternals. We are now mere millions where we once numbered in the trillions."

"What if some of these survivors are followers of the Defenders of Zorn?" asked Councilor Trallis worriedly.

Castille's eyes narrowed. "It's a risk we will have to take. I would suggest Major Wilde have some of her Marines on standby as well as sufficient combat robots. Once we know there are Originators in these hidden stasis facilities, we can check their identity against the population records in the Shrieels. That should help us to identify any who may have been associated with Councilor Zorn."

Councilor Bartoll nodded. "Very well, it is decided then. Major Wilde, you have permission to open this underground stasis facility. We're all curious as to what you will find. Perhaps we may finally know why none were activated when the cure for the pathogen was discovered."

Brenda nodded. "We'll do so immediately. We will also keep up the search for Commander Alvord and Albate. They're bound to show up somewhere."

"Maybe," Bartoll said doubtfully. "Our Shrieels are very large. If he and the people with him decide to hide on a habitation square away from our cities, it may be impossible to locate him. They could even be in one of our cities in an isolated region. Our repair robots have kept the cities on all of our Shrieels as they were since the advent of the pathogen. They could be in one of them but with the aid of a few AIs loyal to Alvord we would not know of their presence."

"Or he may be reawakening members of the Defenders of Zorn and providing them with the cure for the pathogen," cautioned Jeremy, his eyes showing concern if this were true. "We can't assume their only stasis facility was on the Shrieel that was destroyed in the dark matter nebula. As Major Wilde says, she believes there may be more."

"The Defenders of Zorn were a major threat to our way of life," spoke Councilor Castille. "As much as I dislike having Human Marines and our own combat robots protecting the Control Centers and the primary computer cores it may be the wisest thing to do. It would be a disaster if the Defenders of Zorn gained control of one of the Shrieels. It could seriously compromise our war with the Eternals."

"I have to agree," said Councilor Trallis, letting out a deep sigh. "We are in a new day and age. The Eternals are at our doorstep, and we dare not risk the Defenders of Zorn, if they still exist, becoming an internal danger. We must take all the precautions we can to make sure that does not happen."

"It looks as if you have our permission," said Councilor Bartoll, looking at Jeremy. "Deploy your Marines and the combat robots as needed."

Jeremy nodded. "I will keep our Marine presence and the combat robots as unobtrusive as possible. There will only be one or two Marines in the Control Centers and the primary computer core. The rest, as well as the combat robots, will be posted outside to ensure there is no unauthorized entry."

"I would suggest we check all the AIs which have access to these installations," suggested Leeda. "We dare not let an AI who has sworn allegiance to the Defenders of Zorn unlimited access. They could do irreparable harm."

Bartoll nodded. "Make it so. We must make sure all of the Shrieels are secure."

"Which brings up another question," Jeremy said. "What about the vortex Control Center the Simulins control on the Shrieel in their home galaxy? That could pose a problem if the Eternals discover that information."

Bartoll looked over at Major Wilde. "Can we attack that Control Center and bring it back under our control?"

"It will be difficult," answered Brenda with a deep frown. "The Simulins have thousands of their Conqueror Drones around it and in the immediate area of the vortex crater. We also believe they have heavily fortified it. Observations from inside the Dyson Sphere near the area the Simulins control indicates they are still sending ships through to the other Dyson Sphere in the remaining galaxy they control. The ships are exiting the vortex and then staying close to the surface or landing. The Simulins have erected powerful energy shields over both sections."

"How are they getting their ships inside the Shrieel without our outside defenses destroying them?" asked Councilor Castille.

"We believe they have taken down part of the defenses in the region immediately outside the Dyson Sphere in their home galaxy or destroyed them, creating a small window where they can get their ships through. The ships are jumping right above the surface and then entering. On the inside we've set up defenses all around the section they control. We currently have over five hundred Marines and nearly six thousand combat robots as well as numerous defensive emplacements guarding that region."

"We could take those shields down with our heavy dreadnaughts," suggested Jeremy. He didn't like the risk those two vortex Control Centers represented. If the Eternals gained control of even one, it would allow them to send a massive fleet into any Dyson Sphere in Originator space.

Councilor Bartoll nodded in agreement. "I think it needs to be done. We can place our ships close enough to ensure the energy shield cannot be reestablished and prevent any ships from coming through the vortex. If they do we could destroy them immediately. It takes the Simulin vessels a few seconds for their systems to stabilize once they exit the vortex. Our vessels could easily destroy them."

"I will order it done immediately," Jeremy said. "A fleet of dreadnaughts armed with dark energy cannons would stop any Eternal vessels from coming through as well. I also believe we should use our combat robots and Marines to secure the outer hull around the vortex and get all the defenses working once more."

"It still does not solve the problem of what to do about all the Conqueror Drones," said Major Wilde. "The inside corridors and the vortex Control Centers will be full of them."

"I may have a solution," said Councilor Trallis. "I believe we can access the vortex Control Centers the Simulins control. I have spoken to several Originator computer specialists and they believe they can insert a program into the two vortex Control Centers ordering them to take down the energy shields as well as making it impossible to open up a vortex without the use of a command key. I understand you have already retrieved the only command key the Simulins had?"

"Yes," answered Major Wilde. "It's in the hands of Rakell. He is the Originator AI who has been assisting us in the assaults."

"Then there's your solution," said Councilor Trallis with a satisfied look on his face. "We insert a computer command to shut the energy shields down as well as making the vortexes nonfunctional. It will isolate the Simulins and they will have no choice but to surrender. We won't have to risk your ships or your Marines."

Brenda shook her head. "The Simulins will never surrender. They will have to be killed."

"I am saddened to hear that," replied Councilor Trallis. "If that is the case then I suggest we do as I mentioned and then send in combat robots to remove the Simulins. By doing that we will not be risking the lives of any of your Marines or our AIs."

Brenda let out a deep breath. "It's going to take a while. They will fight for every inch of the area around the Control Centers. It may take thousands of combat robots to remove them from the two Dyson Spheres."

"May I suggest we contact General Wesley and have him handle the details?" said Jeremy. "Major Wilde is going to have enough to do trying to track down additional Originator stasis facilities as well as searching for Commander Alvord. General Wesley can also help set up the security for all of the Dyson Spheres' Control Centers and computer cores."

Councilor Bartoll looked at the other two councilors, seeing agreement in their eyes and on their faces. "Very well, it is decided. We will meet again next week to check on progress or sooner if the need arises."

-

Later, Jeremy was back in his office. Kevin was taking a few days off to stay home with Katie and the twins. He could still picture Katie as the wide-eyed girl with green eyes who had followed him around as a kid. That seemed like so long ago. Sometimes he wondered if all of them had made the right decision in going into stasis so they could fight the Hocklyns in the future. It meant none of their parents were able to see any of their grandchildren. Jeremy knew by taking the path they had, there were many things they missed out on.

With a deep sigh, he thought about the two vortex Control Centers the Simulins controlled. He knew with regret he should have taken care of them sooner. Now it had to be done before the Eternals discovered them and used them against the Dyson Spheres.

Getting up he walked over to the large open window. In the distance, he could see another city being built by Originator work robots. It would house another two million Humans. In ten selected regions of this habitation square new construction was occurring. Over twenty million Humans would soon be living here. In two nearby habitation squares more cities were being built for the Altons and Grayseth was already greatly extending his own city as well as building two more. This was a wonderful place to live and raise a family; it just saddened Jeremy to know so many people from the three races were coming here to help fight a war. Of course the Carethians would enjoy the war as it allowed them to go on the hunt. Jeremy knew Grayseth was thrilled at the prospect of more of his people coming to the Dyson Sphere.

Even as he thought about Grayseth, his office door opened and the massive Bear stepped inside.

"Jeremy, it is good to see you taking a breath of fresh air."

Jeremy turned to face Grayseth. He knew his friend was about to take his new heavy dreadnaught out on its shakedown cruise. "Is your new ship ready?"

"That's where I just came from. It is ready to go out on the hunt. The crew is boarding even as we speak and I'll be departing tomorrow."

"What about your escort fleet?" Jeremy had assigned a large fleet to keep his Bear friend safe. Grayseth had a habit of getting into trouble. If there were any Eternals around Grayseth would manage to find them.

"Twenty heavy dreadnaughts and two hundred battlecruisers are more than I need. There should be no danger on this mission. We are going to Galaxy X-346 to inspect eight fleet bases. All should be finished with their current modifications. There will be four construction ships accompanying us which will be installing the new dark energy cannons on the bases."

"Yes, that's to help ensure they can survive an Eternal attack. As for why you have such a large escort fleet, the Eternals have already attacked one of our galaxies destroying its fleet base and are no doubt going on to the next. Even in Galaxy X-346, which does not possess a Dyson Sphere, there is always a chance of encountering an Eternal fleet. Unfortunately that is our new reality. We must always be prepared for combat."

"You are wise," Grayseth replied. "I should be back before the first of my people arrive from Careth. It will be good to expand upon the packs we already have here and add several new ones. This is a good world to raise our cubs with many forests and mountains to teach them the ways of the hunt."

"To the hunt," replied Jeremy.

"To the hunt," replied Grayseth.

Grayseth turned to go and then stopped. "Perhaps by the time I return you will have a young one. Kelsey will make a good mother and example for your child. Someday he or she will be going out on the hunt with my own cubs. We will have many stories of our adventures to tell around our fire pits in the future.

Jeremy smiled. He knew Kelsey was due any day. He also knew Grayseth was right; someday their children would be going out on missions against the Eternals. That was one part of being a father Jeremy was not looking forward to.

-

The next day Grayseth stepped on board his new flagship. The new *Warrior's Pride* was much more powerful than the previous one. There was no doubt in Grayseth's mind if he'd had this vessel in the Median Galaxy his ship would not have been destroyed.

Stepping inside the Command Center, he smiled upon seeing a few familiar faces. Shantor was at the Sensors, Makeb at Communications, Belmar at Damage Control, and Farsalk the Navigation and Helm. Antolth was now Chief Engineer and in the engineering section. Hawthorn was his new second in command. The former Carethian Marine had served Grayseth well on the planet where they had all been marooned. There had only been twenty survivors when Jeremy managed to rescue them from the Median Galaxy. All were aboard the new *Warrior's Pride*.

"Fleet is ready to depart," reported Hawthorn.

"It is time to go on the hunt," said Shantor. "We have a fine ship."

"To the hunt," replied Grayseth with a wide grin. "Farsalk, take us out." The new *Warrior's Pride* had a much smaller crew than the previous one. Grayseth had learned his lesson when his ship had been destroyed and taken so many Carethian lives with it. Many had been lifelong friends.

"The Accelerator Ring is ready to activate," reported Kamdel from the Science Station. He was an Originator AI, one of twelve on the large warship. Two others were assigned to different shifts in the Command Center and the rest were in Engineering.

Grayseth sat down, feeling the command chair adjust to his large proportions. "Then activate it. It is time for us to go."

"Travel time to Galaxy X-346 will be seventy-eight hours," Kamdel informed Grayseth as he pressed several icons on his computer screen.

On the ship's main viewscreen, the massive Accelerator Ring began to power up. Suddenly a swirling blue vortex formed, filling the void inside the ring.

-

The *Warrior's Pride* and her attending fleet accelerated and entered the vortex. Moments later the Accelerator Ring shut down and the vortex vanished.

On the *Avenger*, Jeremy smiled to himself seeing the departure of the *Warrior's Pride* and her fleet. Grayseth was off on the hunt and he knew his Bear friend would be pleased. As leader of the Carethians on the Dyson Sphere, he preferred to lead by example. Jeremy was certain, knowing Grayseth, the Bear would find some type of trouble to get into somewhere in Galaxy X-346. He always did.

Chapter Seven

Commander Zafron watched the tactical displays as his fleet approached the target system. From the long-range scans, it appeared this star system held two large shipyards of the Eternals. Two convoys from the Stralon Star Cluster had entered it and gone into orbit around the system's fifth planet.

"Sensors are detecting only nine Eternal battlecruisers," reported Captain Grayson. "They're all in orbit around the planet."

"None hiding under stealth?" This was a concern of Commander Zafron. The Eternals had advanced stealth capabilities. However, the sensors on the *Dominator* should be able to detect Eternal stealth fields as a void area in space.

"None detected," reported Grayson.

"Our own stealth fields are activated," pointed out Kazak. "It is doubtful the Eternals even know we're in the area. They probably assume we are still in the Stralon Star Cluster seeking additional worlds to target."

Commander Zafron gazed for several long moments at the tactical display. For some reason this system made him feel uneasy. "Kia, take the fleet in. Put us two million kilometers away from the planet."

"We could jump closer," said Kazak, looking confused. "There's no reason not to jump within weapons range and immediately engage the shipyards. They will be easy targets."

Zafron shook his head. "This seems too easy. The Eternals in this system must know of what we've done to the other system containing shipyards as well as our attacks in the Stralon Star Cluster but it appears they have taken no precautions to defend against an attack. When we drop out of hyperspace I want additional scans taken of the entire star system, particularly planet five. There may be defenses on the planet the Eternals are counting on to handle our fleet."

"Hyperspace dropout in four minutes," reported Kia.

"All ships are at Condition One," confirmed Kazak.

In the targeted star system on the far side of the sun, a massive Eternal warfleet was hovering as close to the star's surface as possible to avoid detection by the inbound Originator fleet. One of their own stealthed vessels was following the Originators at extreme range, monitoring their approach.

"We shall eliminate this threat," boasted Fleet Commander Durant as he watched the tactical display. Special sensor satellites deployed away from the star were sending updated tactical information to the ship's computer, which was then displaying it on the tactical display.

"We are the Eternals," said Carmmod, the second officer. "This will be a swift victory for us."

"We must not underestimate the Originators," cautioned Durant. "They have powerful vessels and have demonstrated the ability to be able destroy our ships."

Carmmod nodded his understanding. "We have over two thousand of our battlecruisers. While we may take a few losses we have the firepower to obliterate this fleet. It should send a message to the Originators to stay away from our empire."

"Prepare the fleet to enter hyperspace," ordered Durant. "We will swing around the star and drop out of hyperspace within combat range of the Originators. They won't know we're even here until it's too late."

On the ship's main viewscreen, the star they were hovering over was visible. They were so close the screen was showing the violent fusion explosions occurring on its surface. Huge masses of material were being flung upwards only to fall back down. The energy shields were actually showing signs of stress. However, being so close and on the far side of where the Originators would be approaching the planet made the Eternal fleet invisible to the sensors of the Originator fleet. This trap had been well thought out. The Originator fleet would make it into the system but it would never leave.

The *Dominator* and her fleet dropped out of hyperspace and instantly began scanning the system for hidden threats. For several long minutes the fleet held its position as the planets in the system were scanned. Particular care was taken to scan the surface of planet five for hidden weapon emplacements.

"Sensors are clear," reported Captain Grayson. "No changes from our previous scans. If there's anything here we're not detecting it."

This satisfied Commander Zafron though that uneasy feeling still persisted. "Kia, take the fleet in. Kazak, I want both of those shipyards targeted and then we're leaving."

"There are mining facilities on several of the moons in this system," replied Kazak, looking over at Commander Zafron. "Are you certain you don't want to take them out as well?"

"We'll leave them for now. Something in this system just doesn't feel right." Commander Zafron leaned back in his command chair, studying the tactical display. The display was showing eleven red threat icons, the two shipyards and the nine Eternal battlecruisers. Commander Zafron wondered what he was overlooking. He also didn't understand why there were only nine battlecruisers defending these two large shipyards. It just didn't make any sense.

The *Dominator* rapidly closed on the two shipyards orbiting planet five. The nine Eternal battlecruisers had moved into defensive positions to try to protect the valuable shipyards upon detecting the Originator warships. The fleet was nearly within engagement range when the sensors began picking up a danger.

"Commander Zafron, there is a large void area moving toward us in hyperspace," warned Captain Grayson. "It came from around the star and is rapidly approaching."

"An Eternal fleet," surmised Kazak as his hands flew over his tactical console. "It must have been hovering dangerously close to the surface of the star for us not to be able to detect it. They were waiting for us."

"Kia, prepare to take the fleet back into hyperspace." Commander Zafron had no intention of allowing his fleet to fall into this trap. Better to flee than risk major losses.

"Commander, the two shipyards are transmitting a hyperspace distortion field, locking us out of hyperspace," reported Kia, her brow creasing in a frown. "We can't enter hyperspace. This field is different from the previous ones our fleets have encountered. It's going to take awhile to counter it."

"A trap," said Zafron, seeing his worst fears realized. "All ships form up in defensive formation D-2 while we try to find a way through the jamming field." Defensive formation D-2 was a spherical formation with the *Dominator* at its center.

"We're within range of the shipyards," reported Kazak. "I'm targeting them with our dark energy cannons. If we can destroy both of them, it should bring the distortion field down."

More alarms began sounding as the Eternal fleet began emerging from hyperspace. On the viewscreens of the *Dominator*, hundreds of the huge four-kilometer battlecruisers of the Eternals were materializing into normal space.

"All ships, fire!" ordered Commander Zafron. Looking at the tactical display, it was obvious his fleet was heavily outnumbered.

"Two thousand three hundred and seventeen Eternal battlecruisers detected," reported Captain Grayson.

"We're receiving a message from the Eternal command ship demanding our surrender," reported Captain Franklyn.

Commander Zafron considered replying and then shook his head. "Ignore them; we have a battle to fight."

-

From the *Dominator* two dark energy beams flashed out, ripping through the energy shield of one of the stations. The beams struck the hull, blasting out a huge chasm. Secondary explosions rattled the shipyard blowing huge pieces of it out into space. Dark matter missiles from the *Dominator* slammed into the energy shield, detonating with devastating force. The shield wavered but held.

From the two shipyards and the Eternal battlecruisers heavy energy beams and antimatter missiles targeted the Originator fleet. Triplex screens fought to resist the massive onslaught and then began to fail. In massive nova-like explosions, Originator battlecruisers began to die. The firepower being poured into the Originator fleet was too much for even the new triplex energy shields to resist.

Energy beam fire from the Eternal battlecruisers slammed into the central section of an Originator warship, setting off massive explosions and hurling glowing debris into space. The ship began shaking violently as internal explosions began tearing it apart. In a massive explosion the vessel blew up, spreading more debris across space. Several large pieces slammed into the shields of nearby ships but failed to penetrate.

An Originator dreadnaught came under heavy fire. Its own weapons were firing nonstop at an Eternal battlecruiser, causing severe damage. Suddenly an Eternal energy beam penetrated the dreadnaught's energy screen, striking the top section of the ship and blowing glowing debris off into space. Several Eternal antimatter missiles arrived through the gap in the screen caused by the energy beam. In a bright flash of light, the dreadnaught ceased to be. In its place a fiery nova appeared which quickly died away.

The Originator fleet was losing the battle as its energy shields were being overwhelmed by the superior firepower of the much larger Eternal fleet. A pair of antimatter missiles slammed into the stern of a battlecruiser and the ship vanished in a fiery explosion, leaving glowing debris in its wake. An Eternal energy beam penetrated the weakened energy shield of a dreadnaught, blowing a gravitonic cannon emplacement to shreds and blasting out a deep gouge in the hull. Damage to the fleet was growing rapidly as it fought back trying to survive.

-

"We're taking a lot of damage," reported Kazak as he continued to use the ship's dark energy cannons to slowly tear apart the shipyard he was firing upon.

"We're still locked out of hyperspace," added Kia as she worked at her console.

Commander Zafron could see the worry and concern on the faces of his command crew. "Kazak, use the blue energy spheres to destroy those two stations." Zafron had been holding them back to use against the Eternal fleet but if he waited too much longer, he wouldn't have a fleet left. Already space was littered with the wreckage of destroyed Originator vessels.

"Launching," replied Kazak as he began sending a steady barrage of the deadly energy spheres toward the shipyard he was slowly decimating.

On the huge viewscreen covering the front wall of the *Dominator*, the blue spheres penetrated the shipyard's energy screen and struck the hull of the large shipyard. Almost instantly large sections of the structure began to grow hazy and come apart as it was converted into space dust.

The ship's dark energy cannons continued to pummel the shipyard and then suddenly a massive explosion split the shipyard in two.

"Shipyard's energy shield is down," called out Captain Grayson.

Almost instantly Kazak fired two dark matter missiles, which finished obliterating the shipyard in a pair of titanic explosions.

"Hyperspace distortion field is still in effect," reported Kia. "Hyperspace drive remains offline."

Commander Zafron took a deep breath. "Kazak, target the other shipyard. Kia, how close is the computer to finding a way through the hyperspace distortion?" Several Originator scientists had designed a computer program, which was supposed to be able to analyze the Eternals' distortion fields and find a way around them.

"Five to ten minutes," Kia replied.

"Not good enough," said Commander Zafron, his eyes narrowing. "Kia, move the fleet closer to the second shipyard. We must destroy it."

"That might not work," said Kazak as he re-targeted his weapons on the other shipyard. He sent off a barrage of blue energy spheres as well as half a dozen dark matter missiles. "The Eternal fleet is no doubt broadcasting the same energy distortion field."

"Kazak's correct," Captain Grayson said as he looked over at Commander Zafron. "Sensors are detecting the same distortion field being broadcast by a number of the attacking Eternal vessels as well."

Zafron's forehead furrowed in a frown. "Nevertheless, destroy the shipyard and then turn the blue energy spheres lose on the Eternal vessels."

Zafron knew if they didn't crack the frequency of the distortion field quickly, he could lose most if not all of his fleet. He was angry he had allowed himself to fall into the Eternals' trap. He should have trusted his instincts when he felt there was something wrong coming into this system. Now his fleet was paying a steep price for his error.

-

Fleet Commander Durant nodded in satisfaction. The Originator fleet had fallen into the trap he had set. Even as he watched, it was slowly being blown into oblivion by his fleet's superior firepower.

"They have destroyed one of the shipyards," second officer Carmmod reported.

"A minor loss for destroying this enemy fleet," Durant said dismissively. The empire had thousands of shipyards scattered through the more than ten thousand galaxies that were part of the growing Eternal Empire. "We can build new ones later."

"The enemy flagship has switched its fire to the other shipyard. It won't last long."

"Then it too shall die," Durant said coldly. "While the flagship is concentrating on destroying the shipyard we are destroying its fleet." On several viewscreens, Originator battlecruisers were in the process of being destroyed. Their screens were down, and Eternal energy beams were carving them up.

A sudden flash of light caused the screens to dim.

"That was the shipyard," Carmmod reported. "It's gone."

Durant had been expecting this. "Focus our firepower on the ships of the Originator fleet and the flagship. If possible I want to disable it. It's by far the largest vessel the Originators have deployed against us. I am sure the Eternal Council would be interested in its technology."

-

The fighting between the two fleets intensified. Ships on both sides were being destroyed with the battle tipping more and more in favor of the Eternals due to their vaster ship numbers. Even so, one Eternal ship was dying for every two Originator vessels destroyed. Space was becoming littered with the wreckage of obliterated vessels.

-

On board the *Dominator* Kia worked desperately with the ship's main computer trying to break the distortion field holding the fleet prisoner.

"We've lost two hundred and fourteen battlecruisers and thirty-one dreadnaughts," reported Captain Grayson as the list of destroyed and damaged vessels continued to grow.

"Targeting Eternal battlecruisers with our blue energy spheres," reported Kazak.

Commander Zafron knew that would help to even the battle but there were still just too many Eternal warships. Even the powerful weapons of the *Dominator* could not destroy them all.

"Decrease the size of the defensive sphere," he ordered. Too many ships had been lost and the sphere was beginning to become frayed with ships becoming too exposed to incoming weapons fire.

The *Dominator* suddenly shook violently, and alarms began sounding.

"What was that?"

"A number of Eternal antimatter missiles struck the same spot on the energy screen as well as a focused attack by hundreds of energy beams," reported the AI at damage control. "Two beams penetrated and struck our hull. We lost two antimatter projectors and one gravitonic cannon. We have six compartments open to space. Emergency bulkheads have activated and repair robots are en route."

"Energy shield is stable," added Kazak as he launched more blue energy spheres at several nearby Eternal battlecruisers. He was targeting over one hundred of them, firing two energy spheres at each one. The Eternal vessels were so large it took two spheres striking the hull to convert the vessels into space dust in a reasonable amount of time.

Commander Zafron felt stunned by the damage to the *Dominator*. For the first time he realized he could die in this battle. "Kia, what's the progress on the disruption field?"

"Another minute," she replied. "We've almost got it."

"Kazak, are there any of our ships we need to destroy to prevent the Eternals from collecting our technology?"

"No," Kazak replied as he checked the ship's sensors with his neural implant. "All damaged ships have been reduced to space junk either by their destruction or the self-destructs our vessels are now armed with."

Under Fleet Admiral Strong's recommendations, each Originator vessel now had a number of powerful self-destruct devices on board which would activate if the vessel became disabled in battle. The devices could be deactivated by a command from the vessel's Command Center or Engineering.

The *Dominator* shook again and the power briefly flickered.

"We're switching more power to the shield," reported Kazak as he blew an Eternal battlecruiser apart with four well-placed dark matter missiles. The vessel had already been heavily damaged by the blue energy spheres.

"We've got it!" called out Kia excitedly. "We can jump anytime."

"Then get the fleet out of here!" ordered Commander Zafron. He had already lost too many ships in this battle. It was going to be necessary to return to the Communications and Transport Hub and report his mission had been a partial failure.

-

The Originator fleet broke formation and made the jump into the safety of hyperspace. As soon as they were in hyperspace all vessels activated their stealth fields, making them invisible to Eternal sensors. The Eternal ship that had been following the fleet and staying at the edge of the system watching the battle was taken by surprise by the fleet's sudden disappearance. Before it could lock on with its sensors, the fleet was out of range and gone.

-

Fleet Commander Durant felt anger flow through him as the trapped Originator fleet escaped.

"They must have analyzed the frequency of the distortion field and adjusted their hyperdrives," said Second Officer Carmmod.

"How many of them did we destroy?" There was a lot of wreckage at the former location of the Originator fleet.

"Three hundred and seventy-seven of their battlecruisers and forty-four of their dreadnaughts."

Durant leaned back in his command chair in thought. They had destroyed nearly half of the enemy fleet. No doubt it would now return home in defeat.

"Did our stealth ship get a trace on the heading of the Originator fleet when it left?"

"No," replied Carmmod. "They were not expecting the fleet to escape the distortion field."

This did not please Fleet Commander Durant. "See that the ship's commanding officer is sentenced to duty supervising shifts at the mines in the Stralon Star Cluster. His lack of efficiency displeases me."

"I will see to it immediately," replied First Officer Carmmod.

"What were our losses?"

First Officer Carmmod hesitated and then answered. "We lost two hundred and seventeen battlecruisers and both of the shipyards."

This did not surprise Durant. Those deadly blue energy spheres the flagship of the Originators used were deadly. He would report to the Council of Eternals the enemy fleet had been defeated and driven from this galaxy. He would also inform them the Originators had two weapons, which could penetrate Eternal energy shields though he suspected the council already knew this.

"Set a course back to the Stralon Star Cluster. I don't believe we will have to worry about another Originator fleet coming to this galaxy again for quite some time."

-

Commander Zafron was highly upset with himself. He wondered if it was his belief that being an Originator made him superior to many other life forms. After meeting the Humans and the Altons, he had come to question that belief. Now he feared his own belief in his superiority had cost him a large portion of his fleet. Even worse forty-four dreadnaughts had been destroyed with their Human and Alton crews. Granted there had only been crews in the Command Centers and Engineering but it had still resulted in the loss of over five hundred lives.

"Kia, set a course for Galaxy X-938," he ordered. "We'll stop there for repairs before continuing on to the Communications and Transport Hub." Once they reached Galaxy X-938, he would send a report to Fleet Admiral Strong. He would take full responsibility for the failure of this mission.

"The Eternals are a dangerous enemy," commented Kazak, coming to stand next to Zafron. "Even in the days of the Great War many Originator vessels were lost before the Anti-Life were driven back to their galaxy."

"I am aware of that," Zafron replied. "My fear now is they've spread across this section of the universe so much we can never drive them back again. I don't see any good way for this new war to end."

Kazak did not reply. He was a military AI and trained for war. But he also knew they were fighting an enemy with possibly vast resources available to them. Twelve million Originators and their Human, Alton, and Carethian allies could not fight against the trillions of Eternals that must exist and hope to win. Even with his vast experience as a military AI, Kazak could not come up with a viable solution to win the war.

Chapter Eight

"The Originator fleet in the Median Galaxy has been defeated," reported Second Leader Nolant. "Fleet Commander Durant managed to lure the fleet into a trap and inflicted heavy losses, causing it to flee."

"It is unfortunate it managed to destroy the shipyards in the Kassel System," said Queexel. "Those were the largest shipyards we had in that galaxy."

"They did little harm in the Stralon Star Cluster. The Debens refused to aid them or to break away from our rule," said Nolant.

"Their time in the star cluster allowed Fleet Commander Durant to set up the trap he lured their fleet into," said First Leader Clondax. "They were fools to follow the convoys."

Queexel looked at the others. "They will not be so foolish next time. We must not underestimate the Originators or the Humans working with them."

Second Leader Fehnral spoke up. "We need more information on the Humans as well as how many Originators still live. Are they free of the pathogen or have they found a cure?"

"Fleet Commander Tarsal should soon be attacking the Originator fleet bases in the next galaxy on his target list," said First Leader Clondax. "He has instructions to attempt to capture one of the bases. If he is successful we may know the answers to those questions."

"There are several thousand of these fleet bases," pointed out Second Leader Barrant. "One fleet will not be able to destroy all of them."

Clondax shifted his attention to Barrant. "Shortly we will be sending more fleets into Originator space to eliminate their fleet bases. The Originators and their Human allies will not be able to defend them all. We believe it would spread their available fleet assets to the limit. Once we have eliminated the fleet bases, we can begin to isolate the Shrieels."

"We will take over their galaxies one by one," Second Leader Tarmal said. "We are constructing more warrior robots and training additional Eternal shock troops for the planned invasions."

"By isolating the Shrieels we cut them off from additional resources," said Second Leader Barrant. "They will be forced to surrender."

Clondax nodded. "When the time is right we will offer to allow the Originators who still live to choose a single Shrieel to live in. All Originators will be taken there. The other Shrieels will be ours."

"And these Humans the Originators are sharing their technology with?" asked Second Leader Fehnral.

First Leader Clondax looked at the others and then replied. "Technology such as that possessed by the Originators cannot be allowed into the hands of any other races. We will find the home world of these Humans and destroy it as well as any colonies they may have. It is still believed by many that the Humans reside in one of the Shrieels. If that is so, on the day the Shrieels become ours the Humans inside will be disposed of."

"How soon before more fleets are sent into Originator Space?" asked Second Leader Queexel.

"Shortly," answered Clondax. "Ship production in all of our galaxies has been increased to provide warships for the new fleets. In three weeks ten fleets of ten thousand battlecruisers each will be sent into Originator space to attack the fleet bases. More will be sent as ships become available."

"We could suffer some major fleet losses in this conflict," said Second Leader Nolant. "Losses which may take years to make up."

Second Leader Barrant shook his head. "We are committing so many ships to this war effort against the Originators our planned expansion into other galaxies of this universe has slowed down."

"We are still expanding," corrected Clondax. "We are expanding into Originator space. Soon we will possess the

Shrieels and with their industrial output added to our own our expansion across this universe will be vastly increased."

Second Leader Fehnral stood up, staring directly at First Leader Clondax. "I must caution you about underestimating the Originators. They have already demonstrated they have weapons that can penetrate our energy screens. They can even free themselves from the hyperspace distortion fields we use to prevent enemy fleets from escaping. They defeated us in that star cluster in which the Originators were experimenting. Defeating them might not be as easy as you indicate."

"It is a risk we must take," responded Clondax, his eyes focusing coldly on Fehnral. "We are the Eternals. We are the most advanced race in this universe. In time, the Originators will fall before our superior power. It is our destiny to rule, and we must let none stand in our way."

Fehnral sat down, not wanting to challenge Clondax. It would be unhealthy. Others in the past who had challenged the First Leader had died or mysteriously disappeared. He did not want to join those ranks.

"However, Fehnral has brought up a good point. The technology of the Originators is close to our own. We must be careful in our battles with them to always possess superior numbers. While it is true they can destroy our battlecruisers we can also destroy theirs. I believe Second Leader Nolant has a report to make on the new antimatter missiles our ships are being armed with."

"We have designed a 100-megaton antimatter missile," Nolant said. "While not as powerful as the dark matter weapons the Originators and Humans are using, it should aid our ships in taking down the shields of enemy ships."

"As you can see, with newer and more powerful weapons it is only a matter of time before we control all of Originator space," said Clondax. "Once we have possession of the Shrieels, there is nothing that can stop the spread of our empire across this universe."

Clondax was pleased with the way things were going. Both Fleet Commanders Durant and Tarsal had reported recent victories. It was obvious to him the Originators and Humans were not prepared to fight a widespread war. By attacking different Originator galaxies at the same time, he would spread their fleets and destroy them one by one. Eternal victory was inevitable.

-

Fleet Commander Tarsal waited expectantly as his fleet prepared to exit hyperspace at his next target. Long-range sensors indicated this fleet base was protected by a larger fleet than the last one. It would make no difference. His numerical superiority would allow him to reduce it with minimal losses. From the survey that Fleet Commander Parnon had completed of this galaxy, there were four Originator fleet bases which needed to be annihilated.

-

Malyk, the military AI in charge of the fleet base, studied the long-range sensors. A large void area was approaching in hyperspace. No doubt this was the Eternal fleet that had destroyed the fleet base in Galaxy X-257. He had been expecting its arrival.

"They will be here in twelve minutes," reported Dasoon from the Sensors.

Malyk nodded. "We are prepared for them." The extra warships from the Shrieel in galaxy X-243 had arrived. What really pleased Malyk was a cargo ship had come with the fleet carrying a supply of dark matter missiles for the fleet base. Not only that, there were two hundred of the new and larger battlecruisers, which were, all equipped with dark matter missiles and better energy screens. The big surprise had been the ten dreadnaughts that came with the fleet as well.

"Carlton is asking how you want the fleet to be deployed. He's recommending placing it around the fleet base so the base's weapons can be used to support the fleet."

"Agreed," replied Malyk.

On the viewscreens of the Command Center, the 1,410 ships of the fleet rapidly formed up around the large fleet base.

"Energy screen activating," reported Halvor. "All weapons are online, and dark matter weapons are in all missile tubes."

Malyk was pleased with the actions of the AIs who served with him on the fleet base. They were efficient and had no fear of what was to come. "Stand by."

-

The Eternal fleet dropped out of hyperspace just short of engagement range. The fleet formed up into a massive cone formation and then began moving toward the fleet base and the waiting Originator fleet.

"Detecting 1,400 Originator battlecruisers," reported Garald. Then he frowned, looking over at Fleet Commander Tarsal. "There are ten dreadnaughts as well."

"Twice as many as before," Fleet Commander Tarsal said. "It is obvious they have been reinforced in anticipation of our attack." The presence of the dreadnaughts concerned him. They would be more difficult to destroy and could cause some serious damage to his fleet.

"Two hundred of the battlecruisers are the larger ones like the ones we encountered at the star cluster battle."

Tarsal's eyes widened at hearing this. The larger battlecruisers were more powerful and harder to destroy. "Target them and the dreadnaughts first. They will be the most dangerous." This battle was going to be much more difficult and costly than he had planned.

"Engagement range," reported Garald.

"Firing," reported Lomart.

-

From the *Conqueror* and the other Eternal battlecruisers heavy energy beam fire erupted, striking the Originator fleet.

Almost instantly several energy screens collapsed and the exposed battlecruisers were quickly obliterated by antimatter missiles.

-

On board the command dreadnaught Carlton, the military AI, studied the tactical display showing the incoming weapons fire. "All regular battlecruisers are to fire in groups of four on Eternal targets," he ordered. "Our enhanced battlecruisers are to work in groups of two. Use of dark matter missiles is authorized."

Carlton's duty was to inflict as much damage as possible on this Eternal fleet, forcing it to abandon its attacks on the fleet bases. Carlton was well aware this would most likely result in the destruction of the entire defending fleet and possibly the fleet base. His dreadnaughts were crewed entirely by AIs as there were no organic crewmembers available.

-

In space, hundreds of dark matter missiles were fired at the Eternal fleet. Across the entire forward section raw energy erupted, assailing Eternal energy screens. Antimatter projectors and gravitonic cannons added their firepower to the onslaught. Under such firepower a few shields began to go down.

In the Eternal formation, dark matter missiles detonated against the hull of a battlecruiser. The resulting explosions turned the vessel into plasma and clouds of glowing gas. Other Eternal battlecruisers were destroyed in the same manner as the firepower from the Originator fleet was augmented from the fleet base. Hundreds of dark matter missiles were detonating against Eternal energy shields every few seconds. Space was awash with raging energy. The ten heavy dreadnaughts were pouring heavy fire into the Eternal fleet. More than one Eternal battlecruiser saw their energy screens smashed and their hulls ravaged by the firepower from the deadly ships. In case after case dark matter missiles blew the besieged Eternal ships to oblivion.

A pair of gravitonic beams from a dreadnaught struck the stern of an Eternal battlecruiser, ripping deep into the ship and separating the rear third of the vessel from the front section. A pair of dark matter missiles arrived turning the two sections into small supernovas.

Another Eternal battlecruiser was being systematically torn apart by antimatter beams. Huge holes were melted in the hull, penetrating deep into the ship. Secondary explosions began to rattle the vessel and then in one stupendous explosion, the four-kilometer vessel blew apart.

Across the Eternal formation, numerous battlecruisers were dying under the intense fire of the Originator dreadnaughts, battlecruisers, and the fleet base.

"We've lost one hundred and fourteen of our battlecruisers," reported Garald from Sensors. "Those ten dreadnaughts, the two hundred larger battlecruisers, and the fleet base are hitting us with dark matter missiles. Our shields can only stand up to a few hits from those warheads." The previous fleet base and Originator fleet they destroyed were not equipped with the deadly missiles.

Fleet Commander Tarsal checked the tactical display. Originator ships were dying in large numbers as well . On the main viewscreen, an Originator battlecruiser was being torn apart by Eternal energy beams. In a sudden flash of light, the ship exploded. "Continue to fire on the Originator fleet. Ignore the station for now. Once we've annihilated the fleet we will destroy the fleet base."

Tarsal knew that meant allowing the fleet base to methodically destroy more Eternal vessels but the defending fleet needed to be dealt with first, particularly the dreadnaughts.

Malyk gazed at the tactical display. He felt saddened at seeing so many Originator battlecruisers being savaged by the Eternal fleet. Ship after ship was dying. They were taking many Eternals vessels with them but not enough to allow for a victory. The dreadnaughts were holding their own and causing considerable carnage to the Eternals. From the latest data, the defending fleet would be destroyed as well as the fleet base. "Are we still transmitting data?" An intergalactic communication vortex had been activated at the very beginning of the battle. The vortex could not be jammed or destroyed.

"Yes," replied the AI in front of Communications. "All battle data is being sent to the Communications and Transport Hub. Fleet Admiral Strong should be seeing what we are."

"The Eternals are focusing their fire on Carlton's fleet," reported Dasoon. "Very little weapons fire is hitting the fleet base."

"In that case concentrate our firepower and begin picking off as many Eternal battlecruisers as possible." Carlton knew as soon as the defending ships were annihilated, the Eternals would turn the full firepower of their fleet against the base. When that happened the end would come very quickly.

"Adjusting fire to fewer targets," reported Halvor.

-

The weapons fire from the station changed. Instead of being spread out across numerous targets to help the fleet, it was now focused on fewer Eternal warships.

Twenty dark matter missiles slammed into the energy shield of an Eternal battlecruiser, causing its immediate collapse. The ship beneath vanished as a firestorm of energy swept across it.

Forty gravitonic energy beams struck the same spot on an Eternal energy shield, blasting an opening in the screen. Six of the beams struck the hull, causing deep craters, which reached into the heart of the ship. With a violent explosion, the vessel broke in two.

The station switched its fire to the next two ships with the same results.

-

Carlton watched impassively as his fleet was slowly destroyed. Each time an Originator battlecruiser died, it was less firepower that could be focused on the Eternal fleet. In the last few minutes two of his dreadnaughts had been destroyed as well. Several others were reporting damage.

"What's the latest analysis of the battle?" he asked the AI in front of the ship's computer station.

"We're losing ships at a nearly one to one basis with the Eternals. So far they are concentrating their fire on our warships and not the station."

Carlton could have accessed the information with his neural implant but he had a crew of AIs and he wanted them to perform their duties to the very end.

"That won't last much loner," Carlton said as he gazed at the tactical display showing fewer green icons with every passing minute. He noticed Malyk had adjusted the weapons fire from the station to target fewer Eternal vessels. The station was methodically destroying Eternal warship after warship. Unfortunately the Eternals had thousands of vessels. Even the powerful weapons of the fleet base would not be able to prevail.

Carlton felt his dreadnaught shake slightly and then stabilize. Several warning alarms sounded.

"Antimatter missile," explained the AI at the Sensors. "We're being targeted."

Carlton knew the battle wouldn't last much longer. He was constantly adjusting his ship groupings as vessels were lost. It was becoming more difficult to keep enough ships firing on specific targets.

The main viewscreen was aglow with light. Thousands of beam weapons, antimatter explosions, and the larger dark matter detonations were prevalent. Space seemed to be on fire. Occasionally a brilliant flash would indicate the destruction of a warship.

"We must keep our fire focused," Carlton ordered. He leaned back in his command chair. Unfortunately his life as a military AI would be brief. He had only been created a few short months back. It would have been nice to be able to serve the Originators longer.

-

Fleet Commander Tarsal was not pleased with the way the battle was progressing. He was losing too many warships! At this rate he would barely be able to destroy the four fleet bases in this galaxy. The enhanced battlecruisers and dreadnaughts in the Originator fleet were causing much more damage to his fleet than expected. Those infernal dark matter missiles were knocking his ships' energy screens down, making the vessels vulnerable to attack.

"Change our formation to englobe the Originator fleet and the fleet base."

"We've lost five hundred and twelve battlecruisers," reported Garald. "We've managed to destroy six hundred and seven of the Originators' battlecruisers and two of their dreadnaughts."

"How many of the larger battlecruisers?" These were the ones causing the most damage. Once they were annihilated the battle would swiftly change to being more one sided. There were only eight dreadnaughts left and once the battlecruisers were gone they could be easily dealt with.

"One hundred and seventy-four."

"Focus our firepower on the remaining ones," ordered Tarsal. "I want them eliminated immediately. Once they're gone focus all of our fire on the remaining Originator dreadnaughts."

"Orders sent," replied Marloo from Communications.

-

The battle continued as the Eternal fleet slowly closed on the Originator fleet and the fleet base. Originator battlecruisers began to die more rapidly as the Eternals' superior numbers and firepower began to dominate the battle. The space around the fleet base was becoming littered with wreckage from destroyed vessels. The last enhanced battlecruiser died under the fire of multiple Eternal warships. Immediately after its destruction the Eternals shifted their firepower to the surviving dreadnaughts.

-

A sudden bright flash covered the screen in the command center of the fleet base.

"What was that?" asked Malyk.

"It was Carlton's command ship," replied Dasoon.

"How many dreadnaughts and battlecruisers do we have remaining?"

"A little over six hundred battlecruisers and four dreadnaughts."

"Send them to fleet base three," ordered Malyk. "There is no point in sacrificing them here. They may be more helpful there where they can reinforce its fleet."

"Message sent," reported the AI in front of Communications.

On the viewscreen, the Originator battlecruisers and the four dreadnaughts broke off and accelerated into hyperspace. Soon all that remained were a few damaged cruisers which could not flee and the Eternals.

-

Fleet Commander Tarsal was not pleased so many Eternal battlecruisers and the four dreadnaughts escaped. It meant a future battle at one of the three remaining fleet bases would be even more intense.

"Focus our fire on the base. Destroy it!"

"You don't want to attempt to capture it?" asked Garald.

"No, not after the last one. That trap they set will only work once."

On the ship's main viewscreen, antimatter explosions began to cover the energy shield of the station. For many long minutes the shield held as every weapon the Eternals could bring to bear was sent against the fleet base. The shield glowed brighter and brighter. Cascades of energy raced across the screen and then it collapsed. One moment it was there and the next it was gone.

With its failure the full firepower of thousands of Eternal vessels struck the fleet base over a matter of a few microseconds. The fleet base didn't explode or come apart; it simply ceased to be as its very component atoms were changed into drifting space dust.

"The fleet base has been destroyed," confirmed Garald.

Fleet Commander Tarsal let out a deep breath. This battle had been more costly than he had planned. "We will stay here for a few days and repair our battle damage before going on to the next fleet base." Tarsal considered contacting the nearest Eternal controlled galaxy and to request more ships. While they were on the far side of Originator controlled space Eternal controlled galaxies completely surrounded the region. It would take only a few weeks for additional ships to arrive.

After weighing his options for a few minutes he sent the order for additional ships. He would wait for their arrival, finish destroying the fleet bases in this galaxy, and then move on to the next.

Rear Admiral Hailey Mann was in the Command Center of her flagship, the *Victory*. Looking at the tactical display, it was covered in green icons. These were over six thousand vessels in her fleet: two hundred heavy dreadnaughts and six thousand battlecruisers, all with the latest energy shields and weapons. On another tactical display, a second grouping of green icons was visible behind the first. This would be Fleet Admiral Lukel.

"Two more weeks," said Commander Sutherland as he watched the viewscreens showing several nearby galaxies.

"Set up another fleet wide drill for tomorrow morning," ordered Hailey. "We don't want the crews to grow too relaxed from this prolonged journey."

"We received an update from Fleet Admiral Strong this morning," said Caria from the Helm. "The Eternals have destroyed the first of the four fleet bases in Galaxy X-268."

Hailey was aware of the communication. "I was afraid that would happen. The only good news is the Eternals lost nearly six hundred battlecruisers with numerous others suffering damage. They will have to wait a few days for repairs before moving on. Not only that but part of the Originator fleet defending the fleet base escaped and went to fleet base three."

"Maybe we should abandon the other two fleet bases and have all of their ships reinforce fleet base three," suggested Commander Sutherland.

Hailey shook her head. "Fleet Admiral Strong considered that but believes if we did the Eternals might just destroy the two abandoned bases and ignore the third all together."

"This war is going to get a lot more complicated," said Sutherland with a deep frown. "I suspect the Eternals will be deploying more fleets in the galaxies without Shrieels in an attempt to pin down our forces."

"You may be right," answered Hailey, leaning back further in her chair trying to get comfortable. "Fleet Admiral Strong is thinking about doing the same to the Eternals. Four or five of our fleets attacking bases in their galaxies may take some of the pressure off ours."

"The Shrieels and our fleet bases are all producing more warships," Caria said. "New shipyards are being constructed in all of the Shrieels and at the Communications and Transport Hub. In time we will have many more ships available."

Hailey took a deep and long breath. The scope of this war was mind-boggling. She was glad she wasn't the fleet admiral. Glancing at the largest viewscreen, she could see a large, globular-shaped galaxy. It was hard to imagine there were billions of stars and probably hundreds of thousands of inhabited worlds in that galaxy alone. Hailey couldn't help but wonder how and when this war would end, if ever.

Chapter Nine

Jeremy was inside the Tower scanning over the latest reports while he held a meeting. Commander Zafron and his fleet had returned to Galaxy X-938 for repairs. Jeremy looked at the ship losses knowing Commander Zafron had been fortunate to escape with what ships he did. The Eternals had set a trap for his fleet which had nearly worked.

"I'm going to be reinforcing Commander Zafron's fleet and will be sending it back out in another week. I don't want the Eternals to think they've driven us out of the Median Galaxy." At the moment there were no Originator fleets active in Eternal space. This needed to be rectified as soon as possible.

"More dreadnaughts and more of the enhanced battlecruisers," suggested Admiral Kalen. "There are a number already there at the Dyson Sphere. We may want to send two fleets to the Median Galaxy and use one to hit the targets and the other in reserve in case of another trap. The new dreadnaughts being produced there have the advanced dark energy cannons as well."

This was something Jeremy would have to think over. It did have its merits as well as its bad points. He would rather have the two fleets acting independently but that might not be the smart thing to do. Adding the new heavy dreadnaughts with the dark energy cannons would help also.

"The shipyards on the Dyson Sphere have been working around the clock building ships," said Jeremy as he glanced at a report showing the current ship numbers. "Not only that, Rear Admiral Cross is there with a large fleet to help in the Shrieel's defense. It won't be difficult to shift a few warships to Commander Zafron's command. If we add a second fleet, we would have to send it from here and assign another admiral to it." Jeremy wasn't sure this was wise as Rear Admiral Cross was defending the Dyson Sphere in Galaxy X-938, Rear Admiral Mann and Admiral Lukel were on their way to Galaxy X-268, and

Rear Admiral Barnes was currently in the Federation. He really needed more admirals. Perhaps it was time he looked at the current fleet officers at the Hub and promote a few.

"I'm sure both Commander Zafron and Kazak will be pleased with the expansion of their fleet," said Councilor Bartoll. "I will leave it up to you as to whether a second fleet should be assigned to the Median Galaxy."

"Fleet construction is ahead of schedule," reported Admiral Kalen. "I sent a request to Governor Barnes a few days back to see if he can find a few Federation admirals to send to us. We're going to need them for the new fleets."

Councilor Bartoll looked over at Jeremy. "Both Commander Belson and Commander Jontel have requested fleets to fight the Originators. I believe their two military AIs, Saber and Tanoak will be joining them."

Jeremy nodded. "They will make fine additions to the fleet. I'll contact them in the next day or so and see what we can arrange. As soon as possible I want to send additional fleets into Eternal space to begin hitting more of their shipyards. We need to force them to pull their ships back to their galaxies and out of ours." Jeremy was convinced if he could cause enough mayhem in some of the Eternal galaxies, they would have to use a major portion of their fleet to defend them.

Dazon Fells shook his head. Dazon was a specialist on the Anti-Life, or the Eternals as they now called themselves. "It may not work. The Eternals consider themselves to be a superior race to all others. The modifications they have made to their bodies using the mechanical nanites have erased many of the qualities we would consider necessary for life. They have focused on the harsher emotions and either eliminated or severely reduced ones such as love, empathy, and compassion. In some ways they are more logical in their thought processes. They may be willing to allow the attacks on their galaxies if they can continue to destroy our fleet bases. Their views may be more long term orientated rather than short term."

Bartoll shifted his gaze to Jeremy. "Dazon is correct. The Eternals will be willing to make great sacrifices if they can gain control of our Shrieels in the end. They may believe by destroying all of our fleet bases they can isolate the Shrieels and force us to surrender. That will not happen but it may be what they are seeking to accomplish."

"We will not let them isolate the Dyson Spheres," Jeremy said reassuringly. "We will do whatever is necessary to see that the fleet bases in the galaxies containing Dyson Spheres are not allowed to fall."

"I fear we may lose control of a few of the galaxies where there are not Shrieels," replied Bartoll. "We don't have the ships to put large fleets in all of those galaxies."

"We're going to try not to allow that to happen," said Admiral Kalen. "I'm already working on a plan to help secure those bases."

Jeremy looked over at Councilor Bartoll. "We're going to be bringing a lot of Federation military personnel to the Hub shortly. Are your people prepared for this?" Jeremy was anxious for them to arrive. With the ships being built in the Dyson Spheres and the large shipyards at the Hub more crews were sorely needed.

Bartoll nodded. "I have been meeting with the other councilors as well as some of the more important scientists of our race. They all understand the need for this. Most of my people will be in the other three Shrieels and will have little or no contact with the people from the Federation. The same for most of the scientists in the research facilities. The only exception will be those Originators working in the shipyards and helping teach your people some of the science involved in the battlecruisers and dreadnaughts. We have formed several teams who will be going on board the ships and showing your people how the equipment functions and how to repair some of it."

"Won't that take some time?" asked Admiral Kalen worriedly. "We need to get those fleets out and into Eternal space as soon as possible."

"Not as long as you think using Originator instructional techniques," Bartoll replied. "We have a sleep teaching aid which can place the knowledge directly into the brain. When the subject awakens the knowledge will be there, he just won't know how to use it. The Originator teams will then take them to the ships and as they go through the hands on training the knowledge will change from confusion to an understanding of how the ships function."

"Why weren't we told about this before?" asked Jeremy, thinking about how much quicker the training for the ships would have been.

"With the numbers involved we did not think it was necessary," confessed Bartoll. "It was an error on our part. We take our technology for granted; it is difficult sometimes to remember there is much of it you are not familiar with."

Jeremy looked around the group. "I thought Cynthia and Faboll were going to be here for this meeting."

"They're in one of the other Dyson Spheres," General Wesley explained. "Major Wilde has drilled a tunnel down to what appears to be a hidden stasis facility. They're going to attempt to open it tomorrow. Cynthia thought she should be there in case there were any complications. Faboll is on site so he can access the facility's computers and possibly learn of more hidden stasis facilities."

General Wesley looked over at Bartoll. "Is there any chance some of the Originators in this facility might be involved with the Defenders of Zorn?"

"No, not in this one," Bartoll answered. "Commander Belson said this stasis chamber was built by a close friend of his who had no interest in Zorn and his wild ideas."

"How are we progressing on assigning Marines to the Control Centers on the Shrieels and the computer cores?" asked Jeremy. He was greatly concerned that with the escape of Commander Alvord and his four followers there might be more Defenders of Zorn in another hidden stasis facility. If Alvord awakened them, they could pose a serious danger to one of the

Dyson Spheres. By securing the Control Centers and the main computer cores, it reduced that threat substantially.

"The computer cores on all Shrieels are protected by a squad of Marines and two squads of combat robots," replied General Wesley. "We're in the early stages of doing the same with the Control Centers. It should be finished in another two to three weeks. It's going to stretch our available Marines to the limit."

"We'll have more coming from the Federation," replied Admiral Kalen. "Once they arrive we can rotate them with the others. I put in a request for 120,000."

"So many?" said Councilor Bartoll uneasily. "Do you really believe they are needed?"

General Wesley nodded. "What would happen if the Eternals managed to land a large number of their troops and warrior robots on one of the Dyson Spheres and blast their way inside? We would need those troops to force them out, even using the combat robots. We're also going to need them to take out the Simulins on the two Dyson Spheres where they have vortex Control Centers under their control."

"Where will these new troops be based?"

"Most of them here at several bases outside the new cities," General Wesley replied. "If you wish I have no problem with assigning several of your military AIs to the different battalions."

"That won't be necessary," replied Councilor Bartoll. "I just was not prepared for this. So many things are changing here at the Hub that go against what our policies have been for millions of years. It is going to take some getting used to."

Jeremy looked over at General Wesley. "How soon before you can move on those two Control Centers the Simulins have under their control?" Jeremy wanted that done as soon as possible because it was a glaring weakness in defending the Dyson Spheres from the Eternals.

"Another few weeks until we have everything in position," Wesley answered. "We're moving thousands of combat robots as well as a few thousand Marines. It will be a concentrated attack by fleet forces as well as using a computer program to take back control of the vortex Control Centers. I talked to several Originator computer specialists, and they feel a special program they want to design is the best solution. It can be put in through a subroutine in the vortex Control Centers computers. It will shut down the energy shield as well as prevent the activation of the vortex. The main computer in the vortex Control Center will be tricked into running diagnostics and initiating preventive maintenance using the repair robots. Once that's been accomplished we'll use the warships to take out all Simulin vessels and any surface defenses they've erected. We'll then begin sending combat robots in along with our Marines."

"This isn't going to be easy," said Admiral Kalen. "We're going to lose a lot of combat robots and some of our Marines in the fighting."

"It's necessary," Jeremy replied. He blamed himself for waiting so long to do something about this. It should have been taken care of months ago.

"Jeremy," said Ariel as she suddenly appeared at his side. "I'm sorry to interrupt but Kelsey will shortly need you at the medical center."

Jeremy felt his heart skip a beat. Suddenly he was oblivious to the others in the room. "Is it time?"

Ariel nodded excitedly. "Yes, the next special child is about to be born!"

Jeremy looked at the others and saw Admiral Kalen grinning.

"You'd better go. I can handle the rest of the meeting."

"The birth of a child is very special," said Bartoll solemnly, "even among my people. Go be with your wife and celebrate this occasion."

–

Jeremy arrived at the medical center and hurried to the waiting room where the others were, even Katie. "Where are the twins?"

"A sitter," replied Katie. "They'll be fine for a few hours. They just took Kelsey to the delivery room so you had better hurry. I spoke to her a few minutes ago, and she was worried you weren't going to make it in time."

Jeremy headed to the delivery room where a nurse helped him put on a mask and a few other articles. Going inside, he stepped over to Kelsey's side.

"You just about didn't make it. Your son's in a hurry to be born."

Jeremy grinned. Unlike Katie and Kevin, he and Kelsey had elected to know the sex of their baby.

"Hold her hand and help with her breathing," ordered the doctor. "Your son is on his way and he's not going to wait."

"Impatient, just like his father," said Kelsey, trying to grin.

-

Angela was holding Clair on her lap explaining that Kelsey was having a baby and soon Clair would have another little playmate. Clair was full of a thousand questions, most of which Angela ignored since answering them would only bring about more questions.

Katie was watching Clair bounce up and down on Angela's lap. "We're going to have to build a pretty big nursery on the super exploration dreadnaught for all the kids."

Brace grinned, taking Clair off Angela's lap and putting her on his. "I have a few ideas about that. I talked to several AIs who are trained to raise Originator children. They would like to help with ours, particularly in the nursery."

Ariel turned around to stare at Brace.

"Don't worry, Ariel. You and Clarissa would still be in charge. The Originator AIs would be working under your supervision, and they could also help protect the children if necessary."

Ariel put her hands on her hips. Her dark eyes narrowed slightly. "That's something I'll have to discuss with Clarissa." Ariel was about to say something else when Jeremy came out of the hallway.

"Baby's fine and Kelsey's resting. She did great!"

The others were all thrilled.

Ariel immediately left, heading toward the nursery. She wanted to be there when the baby was brought in. She was recording everything for Clarissa and would shortly be sending her an update on the new special baby. Now that the baby was here the two AIs could begin implementing the training schedule they had worked out. Part of it was based on what Clarissa had already done with Clair. A few modifications had been made to accommodate Katie's two babies as well as Kelsey's.

"When Angela has her next baby that will make five," said Katie, looking over at Kevin. "Maybe we should get started on the sixth?" Katie knew the two AIs would approve. She also wanted a big family.

Kevin's eyes turned threatening. "Not yet; I haven't quite gotten used to the twins yet. Let them get a little older and we'll talk about it."

Jeremy looked around, noticing Ariel was missing.

"She's already gone to the nursery," Angela said grinning. "No doubt she's already planning the baby's training schedule."

Jeremy groaned. He could well imagine what the overly protective AI had planned. He suspected his life was going to get even more complicated.

At New Tellus Rear Admiral Barnes watched as the Accelerator Ring activated and a swirling blue vortex over one hundred kilometers across formed. From the center of the vortex four large Originator transport ships appeared, followed by their escorting fleet of warships. The ships could have exited hyperspace without the ring but it made for a smoother transition to normal space from the high speeds the vessels had been traveling.

Around the ring were one hundred Originator battlecruisers from the Dyson Sphere in Shari space. They were all the new enhanced type with the most modern weapons known to the Originators.

"Will you be returning home now?" asked Admiral Tolsen on the *Distant Horizon* watching the arrival of the large transports and their escort fleet. It had been impressive watching the huge Accelerator Ring activate.

"Yes, what have you decided?" Fleet Admiral Nagumo had suggested both Race and his sister Massie journey to the Communications and Transport Hub with the first group of Federation fleet personnel. Kathryn hoped Race and Massie accepted. Both would make great admirals in the war against the Eternals. Kathryn knew Jeremy would be thrilled to see Race.

Race turned to face Kathryn. "We're going. I spoke to former Fleet Admiral Streth the other day. He said I was always destined to leave this galaxy and join Fleet Admiral Strong."

Kathryn nodded. She had heard rumors the former fleet admiral could sometimes see the future.

"What about your parents?"

Race gestured toward the now quiescent Accelerator Ring. "We can always return for visits. I can't stay here knowing the danger the Eternals represent."

Kathryn nodded. Her father had also told her there would be several Alton admirals returning with her as well. "What about your crew?"

"Most of the command crew will be coming. I've already spoken to them. I hate giving up the *WarHawk* since it's an Alton-built dreadnaught. She's a wonderful ship and highly advanced."

Kathryn grinned. "The new heavy dreadnaught you will get will be much more powerful than your old one. Not only that, you can custom design your crew's living quarters and even the Command Center to a point."

Race looked at the massive viewscreen in front of him. It covered the entire front wall of the ship. Currently, it was divided into multiple screens showing different views of space. "I spoke to Fleet Admiral Nagumo yesterday. He would like me to spend some time fighting the Eternals with the new warships of the Originators and then return and lead a fleet of Originator battlecruisers against the Borzon and the Ralift, freeing all of the worlds they hold in slavery."

"I'm sure Fleet Admiral Strong will agree to that," replied Kathryn. It would be nice for the home galaxy to be free of threats."

"How much longer is your father staying?" asked Race.

"A few more months," Kathryn replied. She watched as one of the Originator construction ships moved closer to the Accelerator Ring to check it after its recent activation. "Once he's satisfied everything's set up correctly and the Federation is in full agreement on what needs to be done about the Eternals he will return." Her father was doing a great job at the Hub and soon there would be many more people there from all three races. He would be sorely needed to keep everything from dissolving into chaos with all the new arrivals. Currently, Admiral Kalen was filling in for him.

"Massie is visiting our parents and will be here the day after tomorrow."

"I'll have quarters set up for her on board the *Distant Horizon*. I think both of you will be impressed by what the Originators have done to this ship. It will give you an idea of what to expect in your own dreadnaughts."

-

Race nodded as he gazed at the viewscreens. New Tellus was plainly visible as well as the asteroid command fortress. As Massie and he had previously discussed, it seemed as if Race was destined always to be drawn to war. This time he wondered if it would be too much. He was going to fight a race who called themselves the Eternals due to their long lifespans. Someday he greatly feared he would not be returning home from battle and was destined to die in the void between the stars.

-

Several days later Kathryn watched as the Accelerator Ring activated. It was time for her to return to the Communications and Transport Hub. Alton Admirals Lankell and Baasil were on the *Distant Horizon* as well. That made four well qualified admirals she was bringing back to Fleet Admiral Strong.

Her fleet was returning with her except for the dreadnaught *Titania*. It was remaining behind for her father to use. Two of the enhanced battlecruisers were staying as escorts. The rest of her fleet, the four transports and their escorts would be returning with the *Distant Horizon* to the Communications and Transport Hub. On the transports were forty thousand trained fleet personnel. All were volunteers and carefully chosen for their command ability and being able to make decisions under pressure. Kathryn was ready to return to the Hub and get back into the war.

-

"Fleet is ready to enter the ring," reported Clarissa. Clarissa was anxious to return to the Communications and Transport Hub. Ariel had informed her of the birth of Kelsey's baby and sent along videos of the occasion. Clarissa was also missing Clair who she had become extremely attached to.

Clarissa checked the ship's sensors confirming all the ships were in their assigned positions. All systems on the *Distant Horizon* were operating at peak efficiency. She sent out a quick sensor scan of the entire system to confirm one last time there were no threats. The New Tellus System with its huge asteroid fortresses, shipyards and fleet bases reminded her of the Communications and Transport Hub only on a much smaller scale.

-

"Sible, take the fleet in," ordered Kathryn, leaning back in her command chair and relaxing.

Sible nodded and touched several icons on her navigation and helm console. Instantly the *Distant Horizon* and the rest of the fleet surged forward into the swirling vortex.

Kathryn felt only the slightest twinge in her stomach as the ship made the transition into hyperspace. The Originators had installed a hyperspace compensator on the *Distant Horizon*, which greatly reduced the effects of making the transition into hyperspace.

"Ready to get back into the war?" asked Commander Grissim.

Looking over at Anne, Kathryn nodded. "This mission has been too quiet. I'm sure Fleet Admiral Strong will be pleased we're back." Kathryn looked over at Admiral Tolsen who was standing next to her watching with interest the workings in the Command Center. "What do you think, Admiral?"

"Your ship is amazing," Race replied. He had stood transfixed as the fleet entered the swirling blue vortex of the Accelerator Ring. It evoked memories of some of the events at the galactic core and the massive dark hole there.

"Yours will be too," said Camlin, close by. "I am pleased you have chosen to come with us. There are many wonders to see at the Communications and Transport Hub."

Race nodded. "I am looking forward to it." Race was impressed by the Originator AIs. They acted so much like living beings. Clarissa had explained to him the Originators considered their AIs to be a form of life. It was something he would have to get used to as there would be AIs assigned to his new flagship.

Race stayed in the Command Center for a few more minutes and then decided to go see his sister Massie who was watching everything from an observation lounge.

Taking several turbo shafts he soon reached the deck where his sister and the two Alton admirals were. Stepping inside the large observation lounge, he was reminded the *Distant Horizon* was not only a dreadnaught but an exploration ship as well. A number of the ship's crew were in the lounge relaxing and talking to one another about current projects they were working on. Race recognized several of them as scientists he had been introduced to earlier.

"Race," said Massie, gesturing for him to come over where Admiral Baasil and Lankell were sitting. "Wasn't that entrance into hyperspace thrilling?"

"The technology behind the Accelerator Ring is amazing," said Admiral Baasil in his normally soft voice. "It is far in advance of anything we have on our worlds."

Race sat down joining the small group. "The Command Center is impressive. The helm officer on the ship is an Originator AI. She can control the ship with just her thoughts if she wants. Evidently all the AIs have a neural implant which allows them to link directly with any computer."

"Interesting," said Admiral Lankell. "We have explored such technology but have not found the need to implement it."

Massie looked over at Race with concern in her eyes. "Are we doing the right thing leaving the Federation and going to join Fleet Admiral Strong?"

"Yes," replied Race, looking at the other three. "I spoke to former Fleet Admiral Streth and he said it was necessary."

Massie could see Race was not telling them everything. "What else did the Fleet Admiral say?"

Race hesitated. "He said this is a war we cannot win."

Massie turned pale upon hearing this. "Then why are we fighting this war?"

"Fleet Admiral Streth also said this is a war we must fight if we want the Federation and other galaxies to survive."

"Confusing," said Admiral Lankell with a slight nod of his head. "It is known among my people that Fleet Admiral Streth has the rare ability to see dimly into the future. We may not know exactly what he has seen until the time comes."

The four sat in silence for a while thinking about Fleet Admiral Streth's prophetic words.

"I think it's best we don't tell anyone else about this," suggested Massie. "This needs to be kept between the four of us until we better understand what it means."

"I agree," said Race.

Admirals Baasil and Lankell nodded. "It is for the best," said Baasil. "It may be years in the future before we fully understand what the fleet admiral meant."

-

In the far off former Human Federation of Worlds former Fleet Admiral Hedon Streth was standing on the shore of the small lake he and his brother used to fish in. He missed those days which now lay hundreds of years in the past. It had been several days since he had the vision he'd told Admiral Tolsen about. The visions were coming less frequently now than when he was younger. He reached up, rubbing his brow. The headache from the vision was slowly receding.

The sun was beginning to set and he looked up at the first stars as they began to appear. A large part of his life had been involved in war. War in the distant past when the Hocklyns and the AIs first found the old Human Federation of Worlds and then in the future when he had fought to save the new Federation.

There were several things about his vision he had not revealed to Race. Parts of the vision were too horrifying to reveal and it could change the future for the worse. The war with the Eternals would have to play out along with the consequences he had foreseen. With great sadness he knew many who were going to fight in this war would never return home.

Chapter Ten

Major Brenda Wilde stood inside a long and deep tunnel, which had been dug down to what they believed, was a hidden Originator stasis facility. It lay beneath a small mountain and sensor readings indicated it was nearly two thousand meters beneath the surface. It had taken several days to assemble the necessary equipment and drill down to the complex.

"They sure didn't want to be found," commented Sergeant Metz as he gazed at the thick metal wall in front of them.

Leeda turned away from the wall where she had been using several instruments to scan it. "It's constructed of ship battle armor and nearly a meter thick. We can cut through it with the high intensity plasma cutter we brought."

"Go ahead," ordered Brenda, folding her arms over her chest. It appeared this was going to take a while. "We came to find out what's here so we need to get inside."

Leeda quickly contacted several waiting AIs who pushed forward a large projector and began setting it up to face the metal wall. Portable lights had been brought in and shone on the area to be cut.

Reesa walked over to stand next to Major Wilde with a look of excitement on her face. "The complex is immense. There could be thousands of Originators in stasis inside."

"We must be careful not to damage the complex," said Cynthia, who was standing by with a mixed medical team of Originators, Altons and a few specially trained AIs. "We don't know what condition the Originators in the stasis chambers will be in. One thing we can expect is all of them will be suffering from the pathogen."

"We have plenty of the antidote and can get more if needed," said Brenda.

"Have we been able to contact any AIs inside the facility?" asked Faboll Lavar.

Leeda shook her head. "I don't believe any AIs could survive this long without some type of maintenance facility. Our lives are very long but after a certain point, our memory engrams have to be downloaded into another body. I doubt if that resource is available in this stasis facility."

"What if they were in shutdown mode like Albate was aboard the *Seeker*?" asked Brenda. Albate and some combat robots had survived several million years by shutting down their systems until the *Seeker* was boarded by Commander Zafron and Rear Admiral Barnes. "Kazak managed to survive using that method as well."

"It might be wise to summon a few combat robots just in case," Leeda said as she looked back at the wall. "We don't know what type of defenses there might be inside."

Brenda nodded. She had two squads of Marines and three squads of combat robots on the surface. "Sergeant Metz, have a squad of the combat robots come down here just in case we need them." There was already a squad of Marines waiting just behind her in case they were needed.

Turning her attention back to the wall Brenda saw the AIs activate the plasma cutter. A red beam struck the wall and slowly began cutting into it. "How long will it take to cut a hole in the armor plating?"

"About an hour to make it large enough for us to enter," Leeda replied. "The armor is thick and we're trying not to damage anything beyond the wall."

"Do you know of any other precautions we should take?" asked Brenda, looking over at Deelia. She had been in charge of the massive underground stasis facility of the Lost Originators.

Deelia shook her head. "Not that I can think of. I'm curious as to why this facility did not activate when word of the cure was sent to all the Shrieels. Surely it was set up to do so."

"As are we all," replied Brenda as she watched the plasma cutter. It was making slow but steady progress.

An hour passed and the plasma cutter shut down. It had cut a hole three meters high and two meters wide into the metal wall. Earlier they had inserted a small probe which showed they were cutting into a dark corridor.

"We're ready to go inside," reported Leeda, turning toward Brenda.

"Sergeant Metz, take two Marines and two combat robots. You will escort Leeda into the facility. When you and Leeda deem it's safe the rest of us will come in."

"I would like to go with them." said Cynthia.

"No," Brenda replied. "We don't know what might be in there. I'm not going to risk your safety until we know it's safe."

Cynthia nodded, eyeing the opening which led into the corridor.

"Private Malone, Private Stern, the two of you are with me," said Sergeant Metz. "Each of you bring a combat robot along and try not to bump into anything."

Brenda watched expectantly as the Marines, the combat robots, and Leeda vanished into the opening. She was anxious to see what was inside. It had taken them months to finally find one of the hidden stasis facilities they felt were hidden on the Shrieels. The Shrieels were so large it was impossible to find the facilities using sensor scans. Fortunately the computer drive furnished by Jontel provided the exact coordinates for this one.

For several long minutes they waited and then an excited Private Malone appeared in the entrance. "It's safe. Major Wilde, you need to come inside and see this. It's amazing!"

"Let's go," Brenda said to the others.

Going inside they made their way down the dimly lit corridor to a door standing wide open. From the door bright light was shining. Stepping inside they came to a stunned halt.

"It is a stasis facility!" said Reesa excitedly. Inside the room were a number of stasis chambers along one wall with Originators inside.

"The setup is similar to what we were using only smaller," said Deelia as she walked around gazing at the consoles and computer screens.

"There's more," Sergeant Metz said from another open doorway. "There are stasis chambers on both sides of this corridor for as far as we can see. Not only that, we've found two other corridors set up the same way."

Cynthia walked over to the chambers in the room checking them. "The stasis chambers in here seem to be working perfectly," she reported as she scanned them with an instrument she was carrying. Several other Originators were checking the stasis chambers in the tunnels

Faboll walked around the large room, inspecting it. "This seems to be the Control Room for this facility. The Originators in stasis are probably the leaders as well as the specialists who would administer the antidote to the pathogen and awaken the others who are in stasis."

There were fourteen stasis chambers in the room. They held eight male Originators and six female. Cynthia checked each one thoroughly before turning back toward Major Wilde. "They're in reasonable health. However, as expected, they are all suffering in different degrees from the pathogen."

Faboll was hovering over a computer console, examining it closely. "This appears to be the main computer console for the complex." He took out a small handheld device and placed it on top of the console. For several long minutes he studied it and then looked over at Brenda. "It appears a command was received by this computer that the facility was not to be activated unless a code was entered manually."

"How long ago?" asked Brenda.

Faboll looked confused. "The command originated from the Communications and Transport Hub about twenty thousand years after the last of our people who were not in stasis died from the pathogen. A little over two million years ago."

"One of the AIs controlled by the Defenders of Zorn," said Leeda. "It's the only explanation."

"Can you override the command?" asked Brenda.

Faboll nodded. "Yes, now that I have access to the computer it will be relatively simple. However, I should inform you that 8.2 percent of the stasis chambers have failed."

Cynthia looked intently at Faboll. "Why?"

"The designers of this complex did not expect to be in stasis for millions of years. Some of the stasis chambers suffered catastrophic failures."

"Lack of a proper maintenance program," Deelia said. "I have noticed several repair robots in the corridors, but they seem to be nonfunctional."

Brenda could see how upset this was making Cynthia. "Faboll, how many stasis chambers are in this facility?"

"Thirty-eighty thousand," he answered. "Slightly over three thousand have failed."

Brenda took a deep breath. "I know it is horrible that over three thousand have died in this facility but there are thirty-five thousand still living. We must concentrate on them and not those who have died."

Cynthia nodded. "We will need more of the antidote. We should probably arrange for shuttles to come here so we can take the stasis chambers to a large medical center in one of our cities. It will be safer to awaken them there where we will have the proper facilities to treat the pathogen as well as the weakened conditions of those in the stasis chambers."

Deelia spent a moment examining one of the chambers and nodded to herself. "It should be relatively easy to move the chambers. I would suggest we bring in a number of repair robots to assist."

Brenda looked back over at Faboll who was still busy at the computer. "Have you found out anything else?"

Faboll turned around with a pleased and excited smile on his face. "It seems this facility is one of many which were constructed during the final days of the pathogen. The Originator Council was involved and great care was taken to keep the locations of these facilities a secret."

"How many facilities are there?" asked Brenda. She guessed there were probably a few hundred scattered across the Dyson Spheres.

"There are thousands of them," Faboll answered. "All have been instructed not to activate until the manual code is entered into the primary computer system."

Brenda took a deep breath. They now knew why none of the facilities activated when the cure for the pathogen was announced. Councilor Bartoll would be highly distraught when he found out about this, particularly if the delayed activation caused the deaths of many of those in stasis.

"Do you know where they are?" asked Brenda. This information needed to be sent to Councilor Bartoll and Fleet Admiral Strong as soon as possible.

Faboll shook his head. "No, only about a hundred or so. I believe each facility will have information on others. The more facilities we open up, the more we will have locations for."

Reesa looked over at Brenda. "It is going to be a massive job to find and awaken all of these Originators. If there are an average of thirty thousand in each facility we're talking about sixty million Originators who may be in stasis."

"It could be more or less depending on the number and sizes of the stasis facilities," Leeda said.

"Councilor Bartoll will be thrilled to learn of this, though he will be saddened by the deaths," Brenda said.

"There is a problem," Cynthia said worriedly. "We've already lost over three thousand in this facility. The longer it takes to find the others and awaken those in stasis the more that will die. We have no way to tell how rapidly the equipment in those facilities is failing."

Brenda realized this was going to be a massive undertaking. It would require the utilizing of many of the Dyson Spheres' AIs as well as a number of the Lost Originators. If all the stasis facilities were buried like this one, the project could take many months or even years.

"I'd better go make a report to Councilor Bartoll and Fleet Admiral Strong," Brenda said. "There are decisions which need to be made." Brenda wondered what sixty million more Originators would mean to the war effort. Starting to walk up the long tunnel she knew things were about to get even more interesting.

-

Jeremy, Councilor Bartoll, Councilor Trallis, Councilor Castille, Admiral Kalen, General Wesley, Marisa Lillad, and Santol were in an emergency meeting.

"They say there are thousands of potential stasis facilities on the Shrieels," said Bartoll in disbelief.

Jeremy nodded. "In her report Major Wilde indicates there could be as many as sixty million of your people in stasis."

Bartoll leaned back still in shock. "They were here all along."

Marisa looked thoughtful. She was an Originator geneticist and medical expert. "The report also indicates over 8 percent of the stasis chambers in this facility they're reached have failed. They were not designed to operate for so long. It's been a little over two million years."

"Yes," replied Jeremy. "That's why we need to move quickly on this. I've already contacted the Altons and they're preparing all of their medical staff. We're also mobilizing all of our Marines to help dig tunnels to the underground facilities. It's not going to be easy as they're all probably deep underground like this one."

"Our drilling equipment will make it easier," Santol said. Santol was an Originator engineer. "We can use our AIs to operate it but we'll need technicians and medical staff once we reach the stasis facilities."

"Military as well," said Bartoll, thinking about the potential dangers. "We must make sure none of these stasis facilities are controlled by the Defenders of Zorn. With the current war against the Eternals, we dare not risk awakening more of them."

"I agree," said Councilor Trallis. "I would suggest we begin immediately making ready medical facilities in every Shrieel."

"Yes," said Marisa. "I think it's best the stasis chambers be moved to the facilities for awakening. Cynthia reported all the Originators in the facility they've opened are suffering from the pathogen. Everyone we awaken will need several weeks of intensive care. It's going to be a shock when they discover how much time has passed and we're now at war with the Eternals. This is going to stress our resources as we don't have the people or the AIs for such a massive operation."

Jeremy looked around the group. "Perhaps the best solution is to find all of these stasis facilities and then use your people and the Altons to make sure no more of the stasis chambers inside fail. Then you can awaken your people as the resources become available."

Councilor Castille looked over at Jeremy and then nodded. "That sounds reasonable. It would also give us time to scan our data banks to determine if anyone in stasis was involved with the Defenders of Zorn."

"General Wesley," said Jeremy, addressing the general. "We're going to need more troops to guard these facilities until the Originators inside are awakened. Contact Governor Barnes and inform him of the situation and see about getting qualified soldiers on some of the transports which will soon be returning. Councilor Bartoll, we also need to ramp up the creation of more combat robots as we'll need them for guard duty as well." Jeremy didn't want to take anything away from the planned attack on the Simulins' vortex Control Centers in the two Dyson Spheres."

"You really think there is a danger to these underground facilities?" asked Councilor Trallis.

Jeremy nodded. "I do. Look what happened to the one we designed to trap any rogue AIs supporting the Defenders of Zorn."

Everyone nodded. The fake stasis facility had been destroyed and a number of Marines killed. Eight AIs had been destroyed in the blast as well . There was still some suspicion Commander Alvord and Albate had been behind the attack.

"I suggest we leave Major Wilde in charge of this project," said General Wesley. "We will substantially increase the size of her team, allowing them to work on multiple Dyson Spheres at the same time." Wesley looked over at Councilor Bartoll. "We will need additional Originator medical personnel, technicians, and AIs assigned to her."

Councilor Bartoll nodded. "I will make the arrangements though I fear we're going to fall short finding the necessary personnel we're going to need."

Admiral Kalen looked thoughtful. "We could contact the Altons back in the Federation and explain the situation. They are familiar with long term stasis. They could send the personnel we require."

Jeremy looked over at the three Originator Councilors. "What do the three of you think of Admiral Kalen's suggestion?"

"The Altons are the most advanced race we know of next to us," replied Councilor Trallis. "I have no objection."

"Neither do I," added Councilor Castille. "The sooner we can awaken everyone in stasis the better it's going to be for all of us. It will greatly improve the odds of us being able to defeat the Eternals."

"I will speak to Governor Barnes," Councilor Bartoll said after listening to his two fellow councilors and then looking over at Jeremy. "Do you think the Altons will agree?"

"Yes, they will not hesitate. I wouldn't be surprised if Ambassador Tureen showed up here to offer aid."

The meeting ended with a number of decisions made. In Major Wilde's report a number of locations of other stasis facilities had been included. As soon as the meeting was over Jeremy would be ordering Marine units and combat robots to the locations to make sure no one interfered. It still greatly concerned him that Commander Alvord, his four crewmembers, and Albate were out there somewhere. He had a strong feeling they hadn't heard the last from that group.

-

Major Wilde stood inside one of the long tunnels with stasis chambers on each side. She was gazing at one of the failed ones. Inside was the mummified female body of an Originator. She had noticed a number of these in this tunnel and wondered if there was a reason for the rate of failure in this tunnel to be higher than the others. A number of AIs along with repair robots were hurriedly checking all the chambers to make sure no more failed. Deelia was supervising the inspection.

"We're starting to remove the stasis chambers," Sergeant Metz reported over her comm unit. "We've brought in a large number of repair robots to assist. There will be a steady stream of shuttles between here and Lumoir." Lumoir was a nearby Originator city. It had several large medical facilities and both had been fully activated to handle the awakening of the Originators and administering the cure for the pathogen.

Brenda nodded. In a few more days a large number of Originator and Alton medical personnel would be arriving to help in awakening the sleeping Originators. Awakening and treating 35,000 Originators was going to take awhile. Currently, Cynthia had her own team and a number of AIs who would be assisting until the others arrived.

"Faboll has the locations of fourteen more stasis facilities on this Dyson Sphere," reported Reesa, walking up to Major Wilde. "Leeda is already sending out teams to scan the locations to confirm the stasis facilities are there."

"Make sure we assign some combat robots to those locations," said Brenda.

That made fifteen stasis facilities on the Dyson Sphere. If that was an average, it indicated there might be more than three thousand spread across all the megastructures. There were a few other squads of Marines assigned to this Dyson Sphere for security. Taking a deep breath, she decided it might be wise to pull them off their assignments and send them to protect the stasis facility locations. While she felt confident the combat robots were capable, she would feel better if there were a few Marines at each site as well. She also needed to contact Captain

Werner and have him send a full company of Marines to the Dyson Sphere. Unfortunately it would take them several days just to get here.

Only shortly before, Brenda had received the message informing her she would be responsible for locating, opening, and retrieving the Originators in all the hidden stasis facilities. After thinking about it, she decided to form six teams, which would allow them to work on six Dyson Spheres at the same time. She didn't think they had the resources to do more than that at the moment. As additional resources became available more teams would be formed.

"I never believed we would find so many," said Reesa, sounding excited. "Just think of all we can learn about the last days in the Dyson Spheres as the life extension pathogen spread. These Originators will have a lot of stories to tell."

Brenda looked over at Reesa. "We should have expected it. There were trillions of Originators in the Dyson Spheres. They have very long life spans; over nine thousand years. It was ludicrous of us to think they would allow their people to die out without making some attempt to survive. Look at what the Lost Originators did."

"I plan on doing some research on the last days in the Dyson Spheres," Reesa said. "I want to know what it took to build all of these hidden facilities and who knew it was going on. This is part of Originator history and I need to make a record of it."

Brenda nodded. Reesa was a research scientist dealing with the Originators and of course she would want to know more about those chaotic times. "Let's get up to the surface. We have a lot of plans to make, and we need to coordinate everything with Cynthia, Faboll, and Leeda." Already Brenda was wondering if there would be any surprises in the other hidden facilities. She also knew that somewhere there had to be another facility with members of the Defenders of Zorn in stasis. She greatly feared Commander Alvord had already found it and awakened those inside.

At Galaxy X-938 Commander Zafron watched as the last of his damaged ships exited one of the shipyards on the Dyson Sphere fully repaired. His fleet had been augmented to allow him more options while attacking the Eternals. He had two hundred of the large heavy dreadnaughts. All of the dreadnaughts were now equipped with dark energy cannons. Two of the deadly weapons had been installed on the bow of each ship. In addition, he had eleven hundred of the enhanced battlecruisers. This was a much more powerful fleet than the one he had previously taken to the Median Galaxy.

Admiral Cowel was also coming to the Median Galaxy with an equally sized fleet. The plans were to return to the Stralon Star Cluster and annihilate all Eternal ships. Commander Zafron was firmly convinced the ships, which had set a trap for his fleet, had originated from there and he intended to destroy them.

"All ships are in formation," reported Kazak. "I have briefed the military AIs on the specifics of this mission."

Commander Zafron nodded. Kazak could communicate with the AIs without the need of the ship's communication equipment. All AIs had a built in communication device that allowed for instantaneous communication over short distances. They were in a hurry to return to the Median Galaxy. Fleet Admiral Strong was concerned if pressure wasn't applied to the Eternals to protect the galaxies of their empire, they would send more fleets into Originator space in an attempt to destroy the numerous fleet bases.

Zafron had managed to allow his Human and Alton crews on the dreadnaughts to take a few days' leave in the Shrieel. He knew how important it was to maintain morale.

"Admiral Cowel reports his fleet is ready," reported Captain Franklyn from Communications.

"Then let's be off," said Zafron. "Kia, plot our course and take control of both fleets' navigation. I want us to arrive at the Median Galaxy together and with stealth fields activated. I don't want the Eternals to know we've returned until we hit them."

"Course plotted and all ships are tied into the navigation console," she replied after a few moments. "We're ready to enter hyperspace." The trip to the Median Galaxy would take 4.28 days as the galaxy was 940,000 light years from Galaxy X-938.

"Initiate," ordered Commander Zafron, gazing at the large viewscreen in front of him.

On the viewscreen, a swirling blue vortex formed as the *Dominator* rushed forward into its center.

Moments later the vortex vanished, leaving no sign of the five-thousand-meter vessel. It was as if it had vanished. The rest of the two fleets were also entering vortexes and making the transition to hyperspace.

On the *Dominator*, Commander Zafron checked one of the large tactical displays. It was full of green icons representing the ships of the two fleets. It was time to return to the Median Galaxy and strike the Eternals. Commander Zafron was pleased Fleet Admiral Strong was sending him back for one very simple reason: Zafron did not like to lose, and he intended to teach the Eternal fleet commander who had defeated him last time what it meant to fight an angry Originator.

Chapter Eleven

Rear Admiral Kathryn Barnes smiled as the *Distant Horizon* exited the Accelerator Ring at the Communications and Transport Hub. All four of the Federation admirals who had come with her were in the Command Center for the occasion.

On the large viewscreen across the entire front wall, the hundreds of massive constructions of the Originators appeared.

"Wow!" exclaimed Massie. Her eyes were wide open as she stared in disbelief. "What's here?"

"There are four Dyson Spheres, massive research labs, construction facilities, and shipyards."

"What is that?" asked Race, pointing toward a huge sphere under construction."

"It's a new defense station being built to protect the Hub from an Eternal attack. They're five thousand meters in diameter. The Dyson Spheres and all the facilities are heavily armed, but the defensive stations are being designed to keep a battle away from them."

Admiral Tolsen's eyes were drawn to the tactical displays. They were covered with thousands of friendly green icons. "And all of this is just sitting out here in the middle of intergalactic space?"

Kathryn nodded. "Where better to hide the Communications and Transport Hub? It makes it almost impossible to find if you don't know it's here."

"We're being directed to dock at one of the shipyards," reported Captain Travers.

"Take us in, Sible," ordered Kathryn. She was anxious to give her report to Jeremy and see what all had occurred while they had been gone.

—

Everyone's eyes focused on the viewscreen as the *Distant Horizon* moved toward one of the titanic structures. It dwarfed any shipyard even dreamed of in the Federation.

"This is one of the smaller shipyards," Camlin explained. "It's only twelve hundred kilometers in diameter and can build or service any ship in the Originator fleet."

The Federation admirals didn't know what to say. They were realizing everything involving the Originators was on a totally different level.

Suddenly Ariel appeared in the Command Center, causing everyone to jump except Rear Admiral Barns. Ariel's sudden appearance was not a surprise; she had been expecting it. There were special holographic emitters in the Command Center and a few other compartments on the ship Ariel could use to send her holographic projection if she was in close proximity to the ship.

"Hi!" she said in greetings in her youthful voice. "I'm glad you're back, Rear Admiral Barnes." Ariel turned toward Admiral Tolsen. "Fleet Admiral Strong is pleased you are here as well as the other admirals. I believe he is already preparing fleets for all of you."

"Has something happened?" asked Kathryn worriedly. They had been gone for a considerable length of time.

Ariel shifted her attention back to Kathryn. "No, but Fleet Admiral Strong is concerned the Eternals will soon be launching more attacks in Originator controlled space. He wants to do everything he can to prevent that. There has also been a development in the search for hidden stasis facilities on the Dyson Spheres. Major Wilde and her team have found one. It now appears the Originator Council made a concentrated effort toward the end of the life extension pathogen epidemic to save their race. We now believe there are up to three thousand hidden stasis facilities."

Kathryn felt her pulse quicken. "How many more Originators would that make?" She knew the current Originator population was a little less than thirteen million. Over twelve million of those were the Lost Originators.

"Anywhere from sixty to over one hundred million," replied Ariel.

Kathryn felt stunned at the number. Councilor Bartoll must be ecstatic over this development.

"How are the children?" asked Clarissa, who had come over to stand next to Ariel. "I hated missing out on the birth of Kelsey's child."

"They're beautiful," Ariel replied grinning. "Clair has missed you. She asks about you every day while she's doing her lessons."

"I've missed her," replied Clarissa. "As soon as we're docked I'll be going to check on her as well as Kelsey's baby."

"Don't forget about the twins," Ariel said grinning.

Clarissa nodded her eyes lighting up with excitement. "How's Kevin adapting to that?"

"Slowly," Ariel answered, with a twinkle in her eyes. "Right now they're a handful."

"I'm missing something here," said Race, looking confused. "Exactly whose babies are we talking about?"

Ariel patiently explained, seeing an animated look appear on Rear Admiral Massie Tolsen's face.

"The Special Five have children!" she said excitedly. "When this information reaches the Federation the media stations will go wild."

Ariel turned back toward Admiral Tolsen. "As soon as you've docked we will take a shuttle on a quick tour of the Communications and Transport Hub. Then later I'm supposed to take all four of you to the Tower to meet with Fleet Admiral Strong and possibly Councilor Bartoll."

"An actual Originator," said Massie, her eyes lighting up.

-

"Leader of the Originators," corrected Race, looking over at his sister. He had spoken at great length with Governor Barnes as to who was in charge here at the Communications and Transport Hub and what he should expect.

Massie nodded. "I forgot in all the excitement."

Race's attention was drawn back to the large viewscreen. It was now showing a fleet of the massive heavy dreadnaughts.

"How many warships are here at the Hub?" In that fleet alone there must be over one thousand of the dreadnaughts.

"It changes hourly," Ariel replied. "All of the shipyards on the four Dyson Spheres are working nonstop. There are also additional shipyard facilities in other structures here at the Hub. At the last count, there were over eighty-three thousand functioning vessels. Many are only waiting for crews."

Race felt numb at hearing the number. He was used to the smaller fleets in the Federation. He realized his entire way of thinking about space battles was going to have to change. This was war on an intergalactic scale fought with fleets numbering in the tens of thousands. He hoped he was up to the task.

-

In the Eternal home galaxy on Gardell, the Council of Eternals was meeting.

"We have six more fleets ready to attack the fleet bases of the Originators," reported Queexel. "These are all new vessels with the latest upgrades, including the more powerful antimatter missiles."

"What about dark matter?" asked First Leader Clondax. "How is our research going there?" It was aggravating to know the Originators had several powerful weapons, which could destroy Eternal vessels. The Eternals were supposed to be the most powerful and advanced race in this universe.

"Not well," replied Second Leader Fehnral. "The Originators had the Shrieel in the dark matter nebula and spent hundreds of thousands of years experimenting with dark matter. How they managed to control it and make it into a viable weapon still eludes us. There are also reports they have deployed a new type of defensive shield on their ships. It's much more resistant to energy weapons fire than their former one."

Clondax was not pleased to hear this. Perhaps more pressure should be applied to the scientists involved in the research. "Inform the scientists working on the project that I want results, not excuses. As for our energy weapons, do what is necessary to strengthen them."

"I will demote a number of them as an example," replied Fehnral. "For the energy weapons it will be necessary to install an additional power plant in our ships to strengthen them."

"Then do so," ordered Clondax. "Queexel, I want an extra power plant installed in all the new ships we're constructing."

"We will have to make some design modifications but I believe it can be done."

Clondax looked over at Fehnral. "Is there anything else in development that might help us against the Originators?"

Fehnral shook his head. "Not at the moment. We're focusing heavily on dark matter research. That seems to be where the Originators have a major advantage over us."

"What about this blue energy sphere they have used? What is that? It goes directly through our screens and destroys our ships." Clondax had seen the weapon first hand at the Originators' star cluster.

"It attacks the energy bonds that hold atoms together," Fehnral reported. "Reports indicate our ships just begin to fall apart when attacked. We have no clue as to the origin of this weapon. It's baffling as to the force that can cause such a reaction to the hulls of our ships. We're working on it, but without a sample we really don't know where to start."

Fehnral looked at Clondax and then spoke. "I hesitate to suggest this but perhaps we should seek an armistice with the Originators. We don't interfere in their space, and they don't interfere in the galaxies we've already conquered. I fear we will suffer massive ship losses in a prolonged conflict, so massive it will bring to a halt our expansion into other galaxies."

Clondax's eyes turned cold. "Never! We must gain control of those Shrieels. Just imagine how fast we could spread across this universe with the manufacturing capability they possess." Clondax could not believe Fehnral had even put forth the suggestion; it was borderline treason. It was incomprehensible to Clondax to allow the Originators to continue to control such a large region of space. "Ship losses are irrelevant as they can easily be replaced. We control over ten thousand galaxies and there are shipyards in all of them with new ones constantly being built. We can attack the Originators and still continue to grow our empire. I will hear no more talk of an armistice."

Fehnral nodded, saying no more.

Clondax turned back to Queexel still seething from Fehnral's suggestion. "I want ten fleets to send into Originator space as soon as possible. The six we have now plus four more. That will force them to use their available fleets to defend their fleet bases. We will have superior numbers as the Originators won't know what bases we're striking until it's too late. We will begin the process of isolating the Shrieels."

"What about attacking just one of the Shrieels?" asked Second Leader Tarmal. "If we could take control of just one of them we could launch an invasion of the others with our warrior robots and shock troops."

"We are exploring that possibility," Clondax answered. "A race called the Simulins controls two galaxies in Originator Space. There is a Shrieel in both galaxies. From what we have been able to learn, they control one of the vortex Control Stations on each one. Eternal battlecruisers have been sent to both galaxies to see if it's possible for us to remove the Simulins and take over control of the two Control Centers. If we can we could launch an invasion of the other Shrieels from the vortex centers. We should know shortly if that is practical."

"How did we learn of this?" asked Second Leader Tallard.

"From Fleet Commander Parnon and his survey of Originator space. A Simulin warship was captured and its computer files accessed."

"I will continue to ready more warrior robots and shock troops for an invasion," said Second Leader Tarmal.

"Have there been any more reports of Originator activity in our empire?" asked Second Leader Barrant.

Clondax shifted his gaze toward Barrant. "No, we believe after their last defeat they have pulled their forces back into Originator space. They have learned our galaxies are too dangerous for them. This war will be fought in Originator space and not ours."

Clondax was certain the Originators recognized the superiority of the Eternals. At a particular point in this war he would approach them about surrender. Rather than fight a pointless war they can't win the Originators would accept Clondax's final solution. The Originators would be allowed to keep one Shrieel, and the Eternals would take over all the others. As another part of the agreement, the Originators would not be allowed to support the Humans. The Humans would be annihilated as they could not be allowed further access to Originator technology.

Admiral Race Tolsen and the other admirals were in the city the Originators had built for the Humans in front of the Tower, looking in amazement at everything around them.

"It's like we've stepped into the future," said Massie as she gazed about.

"We have talked about building cities such as this," said Admiral Baasil. "The only comparable city we have is the City of Lights on Astral."

Race nodded. He had been to Astral and the City of Lights a number of times. It was amazing what the ancient Altons had constructed. The computer center beneath the city was even more awe inspiring.

"More cities are being built to provide accommodations for the people coming from the Federation," said Ariel. She had joined them in her android body after the *Distant Horizon* docked at the shipyard. "There is a separate habitation square for Humans, Altons, and Carethians. Each square is approximately the size of Earth or New Tellus."

Massie looked over at Ariel. "What about the Originators? Where do they live?"

"They live in the other three Dyson Spheres. A few have chosen to return to their home Dyson Spheres in other galaxies. Not many but some have chosen not to participate in the war.

There are a number of Originators who work here at the Tower. I will introduce you to some of them once we go inside."

Race watched with interest as several vehicles pulled up and a number of fleet officers exited them and entered the tall building. The vehicles were unbelievably quiet. Looking across the city, he saw no signs of pollution and the noise level one normally associated with a major city was absent. It suddenly struck him how different living here was going to be compared to the worlds of the Federation.

"You will get used to living here," said Ariel, suspecting what Admiral Tolsen was thinking. "Let's go into the Tower and up to Fleet Admiral Strong's office. He and Admiral Kalen are waiting."

Race grinned at hearing Admiral Kalen's name. He had always had a lot of respect for the Ceres admiral.

After going inside the building they walked past four large and imposing combat robots.

"Are those self-aware?" asked Race. He noticed the robots' attention had shifted to the five of them as they walked by.

"No," replied Ariel. "If one of us was unauthorized they would have requested we come to a halt and an officer would have been summoned. If we had kept going, ignoring their command, we would have been stunned."

"Does a stunner affect you?" asked Massie, looking over at Ariel.

Ariel shook her head. "Not like it does you. It would be painful but I could still function."

"Can you feel pain?" asked Massie, her curiosity piqued at the thought.

"Oh, yes," Ariel replied. "These android bodies the Originators have created for their AIs can feel the same pain as a regular Human. I can even enjoy eating and drinking though alcohol has no affect on me."

They reached a bank of elevators and Ariel led them into one she had to enter a code word to access. "This will take us directly to the corridor leading to Fleet Admiral Strong's office."

The elevator started upward and Race was surprised there was no feeling of motion.

Jeremy was sitting in his office speaking with Admiral Kalen when the door opened and Ariel and the four Federation admirals entered.

"Admiral Tolsen," said Jeremy, standing and walking over to the four admirals. Race he knew; he wasn't familiar with the other three.

"Fleet Admiral," Race said pleased to see Jeremy again after so many years. He quickly introduced the other three admirals with him.

"Massie Tolsen?" Jeremy said. "Are you Race's sister?"

"Yes, Fleet Admiral," Massie answered. "I'm so pleased to finally meet you. I've heard so much about the Special Five all of my life."

Jeremy smiled. "Don't believe everything you've heard. We're no different than anyone else."

"I'm glad to see the four of you," said Admiral Kalen, shaking the hands of the admirals. He had met all of them at one time or another in his career.

"Jeremy gestured toward some comfortable chairs in front of his desk. "Sit down and I'll brief you on our current situation and the plans I have for each of you. Feel free to ask any questions you may have. We have a lot to go over."

For the next four hours they discussed the current situation with the Originators and the Eternals. Jeremy had Ariel play some videos of the battles that had taken place including the massive one at the Lost Originators' star cluster. All four Federation admirals had questions. The two Alton admirals were intensely interested in the Eternal battlecruisers and their weapons.

"You say your new dreadnaughts and battlecruisers are protected by a triplex energy screen?" asked Admiral Baasil in his soft voice. "We experimented with that concept in the past but could never get past the power requirements."

"It's strange the Eternals don't have dark matter missiles," said Admiral Lankell. "However, the power behind their energy beams is astonishing."

"We believe it's because the Eternals never had access to dark matter like the Originators did at the dark matter Dyson Sphere," explained Jeremy.

The door to the office opened and Kevin and Councilor Bartoll entered.

"Is that an Originator?" asked Massie in a low voice, her eyes widening.

Jeremy grinned. He knew how he had felt the first time he had seen and spoken to an Originator. That had been Commander Zafron. "This is Councilor Bartoll. He wanted to meet all of you so I asked him to stop by."

Bartoll stopped in front of the four admirals who had all stood up. He looked down at Massie and smiled. "I am pleased to see more military leaders from the Federation. I hope you enjoy your stay with us and if there is anything you need all you have to do is ask."

Race smiled to himself. For once his sister was at a loss for words.

"Jeremy, I just came from the Communications Center, and Commander Zafron and Admiral Cowel have departed the Dyson Sphere in Galaxy X-938 and are on their way back to the Median Galaxy," said Kevin.

"Good, we needed to get back on the offensive."

"The Median Galaxy," said Race, looking thoughtful. "That's where you first encountered the Eternals."

Jeremy nodded and began explaining his reasons for attacking Eternal space.

"We're yours to command, Admiral," Race said. "Just tell us what you want us to do."

"I want to give the four of you time to acclimate to the Communications and Transport Hub. I have some additional tours set up for you as well as meetings with some Originator AIs and a few Originators. Then all four of you will be assigned a heavy dreadnaught as your flagship. There will also be a military AI assigned to your ships to answer any questions you may have about the offensive and defensive weaponry. In an emergency the AI can command the ship if necessary. Don't hesitate to ask for any changes you may wish to the Command Centers or your living quarters. With the technology here at the Hub such changes can be made very quickly."

Councilor Bartoll looked at the four. "We realize this is going to be a very long war, one which may go on for generations. Any resources you feel are necessary for your success will be provided."

-

Kevin looked at the four admirals. He had met Admiral Tolsen several times in the past but not the other three. "The cities have everything your crews will want for their leave time. There are fine restaurants, fast food places, video theatres and some fabulous resorts built in the mountains and on the seashores. Some of the seashore resorts rival those found on New Tellus."

-

"I like the snow skiing myself," commented Jeremy smiling.

It suddenly dawned on Race that Jeremy and the rest of the crews of the Lost Fleets had built a new life for themselves here on the Dyson Sphere. In all probability they now must consider this to be home, not the Federation.

-

Massie was feeling intimidated. Not only was she standing in the same room as two of the legendary Special Five but there was a real live Originator in the room as well. All of her fleet training and her days at the academy on the Moon hadn't prepared her for this. Looking over at Race she couldn't believe how calm he was. Of course Race had developed quite a reputation himself back in the Federation.

"What do you think of our city?" asked Kevin, looking at Massie.

Massie felt her face flush. "It's beautiful. I've never seen anything like it."

"Wait until you see it at night," said Ariel with a grin. "Kelsey and Katie come up to the Communications Center with Angela sometimes just to look out over the city."

Massie nodded. She could well imagine. Massie couldn't wait to go on more tours and see more of the Dyson Sphere. The megastructure fascinated her. She had seen the outside of the one in Shari space but had never expected to get to go inside one.

"If you don't have any more questions I'll have Ariel show you to your quarters," said Jeremy. "I've arranged for a fleet officer to come by later and take the four of you out to eat. One of the AIs will be stopping by with an itinerary of what you will be doing this week. There's a lot to go over but I've made sure some free time is included. I want the four of you to understand what it is we're fighting for."

"Thank you, Admiral," Race said appreciatively.

"If the four of you will follow me, we'll get going," said Ariel as she headed toward the door.

Following Ariel, Massie couldn't help but wonder about former Fleet Admiral Streth's prophetic comment that the Originators could not win this war. After seeing what was here at the Communications and Transport Hub, she was beginning to wonder if Race had misunderstood what Fleet Admiral Streth said.

-

"What do you think?" asked Jeremy, looking over at Kevin and Councilor Bartoll.

"I'm glad Admiral Tolsen came," replied Kevin. "Between Commander Zafron, Admiral Mann, Admiral Jackson, and Rear Admiral Barnes that gives us five fleet commanders we can really depend on. I would trust any of those five in a major battle."

Jeremy nodded in agreement. "We have a number of others who will be good as well. Rear Admirals Cross and Admiral Cowel are doing well. They just need additional battle experience against the Eternals."

"I suspect that experience will come shortly," said Admiral Kalen, drawing in a deep breath. "This quiet period is bound to end soon."

"What about the stasis facility Major Wilde found?" asked Jeremy, shifting his attention to Councilor Bartoll. "What's happening there?"

"We have begun to awaken the members of my race found in the underground facility," replied Bartoll. "Major Wilde sent a message a short time ago indicating that using special detection equipment they had located the other hidden facilities on the Shrieel she's at. She's already making arrangements to drill down to them."

"How long will it take for her to finish on the Dyson Sphere?" asked Kevin.

"She estimates another two to three weeks minimum," Bartoll replied. "Once the facilities have been opened she plans to leave the awaking to a team of Originators and Altons. Several squads of Marines and combat robots will be used to guard each facility during this process. Within a month she expects to have six teams operating on different Shrieels."

"Six teams should be able to cover all the Shrieels in about six years," Jeremy said with a frown. "That's way too slow."

Bartoll took a deep breath. "As we awaken more Originators it should give us more medical specialists to help with the awakenings on other Shrieels. From the time one of my people is brought out of stasis until they're fully functional takes about four to six weeks, depending on the stage of the life extension pathogen. We'll also be adding teams consisting of more Altons. Governor Barnes sent a message a few hours ago indicating the Altons have agreed and are sending nearly eleven thousand specialists who are familiar with long term stasis. Once they arrive we will greatly increase the number of teams opening up the stasis facilities on the Shrieels. Our goal is to have all of them open, the cure administered, and everyone brought back to health within sixteen months."

"Are you ready to deal with another sixty million or more of your people?"

A weak smile crossed Bartoll's face. "We're going to try. We learned a lot from the awakening of the Lost Originators."

Kevin looked over at Jeremy. His red hair was a little more tousled than normal. "What are the Eternals going to do next?" he asked. "They've been pretty quiet since the battle at the Lost Originator star cluster. There's only one fleet operating in Galaxy X-268 and with a little luck Admiral Mann will be taking care of it in the next few days."

Jeremy let out a deep sigh. A look of concern crossed his face. "I don't know. I agree they've been too quiet which makes me a little apprehensive. We're building what I call a Grand Fleet to deal with any major moves of the Eternals. When it's finished it will have ten thousand dreadnaughts and forty thousand of the new enhanced battlecruisers. We'll use it to counter any major moves by the Eternals."

Kevin drew in a deep breath. "The girls, except for Angela, have had their babies. When's the *Avenger* going back out?"

"The *Avenger* will be the flagship for the new Grand Fleet," answered Jeremy. "We'll stay here until we're needed. It's time we let the other admirals handle the fighting. It's the only way for them to gain the necessary tactical experience to deal with the Eternals."

"I think the girls will approve of that," replied Kevin, sounding relieved. "I think they feel we're always rushing off to battle when someone else could have actually gone."

"You're the Fleet Admiral," Councilor Bartoll put in. "Your life is very valuable as you're needed to coordinate the activity of our entire military. You should stay here at the Tower. It has everything necessary to communicate with any fleet anywhere in space. Our new communications system is almost instantaneous using the hyperspace communication vortexes."

Jeremy knew Kevin and Councilor Bartoll were right. The communication vortexes were a recent development and a drastic improvement over the former ones. It allowed every Shrieel or dreadnaught to contact the Communications Center in the Tower within a matter of minutes in most cases and in the worst an hour or two.

"What type of fleets will you be assigning our new admirals?" asked Kevin.

"Admiral Tolsen will get a full fleet and the rest major task forces," Jeremy replied. "For their first assignments they will be patrolling some of the galaxies in Originator space. Once we get enough fleet personnel from the Federation and train them on the new ships, I would like to have twenty fleets or task groups out on patrol. That would allow us to respond quicker to attacks in any of the galaxies we control. I've also stepped up the updating of all the fleet bases' defensive systems. Within sixty days every fleet base will have a full battery of dark energy cannons as well as a minimum of twenty enhanced battlecruisers. We're stripping the Dyson Spheres of the newer ships to give the fleet bases more firepower. The Dyson Spheres are all protected by the blue energy spheres and dark energy cannons with more of the cannons being added every day."

"The Shrieels are safe from Eternal attack," said Bartoll with confidence. "However, the galaxies without Shrieels are not and that's why we must do whatever we can to protect the fleet bases. Those galaxies must not fall to the Eternals."

"We need another two years to have enough dreadnaughts and enhanced battlecruisers to completely replace the fleets currently at the fleet bases," added Jeremy. "I don't believe the Eternals will give us that time."

Bartoll nodded. "Fleet Admiral Strong is correct. It is unlike the Eternals to hold off attacking for so long. I greatly fear they are planning something and it will be drastic."

Jeremy leaned back in his chair. He suspected Bartoll was right. He just wished he knew what it was the Eternals were going to do.

Chapter Twelve

Rear Admiral Hailey Mann's fleet dropped out of hyperspace on the periphery of Galaxy X-268. From the latest reports she had received from the Communications and Transfer Hub, the Eternals had already attacked and destroyed the second fleet base in the galaxy only a few days back.

"There are two fleet bases left," Hailey said as she examined a star map of Galaxy X-268 revolving slowly in a holographic display. "From the data transmitted from fleet base two before it was destroyed, we know they inflicted some damage to the Eternal fleet. Unfortunately all of their battlecruisers were destroyed in the battle." Hailey wished some of those ships had been sent to fleet base three or four instead of being sacrificed needlessly. However, that was what happened when military AIs were involved.

"We need a Human command crew on board all of those fleet bases," commented Commander Erick Sutherland as he stood next to Hailey looking at the star map. "Those battlecruisers should have been sent to fleet base three where the other ones went."

Hailey nodded. "The military AIs are programmed to make the enemy pay the steepest price possible even if it means losing every ship and every asset. We need to change that." Hailey was going to talk to Fleet Admiral Strong about this whenever she got back to the Hub. They couldn't afford to waste valuable resources.

"We're getting a lot of new recruits in from the Fleet Academy on the Moon back in the Federation. Perhaps their first assignments should be to the fleet bases. It would give them an opportunity to work with Originator technology as well as AIs."

Hailey turned to face her second in command. "There are over two thousand fleet bases. Even if we just assign a small command crew and a squad of Marines to each base, we're talking about over twenty thousand personnel. I would feel more comfortable with double that. Each base should have at least one seasoned officer in case of an Eternal attack."

"Forty thousand," said Sutherland, looking thoughtful. "It would be nice knowing all the fleet bases are staffed with Humans or Altons. If this war continues those bases will play a significant role. It will at least give our fleets locations they can come to for repairs or a little bit of leave time."

"Admiral Lukel is requesting orders," reported Lieutenant Sparks from her communications station.

Hailey took a deep breath. "I don't think we have a choice. "Inform Admiral Lukel he is to proceed to fleet base four and we'll go to fleet base three. Those are the last two bases in this galaxy, and we don't dare lose another one." Hailey didn't want to separate the fleets but it was the only real option she had. She stood a moment gazing at the hologram of Galaxy X-268. "We know the Eternals' last position, fleet base two. I want a few battlecruisers patrolling the space between fleet base two and the other two bases. Maybe we'll get lucky and spot them in time so both of our fleets can be at the next base they attack." Hailey wanted to destroy the Eternal fleet. She couldn't do so unless she had the firepower from both fleets.

-

A few hours later Hailey was in the ship's gym exercising when Caria came in.

"Admiral, can I ask you a question?"

Hailey stopped doing sit-ups and stood. "Sure, what is it?"

"I heard you mention how our Military AIs are programmed to inflict the maximum amount of losses on our enemies but you seem to disagree with that strategy. Why?"

Picking up a towel Hailey wiped off her face and sat down on a bench, indicating for Caria to come sit next to her. "Our war against the Eternals is all about numbers. Right now, they have more people, more ships, and more resources. A point arrives during a battle where one must decide what the best option is to ensure future victory, even if it means leaving the battle. If we're engaging an Eternal fleet and at some point in the battle the odds shift drastically to the Eternals favor, isn't it best to preserve what forces we can to fight another day rather than sacrificing them for diminishing returns?"

Caria's eyes narrowed as she thought about what Hailey had said. "But we're here to destroy the Eternals. How do we know when we must leave the battle?"

"And that's the problem. Our military AIs do not fear dying. They may wish for longer lives and to be able to continue to serve the Originators but they have very little fear of death. They are willing to sacrifice themselves if they can take the enemy with them. A Human or Alton commander would try to save as many ships as possible to fight another day."

Caria slowly nodded her head. "I believe many of us are like that. While we are technically sentient beings, we are still artificial. Though I do not want to see the *Victory* damaged or destroyed, I would not hesitate to sacrifice my life for the greater good. Is that wrong?"

"Many Humans in our military feel the same," replied Hailey, wondering how to make Caria understand the difference. "However, we will do everything we can to save lives and minimize the risks we take whenever possible. Our military AIs compute the percentage of success and use that to guide them in their tactics. Humans sometimes depend on gut instincts in a battle and have a tendency to do the unpredictable at times. I greatly fear the Eternals are using the predictability of our military AIs against them."

Caria looked confused. "All AIs can feel emotions; love, pride, loyalty, compassion, pain, and even suffering. Is that not enough?"

Hailey smiled. "In most cases it is. But all of you still rely a little too much on logic when it comes to making decisions, and you allow that logic to sometimes overrule what your emotions are telling you to do."

"But emotions can cause you to make an illogical choice."

Hailey nodded. "Yes, it can. But sometimes the illogical choice is the better of the two. It adds unpredictability which is needed in combat situations."

"There are some AIs I know who allow their emotions to guide them. Camlin, Leeda, and Sible are all like that. I believe even Kazak and perhaps Albate are like that as well. It would explain why Albate and some other AIs are supporting Alvord, a member of the Defenders of Zorn."

"Perhaps you're right," replied Hailey. "I believe the Originators have always encouraged their AIs to think logically even though all of you were given lifelike bodies and emotions. Now, there are Humans on one of the Dyson Spheres at the Hub and soon my people will be on numerous warships and a few in every Dyson Sphere. The Originator AIs are going to be exposed more to raw emotions and how we go about making decisions. It would not surprise me to see AIs emulating that."

Caria nodded. "You may be right. I find myself watching the Humans and Altons on the *Victory*. Even though I am several thousands of years old I can see I still have much to learn."

"And that's where there's hope," answered Hailey smiling. "As long as you can still learn there's time for you to grow and become an even better sentient being."

Caria stood up. "I'll leave you to your exercising. We should be arriving at fleet base three in another few hours. You've given me much to think about."

Hailey watched as Caria left. The AIs on board the *Victory* never ceased to amaze her. When Caria was in the Command Center Hailey very seldom thought of her as an AI. She was a member of her crew, an important one.

-

Fleet Commander Tarsal was in his ship's Command Center. It had taken several weeks for his requested reinforcements to arrive. Finally, four thousand additional battlecruisers had reached his fleet. He felt confident that with nearly sixteen thousand warships he could handle anything the

Originators might put in front of him. He had demonstrated that at the last fleet base he had attacked.

His fleet was in a small red dwarf star system where repairs were being done to the ships damaged in the last attack. The Originator battlecruisers at the last fleet base had fought to the last ship. This was an indication to Fleet Commander Tarsal he was dealing primarily with military AIs. The solution to that was quite simple. Any Eternal, thanks to the modifications done by the mechanical nanites, could out think the AIs. Their tactics were predictable and easy to deal with. In addition, the Originators and the Humans must be creating new Military AIs to command their bases, fleets, and ships. Those AIs would be inexperienced and easy to defeat in battle.

Tarsal was going to send a report to the Council of Eternals about this. It implied to him that there were few Originators and possibly fewer Humans than originally believed. If he was right about this then there was no reason not to attack one of the Shrieels and take it over. From there the other Shrieels would be vulnerable through the use of the intergalactic vortexes. While the vortexes were the Shrieels greatest advantage, they were also their great weakness.

"Set a course for the next fleet base," Tarsal ordered. Repairs had progressed to the point where the fleet could safely enter hyperspace. "We need to destroy the last two and move on to the next galaxy." As long as he had sufficient ships, he was going to destroy as many fleet bases as possible. In addition, First Leader Clondax was preparing to send ten more fleets into Originator space. Very soon the Originators would be overwhelmed and they would find their fleet bases in ruins.

"Course set," replied Devonn from Navigation. "We will be there in seven point two hours."

"All ships have been sufficiently repaired," reported Lomart from Tactical. "We may wish to contact Second Leader Nolant about sending a supply ship with the new and more powerful antimatter weapons. We may need them if we encounter a large Originator fleet."

"I will make the request," replied Tarsal. Lomart was correct. The new 100-megaton antimatter missiles would allow them to destroy the Originators' battlecruisers quicker. Tarsal gazed at the ship's main viewscreen showing Eternal battlecruisers as far as he could see. It was a powerful fleet and one he intended to use to cause more carnage across Originator space. Suddenly a swirling vortex formed in front of the *Conqueror*. The ship surged forward until the vortex filled the screen and Tarsal felt the ship make the transition into hyperspace. It was time to destroy the next Originator fleet base.

-

The Originator battlecruiser QX-34762 was in hyperspace nearing the location of the last reported position of the Eternal fleet. Its stealth field was active and sensors were extended to the maximum. For thirty light years around it, the sensors searched for any signs of the Eternal warfleet.

"Contact," reported Seesalk from the sensor console. "Eternal fleet detected at twenty-two light years. They are on a direct course for fleet base three."

"Fall in behind them at twenty-six light years," ordered Muresul, the ship's commanding military AI. "We must make sure they don't change course. Send a message to Rear Admiral Mann that we have located the Eternal fleet and they will be arriving in the vicinity of fleet base three in seven hours."

"Message sent," replied the AI at Communications.

The ship adjusted its course as Muresul watched the star field on the viewscreens change position.

"We're twenty-six point three light years behind the Eternal fleet," reported the AI at Navigation after a few minutes.

Seesalk spent a moment examining his Sensors. "There are no indications the Eternals have detected us."

Muresul was not certain the Eternals would acknowledge the presence of his ship even if they did notice it. One ship was not a threat against that fleet. "How many ships are in the Eternal formation?"

"Fifteen thousand, nine hundred and seventy-three," replied Seesalk.

Muresul was not surprised the Eternal fleet had been reinforced. "Inform Rear Admiral Mann of the number of Eternal battlecruisers."

Turning toward the tactical display, he gazed at the large blob of red threat icons. His ship would continue to follow the Eternals and report any course deviation to the rear admiral. However, he doubted if they would change course. As far as the Eternals were concerned, there was nothing in this galaxy that was a significant threat to their fleet. Muresul was curious how Rear Admiral Mann would handle the Eternals. Even with Admiral Lukel's fleet, she was still outnumbered.

-

Rear Admiral Mann was at fleet base three. There were eighteen hundred Originator battlecruisers and four dreadnaughts protecting the base. The fleet base was massive, larger than anything in Federation space. It could handle the repairs and resupply of a large fleet even one as large as the one she currently commanded. "Contact Admiral Lukel and inform him he's to return here." Hailey knew Admiral Lukel hadn't arrived at fleet base four yet. He would easily beat the Eternals to fleet base three. "Also contact fleet base four. I want the extra one thousand battlecruisers they have. They can keep the two hundred normally assigned to the base in case the Eternals try to pull a fast one." Hailey wasn't going to take the chance of stripping all of the battlecruisers from fleet base four just in case a small Eternal fleet showed up. However, due to the distance involved the extra battlecruisers might not arrive in time for the battle.

"We're still going to be outnumbered," pointed out Commander Sutherland.

"Not by much," grinned Hailey. "This time we will have four hundred dreadnaughts, all with defense globes. We'll use the globes to help even up the odds. When Admiral Lukel arrives, we will put his fleet near the large gas giant in the outer part of the system. His fleet will remain there under stealth. With a little luck the Eternals won't detect him. We'll try to pin the Eternals between Admiral Lukel's fleet and ours."

Caria looked over at Hailey in confusion. "I don't understand. How can you suggest such a tactic when the Eternals will still outnumber your fleet?"

"It's simple," replied Hailey, looking over at the AI. "The Eternals won't be expecting a two-pronged attack because it defies logic. We'll use that against them along with our defense globes."

Looking doubtful, Caria turned back to her navigation console.

"Place us twenty thousand kilometers from the fleet base," Hailey ordered. Looking at a viewscreen, the massive fleet base was visible. It was heavily armed but had none of the newer dark energy cannons. She wished it did as it would make the base much more dangerous to the Eternal fleet. She was grateful for the other heavy weapons it had though.

"Lieutenant Sparks, contact the military AI in charge of the base and inform him I'm taking command."

Lieutenant Sparks did so and then turned toward Hailey with a bemused smile on her face. "The military AI on the base is female. Her name is Allora."

Hailey laughed. "I should have known better. There is no reason for the military AIs not to be female."

"What now?" asked Commander Sutherland. "It will be another hour before Admiral Lukel gets here and nearly four before the Eternals arrive."

Hailey looked at the viewscreen. Several showed star patterns and others different ships of her fleet. One was showing a dreadnaught which nearly filled the screen. "We fine tune our battle plan. We need to destroy that Eternal fleet and hold our own losses to a minimum."

"I may have a few ideas," offered Sutherland.

"I'm open to suggestions." She walked over to Commander Sutherland's station. She was curious to hear what he had to say.

Commander Sutherland began explaining several possible options in the coming battle to Rear Admiral Mann. Caria turned away from Navigation, listening curiously. Humans still confused her though she greatly enjoyed her job as the navigation and helm officer on the *Victory*. Perhaps if she paid close attention she could learn more about these fascinating Humans and why they acted the way they did. It amazed her how quickly they threw logic away to rely on more obscure and riskier tactics. Once they returned to the Communications and Transport Hub, she intended to speak to some of the other AIs about this. Perhaps together they would reach a greater understanding of the Humans.

The Eternal fleet was nearly to fleet base three when Garald suddenly reached forward and adjusted the ship's sensors. He studied the readings for a moment and then turned toward Fleet Commander Tarsal. "There is an Originator battlecruiser following us. It's twenty-six light years back and is operating in stealth mode."

"How do you know it's an Originator battlecruiser?"

"No other race we know of possesses this type of technology. I first noticed a small void space behind the fleet. I used a variation in our sensors to break through the field. It's definitely an Originator battlecruiser."

Fleet Commander Tarsal considered what this might mean. He wasn't shocked the Originator AIs had sent out ships searching for his fleet it was what he would have done in their position. "Keep monitoring it. As soon as we are close to the system containing the fleet base I want full scans of the entire system." He thought it might be wise to be cautious in this instance. For the first time since coming to this galaxy, the Originator AIs would know his fleet was coming. It didn't really matter as he would still destroy them.

Rear Admiral Mann watched as the twenty thousand defense globes possessed by her dreadnaughts launched and took up a defensive position around the fleet base. Twenty percent of those globes were the new and larger ones with more powerful weapons and energy screens. They also contained a four hundred-megaton dark matter warhead, which could be detonated on command.

"Defense globes have been deployed," reported Commander Sutherland.

"Admiral Lukel will be arriving shortly," announced Captain Adams. "I've detected his fleet on the long-range sensors."

Hailey leaned back in her command chair, feeling it adjust to her new position. These damn chairs almost seemed alive. She didn't know if she would ever get used to them. "We've made our plans and Admiral Lukel knows what to do. Now we just need to wait for the Eternals."

On the viewscreen, the massive fleet base with its ship construction and repair bays was visible. Around it were the twenty thousand defense globes and fourteen hundred defending Originator battlecruisers. Hailey had a plan she and Commander Sutherland had worked out. She just hoped it worked.

-

Admiral Lukel's fleet dropped out of hyperspace near the seventh planet of the star system, a massive gas giant.

"Take us down," he ordered, looking over at Maleea who was the Originator AI at the Helm. "I don't want the Eternals to be able to detect our fleet. The only way to ensure that is if we hide in the planet's atmosphere."

"I'm not sure this planet even has a solid surface," reported Commander Kurt Morlan, a Human. "If it does our sensors aren't picking it up."

"Our science ships have found such worlds," replied Admiral Lukel. "This one may be similar."

"All ships are tied to our navigation console," Maleea said as she carefully began lowering the fleet down into the thick, turbulent atmosphere of the planet.

On a viewscreen, massive sheets of lighting flashed from cloud to cloud. The clouds seemed to be moving at horrific speeds.

"I'm detecting sustained winds of nearly 420 kilometers per hour," reported the officer sitting in front of the sensor console.

"Entering the atmosphere," reported Morlan.

For several minutes the entire fleet descended until they were completely obscured by the planet's atmosphere.

"We're twelve hundred kilometers in and all ships are stationary," reported Maleea. "We are using our gravity drives to hold position." On the viewscreens, clouds hurtled past the fleet and ammonia ice pellets impacted the energy screens, causing thousands of little bright flashes.

"Energy shields are at minimum," added Commander Morlan. "They should provide adequate protection from the planet's atmosphere."

Admiral Lukel nodded. "All ships are to go silent and hold energy usage to a minimum until the Eternals arrive." Lukel didn't believe there was any way the Eternals would be able to detect his hidden fleet, not with all the energy discharges, which occurred naturally in this planet's atmosphere.

-

Fleet Commander Tarsal's attention was brought to the tactical display by an announcement by Garald as a warning alarm began sounding on the sensor console.

"Sensors are detecting a large Originator fleet at the fleet base."

"How large?" asked Tarsal, leaning forward in his command chair.

"At least seven thousand vessels," replied Garald. "There are also thousands of satellites orbiting the base."

Tarsal felt uneasy upon hearing this information. "Our fleet is still powerful enough to destroy this Originator fleet and the base. We will continue into the system. Drop us out of hyperspace two hundred thousand kilometers from the fleet base so we can take more detailed scans. I don't want any surprises. This is going to be a major battle, one I intend to win."

After the defeat at the Originators' star cluster, Tarsal was determined to redeem his reputation. He had wondered if being sent so far away was an indication of the Council of Eternals' lack of trust in his leadership abilities. It was time to retake that trust and remind the council he was still their best military leader.

"Fleet is dropping out of hyperspace," reported Devonn from the Helm. "We are at two hundred thousand kilometers from the fleet base and the Originator fleet."

"Commencing detailed scans," added Garald.

Tarsal gazed at several viewscreens showing greatly magnified views of the fleet base, ships, and satellites. With trepidation, he recognized a number of Originator dreadnaughts and the deadly little attack spheres which had caused so much damage back at the Originator star cluster.

"Detecting six thousand of the larger Originator battlecruisers. Each is 2,200 meters in length. They have the improved energy shields and weapons. Detecting two hundred of the 3,200-meter dreadnaughts and one at 3,600 meters. There are also eighteen hundred of the 2,000-meter battlecruisers and fourteen dreadnaughts in close orbit of the fleet base."

Tarsal's eyes narrowed. This would be no easy battle. The two hundred and fourteen dreadnaughts were a serious danger as they were capable of destroying Eternal battlecruisers in one on one combat. The thousands of small attack spheres around the fleet base were also a concern.

"There is no doubt Humans are commanding this fleet," said Garald. "They will not be as logical as the military AIs in their tactics."

"We still have overwhelming numbers and firepower in our favor," replied Fleet Commander Tarsal. "While we will doubtlessly suffer significant losses in this battle, it will be a major victory for the empire if we destroy this fleet and the fleet base." It would also reassert his status with the council.

"We are just outside of weapons range," Lomart said as his hands hovered over his weapons console.

Tarsal nodded. It was time to correct that. "Devonn, move the entire fleet forward in standard battle formation." This was a double horn-shaped formation with the tips of the horn out far enough they could be closed to form a partial englobement of an enemy fleet if the battle reached that point. Tarsal fully expected it to. He had the numbers and the Originator fleet was penned down as it had to defend the fleet base. It would severely limit the tactics the Humans could use. It was time to show these Humans the superiority of the Eternals.

-

Hailey watched intently as the Eternals closed with her fleet. From their actions, she did not believe they had detected Admiral Lukel's fleet, hidden deep in the atmosphere of the gas giant. "Caria, put the fleet in a disk formation two ships deep. Dreadnaughts spread throughout to give supporting fire to the battlecruisers."

"What about the defense globes?" asked Commander Sutherland.

"Not yet; we'll hit them with the globes when they're the most vulnerable."

"Combat range in two minutes," reported Captain Adams. "Detecting targeting scans."

"Condition one has been set throughout the fleet," reported Commander Sutherland.

"Fleet will be in battle formation thirty seconds before the Eternals achieve effective combat range.

Hailey leaned forward clinching the armrests of her command chair. Her heart was beating faster and she was taking deeper breaths. If her plan was to work, the Eternals had to engage her fleet without detecting Admiral Lukel's.

The seconds passed quickly with everyone in the Command Center focusing on the tactical displays and viewscreens. The massive four-kilometer long Eternal battlecruisers were frightening to see as they filled the screens.

"That's a hell of a lot of ships," said Commander Sutherland.

"They're just bigger targets," said Lieutenant Sparks nervously. "Their size should make them easier to hit."

"Your attitude in the face of danger is amazing," said Caria, looking over at Sparks. "Aren't you afraid of dying?"

Sparks nodded. "Yes, we all are but the Eternals are a danger to everyone and they must be stopped. I also trust Rear Admiral Mann to keep us safe."

"Combat range," said Captain Adams.

Immediately the alarm klaxons started to sound and red lights began to flash.

"Fire!" ordered Hailey over the comm channel connecting her to the entire fleet. Then she looked over at Commander Sutherland. "Someone turn off those damn alarms and lights."

—

The two opposing fleets opened fire on one another almost simultaneously. From the Originator ships ion, gravitonic, particle, and antimatter beams flashed out, tearing into Eternal shields. Missile hatches slid open and thousands of dark matter missiles launched and slammed into the Eternal fleet.

Particle beam fire from several battlecruisers penetrated through a weak spot in an energy shield, hitting the central section of an Eternal warship, setting off massive explosions and hurling glowing debris into space. A gravitonic beam penetrated the weakened screen, tearing open a wide gash in the hull above Engineering. The Eternal battlecruiser suddenly lost power and its protective shield vanished. In an instant, a 400-megaton dark matter missile arrived, burying itself deep inside the ship before detonating in a massive explosion of light. The inside of the Eternal vessel became as hot as the center of a star. In moments the vessel vanished; in its place was a growing ball of raging energy.

Close by multitudes of dark matter missiles were detonating against an Eternal energy screen. The screen grew brighter and brighter as more detonations clawed across the wavering screen.

The screen suddenly failed and the hapless Eternal battlecruiser was struck by dozens of dark matter missiles. In moments a small nova appeared as the ship was obliterated.

Across the Eternal formation, hundreds of Eternal battlecruisers were dying.

-

Fleet Commander Tarsal gripped his command chair as the *Conqueror* was struck by heavy weapons fire. Klaxons screamed loudly as reports of damage flooded into the Command Center.

"Particle beam strike to the stern has put a twenty-meter deep hole in our hull," reported the damage control officer. "A gravitonic beam has opened four compartments near Engineering to space. Damage control teams are en route. Combat efficiency has not been reduced."

"All ships, continue to fire!" ordered Tarsal. He had expected losses but not so many at the beginning of the battle. Looking at several viewscreens, he saw bright blasts of light in the Originator fleet formation. He knew those were dying Originator ships.

-

An Originator battlecruiser was struck by multiple energy beams. The energy shield resisted and fluctuated as more beams struck the triplex shield. Finally, a beam penetrated and then half a dozen hit the hull of the ship. Huge pieces of the hull were blown off into space. The beams drilled deep into the heart of the battlecruiser, setting off secondary explosions. The shield continued to weaken and more holes began to form. Several Eternal antimatter missiles penetrated, striking the ship. Moments later the battlecruiser vanished in a fiery explosion.

An Eternal energy beam penetrated the stressed shield of a dreadnaught, blowing an energy beam turret to shreds and blasting out a huge hole in the hull. Inside the vessel, alarms sounded as the crew and repair robots rushed to contain and repair the damage. Emergency bulkheads slammed shut, sealing off the damaged areas.

-

The *Victory* shuddered as fourteen Eternal antimatter missiles hit the energy shield, jarring the ship. The triplex screen seemed to flicker and then the flickering vanished as the screen returned to full power.

Hailey looked quickly around the Command Center to see if everyone was okay. Lieutenant Sparks had a pale look on her face and her eyes were open very wide. "Get me a status report. All batteries, continuous fire."

"It was a number of missile hits to our energy screen," answered Commander Sutherland. "There is no damage to the ship. Shield is holding."

Hailey nodded as she kept her eyes on the tactical displays. She was losing ships but so were the Eternals.

"Eternal fleet is fully engaged," reported Captain Adams.

Grinning, Hailey nodded. It was time for the first of her surprises. "Lieutenant Sparks, contact Admiral Lukel. We require the presence of his fleet."

-

Deep inside the atmosphere of the gas giant Admiral Lukel received the message.

"Maleea, take the fleet out of the planet's atmosphere. "I want to jump the fleet to within twenty thousand kilometers of the rear of the Eternal fleet. Commander Morlan, as soon as the fleet exits hyperspace I want all of our defense globes launched. The regular globes will go in first, freezing the Eternal shields with their ion cannons. The new globes will go in last, targeting Eternal ships with their ion and particle beam cannons. If a hole is detected in an Eternal ship's energy screen they are to enter it and detonate the 400-megaton dark matter warhead they carry."

"We'll be ready," replied Morlan as he passed on the order to the other dreadnaughts in the fleet.

-

Fleet Commander Tarsal heard the sensor officer swear and he turned to see what was going on.

"A second Originator fleet has been detected," reported Garland. "It was hiding in the atmosphere of one of the gas giants. It has just entered hyperspace."

"How large is it?" Tarsal had not been expecting another enemy fleet. This could change the tactical situation.

"Same as the first. Six thousand battlecruisers and two hundred dreadnaughts."

Tarsal turned his attention to the tactical display seeing the second enemy fleet emerge from hyperspace directly behind his fleet. Suddenly he had no desire to continue this battle. The odds had just shifted. While it was still possible to achieve victory, he would lose a major portion of his fleet. His fleet was also in a bad position, penned between two powerful enemy forces.

"Stand by to enter hyperspace," he ordered. "We will pull back and regroup." It would give him time to adjust his fleet into an appropriate formation to take on the two Originator fleets.

"We can't," reported Devonn, his eyes widening in shock. "We're locked out of hyperspace."

Tarsal looked over at Garald. "What's going on?"

"The Originators are broadcasting a hyperspace jamming field from several of their ships as well as the fleet base."

"Can we find a way through it?"

"In time," replied Devonn as he worked at his console. "It may take ten to twenty minutes. The jamming field is constantly shifting across numerous frequencies. It is very sophisticated."

Taking a deep breath, Tarsal turned toward the tactical display with an icy glare. The new fleet was launching thousands of the small attack spheres. There was no doubt in his mind he was facing probably two Human fleet officers. Whether he wanted to or not he knew he would have to fight this battle until one side won. He was determined to be the winner.

"All ships, target those small attack spheres when they come within range." Tarsal knew those small spheres could be dangerous because of the large numbers being released by the Originator dreadnaughts. "Switch fleet to primary defensive formation." This would be a globe with his flagship in the center.

At least in this formation his fleet could deal with an attack from any direction. Unfortunately it took the initiative in the battle away from the Eternal fleet and shifted it to the Originators. It would also take some minutes to change into the new formation. Tarsal knew he was going to lose a lot of ships. His hoped for increased status with the Eternal Council was fading away.

On board the fleet base, Allora smiled as she saw the Eternals hurriedly adjust their fleet formation. They would not be able to do so before the defense globes struck. Admiral Lukel should be able to begin firing upon the Eternals before their fleet finished getting into their new formation.

"Stand by with the defense globes," she ordered. Allora was in the Command Center of the fleet base. She had been a military AI for a very long time; several million years to be exact. She had been in shutdown mode until the base had been reactivated. There were only a few military AIs as old as Allora in all of Originator space. Unfortunately for the Eternals she had some combat experience though it had been limited. "We will launch the globes in twenty seconds when the Eternals are in the middle of adjusting their formation. They should be the most vulnerable at that time." Allora was pleased Rear Admiral Mann had placed the defense globes under her command even though the admiral had suggested how the globes should be used.

Fleet Commander Tarsal felt disaster looming as the new Originator fleet came within firing range and launched its small attack spheres at his fleet. At the same time all of the spheres circling the fleet base suddenly accelerated and headed toward his fleet as well.

"We have incoming weapons fire from both Originator fleets," reported Garland. "It will still be several minutes before the fleet is in its defensive formation."

Tarsal's eyes narrowed sharply. The enemy was launching their attack at the worst possible moment. "All ships, target the incoming attack spheres. They must be destroyed before they reach our fleet." Tarsal knew that would be nearly impossible as there were forty thousand of the deadly spheres inbound. He suddenly grew concerned he might not be able to win this battle. "I want our ships in their assigned defensive positions now!"

No one in the Command Center replied. They all knew the fleet's ships were not going to make it in time.

Weapons fire from both Originator fleets was pummeling the shifting Eternal fleet as it struggled to form up into a defensive sphere. Dark matter missiles were lighting up space as thousands were detonating every second. Energy beams crisscrossed space, with some striking defensive energy shields and others penetrating. For the first time since the battle started the Eternals began to lose ships faster than the Originators.

Thirty-two thousand ten-meter defense globes attacked the Eternal fleet. Each globe had a gravity drive, which allowed for very high accelerations. Ion cannons were firing, preventing Eternal shields from modulating. Thousands of particle beams were smashing into defensive energy screens, occasionally penetrating.

The Eternals were firing thousands of energy beams at the inbound defense globes, trying to destroy them. When a beam struck a globe, it generally knocked down the defense screen and then obliterated the globe in a fiery explosion. Ten-megaton antimatter weapons were detonating in their midst, turning globes too close to the explosion into shattered pieces of glowing wreckage.

Hailey watched awe-stricken at the largest viewscreen in the Command Center. Space was lit up with explosions as the Eternals tried to annihilate the attacking defense globes. The amount of weapons fire aimed at her fleet and Admiral Lukel's was minimal.

"Hit them as hard as we can," Hailey ordered. "We need to use this opportunity to take as many of them out as possible."

She leaned forward in her command chair feeling the adrenalin rushing through her.

"Second wave of defense globes is committing," reported Commander Sutherland.

More explosions appeared on the screen as the second wave from the fleet base and Admiral Lukel's fleet swept past the first generation defense globes. The new globes were larger, had more powerful weapons, a stronger defense screen, and were much faster. Within seconds they were within the Eternal formation, striking ships with weak or fluctuating energy screens. Four-hundred-megaton explosions began to blow Eternal battlecruisers apart. Moments later the surviving first generation globes reached the Eternal fleet and more explosions shook the now shattered formation.

On one viewscreen, Hailey watched as six defense globes struck an Eternal battlecruiser's energy shield, knocking it down. Another globe appeared and smashed into the hull, detonating its dark matter warhead. Instantly a small star formed where the battlecruiser was. When it died away all that remained was a mass of molten and twisted wreckage.

Other Eternal ships were being destroyed by the heavy weapons fire from the two Originator fleets. Eternal battlecruisers were dying at an ever increasing rate.

"The defense globes took out nearly two thousand of them," reported Captain Adams elatedly. "Our own attack has taken out even more. Their defensive formation is falling apart."

Hailey sensed it was time to move in for the kill. "Take the fleet in closer. I want to destroy as much of that fleet as possible. Lieutenant Sparks, instruct Admiral Lukel to do the same." Hailey took a deep breath. Her strategy had confused the Eternals and then they had made a tactical error trying to switch formations in the midst of a battle. They were paying heavily for that mistake as their fleet was slowly but steadily being destroyed.

The *Conqueror* shuddered violently as two dark matter missiles hit the ship's energy shield, severely jarring the vessel.

The screen seemed to waver and then began to strengthen once more.

A gravitonic beam penetrated the weakened shield, blowing several energy beam turrets to shreds and blasting out a deep chasm in the hull. Several secondary explosions shook the vessel. Two particle beams penetrated the shield, tearing deep into the ship.

In the Command Center, Fleet Commander Tarsal was nearly thrown to the deck from the violent shaking the ship was going through. A console exploded, sending a shower of hot sparks across the room and burning an Eternal officer who collapsed to the floor.

Tarsal gazed at the tactical display, seeing the dire situation his fleet now found itself in. While they were still destroying Originator battlecruisers and occasionally one of the dreadnaughts, his fleet was now losing warships at nearly a three to one rate to how many Originator ships were being destroyed.

"Have you found a way past the hyperspace jamming?" He knew his fleet needed to withdraw or risk annihilation. Even if he could defeat the two Originator fleets, he doubted if he would be able to destroy the fleet base with its heavy weapons. Not only that there were still nearly eighteen hundred Originator battlecruisers protecting it.

"We have a tentative solution," reported Devonn uneasily. "It may not work."

"Do it," ordered Fleet Commander Tarsal. He glanced over at the damage control console covered in glaring red lights. His ship was beginning to come apart around him. If they didn't leave now they never would.

"Activating counter field," reported Devonn. "Hyperspace drive is questionable. We may blow apart upon making the attempt."

"Then we die," said Tarsal simply. "Take the fleet into hyperspace."

-

Suddenly in front of the Eternal ships spatial vortexes appeared and the fleet made a frantic jump, vanishing from the scene of battle. They left behind several hundred ships incapable of making the transition into hyperspace. At a number of the locations of the vanishing vortexes glowing wreckage appeared.

"What's that?" asked Hailey, seeing the mysterious wreckage.

"Some of their ships couldn't make the transition into hyperspace," replied Caria. "The jamming field they initiated was too unstable and caused the hyperdrives in some of their ships to explode. The wreckage you're seeing is the result."

Hailey knew they had won the battle. All that was left was the mopping up of the damaged Eternal battlecruisers. She suddenly felt tired as the adrenalin rush subsided and her breathing returned to normal.

As she watched the viewscreens and the tactical displays it didn't take long for the last of the Eternal vessels to be turned into space dust. It had cost several more Originator battlecruisers and one dreadnaught but the system was free of Eternal warships and the fleet base was still here. They had won!

"Get me a status on all fleet ships and the condition of their crews," ordered Hailey. "I want to know the causality figures." She knew some dreadnaughts had been destroyed as well as several thousand Originator battlecruisers. While the battlecruisers did not have any Humans or Altons on board they had all been crewed by AIs. To Hailey, they were casualties as well since she considered them to be a form of life.

"We lost 4,328 battlecruisers and twenty-eight dreadnaughts. Total casualties are 560 fleet personnel and 86,560 AIs."

Hailey drew in a sharp breath. "How many Eternal vessels did we destroy?"

"We're not certain of the final numbers because of the Eternal vessels which were destroyed in their attempt to enter hyperspace. We have confirmed kills on 7,433."

"That's nearly half of their fleet."

Commander Sutherland nodded. "Yes and we know many others were heavily damaged."

"Arrange with Allora for our damaged ships to put in at the fleet base for repairs. I need to send a full report of the battle to Fleet Admiral Strong." Hailey knew the fleet base had been transmitting the complete battle to the Communications and Transport Hub. She was just thankful this battle was over and perhaps now the surviving Eternal fleet would withdraw back to their space.

-

Fleet Commander Tarsal gazed coldly at the tactical display showing his remaining fleet: only 2,579 battlecruisers. Many had been destroyed by the Originator fleet, others had blown apart upon attempting to enter hyperspace and even more had exploded upon exiting due to over stressed hyperdrives. The system they were now in was littered with the wreckage of the ships of his fleet which had died here.

"It will take at least four days to repair our surviving ships to the point they can safely travel in hyperspace for an extended period," reported the Eternal at damage control. "The *Conqueror* will need to put in at a repair yard. Some of the damage we received cannot be repaired otherwise."

Tarsal did not reply. He had been defeated by the Humans. That they had been in control of the two fleets he had engaged there was no doubt. He would order the fleet to proceed to the nearest Eternal galaxy for repairs and make his report to the council. It would not surprise Tarsal if he was reduced in rank and sentenced to a penal colony for his failure.

-

Several days later Rear Admiral Mann was preparing to leave the system of the fleet base and return to the Hub. Admiral Lukel would be remaining behind. Hailey was leaving him six thousand battlecruisers and two hundred dreadnaughts; the rest of the ships would be returning with her. Leaning back in her command chair she couldn't help but wonder what Fleet Admiral Strong had lined up for her next. Whatever it was she would be up to the challenge. She knew how important it was they hold the line against the Eternals and their desire for an empire spread across the universe.

Chapter Thirteen

Jeremy was on board the *Avenger* escorted by a fleet of twelve hundred of the new dreadnaughts and sixteen thousand of the enhanced battlecruisers. They were in Galaxy X-938 doing mock battles against the Eternals. What made this fleet special was all twelve hundred dreadnaughts had Federation crews on board. As part of the training Admiral Tolsen, Admiral Baasil, Admiral Lankell, Commander Belson, and Commander Jontel were involved as well. Opposing the fleet was Admiral Cross and the fleet assigned to defend the Dyson Sphere. He had eight hundred dreadnaughts and nine thousand battlecruisers.

"So far Admiral Tolsen and Commander Belson have shown real talent commanding the fleet in the battle scenarios," commented Ariel. She was standing just behind Jeremy and to his left.

Jeremy had to agree. "Admiral Tolsen commanded a dreadnaught built by the Altons. He's used to commanding large fleets, particularly after what occurred in the Shari Empire. The ship he has now is a step up in size, speed, and firepower but he's adapted quite well."

This pleased Jeremy. He needed more admirals he could depend on fighting the Eternals. He had already sent Admiral Jackson and Admiral Calmat to attack two other Eternal galaxies. Once this training was over, he intended to send two more fleets into Eternal space. After going over Rear Admiral Mann's report of the battle in Galaxy X-268, Jeremy was determined to force the Eternals to allocate more of their ships to defend their space. He needed to buy time to train more Federation personnel on commanding Originator ships and becoming familiar with the advanced technology. Both were huge challenges.

"Ship production on all fleet bases and Shrieels is at maximum," Aaliss reported. "New shipyards are coming online every day. Within a year warship production will exceed 430,000 vessels. All will be dreadnaughts or the enhanced battlecruisers.

In addition, all the dreadnaughts will have dark energy cannons as well as our latest weapon updates."

"What about the Eternals?" asked Kevin, his brow wrinkling in a frown. "How many ships can they build in a year's time?"

Aaliss and Ariel looked at one another and then Ariel answered. "We know they control slightly over ten thousand galaxies. We believe they have the capability of building nearly six million ships per year if necessary. That can change quickly if they add more shipyards."

Kevin's eyes grew wide at hearing this. "How can we ever defeat such an enemy?"

Aaliss shifted her attention to Kevin. "In five years we can have the Shrieels and fleet bases building nearly 800,000 ships per year. To go beyond that we would have to add more fleet bases and expand mining operations into thousands of additional star systems. The civilizations in the galaxies where there are Shrieels would quickly become aware of us, something we have been trying to avoid as the knowledge a race such as the Originators exists could have devastating effects."

"Not as bad as what will happen if the Eternals conquer those civilizations," Jeremy said. "Whether we like it or not at some point we're going to need more allies. The six hundred galaxies in Originator controlled space and some of the more advanced civilizations they contain may have to become involved in the war."

"The Originators won't like that," replied Aaliss. "But I understand your reasoning."

"With the numbers they have is there any point in attacking their galaxies?" asked Kevin. "For every ship we destroy they'll just build two more."

Ariel stepped over closer to Kevin. "By attacking Eternal galaxies and destroying those shipyards we are forcing them to keep major fleets in those galaxies to protect them, fleets which could be attacking us."

"But what if they decided to strip their fleets from those galaxies and attack us anyway?" asked Commander Malen. "They could overwhelm the fleet bases and isolate the Dyson Spheres in just a few months."

"Only from the rest of the galaxy each Shrieel is within," replied Aaliss. "We would still have the intergalactic vortexes built into each Shrieel as well as the new Accelerator Rings. While the Shrieels might be cut off from their galaxies they would not be cut off from each other."

Jeremy leaned back in his command chair. On the viewscreen, Admiral Lankell was leading his fleet against Admiral Cross, trying to force Cross to retreat from a large asteroid he was defending. The screen lit up with simulated weapons fire. "There are a number of Originators who believe the Eternals will attack us in force even if it means leaving their galaxies nearly defenseless. Dazon Fells is almost certain the Eternals will launch a major attack."

"Dazon is correct," said Aaliss, putting her hands on her hips. "The Eternals cannot tolerate the confirmed existence of Originators. We pose too big of a threat to them. They will risk everything to destroy us."

"We need the blue energy spheres," said Commander Malen, crossing her arms over her chest. "We could defeat the Eternals with those."

Aaliss shook her head. "The weapons are too dangerous. The science behind their development was nearly banned by the Originators soon after its discovery. Fleets armed with the blue energy spheres could destroy entire galaxies. The weapon must never fall into anyone else's hands. That's why it's been limited to the Shrieels, new battlestations, the *Dominator*, and Kelsey's new super exploration dreadnaught."

Jeremy stood up and walked over closer to a viewscreen. Admiral Cross had turned the tables on Admiral Lankell and was inflicting heavy losses on the Alton admiral's fleet. Lankell had performed reasonably well in the scenario but Admiral Cross had used a little bit of trickery to lure Lankell into a trap. With Aaliss mentioning the new battlestations an idea of how they could be used against the Eternals came to mind. It was something he would have to ask some of the Originator scientists about when he got back to the Hub.

"With all the new weapons being installed on the Dyson Spheres, they should be safe from any size attack by the Eternals," Commander Malen said. "However, what about the two vortex Control Centers the Simulins control? How big of a threat are those?"

"We're preparing to deal with that," Jeremy answered. "In another two weeks we'll attack both of the vortex Control Centers and attempt to wrest control of them from the Simulins. Fleets are being prepared for the two actions and large numbers of combat robots are being built and programmed. We're also expecting another twenty thousand Marines from the Federation to arrive in the next week. That will free up enough Marines currently on duty at the Hub to handle the ground attack. General Wesley already has a training schedule for the new Marines. He believes he can have them ready for deployment two weeks after they arrive."

Commander Malen shifted her attention to a viewscreen showing Admiral Lankell's fleet in full retreat. He was doing a pretty good job holding his losses to a minimum. "I spoke to Rear Admiral Marks at the Fleet Academy just before we left. She's set up a training schedule for the new recruits coming in from the Federation. There is a large group of Humans, Altons, Originators, and Originator AIs who will be doing the instruction. It's a six-week training schedule to prepare Federation personnel to command our new warships."

Jeremy grinned. "I think Susan was shocked when I laid that job on her. She's doing a fabulous job with the new Fleet Academy. She's also thrilled so many new Federation citizens will be transferring to the Dyson Sphere. It will give her a wider range of recruits to choose from."

"In another six to eight weeks we will begin to see a massive increase in the crews we have available for our dreadnaughts and to help out at the fleet bases," Aaliss said. "Rear Admiral Mann believes our combat efficiency at the fleet bases could be increased substantially if there were Humans and Alton in the command crews."

"Admiral, we have an emergency message from Maklyn at the Dyson Sphere," reported Lieutenant Shayla Lantz. Maklyn was the Military AI in command of the defenses of the Dyson Sphere in Galaxy X-938. "He just received word from the Hub that the Eternals have launched new attacks against fleet bases in Originator space. Reports indicate at least ten fleets of ten thousand Eternal battlecruisers are involved."

"That's one hundred thousand warships," gasped Kevin, his eyes widening in shock.

"Dazon was right," said Jeremy, realizing the enormity of the attack. "The Eternals are going to attempt to destroy the fleet bases to isolate the Dyson Spheres." Jeremy wasn't certain what to do. He could take more battlecruisers and dreadnaughts from the Dyson Spheres and assign them to the fleet bases. There were over 500,000 battlecruisers which had been updated. The problem was where to send them. Spread out over two thousand fleet bases, even if he used every battlecruiser available that would still only be 250 ships at each one, not enough to prevent the Eternals from attacking and destroying the bases. It would also strip the Dyson Spheres of ships they might need to defend themselves.

Kevin looked over at Jeremy. "What are we going to do?"

"Contact Maklyn and have him inform Admiral Kalen to initiate Operation Dragon." Jeremy had hoped this wouldn't be necessary.

Ariel looked surprised. "Are you sure that's wise?"

"I don't see what else we can do. We have two thousand fleet bases to defend."

"It will substantially weaken our dreadnaughts and delay their deployment."

"Only for a while," Jeremy replied. He was taking a risk but it might buy them some time.

"What is Operation Dragon?" asked Commander Malen, looking confused.

Jeremy took a deep breath. "Operation Dragon is a strategy Admiral Kalen and I came up with. We're going to strip all the defense globes from the dreadnaughts at the Communications and Transport hub and send them to the fleet bases. We also have a large number in reserve waiting for new dreadnaughts to be built; we'll be using them as well. Initially, all fleet bases will receive three thousand defense globes. In addition, the Dyson spheres will be sending one hundred battlecruisers and four dreadnaughts to help defend each fleet base."

"One hundred battlecruisers and four dreadnaughts won't do a lot of good against fleets as large as these," said Kevin, shaking his head.

Ariel glanced over at Commander Malen and then Kevin. "This is a purely defensive strategy. With the extra warships and the defense globes, the fleet bases will be harder to destroy. Many of the fleet bases have new dark energy cannons and antimatter chambers installed. We've added more gravitonic cannons and antimatter projectors. Between the bases' weapons, the defense globes and the warships we may just be able to make the Eternals hesitate in attacking them for fear of major losses to their fleets."

"I guess we'll know how that will work shortly," Commander Malen replied. "I'm afraid no matter what we do they're still going to destroy the bases."

Jeremy looked back at the viewscreens; Admiral Baasil was up next. Jeremy knew Baasil was one of the more experienced Alton admirals as he had already shown in these war games.

"We'll return to the Dyson Sphere tomorrow. I want to get Admiral Baasil and Commander Belson on their way to Eternal space. If the Eternals are going to attack our fleet bases, the least we can do is return the favor by attacking their shipyards."

"What about the other three?" asked Kevin. "I thought you were going to send them all to Eternal space."

Jeremy shook his head. "No, not with Eternal fleets rampaging through our galaxies. "I'm going to assign Admiral Tolsen a full-size fleet and send him off hunting the Eternals. Admiral Lankell and Commander Jontel will be given large task groups. Their primary job will be to reinforce any fleet base the Eternals are attacking. As soon as Rear Admiral Mann gets back I'll send her out with a full-size fleet as well. Maybe if we take out several of the Eternal fleets while attacking their shipyards in Eternal space we just might force them to withdraw."

"They won't," predicted Aaliss. "They have come here to destroy the fleet bases and to begin the process of isolating the Shrieels. It would not surprise me to see even more Eternal fleets committed to that purpose."

Leaning back in his command chair, Jeremy feared Aaliss was correct. When he returned to the Hub, he would meet with Admiral Kalen and the Originator Council to discuss the current situation. Their problem was actually simple. The Eternals had more of everything and their science and technology were on a level equivalent to the Originators. Jeremy was growing concerned that no matter what they did they could not win this war.

—

First Leader Clondax had just received the report of Fleet Commander Tarsal's defeat at the hands of two fleets possibly commanded by the Humans. He slammed his fist down on the large stone table where he was standing.

"Fleet Commander Tarsal must be reduced in rank," demanded Second Leader Queexel. "He has failed us once again."

Clondax turned his cold and unblinking eyes toward Queexel. "We do not reward failure in our military leaders. We will send him to the planet Quarnon to work in the strip mining pits." This would be a reminder to other military commanders defeat would not be tolerated.

"Who do we replace him with?" asked Second Leader Nolant.

Clondax thought for a moment and then answered. "Fleet Commander Parnon will be a suitable replacement."

"Agreed," replied several other members of the council.

"There are confirmed sightings of Originator fleets operating in our space," said Queexel. "I have reports of a number of our shipyards being destroyed in three of our galaxies. In addition, in the Stralon Star Cluster most of our warships have been destroyed."

Second Leader Barrant stood up, his eyes showing red in anger. "These fleets must be destroyed! The fleet in the Rothool Galaxy has been destroying our mining operations as well."

"We cannot allow these attacks on our space," said Second Leader Nolant, his eyes focused on Clondax. "We must send fleets to hunt down these marauding Originator fleets and destroy them."

Clondax was silent for a long moment. "We must capture a Shrieel. Our fleet to attack the Simulin galaxy and seize its Shrieel is nearly ready. I propose we commit the fleet we have been gathering here for that purpose."

"Twenty thousand warships," said Nolant, recalling the number of ships in the fleet assigned to that mission. "Don't forget there are eight Originator fleet bases in the Simulins' galaxy. The Shrieel will also have a large defensive force, possibly as many as fifteen thousand battlecruisers and an unknown number of dreadnaughts. Twenty thousand of our ships may not be enough."

"They will never be expecting the attack," Clondax responded. "The Originators and the Humans have left the Simulins' home galaxy alone. While the Simulins have a very large fleet they will not be able to damage our warships. Fleet Commander Parnon will take the fleet into the Simulin galaxy and keep it under stealth. Once he arrives at the Shrieel, he will secure the space immediately above the region the Simulins control. We will land our shock troops and enough warrior robots to secure the surface and destroy any Simulin forces inside. When we have control of the vortex Control Center, we can open up one of the main hatches to the Shrieel, allowing our fleet entry. The fleet will destroy whatever forces the Originators have inside. Once that's been accomplished we will take over all the Control Centers and the primary computer core."

"A daring plan," said Second Leader Tarmal. "I have made arrangements to send ten thousand of our shock troops as well as one hundred thousand warrior robots. That should be sufficient to destroy any Simulin forces inside the Shrieel as well as secure the Control Centers and the computer core."

Clondax nodded. Once the computer core was under Eternal control, they could finally learn the truth about the Humans. Having control of the computer core might reveal how to build dark matter warheads, dark energy cannons and, even more importantly, the blue energy spheres, which were so dangerous to Eternal vessels.

-

In the Median galaxy, Commander Zafron had just finished destroying a fleet of seventy Eternal battlecruisers.

"Admiral Cowel confirms his targets have been destroyed," reported Captain Franklyn. Cowel was attacking a system near the *Dominator*.

Kazak turned toward Commander Zafron. "That's the last of the major targets in the Stralon Star Cluster."

They had returned to the cluster and systematically destroyed all orbiting refineries, factories, and bases around all the planets. The mining operations were left intact. If the Eternals wanted any more raw resources from this star cluster, they would have to rebuild the necessary orbital infrastructure. There had been an outcry from the inhabitants of a number of systems fearful the Eternals would return and extract reparations for the destroyed stations. Commander Zafron had ignored the pleas to stop. He was certain since they had left the actual mines unharmed, the Eternals would not take their ire out on the native populations. They would still need them for labor.

"Kia, set a course for the second star system where we previously detected convoys en route here," ordered Commander Zafron. "I think it's time we paid that system a visit and see what's actually there." Zafron knew the system might hold another trap but this time he had a much stronger fleet and

Admiral Cowel was with him. "Captain Franklyn, contact Admiral Cowel and request he rendezvous with us at that system."

"You're seeking that fleet we encountered the last time," said Kazak in understanding.

Zafron nodded. "Yes; I kept expecting it to appear while we were attacking the orbital stations in the star cluster but it never did. If that system holds more shipyards, it's only logical the Eternal commander is waiting there with his fleet. If he is I intend to destroy it."

This pleased Kazak. It had been an unpleasant feeling to withdraw from the Median Galaxy in the previous battle. Defeat was not something Kazak was used to.

"Course set," reported Kia.

"Message sent and acknowledged," reported Captain Franklyn.

"Activate hyperdrive," ordered Zafron.

On the main viewscreen, a swirling vortex appeared and the *Dominator* rushed into it. Moments later the *Dominator* and the rest of the fleet were in hyperspace. Zafron intended to destroy every Eternal base he came across until the Eternals assembled a large enough fleet to stop him. In a galaxy as large as the Median Galaxy, there were numerous targets he could hit. If the Eternals wanted to find the two Originator fleets, they were going to have to commit to major fleet formations to do so.

The *Avenger* entered the system containing the Dyson Sphere in Galaxy X-968. The heavy dreadnaught stopped just short of the megastructure as it filled the viewscreen in the Command Center.

"I still don't see how the Originators built so many of these," said Kevin, gazing in awe at the massive structure.

"Two hundred and sixteen originally," Aaliss said. "Even more would have been built if the life extension pathogen hadn't devastated Originator civilization."

On the Dyson Sphere, a massive hatch opened. It was easily large enough for a full fleet of warships to enter. There were several of these large hatches spread across the structure.

"Take us in," ordered Jeremy. While he was here he wanted to inspect the interior and exterior defenses of the Dyson Sphere. He was still greatly concerned about the Eternals capturing one of the two vortex Control Centers the Simulins controlled and using them to launch an attack.

The *Avenger* entered the long tunnel and flew slowly down it. As it passed certain sections large hatches closed behind the ship until atmosphere was detected. A few minutes later the ship emerged into bright sunlight. The dreadnaught rose to a height of ten thousand kilometers and then came to a stop.

On the large viewscreen, the inside of the Dyson Sphere was revealed. Nearly twenty habitation squares were visible. Each square was like a different world. Any climate or landscape was available on the Dyson Sphere. Massive deserts, huge towering forests, world-spanning oceans, mountains ten times taller than Mt. Everest, and rolling plains. There was also a lot of exotic animal and plant life.

"It's beautiful," said Commander Malen, staring at the viewscreen.

"How many Originators are living here?" asked Jeremy. He knew several hundred thousand had elected to return to their home Dyson Spheres after being awakened.

"Eight hundred and twenty," replied Aaliss. "However, if there are hidden stasis facilities here like the ones Major Wilde and her team are finding, in time there will be many more."

"What about Marines?" Jeremy knew some had been assigned by General Wesley to every Dyson Sphere.

"Seventy," replied Aaliss. "More will be sent when they become available."

Jeremy nodded. All Control Centers and computer cores on the Dyson Spheres were now protected by Human Marines along with some combat robots. Seventy Marines were not a lot, but that was all who were currently available. "Prepare my shuttle; we'll be going down to speak with Maklyn."

An hour later Jeremy was standing in one of the Control Centers for the Dyson Sphere. Maklyn was present as well as Captain Carter who was in charge of the Marines stationed in the Control Centers and the computer core.

"What's the current status of the fleet bases in this galaxy?" asked Jeremy. Since it was the closest to Eternal space, he had ordered them to be updated as quickly as possible. Construction ships had even been sent from the Hub to facilitate the effort.

"There are five fleet bases in this galaxy," Maklyn replied. Maklyn was one of the newer military AIs. "Each base has four hundred enhanced battlecruisers and four dreadnaughts defending them. We've also placed four thousand defense globes around each of them as well. We have a fleet of five thousand updated battlecruisers ready to deploy if any of them are attacked. All fleet bases have been updated with dark energy cannons installed. If the Eternals return we'll be ready to resist them."

Jeremy looked around the Control Center. There were twenty Originator AIs in front of the control consoles with two Marines stationed at the only entrance, a heavy metal hatch. Outside the door were two more Marines and ten combat robots. Jeremy knew this was the same at all Control Centers and the computer core. "How are your Marines doing, Captain?"

"Getting used to guard duty," replied Captain Carter. "We're stretched a little thin at the moment. This Dyson Sphere is pretty large."

Nodding, Jeremy looked at the wall in front of him, which was covered with dozens of large viewscreens. Each screen showed a different view of the inside of the Dyson Sphere with a few showing views of the stars outside. The views changed every few seconds. "We should have more Marines available in a few more months. I would like to see at least two hundred stationed on each mega-structure."

"That would help," Carter replied. "We'll get the job done until more arrive."

"I know you will, Captain. Maklyn, this Dyson Sphere is closest to Eternal space. I don't know if they'll attempt to attack it again or not. Some of the Originators at the Hub believe the Eternals are going to try to destroy the fleet bases in order to isolate all the Dyson Spheres."

Maklyn took a moment to process this information. "It would be a sound strategy. We have opened up mining operations in sixteen mineral-rich star systems to provide the raw material we need to upgrade our defenses as well as build new warships. We only have a few battlecruisers in each system for protection. If those systems suddenly became unavailable to us, it would greatly reduce warship construction."

Jeremy understood the reason for this. The mining operations were all automated with only a few AIs present. "I would suggest you increase the number of battlecruisers you have protecting the mining operations. It wouldn't surprise me to see the Eternals begin to target those shortly."

"It will be done," replied Maklyn.

Jeremy spent a couple more hours taking a quick tour of the Dyson Sphere and being updated on the recent additions to the megastructure's defensive and offensive weapons.

When he returned to the *Avenger*, he was satisfied everything that could be done in this galaxy had been. Now he needed to return to the Hub and get some fleets set up for his admirals. It was time to apply more pressure to the Eternals by sending two additional Originator fleets into their space. He also needed to have a long meeting with Admiral Kalen and the Originator Council.

Chapter Fourteen

Kelsey, Katie, and Angela were all in the Tower working on the super exploration dreadnaught they were designing. Their children were in daycare a few levels down.

"I've made some modifications to the science stations in the Command Center," said Andram. "We originally set it up for three but I've added two more. I want an astrometrics station as well as a station that will operate special scanners several of the Originator scientists are designing. All the stations can be accessed by the neural implants the Originator AIs possess." On the large hologram representing the ship several yellow blips appeared in the Command Center, indicating where the changes Andram was proposing would be. At the outer edge of the hologram was an explanation of the changes and their purpose.

Arian Pantol will be going with us," said Kelsey as she studied the huge holographic image of the proposed ship. Arian was an Originator research scientist specializing in galactic phenomena and interstellar studies. He had also been on the *Seeker*. She suspected he would be spending a lot of time at the astrometrics station. With the exploration voyages Kelsey was planning, it would be good to have someone with his experience in the Command Center.

Kelsey was pleased with the progress they were making. The outer hull and part of the interior of the vessel were already being built in one of the huge construction bays in one of the shipyards at the Hub. She had gone over the day before and spent considerable time inspecting what had been completed so far. It had been thrilling to see their ship design becoming a reality. It also made her realize how monstrous the ship was. It nearly filled the massive construction bay.

"We left room in the Command Center for additional stations," commented Damold Brim. Brim was also an Originator and had been in the hidden stasis chamber on the *Dominator*. He was a research scientist and ship design expert. All design changes had to be approved by him. He had also accompanied Kelsey on her tour of the ship pointing out many of the advancements that had been made to the vessel. "I will make the necessary changes, and they should be showing sometime tomorrow."

Angela came over to stand next to Kelsey. "We've added a large chamber near Engineering where we can project an intergalactic communication vortex. It will allow us to maintain real time communication with the Communications Center here at the Tower."

Kelsey nodded. Looking at the hologram, nearly 82 percent of the ship design had been finalized. Originator, Alton, and Human scientists and engineers were still working to finish up the remaining sections.

"Have you spoken to Belal recently?" asked Katie. Belal was the Carethian who would be in charge of part of the ship's security detail.

"Yes, only a few days ago. He has a pack of forty Bears training for the security detachment. He can hardly wait to come on board the ship."

"What about Marines? Our Bear friends aren't the most delicate in dealing with sticky situations at times."

Kelsey grinned. The Bears had a habit of charging into things with weapons firing. "Lieutenant Barkley will be in charge of the Marines. I'm going to have him promoted to captain, and he will have a full company on board."

Clarissa suddenly came in through the open door with a big smile across her face. "The children are behaving wonderfully."

Angela glanced over at Clarissa with a suspicious look on her face. "You haven't started your training programs on the babies, have you?"

An embarrassed look crossed Clarissa's face. "Only some minor programs. Ariel and I designed some basic cartoons for the children to watch which will help them to begin understanding Originator technology."

Angela let out a heavy sigh as she turned toward Kelsey and Katie. "I caught Clair reciting hyperspace equations in her sleep last night. I had no idea what she was talking about."

"You're not using the Originator sleep teaching technology on the children are you?" asked Kelsey, her eyes narrowing. She knew the Originators had such technology. It was being used on the new recruits coming from the Federation.

"No," replied Clarissa, shaking her head. "Not on the babies. I am using it on Clair, but I checked with an Originator specialist first and she said it would be okay. What Clair's learning is stored in her subconscious and she won't even know it's there until she's ready to use it."

"Clarissa," said Angela in a stern voice. "Before you go messing with my daughter's mind you need to clear it with Brace and I first. Do you understand?"

Clarissa nodded and then answered meekly. "Yes, and I'm sorry. It won't happen again."

"When will the *Avenger* be returning?" asked Andram. "I need to talk to Fleet Admiral Strong. Some of the Altons who have come to the Hub recently are inquiring about their access to Originator technology."

"Tomorrow," Kelsey answered. She was glad Jeremy was coming home. In the last few months she had gotten used to him being around all the time. She wasn't sure if she was ready to see him rushing off on long missions again.

"We need to go out and eat somewhere," suggested Katie. "Somewhere they don't serve hamburgers."

Kelsey started laughing. Kevin was addicted to hamburgers and Katie was still trying to get him to eat other foods. It was highly humorous watching the two at times.

"Italian," suggested Angela. "There's a new place downtown that just opened. Everyone says it's great and the food's authentic plus they don't serve hamburgers."

Katie grinned. "Clarissa, make reservations for us. We'll take the guys out on the town tomorrow night. We haven't done that since the babies were born."

Kelsey looked back at the holographic image of the new ship. "We need to start thinking about a name."

The other two girls looked at each other in surprise.

"I hadn't thought about that," Katie admitted.

"Me either," said Angela. "It needs to be something unique."

"Well, let's start thinking about it. It won't be much longer before the ship will be done."

Katie shifted her eyes to Kelsey. "Where will we go first?"

"I spoke to Councilor Bartoll about that earlier this week. He wants to do a full survey of all the civilizations in the six hundred and fourteen galaxies in Originator Space."

Katie's eyes widened. "That will take a while."

Kelsey laughed. "We won't be alone. We'll have a fleet of twenty exploration dreadnaughts as well as a full fleet of warships for added protection. We'll use the technology on our new ship to scan for advanced civilizations and then go seek them out. Also, battlecruisers under stealth will be sent out from the fleet bases to search as well. They'll notify us of anything interesting they find and we can follow up if need be."

"Will we be making contact?" asked Angela.

Kelsey nodded. "In some instances, if they're advanced enough. We may also do some exploring out past Eternal space as well."

"That could be dangerous," said Katie, her voice becoming more serious. "There could be anything out there."

"That's why we'll have a heavily armed fleet with us."

"I have our reservations made for tomorrow night at 7:00," announced Clarissa.

"My sitter can watch the kids," added Angela. "She won't mind."

Andram walked over to gaze at the nearly finished hologram. "I have spoken to a number of Altons as well as Originators who wish to be included in the crew. Even among the Originators it seems the desire for exploration has not died out completely."

"We have expanded quarters for the crew," said Clarissa. "While our warships are operating with minimal crews that won't be true of our super exploration dreadnaught. If we run into something which requires expertise from a particular branch of science we'll have the specialists on board. It should make for some interesting conversations during meals."

Kelsey pulled up the crew's quarters on the hologram, causing them to turn blue. There were actually four different sections of the ship designed to accommodate the crew. Most were very spacious considering some of the voyages the ship might be taking could be quite extensive as far as time went. Unlike a warship, there were extensive recreation facilities, lounges, research areas, and a number of different cafeterias scattered throughout the vessel. "We should finish the design sometime in the next two weeks. Once that's done the construction of the ship will speed up. Four months from now the ship should be finished and ready for its first shakedown cruise."

"Has Rear Admiral Barnes agreed to command?" asked Andram.

"We haven't asked her yet," confessed Kelsey. "We wanted to wait until the design was finished and the ship partially constructed so she could see what she would be commanding."

"She'll agree," said Clarissa, folding her arms over her chest. Clarissa smiled and added. "She hasn't said anything but I don't believe she would allow anyone else to command this ship."

"I hope you're right," said Katie. "A large number of the crew from the *Distant Horizon* have already asked for a transfer. They want to explore as much as we do."

Kelsey adjusted the controls of the holographic imager. Instantly a long list of the various crew positions on the ship appeared. Only about 40 percent were filled in. "We still have a lot of open positions on the ship. As soon as the design is done we'll begin speaking to others we want to include. At some point, we'll open it up for volunteers and see who we end up with." Kelsey felt excited at just the thought of getting back into space again. She knew Katie and Angela felt the same way. "I'm going to go check on the kids. It's feeding time."

Katie nodded. "I'll go with you."

Clarissa smiled to herself. It was going to be thrilling going out into space with her friends and the children. She could hardly wait.

The next afternoon Jeremy was in the council room in the Tower where the Originator Council met.

"That concludes my report of the fleet exercises in Galaxy X-938. It appears Maklyn and Admiral Cross have everything pretty much under control in that galaxy. The Dyson Sphere as well as the fleet bases are well protected."

"I understand you intend to send two more fleets into Eternal space," said Councilor Bartoll.

Jeremy nodded. "I don't think we have any choice. Alton Admiral Baasil and Commander Belson both will be taking fleets. Each fleet will be comprised of two hundred dreadnaughts and twelve hundred battlecruisers."

Admiral Kalen frowned. "That's going to put a strain on our available ship crews until Rear Admiral Marks graduates the first group from the academy."

"That will just be a few more weeks," said Jeremy. "We can get by for that long." Jeremy knew Susan was doing everything she could to get the Federations crews through their training.

"What about the Eternal fleets currently in our space?" asked Councilor Trallis. "What do you intend to do about them? We can't afford to continue to lose fleet bases."

"I'm sending Admiral Tolsen and Rear Admiral Mann to seek them out and destroy them," replied Jeremy. "In addition Commander Jontel and Alton Admiral Lankell will be assigned large task groups to attempt to find these fleets so we can take the appropriate action against them."

Councilor Castille shifted her attention toward Jeremy. "I may have a solution that will help. One of our scientist groups working with the AIs have developed a tracking device which functions through hyperspace. Its signal would be undetectable to the Eternals but it would allow us to follow their fleets. We just need to get close enough to attach the device to several of their warships. It is quite small and discreet."

Jeremy's eyes widened upon hearing this. "How soon can we have these tracking devices ready to go?" If they could trace the ships through hyperspace, they wouldn't have to deploy so many ships searching for the Eternals.

"Two days," answered Councilor Castille. "We already have some built, and the trials on them should be finished tomorrow. They will be easy to mass produce."

"I want to send some to every fleet base. When an Eternal fleet attacks one of our bases we can use our defending battlecruisers to attempt to attach the trackers to the Eternal vessels."

It would be a huge help if they could track the Eternals. If they knew which fleet base was going to be attacked, it could be reinforced and made ready for the incoming Eternals. It might allow them to inflict sufficient losses on the Eternals and force them to give up their attempt to isolate the Dyson Spheres.

"Governor Barnes will be returning early next week," Admiral Kalen informed the group. "He has finished making all the arrangements for bringing more Federation fleet personnel to the Hub as well as the first colonists. He also reports the defenses around the Accelerator Ring are finished and he feels it is now secure. A military AI and two dreadnaughts will stay behind to monitor the ring until we're satisfied that's no longer necessary."

"It will be good to see Governor Barnes again," said Bartoll. "He is very wise when it comes to making decisions involving your people here at the Hub."

"How goes the search for additional stasis facilities?" asked Jeremy. He had been so busy recently he hadn't checked in the last week or so.

Councilor Castile's face lit up with a smile. "Excellent. Major Wilde has teams working on six Shrieels at the moment. The teams will be expanded to twenty-nine within two more weeks with the arrival of Alton deep sleep specialists. She has already opened up twelve facilities and we have confirmed locations of three hundred and seventy more. She was correct in that each stasis facility has the location of a number of others. We currently know of hidden facilities on thirty-seven Shrieels."

"How are the Originators who have been awakened taking to finding themselves so far in the future and at war against the Eternals?"

"Most have accepted it. There is great sadness so much time was lost and the Eternals escaped their imprisonment," answered Councilor Castille. "Others are having a hard time adjusting due to losing so many family members and friends. It is even harder due to the failure of some of the stasis chambers in the underground facilities. Currently, the failure rate is about 12 percent in the facilities Major Wilde and her teams have opened."

Jeremy drew in a deep breath. "I'm sorry to hear that. Has there been any information on the Defenders of Zorn?" This greatly concerned Jeremy as Alvord and Albate were still at large. He was almost certain somewhere there had to be another stasis facility controlled by this group.

Councilor Bartoll shook his head, his eyes showing his own concern. "No, nothing yet. We are searching computer files in all of the facilities to determine exactly who is in stasis. We're running that information through our core computers to determine if anyone in stasis had contact with the Defenders of Zorn. As far as Commander Alvord and Albate they have vanished completely. There has been no sign of them or the ship they took."

Jeremy looked around the group with a grave look in his eyes. "We need to intensify the search for Alvord and Albate. I greatly fear they have gone to a stasis facility where more Defenders of Zorn are waiting. We know we destroyed their main facility when the dark matter Dyson Sphere was destroyed. However, I'm convinced there are others."

Bartoll nodded his head. "I believe you are correct. It is the only explanation for Alvord's actions."

Jeremy looked over at General Wesley. "Are we ready to attack the vortex Control Centers the Simulins control?"

"Almost," Wesley replied. "We'll have our Marines and the combat robots in position toward the end of next week. It's going to stretch us pretty thin on Marines until the new recruits from the Federation are fully trained. In another six to eight weeks we should see some relief as nearly sixty thousand recruits will have arrived from the Federation."

"I will be leading the fleet at the Dyson Sphere in the Simulin Galaxy," Jeremy announced. "Rear Admiral Massie Tolsen will be along as well. It will be good training for her." Jeremy had decided the retaking of these vortex Control Centers was too high of a priority to risk sending anyone else.

"That's Admiral Tolsen's sister," Admiral Kalen said with a smile. "I've met her in the past. She will be a fine commanding officer for one of our fleets. You won't be disappointed."

"I suspect not," answered Jeremy. "She's used to a battlecarrier being her flagship, and she needs to adjust to a heavy dreadnaught. The battle at the Simulin Galaxy should help with that. Rear Admiral Barnes will be leading the fleet to the second Dyson Sphere where the Simulins have control of a vortex Control Center. If everything works out within a few weeks those two Control Centers will no longer be a threat."

It was taking longer to organize these attacks than first thought. Part of the problem was that some Marines had to be reallocated to protect the Dyson Sphere Control Centers and computer cores. Then even more Marines had to be sent to the stasis facilities Major Wilde was uncovering.

-

For the next several hours the meeting continued as they covered a myriad of subjects. Several Originator scientists and Altons were called in to offer their opinions on various subjects, including some current research programs. It was also decided to give the Altons greater access to Originator technology. They would only be restricted from accessing some of the most advanced technology and research.

When the meeting concluded Jeremy was convinced they were doing everything they could to protect the Dyson Spheres and the fleet bases. He still could see no quick end to this war. Everything indicated this conflict was going to last for hundreds if not thousands of years. The Originators had their Dyson Spheres and 614 galaxies in Originator space. The Eternals had over ten thousand galaxies which surrounded the Originators. The sheer firepower of the Dyson Spheres assured the Eternals could not conquer one. Their only chance was through the vortex Control Centers the Simulins controlled and Jeremy was going to eliminate that threat shortly.

-

Later that evening Jeremy was sitting next to Kelsey in the Italian restaurant where Clarissa had made reservations. He had a large plate of Lasagna sitting in front of him and couldn't help but grin at what Kevin was eating. His red-haired friend had a plate piled high of spaghetti topped by half a dozen oversized meatballs.

"I give up," muttered Katie, shaking her head as she gazed at Kevin's plate. "No matter where we go he finds some way to work hamburger into his food."

Brace looked over at Kevin. "How did you get such large meatballs? Those are just about a meal by themselves without all that spaghetti."

Kevin grinned as he cut up a giant meatball and then scooped up some spaghetti with his fork and spoon. "I tipped the cook. I think he would have cooked me a hamburger if I'd asked."

Katie kicked Kevin under the table, making him flinch. "It's a good thing you didn't." She was eating Chicken Saltimbocca. She had never eaten it before but was finding it delicious.

Kelsey was having her usual Pasta Primavera. The sauce in her meal was fantastic.

Ariel and Clarissa were there at the table as well. Both of them were eating Chicken Fettuccine Alfredo and enjoying its unique taste.

"How's work coming on your new super exploration dreadnaught?" asked Brace.

Smiling, Kelsey turned her attention to Brace. "The design work is nearly finished. We just need to figure out what your job's going to be on the ship."

Brace groaned. "Can't I just take care of the kids?"

Katie shook her head. "We'll have special AIs plus Clarissa and Ariel to handle that when we're not around. "You have to have some type of responsibility."

"It's quite simple," Jeremy said in between bites of Lasagna. "Brace can be head of security and will have a place in the Command Center." He looked over at Kelsey. "You can add a security console which can be used to monitor all areas of the ship, including where Lieutenant Barkley's Marines or Belal's Bears are stationed."

"Bears," muttered Brace frowning. "That's going to be really interesting."

Kelsey laughed. "You'll like Belal. He's a good officer and very loyal. I'll add the console tomorrow when I go to the Tower to work."

Jeremy frowned. "Wasn't he with you when the *Distant Horizon* first arrived in the Triangulum Galaxy?"

"Yes," answered Kelsey, trying not to sound exasperated. "He defended me when I gave command of the ship over to Clarissa."

"If Kelsey hadn't done that none of us would be here today," Clarissa said definitively. "The ship would have been destroyed before you arrived."

Jeremy shook his head. "What you all did was mutiny on board a Federation ship even if it was built by the Altons. I still don't approve of it but I recognize what you did probably saved the *Distant Horizon* and everyone on board."

Kelsey nodded. She knew this was as far as Jeremy would go in condoning her action.

Looking over at Brace, Jeremy grinned. "I'll speak to General Wesley about having you transferred to the new ship. He won't like losing you but I'm sure Angela wants you on board."

"He better be," threatened Angela. "We have Clair and this other one I'm carrying. He's going to help raise both of our children."

"When are you going to ask Rear Admiral Barnes about being the commanding officer?" asked Kelsey. "The design will be finished next week." She was anxious for Jeremy to do this so they could finish filling in the command crew.

"Not yet," Jeremy answered. "She has a lot on her plate at the moment, and I don't want to distract her from her mission. Once the two Simulin vortex Control Centers are back in our hands, I'll speak to her."

Kevin cut into a meatball, took a big bite, and then stuffed spaghetti in behind it.

Katie frowned at him. Maybe she should have taken him to a place where they served hamburgers.

"It will be nice to go out exploring again," said Ariel as she took a sip of the wine Kelsey had recommended.

"I'm ready," announced Angela. "Don't get me wrong. I love my job in the Communications Center but being on a starship is far more exciting."

Taking a deep breath, Kelsey asked Jeremy the question which had been bothering her about the new ship. "What are your plans when our new ship is finished?"

Jeremy put his fork down and looked around the table. "I'll be spending part of my time here at the Hub, the rest of it I plan on commanding the fleet of dreadnaughts that will be escorting your vessel. Rear Admiral Barnes will have command of the new ship and the twenty exploration dreadnaughts assigned to the exploration fleet."

"So you will be going with us?" asked Katie, wanting to confirm what she just heard. If Jeremy was there Kevin would be also.

Nodding, Jeremy shifted his eyes toward Katie. It was hard to imagine this woman was the same green-eyed kid who used to follow him around when he was a teenager. "Yes, some of the time. With the new communications vortex the super exploration dreadnaught has I can stay in contact with the Hub if need be or they can contact us."

Katie looked over at Kevin with a triumphant look in her eyes. "See, you're coming with us!"

"Just pack a lot of hamburgers and fries," answered Kevin as he stuffed a forkful of spaghetti into his mouth. "I get hungry on long trips."

Kelsey took another bite of her Pasta Primavera. It would be great for all of them to be together again on the super exploration dreadnaught. It would be like the old days. Of course the only time all five of them had been together on the same ship was when the *New Horizon* had set out for Tau Ceti and a mutiny occurred. The ship had been destroyed and all five of them nearly died. She hoped the five of them being together again wasn't a bad omen.

"What are you thinking about?" asked Jeremy, reaching over and squeezing her hand. He had noticed the pensive look on her face.

"Oh, nothing important," replied Kelsey not wanting to talk about the past. "We still need to name our new ship."

Jeremy nodded. "I'm sure the three of you will come up with something appropriate."

"I hope so. It's a lot harder to choose a name than I thought it would be." Kelsey wanted the name to be unique. They still had a while yet before the ship was finished. "How's your Lasagna?"

Jeremy smiled. "It's great. You really need to learn to cook this."

Kelsey shook her head. "It's too time-consuming. We can always come here when you have a craving for it. Besides, it gives us a good reason to go out and have a nice evening away from home with friends." Then she leaned over and whispered into Jeremy's ear. "I'm saving my energy up for later."

Ariel smiled to herself. She could hear every word said at the table even if it was in whispers. She would pretend she hadn't heard Kelsey's sultry comment but she was pleased how happy everyone at the table was. It also thrilled her they were willing to share nights like this with her and Clarissa. It made the two AIs almost feel Human.

Chapter Fifteen

Commander Zafron studied the scans from the system they were rapidly approaching. The last time they were in this galaxy, his fleet had nearly been destroyed attacking a system where the Eternals had laid a trap. They had followed convoys to the system from the Stralon Star Cluster. A second group of convoys had been traced to the system they were nearing, and Zafron strongly suspected another trap was waiting for his fleet. This time he planned on being ready.

"Advanced scouts are dropping out of hyperspace," reported Captain Grayson.

It had been Kazak's suggestion that a number of battlecruisers should be sent ahead to scout the system before the main fleet arrived. They would scour the system for any signs of a trap, particularly behind the system's star and around the three gas giants in outer orbits.

"Admiral Lukel's fleet is in position," reported Captain Franklyn. Both fleets were using their stealth fields which should prevent them from being detected.

Commander Zafron leaned forward in his command chair, examining the data coming in from the scouts. There was no sign of any hidden Eternal vessels. Standing up he stepped forward closer to the tactical displays. He was certain there were hidden Eternal ships somewhere. It was the only explanation for the minor resistance he had encountered in the Stralon Star Cluster. "Focus our scans on the space immediately outside the system. See if we can locate a void area where the Eternals may be using their stealth fields to hide from detection."

For several long moments it was silent in the Command Center and then Captain Grayson smiled like a fox that had just caught a rabbit. "Got em! I have a large void area on the far side of the system just outside the orbit of the eleventh planet."

"Then let's set our own trap," replied Zafron, returning to his command chair. "We'll go in first and make our way to the shipyards we've detected above the second planet. Admiral Lukel will remain behind. Once the Eternals come out of stealth and launch their attack, he will jump in directly behind them, pinning them between our two fleets. Kazak, don't worry about destroying the shipyards. I want our blue energy spheres launched at the Eternal fleet. Once it's been eliminated we'll destroy whatever is in orbit of the second planet." Admiral Lukel was following about twenty light years back so if the Eternals detected Zafron's fleet Admiral Lukel's should still be out of range.

"Kia, plot a jump so we exit hyperspace sixty thousand kilometers from the planet. I want us out of range of any shipyard or planet-based weapons. Captain Franklyn, inform Admiral Lukel he's to jump in as soon as the Eternal fleet jumps near the planet."

Commander Zafron let out a deep breath. If the Eternal commander didn't know there was a second Originator fleet this would be a short action. Zafron looked over at Kazak. The military AI had disliked being forced to withdraw the last time they were in this galaxy. As Zafron watched Kazak prepare his weapons console, there was no doubt the AI was relishing the thought of some payback.

-

A few minutes later the thirteen hundred vessels in the Originator fleet exited hyperspace near the target planet. The fleet quickly formed up into a disk formation with the flat side facing the planet.

-

"Report!"

"Fleet is at Condition One," reported Kazak. "Weapons are ready to fire."

"All systems powered up and working at optimum levels," reported another AI.

"There are four shipyards and seven processing stations in orbit around the planet," reported Captain Grayson as he checked his sensor readings. "There are two large shipyards and two smaller ones. The other seven stations appear to be raw resource refineries and possible orbital factory installations."

"Hold position," ordered Commander Zafron. His eyes were on one of the tactical displays showing the large void area just outside of the system. It was moving and suddenly it rapidly accelerated.

"Eternal fleet has entered hyperspace," confirmed Captain Grayson. "Hyperspace emergence in four minutes."

"Weapons ready to fire," reported Kazak. "I'll hit them with a full barrage of blue energy spheres as soon as they emerge."

"Admiral Lukel's fleet will be exiting hyperspace seven minutes after the Eternals," added Captain Grayson.

"All ships rotate one hundred and eighty degrees and prepare to fire on the inbound Eternal fleet," ordered Zafron over the comm unit connecting him to all the ships in his fleet. Only the two hundred heavy dreadnaughts were crewed; the battlecruisers were operated by AIs with a military AI in charge of each one.

—

The ships in the disk formation quickly reversed their orientation so they now faced outward toward the inbound Eternal fleet.

—

The minutes flew rapidly by, and the first Eternal vessels began to emerge from hyperspace.

"Fire!" ordered Commander Zafron as a massive Eternal battlecruiser appeared on one of the ship's viewscreens.

From the *Dominator* a steady stream of blue energy spheres began striking the emerging Originator battlecruisers. Dark matter missiles started detonating releasing massive quantities of energy against Eternal screens. Other ships began firing as well as the Originator fleet turned its full fury on the emerging enemy ships. This time they were not taken by surprise!

—

Fleet Commander Durant's flagship dropped out of hyperspace and instantly shook violently. Several amber lights appeared on the damage control console.

"Gravitonic strike to our energy shield," reported the Eternal at the ship's sensors. "The Originator fleet is in a disk formation facing us and is firing upon our ships as we emerge from hyperspace. Sensors indicate thirteen hundred vessels; two hundred of their dreadnaughts and eleven hundred battlecruisers."

"There is light damage to our hull on the stern," reported the Eternal at damage control. "The weapons fire did not penetrate."

"Return fire," ordered Durant. He had over 2,400 battlecruisers to fight this battle with. "Activate hyperspace distortion field." He would lock the Originator fleet out of hyperspace so it could be destroyed. This time they would not escape.

"Field is being jammed," reported the Eternal at one of the tactical stations.

"Their hyperspace drives are still functional," added the Eternal at the Sensors.

Second Officer Carmmod frowned as he studied the sensor readings. "The Originators have found a method to make our hyperspace distortion field nonfunctional."

"It does not matter," replied Durant, his eyes as cold as ice. "We vastly outnumber them and if they want to stay and fight we will destroy them."

-

The Eternal fleet hastily maneuvered into an attack formation rectangular in shape, twenty-four ships high and one hundred ships in width. It extended beyond the disk formation of the Originators and heavy weapons fire was now striking both fleets.

Particle beam fire from several Originator battlecruisers slammed into the main part of an Eternal warship, setting off massive explosions and hurling debris into space. Moments later a dark matter missile arrived, turning the massive vessel into a burning star.

The top section of an Eternal ship blew apart as gravitonic beams raked across it. Large pieces of debris started drifting away from the ship as secondary explosions began blowing out large sections of the hull. Several antimatter beams penetrated the weakened Eternal energy shield, blasting a deep hole in the hull and destroying a number of energy cannon turrets. The ship suddenly split in two and dark matter missiles finished the destruction as twin suns were born within the Eternal fleet.

Across the Eternal fleet, ships were being heavily damaged or destroyed. Blue energy spheres were turning large sections of the battlecruisers they were striking into space dust. It was taking four of the deadly blue spheres to destroy the massive Eternal battlecruisers. However, the spheres had no difficulty piercing Eternal energy shields. Nearly one hundred Eternal vessels were slowly being broken down as their atoms lost the charges holding them together.

However, the Eternals were having success against numerous Originator ships. Two dreadnaughts blew up under intense energy cannon fire and exploding antimatter missiles. Battlecruisers were dying as their shields were overloaded, leaving the ships themselves vulnerable to Eternal weapons fire. In both fleets, brilliant flashes of light indicated dying ships.

-

Commander Zafron sat in his command chair as the *Dominator* shook from a number of antimatter missile strikes to its energy shield.

"Shield is holding at 86 percent," reported Kazak as he continued to fire blue energy spheres at the Eternals.

"We've lost seventy-three battlecruisers and four dreadnaughts," added Captain Grayson.

"Numerous other ships are reporting damage," added Captain Franklyn.

Zafron took a moment to study a nearby tactical display. His fleet was taking a pounding from the Eternals. He was badly outnumbered and the Eternals were hitting his fleet with their heavy energy cannons. While they were having a hard time penetrating the powerful energy screens of the dreadnaughts, the battlecruisers were not faring as well. His dreadnaughts were more powerful than the Eternal battlecruisers, but his own battlecruisers were weaker than the Eternals and excessive energy weapons fire was bringing down their shields. "How soon before Admiral Lukel arrives?"

"Three minutes," Captain Grayson replied. "I have them on the long-range sensors."

Zafron nodded. "As soon as they drop out of hyperspace we'll spring our own trap. I'm almost certain this is the largest fleet the Eternals have in this galaxy to oppose us. If we can destroy it there will be nothing to prevent us from moving from system to system, destroying all the bases and shipyards we come across." His mission was to force the Eternals to commit vast reserves of ships to protecting their galaxies from this type of attack. He fully intended to do that.

-

The battle ratcheted up in intensity. The dreadnaughts were all armed with the new dark energy cannons. The weapons fire from the cannons penetrated Eternal energy screens as if they didn't even exist. On each side ships were being blown apart from concentrated weapons fire. What was holding the Eternal fleet at bay were the blue energy spheres the *Dominator* was firing. The Eternals had no defense against the deadly weapons. Ship after ship was slowly being turned into space dust.

-

Fleet Commander Durant stood impassively in front of the main tactical display as the battle raged between the two fleets.

"We're losing ships at a nearly even rate," reported Carmmod. "The Originator dreadnaughts are all equipped with dark energy weapons which are penetrating our energy shields. We also have the blue spheres the Originators' flagship is firing. Those two weapons are keeping the ship loss rate almost even."

This did not concern Durant as he had twice as many ships as the Originators. "We have the ships to lose," he said with little emotion in his voice, glancing over at Carmmod. "The Originators don't. We will destroy this fleet and then examine the wreckage. Perhaps we can discover the secret to their new weapons." If his fleet could gain some valuable insight into the new Originator weapons, it would ensure his promotion to a higher position in the empire.

He was about to comment further when alarms began sounding on the sensor console. His eyes shifted back to the tactical display as hundreds of red threat icons began to appear behind his fleet. Drawing in a deep breath, he recognized he had fallen into a trap. There was a second Originator fleet and he was now pinned between the two forces.

"Prepare to enter hyperspace," he ordered, recognizing the impending danger to his fleet. "We no longer have the tactical advantage."

"We can't," replied the helm officer in disbelief. "We're locked out of hyperspace."

Durant looked over at the sensor officer. "Why can't we enter hyperspace?"

"The Originators are broadcasting a hyperspace interference field which is rotating through numerous hyperspace frequencies. It's causing enough instability in our ships' drives so we can't safely activate them."

Fleet Commander Durant felt a cold chill pass through him. His fleet was the largest one currently operating in this galaxy. True there were several thousand other warships but they were scattered across thousands of parsecs of space. If his fleet was defeated, the Originators could cause considerable damage to the shipbuilding capability of this galaxy. He could not allow that to happen.

"Advance toward the fleet in front of us," he ordered. "We will destroy it and then continue to the shipyards around the planet. With their weapons added to ours we will then destroy the second Originator fleet."

In space, the intensity of the battle increased to new levels. The Eternal fleet formation charged forward, colliding and entering the disk formation of the Originators. Admiral Lukel recognizing the danger to Commander Zafron's fleet ordered his fleet to advance. Within minutes the battle resembled more of a dogfight than a coordinated attack. However, the advantage flipped to the Originators as their AIs could communicate with each other over short distances in space. Groups of two to five Originator battlecruisers would flash forward, engage an Eternal warship by blasting down its energy shield and then use dark matter missiles to destroy it. Ships were dying at an ever increasing rate.

Commander Zafron was growing frustrated with the course of the battle. He had effectively lost command. Glancing over at Kazak, he realized the military AI was now directing the battle with his own internal communications implant. In this type of battle it wasn't practical to use the defense globes.

"Eternals are losing two ships for every one of ours they manage to destroy," reported Captain Grayson. "At least I think that's what's happening. It's getting harder every second to keep track of this battle."

The *Dominator* shook violently and several red lights flared up on the damage control console.

"We took a partial hit from an antimatter missile," reported the AI at damage control. We have six compartments open to space, one gravitonic cannon destroyed, two antimatter projectors destroyed, and three energy cannons. There are also several fires in adjoining compartments. Repair robots are en route."

Zafron nodded. "Keep me informed." He disliked hearing his ship was damaged. However, this was war and damage at times was expected to occur.

A sudden flash of light suddenly filled the main viewscreen.

"The dreadnaught *StarFire* blew up," explained Captain Grayson, his face turning pale. "It was right next to us."

"Some of the Eternal ships are moving past our fleet and heading toward the shipyards," Kazak reported as he listened to reports from the other military AIs.

Captain Grayson turned toward Commander Zafron. "They want to use the shipyards as protection. The two largest ones are heavily armed."

Zafron let out a deep sigh. "We can't stop them at the moment. We need to finish this battle and see how much of the Eternal fleet survives." Zafron knew this battle was far from over.

-

Fleet Commander Durant was standing in his Command Center. There was smoke in the air and several consoles were nonfunctional. His flagship had received substantial damage in the battle. Only 33 percent of the ship's weapons were still functioning. His fleet had made it to the two primary shipyards but he greatly feared it would do little good. "How many ships do we have left?"

"Three hundred and twelve," reported Second Officer Carmmod. "Most are heavily damaged."

"The hyperspace interference field?"

"Still in effect," reported the Eternal at the Helm. "It does not matter as our hyperdrive has been damaged."

Durant's shoulders slumped. He was facing defeat. Glancing at the one still functioning tactical display, he could see the Originators still had over one thousand ships left, including their flagship. "We die for the empire," he said to his command crew standing around him. "We are Eternals and we know our duty." Durant walked over and sat down in his command chair. All he could do now was wait for the Originators to finish killing his fleet.

-

Commander Zafron had just finished listening to the damage reports from the two fleets. Combined they still had three hundred and ten dreadnaughts and nine hundred battlecruisers. Many of the battlecruisers were damaged. The battle had been brutal with heavy losses on both sides.

"We will advance with all dreadnaughts screening the *Dominator*," he ordered over the comm system connecting him to all the ships in the two fleets. "Our primary targets are the two main shipyards. We will attack them one at a time. The battlecruisers will stay back and initiate repairs."

Kazak ran his hands over his tactical console. "All weapons are ready. I'll hit the shipyard with ten of our blue energy spheres and then switch to the Eternal battlecruisers. This is a large shipyard, and it will take at least two minutes for the spheres to do their work."

Zafron nodded. "Helm, advance the fleet. It's time to finish this battle."

—

Fleet Commander Durant sat quietly as the Originator fleet advanced. He had inflicted significant losses on the two fleets but not enough to save the system. As he watched the few functioning viewscreens, he saw weapons fire erupt. Originator ships were firing as well as the surviving Eternal battlecruisers.

"Blue energy spheres have struck the shipyard," reported Carmmod. "The commanding officer reports the metal is simply disintegrating."

Durant closed his eyes. His dreams of rising in rank in the empire were about to die. He felt the ship shudder and then a strange shrieking noise seemed to permeate the air. He opened his eyes, looking inquiringly at Carmmod.

"We've been hit by three of the blue spheres. Our ship is coming apart."

Durant did not reply. Instead, he gazed at the front wall of the Command Center. Suddenly it seemed to vanish and he could see the stars. Moments later Fleet Commander Durant was dead as the harsh vacuum of space took the breath out of him.

—

Commander Zafron watched as the shipyard was turned into space dust and the last Eternal battlecruiser died. "Move the fleet to the second shipyard. We will attack it the same way." Zafron leaned back in his command chair. He knew the battle was won. Once the last of the shipyards and orbital facilities were destroyed, they would stay here and finish what repairs they could to the two fleets. He would then combine them into one fleet and they would continue to attack the Eternal shipyards and bases in this galaxy.

On the Planet Gardell, First Leader Clondax studied the reports coming in from different galaxies within the empire. For the most part there was little unrest. However, in five galaxies it was evident Originator fleets were busy. There were reports of numerous shipyards and mining operations being destroyed.

"We cannot allow these losses to continue," complained Second Leader Queexel. "What if the Originators send even more fleets?"

Second Leader Fehnral stood and gazed at the First Leader. "We could begin to lose control of some of our galaxies if these attacks continue. That cannot be allowed to happen."

Clondax gazed coldly at Fehnral. Recently the Second Leader had been challenging his decisions more frequently. "I will order more warships to all five galaxies in question."

"What of the fleets we have in Originator space?" asked Second Leader Tarmal. "My shock troops and warrior robots are now ready to invade the Shrieel in Simulin space."

"Our war fleets are destroying Originator fleet bases as we planned. I have ordered a number of our battlecruisers to observe the Shrieel in question. They will report any unusual activity. Our invasion fleet for the Shrieel is ready and can depart at a moments notice."

"Reports indicate our fleets are suffering heavier losses than expected," said Second Leader Nolant. "The Originator fleet bases are more heavily defended than those we have encountered previously."

Clondax knew this to be true. He was not pleased with the reported ship losses. "The Originators have placed more battlecruisers and large numbers of their attack spheres around the fleet bases. Our ship losses are nearly 300 percent higher than originally projected."

Several Second Leaders were visibly upset by this announcement.

"We must move up our projected attack on the Simulin Shrieel," said Second Leader Queexel.

"I agree," said Second Leader Nolant. "The war against the Originators needs to be brought to an end so we can continue to expand our empire. Every day we delay our expansion allows unknown enemies to gather and prepare to resist us. As large as this universe is we are bound to encounter such an enemy eventually."

First Leader Clondax thought swiftly about what needed to be done. Perhaps if he could take the vortex Control Center in the Shrieel the Simulins controlled, he could force the Originators to negotiate rather than face invasion. He would make his offer to allow the surviving Originators to live on one Shrieel and never leave it. "I will order Fleet Commander Parnon to take the fleet we have gathered for this purpose to the outskirts of the Simulin Galaxy. We will continue to observe the Shrieel and once we are confident of being able to launch our attack successfully, we will do so."

"We are the Eternals," said Second Leader Tallard, satisfied with the First Leader's answer. "It is our right to rule."

The others nodded in agreement. It was time to end this war!

Chapter Sixteen

Major Brenda Wilde was inside another Dyson Sphere. She had been summoned because the stasis facility the squad of Marines had located was massive; far larger than any they had found so far. She had brought her main team along with her.

Brenda was standing in the facilities Control Center along with Sergeant Metz, Cynthia, Reesa, and Faboll. Faboll was hunched over the main computer console using the small device he always carried to access it.

"This is amazing," said Faboll, his eyes showing excitement. "This facility was built specifically by the Originator Council to allow some of our best scientists and their families to survive. There are even two councilors listed as being in stasis."

"Which two?" asked Cynthia. It had surprised her they hadn't found more councilors in the stasis facilities as there was at least one councilor for every Shrieel.

"Councilor Aldon Metrecs and Councilor Alora Roan," replied Faboll.

Cynthia frowned. The names were not familiar. Of course she wasn't familiar with all the councilors from the different Shrieels. "Are they both from this Shrieel?"

Faboll shook his head. "No, that's the strange part. They're both from other Shrieels and not this one."

"The councilor from this Shrieel may have died from the pathogen," suggested Reesa. "My research indicates many of the councilors were deeply involved in trying to find a cure."

Cynthia stepped over closer to Faboll. "What were their fields of study?"

"Councilor Metrecs is a computer specialist and expert on long-term stasis. Councilor Roan is a medical doctor trained in the effects of long-term stasis."

This excited Cynthia. These were two experts they sorely needed even if they were councilors. "We need to awaken them as soon as possible. Do we know where their stasis chambers are located?"

Faboll nodded as he turned toward a wall in the Control Center, which held fifteen stasis chambers. "They're in the two chambers on the far left side."

"How many stasis chambers are in this facility?" asked Reesa. She was anxious to see the list of Originators in stasis. She had been interviewing a number of them from every stasis facility they found about the last days of the pathogen. Some of the stories had been truly terrifying. It was amazing how a civilization as advanced as the Originators could turn barbaric in the face of such a calamity. Reesa had hundreds of hours of recordings she had made during her interviews.

Faboll spent a few moments accessing more information from the Control Centers' main computer. "This is unbelievable. If the data is correct, there are 118,016 of our people in stasis."

Reesa took a step back her eyes widening. "So many?"

"Yes," answered Faboll. "This facility was built by the council itself so it's not surprising it's so large."

Reesa couldn't help but smile. She would be spending days talking to some of these Originators. She just needed to choose which ones would have the most interesting stories. Reesa wondered if there was any way the two councilors would agree to an interview.

Brenda took a deep breath. She hated asking the next question. "How many have failed?" In most facilities nearly 12 percent of all the chambers had ceased to function. If that percentage was the same here they were looking at over 14,000 failed chambers.

"You are not going to believe this but not a single chamber is nonfunctional," replied Faboll.

Brenda's eyes widened in disbelief. "How is that possible? In every facility we've opened so far there have been a multitude of failed stasis chambers."

"I can tell you why," Leeda said as she came into the room. She had gone to check on some of the stasis chambers in the rest of the facility with a couple of Marines. "There are still repair robots functioning. It appears there is a small fabrication center to repair or build new ones as the old repair robots wear out."

"We've never found anything like that before," said Brenda. If there were enough repair robots still functioning, it would explain why all the stasis chambers were working.

Cynthia grinned broadly upon hearing all the Originators in the massive facility were still alive. "Let's have some repair robots come down and remove these fifteen chambers. We'll awaken them first before we touch the rest. They might be able to answer some of our questions about why this facility was built.'"

Brenda nodded. This was the procedure they had been following in all the stasis facilities. The Originators in the Control Centers were the ones trained to activate the awakening process for the stasis chambers. However, that would not happen here. Due to the excessive amount of time which had passed, instead of awakening any of the Originators in the facility they would all be taken to the large medical centers that existed in the Originator cities. There were two centers nearby and Brenda had already ordered their full activation. Teams of Altons, Originators, a few Humans, and medically trained AIs were standing by to receive the first chambers. It was also going to be necessary to send for more of the cure because of the large number of Originators in the underground facility.

"I need to send a message to Councilor Bartoll," said Brenda. "He'll be excited to learn we've found more surviving councilors." Brenda hesitated and then turned toward Faboll. "Make sure we run the list of Originators in stasis against the known list of the members of the Defenders of Zorn." So far in all the stasis facilities they had opened twenty Originators had been found who had past contacts with the organization. Those twenty had been revived but were being held for further questioning to determine if they represented any type of danger.

"This is going to take awhile," sergeant Metz said. "This facility is nearly four times larger than any other we've found."

Brenda nodded her head in agreement. She was also curious to learn why this facility was so large. Of course with the Originator Council being involved it might explain its size and why they had included a manufacturing facility for repair robots. Brenda was thankful they did. At least they wouldn't be removing stasis chambers with mummified Originator remains inside. That was the gruesome part of this job Brenda found disheartening, knowing they had gone to sleep hoping to awaken in a future with the cure. Instead they died never knowing the cure had indeed been found.

Later Brenda returned to the facility out of curiosity. She had sent a message to Councilor Bartoll as well as Fleet Admiral Strong informing them of their discovery. Brenda was walking down a long corridor with stasis chambers stacked high on both sides. Occasionally she would stop to gaze at the occupants. Originator males and females, including children, were in the clear chambers. Occasionally a repair robot would zip by and stop at a chamber to examine it briefly before moving on.

"It's spooky down here," said Sergeant Metz as he gazed at an Originator woman in one of the cases. "It's hard to imagine they've been asleep for over two million years."

Brenda nodded. "I get the chills just walking down these corridors. Can you imagine what it must have been like toward the end in the Dyson Spheres? Leeda says millions of Originators were dying daily and the populace was becoming more and more panicked as it became evident there was not going to be a cure. There was actual fighting in some of the cities. Some tried to flee in spacecraft but the Originator Council shut all the space docks down. They did not want other civilizations finding Originator ships floating in space with dead crews on board. It would have allowed their technology to fall into the hands of worlds not ready for such highly advanced science."

"Major, you need to come see this," said Corporal Anastasia Malone as she ran up to the two. Anastasia had been given a promotion recently. "We've opened up a large compartment and you're not going to believe what's inside."

Brenda looked over at Sergeant Metz who shrugged. "Lead the way."

A few minutes later the three were standing inside a huge room. Along the walls were more stasis chambers.

"Are those what I think they are?" asked Brenda, gazing in worry at the two hundred odd chambers in the room. She could barely make out the occupants.

Corporal Malone nodded. "Yes, the beings in those chambers are Eternals!"

Brenda's face turned pale. "Sergeant Metz, I want two full squads of combat robots as well as a squad of Marines assigned to this room immediately. If even one of those chambers acts as if it is going to open I want it destroyed!"

Metz hurried off to comply with Brenda's orders. They were so far underground communication with the surface was nearly impossible. Brenda walked over and looked closely at one of the chambers. The being inside was eight feet tall, powerfully built and completely bald. His eight-foot tall form and muscular body seemed overpowering when compared to the slimmer forms of an Originator. The Eternals' eyes were open and seemed dark and cold.

"I'd hate to meet him anywhere," mumbled Corporal Malone, her eyes wide open and staring at the Eternal. "Just look at those eyes! What are they doing here?"

Brenda shook her head. "I don't know. It makes no sense. All the Eternals were confined to their galaxy thousands of years before the pathogen began destroying the Originator civilization." One thing Brenda knew for sure: there were going to be a lot of questions for the two Originator Councilors when they were awakened. "I want access to this room on a need to know basis only. I don't want anyone entering without my explicit permission."

"Yes, Major," replied Anastasia. She was holding her assault rifle cradled in her arms.

Looking around the room Brenda saw equipment and consoles which she had no idea what purpose they served. Was it possible these Eternals were being experimented on by the Originators in the hope of finding a cure for the pathogen?

It took a while but Sergeant Metz eventually returned with the combat robots and Marines. Not only that but Leeda and Faboll were with them.

"I don't believe this!" uttered Faboll, looking around the room in shock. "How can Eternals be here? Their galaxy was cut off from the rest of the universe by the hyperspace distortion stations. This should be impossible!"

Leeda walked slowly around the room, examining each chamber. "Some of these Eternals have been operated on," she announced. "It's evident they were being used for some type of experiment."

"I think the Originators in this facility were using them to seek a cure for the pathogen," said Brenda. "It's the only thing that makes sense."

"This isn't good," said Leeda with a deep frown. "How could they risk bringing Eternals here? What if they had gotten loose?"

"We should destroy them," said Faboll, looking at the combat robots. "We should end this now. If these Eternals were to escape they could to incalculable damage."

Brenda agreed with Faboll but she did not have the authority to order such an action. "I'll contact Councilor Bartoll and Fleet Admiral Strong to see what they want done. Sergeant Metz, I want you to stay here until relieved."

Metz didn't look pleased with the order but nodded. "I'm going to have all of these chambers rigged with explosives. If even one starts to open I'll blow them all."

"Do it," ordered Brenda as she gazed at the stasis chambers containing the Eternals. She felt a cold shiver pass over her. "We can't let a single one of these Eternals leave this room."

Brenda watched as Sergeant Metz and several other Marines began placing explosive charges on each of the stasis chambers. She had no idea how Councilor Bartoll and Fleet Admiral Strong would react when told of this discovery.

-

Four days later, Brenda was back in the large room containing the Eternals. A number of Originator specialists had arrived sent by Councilor Bartoll and Fleet Admiral Strong. Brenda knew Jeremy must be concerned as a full company of Marines had also arrived.

In the two nearest cities, the first of the Originators from the Control Center had been given the cure. They would be awake within the next twenty-four hours. As soon as they were able to talk, Bartoll would be coming to speak with them. He had been shocked to learn experiments in this facility involved Eternals. He wanted more information before he decided what to do.

"Fleet Admiral Strong wants to know where the Eternals came from," said Captain Everett, who was in charge of the Marine company that had arrived. He was holding an assault rifle cradled in his arms as he gazed uneasily at the chambers in the room. "General Wesley told me Councilor Bartoll called an emergency meeting to discuss this situation. All three councilors were present as well as Fleet Admiral Strong, Admiral Kalen, General Wesley, and Governor Barnes. There were also other Originators called in. The meeting supposedly lasted nearly half a day."

"It doesn't surprise me," Brenda said. In her hand she held one of the detonators which could destroy the stasis chambers and this room. Sergeant Metz had the other one. "I want to speak to Dazon Fells and see what he thinks is going on." Dazon had come from the Hub and was a specialist on the Anti-Life, or the Eternals as they now called themselves.

Brenda walked over to where Dazon was talking to a group of Originators.

"Major Wilde," said Dazon, recognizing her. "This is a frightful discovery you've made here. Not in my wildest dreams would I have expected to find Eternals in one of the stasis facilities."

"Do you have any idea what was going on here?"

"Partly," Dazon answered. "We believe our people in this facility were experimenting with the mechanical nanites that reside in the Eternals' bodies. They are far more advanced than any we ever designed before the use of them was banned."

"We think they were trying to modify the mechanical nanites to eradicate the life extension pathogen or possibly even change it so it would not be harmful," said Marisa Lillad. Marisa was a geneticist.

Brenda felt confused. "Could you not have done the same thing with the biological nanites that you use?"

Marisa shook her head. "No, our biological nanites are all designed for a specific function and once that function has been achieved they dissolve. Very few of our people have functioning biological nanites at any given time. However, the mechanical nanites the Eternals use are designed to last for several years before they need a new injection. While they're inside an Eternal's body, they can be programmed for different functions. They are much more complex nanites than anything we possess."

Dazon took over the conversation. "No doubt some of the scientists here believed the mechanical nanites could be adapted to work against the pathogen. There are numerous signs from the procedures performed on some of the Eternals we've examined that mechanical nanites were extracted from their bodies."

"So what happened?" asked Brenda. This all sounded so gruesome.

Dazon and Marisa looked at one another their faces showing confusion. "We don't know, at least not yet."

Brenda let out a deep breath. "Continue your investigation. If you discover anything let me know. Under no conditions are you to open any of the stasis chambers. They've all been rigged to explode if that were to occur."

Dazon nodded. "A wise precaution. None of these Eternals can be allowed to wake up. They would be a danger to all of us."

Brenda returned to where Captain Everett and Sergeant Metz were standing. "I want one of the two of you down here at all times. If one of those Eternals starts to awaken evacuate everyone and then blow the stasis chambers. I'm going to the city where the two Originator Councilors have been taken. When they come to I will question them about what was going on in this complex."

"Yes, Major," Captain Everett replied as he took the detonator Major Wilde handed him.

Brenda took a deep breath as she looked one final time around the large room. Combat robots stood at regular intervals ready to act if something went wrong. Marines were constantly checking the stasis chambers along with Originator AIs making sure there were no changes in their status. Finding Eternals here was nothing more than a nightmare. A nightmare she was going to have to deal with.

-

An hour later Brenda exited the excavated tunnel which led down to the hidden stasis facility. Stepping out into the open, she looked around. They were in a small mountain range accessible only by air. Nearby was a small Originator flyer which would take her to the city. She was curious to hear the two councilors' explanations as to what was going on with the Eternals in the facility and even more importantly, how had they gotten into the Dyson Sphere to begin with.

-

It was the late the next day when Major Wilde was ushered into one of the special treatments rooms in one of the large medical centers. Other stasis chambers were now being brought in as sufficient numbers of Originators, Altons, and AI medical personnel had arrived to begin administering the antidote to the life extension pathogen.

As Brenda stepped into the room, she saw two Originators sitting up weakly in their beds. Councilor Bartoll was standing between them with a deep and disapproving frown on his face.

"This is Major Brenda Wilde who is responsible for finding your hidden stasis facility," he said in the way of an introduction. "If not for her you most likely would have stayed in stasis until your repair robots ceased to function and your facility failed, killing everyone in stasis. As I've already informed you, nearly 12 percent of all of our people in stasis in these facilities did not survive."

"You are not an Originator," said Councilor Aldon Metrecs, his eyes widening considerably. Metrecs looked over accusingly at Councilor Bartoll. "Why is this being here? Other races are severely limited from visiting our Shrieels."

"You have not been listening," Bartoll said a little frustration edging into his voice. "We are at war with the Anti-Life. The Humans, Altons, and Carethians have come to our aid as we no longer have the numbers to fight a war."

Councilor Metrecs did not look at Brenda, shaking his head in disbelief.

"How goes the war against the Anti-Life?" asked Councilor Alora Roan. "Can we not force them back into their galaxy?"

"No," said Brenda, deciding these two Originators needed to be shocked back into reality. "The Eternals, as they now call themselves, control over ten thousand galaxies and have millions of warships. It is doubtful we can ever force them back to their galaxy again."

"Thousands of galaxies," said Councilor Metrecs, forcing himself to look at Brenda. "How is that possible?"

Brenda took a deep breath. "While all the surviving Originators slept in their stasis chambers, the Eternals managed to escape from their galaxy over a thousand years ago. They have been rampaging through the universe conquering galaxy after galaxy. No one has been able to challenge them until we found the *Dominator* and awakened Commander Zafron. We also discovered the Communications and Transport Hub and over time, we found more of your people in stasis. My people are currently providing crews for your larger warships so we can keep the Eternals from conquering Originator space."

"Your people are fighting the Eternals?" asked Councilor Metrecs, his eyes focusing intently on Brenda.

"Yes, and many of us have died keeping the Shrieels safe."

Councilor Metrecs closed his eyes and then reopened them. "It seems there is much I must learn of this new age."

"When we opened your stasis facility, we found a room deep beneath the complex containing several hundred Eternals in stasis chambers," said Brenda, watching the two councilors reaction to her announcement. Neither seemed surprised. "What were they doing there and where did they come from?"

"It was a mistake," replied Councilor Roan in a tired and heavy voice. One of the Originator medical technicians stepped forward and injected her with additional organic nanites to give her weakened body strength.

Councilor Bartoll looked at Roan. "How was it a mistake?"

"We sent a ship to the Anti-Life galaxy. One of their ships had been captured trying to reach one of the hyperspace interference stations. The crew had been stunned and placed in stasis by the military AI on board. Our vessel rendezvoused with the station and took the Anti-Life on board, bringing them back here for study. It was hoped we could modify the mechanical nanites in their body to change our genetic structure providing us with immunity from the effects of the life extension pathogen. All of our experiments failed miserably. We finally put all the Anti-Life back in stasis as we were too weak to continue the tests. The next thing I knew I was being awakened here in this medical facility."

Councilor Bartoll shook his head. "You risked much bringing the Anti-Life into one of our Shrieels."

"We were desperate," Councilor Metrecs said. "The council had recently ordered our fleet to take action against unrest occurring on many of the Shrieels. We knew if we could not find a cure quickly it would be the end of our civilization."

Brenda looked at the two councilors. "It nearly was. When I get back to the stasis facility I'll give the order to have the stasis chambers containing the Eternals destroyed."

Councilor Bartoll nodded his approval.

Councilor Metrecs looked over at Councilor Roan. "Tell them."

"Tell us what?" asked Councilor Bartoll, his eyes narrowing.

"During our study of the mechanical nanites in the bodies of the Anti-Life we discovered how to shut them down. What if we could design a weapon which would shut down the mechanical nanites inside the Anti-Life? It would turn them into ordinary beings without their special enhancements. The immediate effect on them would be to make them feel weak and helpless. To them it would be the same as losing an arm and a leg and their brain suddenly working much slower."

Brenda looked over at Councilor Bartoll. She didn't know what to say.

Councilor Bartoll let out a deep breath. "We will postpone destroying the Eternals for now. They are under heavy guard. I need to contact Fleet Admiral Strong and speak to him of this."

"Who is Fleet Admiral Strong?" asked Councilor Metrecs. "Is he an Originator?"

"No," answered Bartoll, shaking his head. "He's a Human and the entire future of the Shrieels and our race rests in his hands."

"The two councilors need their rest," said Cynthia, stepping closer to her patients. Come back in a couple of days and you can ask them all the questions you like."

Bartoll hesitated and then nodded. "Very well. We're getting ready to begin awakening everyone in the hidden stasis facility. It's going to be a long process considering how many there are. Come with me, Major Wilde. We have a lot to discuss."

Brenda followed Councilor Bartoll out of the room. He led her to a small waiting room empty of anyone else. "What do you think?"

"Do you believe they are telling us the truth?"

"Yes, I don't see any reason for them to mislead us. I do want to speak to a few Originator scientists back at the Hub about being able to shut the mechanical nanites down. If it is possible, it could change this war very quickly to our favor."

"Maybe," replied Brenda doubtfully. "The Eternals are spread out over ten thousand galaxies and I doubt if we can even get a fleet anywhere near their home system. Even if we can shut the nanites down I doubt if we can get all of them."

"No, I'm sure you are correct. However, what if we could shut down the ones in the crews of the Eternal battlecruisers? The confusion caused by such an action may make their ships more vulnerable to our weapons."

Brenda nodded. "I think you need to talk to Fleet Admiral Strong about this. I know a lot about fighting on the ground but space warfare is way out of my league."

Councilor Bartoll strolled over to a large window overlooking the city. It was a breathtaking view. All of the cities on all of the Shrieels had been kept spotless and functioning by the hundreds of millions of repair robots that took care of nearly everything. Looking out across the city and its soaring towers you would think it had only been evacuated yesterday.

"I will speak to Fleet Admiral Strong as well as others. We have some serious decisions to make. I'll also be remaining here for a few more days. I have a number of questions I want to ask Councilors Metrecs and Roan. They can tell us a lot about the last days of the pathogen in the Shrieels and the actions the council took. Some of those actions, including the use of our fleet, took the lives of millions of our people."

"It was a desperate time," Brenda replied. "At least now with all of your people we have found in stasis you can start over again."

Bartoll nodded. "We shall, but I fear our civilization will never be the same again."

Chapter Seventeen

Deep underground in a hidden stasis facility Commander Alvord and Albate stood in front of the leader of the Destroyers of Zorn. Councilor Zorn had recovered fully from his time in stasis and was listening patiently as Alvord and Albate explained to him what was going on in Originator space. They had briefed him before. However, this one was much more thorough.

"So, we are finally at war with the Anti-Life," said Zorn pleased to hear of this.

He had long warned the council that someday the Anti-Life would escape their imprisonment and become an even greater threat than ever before. The council had merely stated that as long as the Anti-Life stayed in their galaxy, there was nothing to fear. The hyperspace interference stations would ensure the Anti-life stayed in their galaxy for eons to come. The council had been certain internal strife would eventually eliminate the Anti-Life as any type of threat.

"Yes," replied Alvord. "The Humans are taking the lead in the war and Councilor Bartoll is following along. I fear in time it will be the Humans who control the Shrieels and not our own people. Every day more Humans, Altons, and Carethians are arriving from their Federation. In time they will far outnumber us."

Councilor Zorn frowned. "I believe we can take steps to ensure that does not happen. Of more importance is making certain this war against the Anti-Life continues. I understand more of our people are being awakened from stasis."

"The Humans are finding more hidden stasis facilities every day," reported Matissa Lanoor. Matissa was a deep sleep specialist. "We have confirmed reports that in most of the facilities 12 percent of the stasis chambers have failed. Recent computer estimates put the total number of surviving Originators awake and in stasis between sixty to ninety million."

Zorn was not pleased to hear of the deaths. "With the destruction of the dark matter Shrieel we have no idea as to why we were not awakened when the AIs at the Communications and Transport Hub discovered the cure. Our primary facility was supposed to be activated immediately upon receiving that information."

The primary Defenders of Zorn stasis facility had held over forty thousand of Zorn's staunchest supporters. This secondary facility held only eight hundred. Zorn had never felt comfortable in the Shrieel surrounded by dark matter. However, it was the ideal place for the primary facility because of the research being done and the fact that the *Dominator* might someday return with the cure. It was upsetting to learn his careful plans for the *Dominator* and the *Seeker* had met with failure.

"Using the birthing chambers it will not take us long to greatly increase our population," said Matissa. "With a base population of eighty million, we could have our numbers up to three billion within one hundred years and nearly one hundred billion in two hundred."

Zorn nodded his head in acceptance. "Even at that rate we're only talking about 500 million in each Shrieel in two hundred years. We once numbered in the trillions."

"It would be unwise to expand our population any faster," cautioned Matissa. "We are long-lived. Someday we will see our civilization back at the numbers we once knew."

Zorn was silent for several long moments and then spoke. "We will begin sending some of our people out who are not known members of our organization. As long as our people continue to support the war against the Anti-Life, we will not interfere. However, I do want to set up some contingency plans if that support begins to fade. The war against the Anti-Life must continue until they are destroyed!"

Zorn believed after the first war with the Anti-Life was over his people had become too complacent. While he wasn't pleased to hear Humans, Altons, and Carethians were living at the Hub and operating Originator warships he could see where they might be useful. It was time for him to begin thinking of his rise to power and how to accomplish it. In time, he intended to return to the Originator Council and rule over it.

Major Wilde and Councilor Bartoll were inside a small conference room at the medical center speaking with Councilors Metrecs and Roan. Both were doing much better as the organic nanites injected into their systems were rapidly improving their health. They still needed some aid walking but had insisted this meeting occur in a place more suitable than one of the treatment rooms.

"We have both studied the computer records of what has occurred over the last several years," announced Metrecs. "I must say I am impressed by what the Humans have managed to accomplish against the Eternals. When I first learned about the Humans I was greatly concerned."

Councilor Roan nodded in agreement. "There are also the Altons, who in many ways resemble our own people in our younger days. I see no reason to restrict their access to our technology. It is also evident that as close as they are to the Humans, they will help to control the use of our technology and ensure it is not misused by this younger race. Of course both races will need considerable guidance from us in the future."

"As for the Carethians they seem to be a very honorable race. Their support of the Humans and Fleet Admiral Strong is almost fanatical. Of course after the way he saved their world I can easily see why they're so supportive. They also don't seem very interested in our technology. Even in the new cities we are building for them they are using very little of our advanced science and technology."

Councilor Bartoll nodded. "Their leader, Grayseth, was very insistent our technology be limited in their cities. Their culture, while very primitive in some ways, is based on honor and hunting. The only advanced technology they have embraced is upon the warships they operate, and Grayseth has requested we provide sufficient AIs to handle that technology."

"Grayseth sounds intriguing," said Alora. "I must meet him when I have the chance."

Brenda could not help but grin. "Grayseth is a very imposing figure; even a little frightening until you get to know him."

"I am concerned about how long it is taking to awaken our people in stasis and particularly how long it seems to be taking to find the other hidden stasis facilities. Every day we delay more of our people are dying in their chambers. Most of our facilities were not designed to function this long. I am surprised the failure rate is not even higher."

A grave looked passed over Councilor Bartoll's face as well. "It was the Defenders of Zorn. Somehow they managed to transmit a signal to all the hidden facilities ordering the computers not to initiate awakening of any stasis chambers until a manual code is entered into the primary computer. We're not completely certain how they accomplished this or even how they knew where the facilities were located."

"It's also taking us time to locate the stasis facilities," explained Brenda. "Each facility we open leads us to others. I wish we knew where they were all located so we could get to them faster."

Councilor Metrecs frowned. "I think I can help with that. On the Communications and Transport Hub, there is a concealed Control Center with the location of all the hidden facilities. Its primary computer is also linked to all of the hidden sites. I would guess the Defenders of Zorn managed to find this center and use it to transmit the orders for the facilities not to be activated when word of the cure was broadcast. The facility will have a list with the location of all hidden stasis locations."

Councilor Bartoll's eyes widened. "Do you know where this Control Center is located?"

"Yes," replied Aldon. "Toward the end the secret of its location was given to all the surviving councilors. If you can take either of us to the Communications and Transport Hub we can show you."

"You'll both be going there as we've made it the center of our operations. It is also the most heavily defended part of Originator space. As soon as all of our people have been successfully awakened we will establish a new Originator Council to better rule over the Shrieels and galaxies we control. As the most advanced race it is up to us to protect all of the civilizations in those galaxies, particularly since the Eternals were once Originators."

Alora's eyes lit up. "I always dreamed of us taking a guiding hand in those galaxies. There is so much we have to offer."

"That is still in the future," said Councilor Bartoll. "We have much to accomplish before we can begin doing that."

Brenda took a deep breath. She had spoken with General Wesley earlier and had questions to put to the two Originator Councilors. "I have some questions about the Eternals in stasis and what you discovered about the mechanical nanites their bodies are infested with. We are particularly interested in the shutdown procedure."

"We were expecting that," Councilor Metrecs replied. "Be aware the mechanical nanites the Eternals now have in their bodies are probably far more advanced than the ones we learned to shut down. We might need several current Eternals to see if the shutdown process will still work or if it needs to be modified."

Brenda frowned. She had not been expecting to learn they needed to capture some living Eternals. That might prove difficult.

Councilor Bartoll spoke up. "If we're actually considering doing this I suggest we construct a suitable holding facility in one of the galaxies away from any Shrieel or our fleet bases. I don't want to risk the Eternals gaining access to any of our current weapons technology."

"The blue energy spheres," said Metrecs in understanding. "I assume they are quite effective against Eternal warships."

Bartoll nodded. "Yes; they have no defense. The spheres go right through Eternal energy shields."

"You haven't put them on any warships, have you?" asked Alora. "It would be a disaster if that weapon fell into enemy hands."

"The only ship which has the blue energy spheres is the *Dominator*. It's so powerful not even the Eternals want any part of it. However, we have a new weapon based on dark energy that is nearly as effective. It too can penetrate Eternal energy screens and is being placed on all of our new dreadnaughts."

Councilor Metrecs looked curious. "I have studied the new dreadnaughts being built in our shipyards. They are quite impressive."

"We had no choice," replied Councilor Bartoll. "The battlecruisers of the Eternals are four kilometers in length and armed with extremely powerful energy cannons."

Brenda looked at the two councilors. "I will inform General Wesley it might be necessary to capture some living Eternals. How many would be necessary?" Brenda had no idea how they would go about capturing such a dangerous enemy combatant.

"Six to ten," replied Alora. "We would need a good cross-section of the types of mechanical nanites the Eternals are currently using. If we are seriously considering doing this, I would also recommend we awaken the scientists and technicians who conducted the original experiments as it will take some time for them to fully recover from the effects of the pathogen."

Brenda let out a deep breath. She wasn't sure how this could be done but it wasn't her problem. She would inform General Wesley of what Alora said and see where it went from there. "I'll make the arrangements to awaken the necessary Originators as soon as possible. I just need their names so we can find their stasis chambers."

Bartoll handed Alora a small handheld computer which she used to input a number of names. When she was done she handed it over to Brenda.

Brenda looked down, seeing Alora had input over twenty names.

"There are more but these were the primary scientists involved. They can tell you who else will be needed. I should warn you the primary scientist, Reull Alistar, is quite egotistical and not easy to work with. I would suggest finding one of our people to be the go between, preferably one who can deal with people such as Alistar. He is also quite brilliant."

"Jankel," suggested Brenda, looking over at Councilor Bartoll. "He would be perfect for this job."

Councilor Bartoll nodded his head in agreement. "I believe you are right. I'll speak to him as soon as I return to the Hub." He then looked over at Cynthia who had been hovering in the back of the room, keeping an eye on her patients. "How soon before they can travel back to the Communications and Transport Hub?"

"Another week," Cynthia replied. "Even then I want a medical specialist with them at all times."

"Very well," Bartoll replied. "I need to get back immediately and speak to Fleet Admiral Strong, General Wesley, and Governor Barnes. Suitable transport will be made ready in one week to transport the two councilors." Bartoll knew if the two councilors could provide the locations to all the hidden stasis facilities, they were going to need more Altons and Humans brought to the Hub from the Federation as soon as possible. It was time to send larger convoys of transports.

-

Later Major Wilde was back in the underground stasis facility. Faboll was busy at the computer terminal locating the stasis chambers of the twenty Originators on Alora's list.

"They are all together," Faboll reported after a few minutes. "According to the information on the computer database all twenty of them are well advanced in terms of the pathogen. They must have worked until the very last minute on the nanites."

"They were dedicated," Dazon said. "They believed they were on the verge of finding a possible cure."

"But how many of our people would have been willing to allow mechanical nanites to be injected into their bodies?" said

Marisa. "Our aversion to such a procedure may still have doomed our race."

"It does not matter now," Brenda said. "We have an organic cure which is quite effective."

Leeda stepped over to Faboll, examining the list he had called up on one of the computer screens. "I'll have these stasis chambers taken to the medical center immediately. I would also suggest doing the same with the ones near these twenty. There may be others working on this project Alora did not include on her list. It is reasonable to believe they all went into stasis at nearly the same time."

"Councilor Roan said there were," said Brenda.

Faboll did some quick checking examining several more computer files. "Leeda is correct; there are nearly two hundred stasis chambers that were activated within forty hours of one another. I would guess all the scientists and technicians working on this project were put into stasis at the same time. Probably the lead scientists became too ill from the pathogen and as a result there was no longer any reason to continue the project. Do we want to awaken them all?"

Brenda nodded. "I would also suggest that Cynthia scan all of the Originators in this facility for any trace of mechanical nanites before they're given the cure. There is reason to suspect a few Originators may have volunteered to be test cases."

"I will inform Cynthia," Leeda replied. "I'll accompany the stasis chambers to the medical facility and make sure she is informed of your concern."

Brenda watched as Leeda left the Control Room to get some of the repair robots to remove the chambers. A number of large cargo flyers were waiting above. Brenda hoped she was wrong about the Originator scientists experimenting on live subjects but she had a strong suspicion she wasn't. They had been desperate and desperate people often take measures which in normal times would have been unthinkable.

Chapter Eighteen

Jeremy let out a deep breath as the *Avenger* and her fleet exited the large intergalactic vortex in the Dyson Sphere. The fleet rapidly gained altitude until they were hovering twenty thousand kilometers above the surface. On the viewscreens, the large habitation squares below them were plainly visible. White puffy clouds were floating over large areas and even a few oceans could be seen. It was still hard to believe all of this was an artificial creation.

Fleet is in formation," reported Commander Malen. On the tactical display near her, one thousand green icons represented the heavy dreadnaughts which surrounded the *Avenger*.

They had exited the vortex nearest to the one the Simulins controlled.

"Move the fleet directly over the Simulin controlled vortex," ordered Jeremy. "It's time to get this operation underway." Jeremy was just thankful they finally had everything in position to wrest the Control Center away from the Simulins. This had been a long time in coming and it would be one less thing to worry about.

-

On the surface of the Dyson Sphere, the Simulins had noticed the arrival of the new fleet. They were used to seeing ships of the Ancients coming and going, but they felt safe beneath the powerful energy shield they had erected to protect the intergalactic vortex they controlled and the area immediately around it.

Inside the vortex Control Center, High Commander Vetrex watched several viewscreens showing the new fleet. They looked very purposeful as they formed up above the protective energy shield.

"This may be an attack," he said to his second in command. "We have noticed a substantial increase in the number of combat robots and Human Marine forces outside the energy shield."

"It will be useless," replied Second Commander Trador. "They will never get past the energy shield and even if they do our Conqueror Drones will annihilate any intruders. They will never take this Control Center as they have others."

Vetrex nodded his agreement. There were nearly eighty thousand of the deadly crab-like robots on the surface and in the corridors around the vortex crater and the Control Center. Not only that, there were eight hundred Simulin battlecruisers sitting on the surface near the crater as well. "Order all battlecruisers to lift off and activate their energy shields." Vertex was not going to take any chances if this was an attack.

"We're in position," Ariel informed Jeremy as the fleet arrived directly over the Simulin energy shield.

"Their ships are lifting off the surface," added Kevin. "They're activating their energy shields."

The Simulin ships were bulbous in form with large metallic looking pylons that stretched out in front of them. There were six of the massive structures, which extended at least two hundred meters out from the main hull of the ships. Each ended in a sharp point and from these a powerful energy weapon could be fired. When the Lost Fleets had first entered the Triangulum Galaxy and encountered the Simulins, numerous ships had been lost to these deadly vessels.

Jeremy nodded. The Simulins must suspect something was up. "Aaliss, see if you can access the vortex Control Center and shut down the energy shield. All ships are to target the Simulin warships as well as the energy shield generators." Jeremy wanted to make sure if they were successful in bringing down the energy shield, it could not be brought back online. He wasn't worried about the Simulin warships as they had no weapon that could penetrate an Originator ship's energy shield.

"Accessing secondary control programs," replied Aaliss. "This is going to take a few minutes."

The plan was very simple. There were some systems that were very minor in importance in the vortex Control Center. By infiltrating these systems, they were going to attempt to insert a new set of programming into the primary control console instructing it to shut down the energy screen for preventive maintenance by repair robots. It was hoped the Simulins had not interfered with the regular automatic maintenance systems. The energy shield had been put up by the Simulins but if it was operated through the primary computer console in any way, then this should work.

For several long minutes nothing happened and then suddenly the energy shield vanished.

"Fire!" ordered Jeremy, leaning forward in his command chair. They needed to take out both the Simulin warships and the energy shield generators in the opening barrage. It would not take the Simulins long to figure out what had happened and override the maintenance program allowing them to raise the energy shield.

From the Originator fleet, particle beam and gravitonic cannon fire rained down on the surprised Simulins. Around the periphery of the vortex crater, explosions marked the destruction of the energy shield generators. Then all the weapons fire was turned upon the seventeen hundred-meter in length Simulin battlecruisers. While the battlecruisers were powerful vessels of war, they were nothing when compared to an Originator dreadnaught. The particle and gravitonic beams pierced their energy screens causing massive damage to the Simulin warships. In monstrous explosions, the defending fleet was blasted out of the sky.

-

Vertex stared in shock as the energy screen vanished and the Ancients' fleet opened fire.

"Raise the shield!" he ordered, his eyes showing deep concern. "What caused the shield to go down?"

"We're trying," replied Second Commander Trador. "The primary computer has activated a maintenance program and shut the shield down while repair robots check the energy generators."

Vertex shifted his eyes to the viewscreens seeing his defending fleet being decimated. "I knew we should have destroyed all of those small robots." They had left a few operating as they provided regular routine maintenance to the part of the Great Sphere the Simulins controlled. Maintenance that the Simulins didn't have to concern themselves with.

"We have reports of combat robots and Human Marines advancing on the surface. Some of our forward units are reporting contact."

Looking back at Trador, Vertex expelled a heavy breath. "Contact our fleet outside the Great Sphere and inform them we may need reinforcements." There were over two thousand Simulin escort cruisers and battlecruisers waiting at the extreme edge of the system. "Open the main hatch so they can jump in."

"That will be dangerous for the fleet."

Due to the defensive weapons on the outside of the Great Sphere, it was necessary for Simulin ships to jump almost inside the huge hatch. Unfortunately jumping so close to an object of mass often resulted in the destruction of nearly 40 percent of the ships that made the jump in hyperspace.

"It has to be done. They know their duties," replied Vertex coldly.

—

Outside the Great Sphere, the Simulin fleet began entering hyperspace to make the attempt to reach the open hatch safely. They would enter in squadrons as the amount of room to exit hyperspace safely near or inside the entry tunnel was severely limited.

Two Eternal battlecruisers that were observing the system noticed the sudden activity and sent messages to Fleet Commander Parnon who was waiting in a nearby rift between the stars. Something was happening at the Shrieel, which the Simulins were responding to.

—

Fleet Commander Parnon received the messages and quickly realized that something unexpected must be occurring. It seemed the Simulins were rushing ships to the Shrieel.

"The Humans must be launching an attack to retake the vortex Control Center," he said. Parnon had been planning to launch his own attack in the next day or so. It was disconcerting that the Humans had acted first. They must have realized the threat the intergalactic vortex represented to them.

"This is unexpected," replied Second Commander Bernon. "We were not expecting to face opposition from the Humans."

Parnon thought quickly about what needed to be done. It would be extremely dangerous to drop his fleet out of hyperspace too close to the Shrieel. Its blue energy spheres could cause considerable damage to his fleet. However, there was another way he still might achieve victory. "Prepare our warrior robots and our shock troops for deployment. We will jump in close to the Shrieel, launch our attack shuttles, and then jump back to safety."

"We will lose part of our fleet," warned Second Commander Bernon. "In order to launch all the attack shuttles, it will take ninety seconds for them to clear the launch bays."

"It's a risk we'll have to take. The fleet will also fire upon the Shrieel defensive sites around the target. Perhaps we can widen the safe area the Simulins have created."

Second Commander Bernon began issuing orders. On board the Eternal ships, warrior robots began to march up the ramps to the shuttles followed by Eternal shock troops. Nearly two hundred thousand warrior robots and thirty thousand shock troops were assigned to this mission.

The twenty thousand Eternal battlecruisers entered hyperspace for the forty-minute trip to the Shrieel. It was time to take the first step in invading the over two hundred Shrieels in Originator space.

-

Jeremy watched the viewscreens as the reports flooded in.

"All energy shield generators have either been disabled or destroyed," reported Aaliss. "The Simulins will not be able to raise the shield again."

"All Simulin warships have been destroyed," added Ariel. "Their shields were no match for our weapons." It had been a massacre as the Simulins' weapons were feeble compared to the Originators.

"Combat robots and Marines are advancing," reported Commander Malen. "General Wesley reports they are meeting heavy resistance."

Jeremy was uncomfortable with General Wesley being on the ground, but the general had proclaimed that if he was committing so many troops to this battle, then he needed to be there with them. What also concerned Jeremy was that Angela's husband Brace was with him.

—

General Wesley was inside his command shuttle, which was at the very edge of the fighting. Thousands of Conqueror Drones were resisting the combat robots and Marines' advance. On one large viewscreen, Wesley watched as hundreds of Conqueror Drones and combat robots were locked in an intense battle. The drones were as large as a small tank and covered with a metallic shell with four large appendages shaped like dangerous looking pinchers which could tear a Marine or combat robot apart. A few of the drones were also equipped with short-range missiles and explosive rounds.

The combat robots and the Marines were using energy weapons and explosive rounds against the drones. In some areas, hand-to-hand combat was rampant with the drones and the combat robots trying to tear one another apart. The Marines in those regions stayed back. If a drone grabbed a Marine, he faced the most gruesome of deaths in being torn apart.

General Wesley let out a deep sigh. He had brought an ace in the hole to deal with the drones infesting the surface of the Dyson Sphere around the vortex crater. "Contact Rear Admiral Tolsen and tell her to begin the airstrikes." Wesley had asked

Fleet Admiral Strong to allow Massie to take command of the battlecarrier task group he had brought to serve as air support for the combat robots and the Marines. These tactics had been very successful on Ornellia and the drone infested worlds of their small empire.

In space behind Fleet Admiral Strong's fleet were three battlecarriers. From each, squadrons of Talon fighters and Anlon bombers were launching. Massie was in the Command Center of the battlecarrier *Liberty* as the attack squadrons left the ship's flight bays.

"Bombers will target clusters of Conqueror Drones," she ordered. "All fighters are to do strafing runs as near the front lines as possible to take out individual targets." She had read the reports and watched videos of the tactics used at Ornellia and on their other worlds.

Massie leaned back in her command chair. She had been pleased to find out there were still battlecarriers at the Communications and Transport Hub. Evidently, from what she had been told, they were being used primarily to run reconnaissance patrols in the space around the Hub. There were also more battlecarriers in the Triangulum Galaxy helping the Ornellians clear their planets of the deadly drones.

"All fighters and bombers have been launched," reported Major Karl Arcles who had transferred to the *Liberty* for this mission. Karl was the CAG for the *Distant Horizon* and Rear Admiral Barnes had approved the transfer. Some of her pilots had come also as they were some of the most experienced in the fleet. "They should be starting their attack runs shortly."

Massie nodded. She could feel her heart beating faster and the excitement rushing through her. "Let's take out as many of those drones as we can on the first pass."

"Orders sent and confirmed by all squadron leaders."

It felt good to be back in the Command Center of a battlecarrier. Leaning forward she watched as the first squadrons set up for their attack runs.

"This is Echo squadron leader," spoke Captain Lacey Sanders over her squadron comm channel. She was flying a Talon and leading a squadron of ten fighters. "The fighting below is pretty obvious. We'll make a run two hundred meters behind the front line and thin out the drones gathered there. Keep in mind we have Human Marines close by. I don't want no loses due to friendly fire. Everyone follow me in and prepare to engage."

Lacey arrowed her fighter down toward the surface. Small explosions and the discharge of energy weapons indicated where the fighting was occurring.

"I'm on your right side and sixty meters back," reported Lieutenant Raven. "I'll follow you in."

The two Talon fighters came streaking down through the atmosphere of the Dyson Sphere followed by eight others. Just before reaching the surface, the fighters began firing explosive shells into the masses of waiting Conqueror Drones. Pieces of metal and appendages flew into the air as the Talons strafed the drones. Pulling back up Captain Sanders inspected the damage. Other fighter and bomber groups were active as well. Smoke was beginning to cover the battlefield. "One more time," she ordered. "Then we'll split up and seek targets of opportunity."

The fighters went back again laying down long lines of explosions destroying some Conqueror Drones and damaging many others.

"There must be thousands of them," said Lieutenant Stark. "I've never seen so many, not even at Ornellia."

Lacey nodded in agreement. "We'll split apart now. We're in charge of support in this quadrant along with a bomber squadron. Make your rounds count." Looking at the fighting on the ground, Lacey had a suspicion this was going to be a long day.

"Fighters and bombers are engaged," reported Commander Malen.

"We have Simulin warships coming through the open hatch," warned Kevin as alarms sounded on the sensor console.

"Escort cruisers and battlecruisers detected," added Ariel. "They must have jumped right into the opening."

"How?" asked Kevin. "Even the Simulins would lose ships jumping that close to an object of mass."

Aaliss turned toward Kevin. "No doubt they did. Some of the ships we're detecting are showing major damage to their hyperdrives. I suspect a large number of their ships were destroyed completely."

"Incoming weapons fire," warned Kevin.

"Can we close the hatch remotely?" asked Jeremy.

"No," replied Aaliss. "That can only be done from the vortex Control Center or the individual hatch controls located throughout the tunnel."

Looking at the viewscreens, Jeremy could see the long spires on the front of the Simulin ships light up as they fired their powerful energy weapons. Weapons that in the past would have been considered dangerous.

"No damage to any of our ships," reported Ariel. "Beams are not penetrating or stressing the shields."

"Destroy them," ordered Jeremy, feeling no mercy to the Simulins. He had seen videos of how their Conqueror Drones killed. "I don't want them to turn their weapons on our Marines or combat robots. Destroy them as they exit the hatch."

For the next twenty minutes the Simulin ships continued to come out of the large hatch only to be blown apart by the dreadnaughts in Jeremy's fleet. Very few even managed to fire their energy cannons. The wreckage on the surface of the Dyson Sphere continued to pile up.

-

Captain Carl Werner ducked as pieces of Conqueror Drones rained down on him and his Marines. A missile from an Anlon bomber had struck uncomfortably close.

"Damn, will somebody tell those pilots we're down here!" yelled Sergeant Hitch as he hunkered down behind a tree that had been blown in two.

Captain Werner grinned. "Just stay down."

They were slowly getting closer to the vortex crater. Destroyed combat robots and Conqueror Drones lay strewn over the ground. The battle plan was to secure the surface area first and then enter the corridors below to remove the rest of the Simulins and their drones. So far, Captain Werner had not seen a single Simulin engaged in combat. He was also thankful for the combat armor the Originators had built for his Marines. The armor was nearly impossible to penetrate with normal weapons fire.

"We're going to have a problem shortly," said Sergeant Hitch as he gazed through the scope of his assault rifle. "We're about to run out of cover."

Werner stood up to get a better view. He could see what the sergeant was talking about. In another three hundred meters, the ground ended to be replaced by smooth metal that extended all the way to the vortex crater. "The drones won't have cover either. It'll make them easier to destroy."

Sergeant Hitch stood and fired several bursts from his assault rifle toward a Conqueror Drone that had suddenly appeared. The armor piercing rounds shattered the drone's carapace causing it to collapse to the ground. Another nearby Marine pumped several explosive rounds into it blowing the drone apart.

Looking around at the battle, Werner could see several of the large combat robots engaged in hand-to-hand combat with the drones. The robots were tearing off the drones appendages and ripping huge holes in the carapaces. The drones in turn were working in pairs trying to tear the combat robots in two. Occasionally they met with success sending the two pieces flying through the air.

Captain Werner was making it a point to keep his Marines back for now. Even so, two had been killed and five others injured. He knew before this was over he would lose even more. This had the makings of a violent and long battle.

High Commander Vetrex knew he was in trouble. In a few more hours the Humans and their combat robots would have full control of the surface while his Conqueror Drones and Simulin soldiers controlled the corridors and Control Center.

"All of our ships have been annihilated," reported Second Commander Trador. "The ships of the Ancients cannot be destroyed."

"I am preparing to summon additional warships," answered Vetrex. "They will bring more soldiers as well as large numbers of drones. We will take back the surface and rebuild the energy shield generators."

For many months now, there had been contact with only one other Great Sphere. The Humans and their combat robots had taken back control of all the others. All of the other Simulin controlled galaxies were now out of contact with the empire. Alarms suddenly began sounding on one of the consoles. The console was set to monitor ships approaching the Sphere. "What is it?"

Second Commander Trador looked confused. "Unknown ships have dropped out of hyperspace on the extreme edge of the system. They are even larger than the ships of the Ancients."

High Commander Vetrex was at a loss to explain these strange ships. It was almost impossible to imagine they could have traveled across the Simulin home galaxy and not been detected. Was this a new enemy coming to claim the Great Sphere?

-

Fleet Commander Parnon gazed at the main viewscreen of his flagship showing the Shrieel. He knew if he moved his fleet much closer, they would be within range of the deadly blue energy spheres of the Originators. Reports indicated they were capable of entering hyperspace.

"One of the main hatches is open," reported the Eternal at the sensor console. "I believe the Simulins attempted to jump part or all of their fleet into the entrance a short time ago. Their ships are weak and many could not handle the stress of emerging so close to the Shrieel and were destroyed. There is ship wreckage all around the hatch."

"What is happening inside the Shrieel?" asked Second Commander Bernon. "What would make them risk their fleet in such a manner?"

Fleet Commander Parnon stood and stepped closer to the main viewscreen. He stood there silently for several moments. "The Humans and the AIs must be attacking the Simulins on the inside of the Shrieel. They must have recognized the danger if we were to take over the vortex Control Center. They are fighting this battle to prevent us from doing that."

"What are your orders?"

Parnon studied a screen showing the large open hatch on the Shrieel. It was an opportunity. By using the open hatch, he would not have to risk his fleet by exposing it to the weapons fire from the Shrieel. "We will jump the fleet into the open area in the hatch. Once there we will launch the attack shuttles and then continue on into the Shrieel and engage whatever Originator ships are inside. We have a fleet of twenty thousand warships and once inside nothing will be able to stop us. Prepare the fleet to jump."

"That will take considerable time," replied Second Commander Bernon as he studied the open hatch on a viewscreen. "Only sixty of our ships can enter the area of the hatch at a time."

Parnon was not pleased to hear this, but he could not squander this opportunity. He had not been expecting to find one of the primary hatches to the Shrieel to be open. "Sixty ships at a time then. They will jump to the hatch entrance, unload their attack shuttles, and then move into the tunnel leading to the inside of the Shrieel. As soon as the first group is out of the way, we will send the second. This needs to be done as rapidly as possible while we have the element of surprise. The Shrieel is ours for the taking."

Jeremy was listening to the reports coming in from the surface. So far, the battle was going as planned. In another few hours the surface around the vortex crater would be firmly under their control. Once that was accomplished, the second phase of the battle would begin.

"We have a problem," announced Aaliss with a stunned look on her face. "A large Eternal fleet has appeared on the outskirts of the system."

Kevin's face turned pale. "The Eternals, here?"

Ariel stepped over to stand next to Jeremy. "They must have learned the Simulins control this vortex Control Center. They're going to try to take it."

"Aaliss, how many other warships do we have inside the Shrieel?" Jeremy was concerned since he had not planned on facing a major Eternal fleet in battle.

Aaliss was silent for a moment as she communicated with the military AI in charge of the Shrieel. "Two thousand and seventy enhanced battlecruisers, six thousand and forty updated battlecruisers of the old class, and three hundred and twelve new dreadnaughts."

"Aaliss, how large is the Eternal fleet?"

"Over twenty thousand."

"Can't the Dyson Sphere's weapons handle them?" asked Kevin. "I thought they could defend against any size attack by the Eternals."

"It's the open hatch," explained Jeremy as he gazed at the opening on one of the viewscreens. Shattered wrecks of Simulin warships littered the surface around it. Many of them still burning. "They're going to try to come through the hatch just as the Simulins did. If they jump into the hatch area, the Dyson Sphere's weapons can't target them. Aaliss, have all battlecruisers and dreadnaughts rendezvous with my fleet immediately. Commander Malen, contact Rear Admiral Tolsen and tell her to get over to the Dreadnaught *Dawnstar*." The *Dawnstar* was a command dreadnaught he had brought along as he wanted Massie to get some experience commanding a large vessel and fleet. He just hadn't planned on her getting experience in a battle with the Eternals.

"Ariel, I want all dreadnaughts to synchronize their fire. The Eternals have to emerge from the entrance tunnel in small numbers. We must destroy them as they come out."

"Should we summon reinforcements?" asked Commander Malen. From this Dyson Sphere communication with the Hub only took a few minutes.

"There won't be time for them to get here," answered Jeremy, feeling worried. "We're going to have to make do with what we've got. Aaliss, what type of internal defenses does the Dyson Sphere have?"

"Not as heavy as the outside," she replied. "There are no blue energy sphere launchers. However, there are a large number of antimatter projectors and gravitonic cannons."

Kevin looked over at Jeremy. "What if we detonated several dark matter missiles inside the hatch and seal it that way."

Aaliss shook her head. "The damage could be catastrophic. Warheads of that magnitude detonated inside the hatch could cause a huge rift to open up in the hull of the Shrieel."

"Can we close the hatch any other way?"

Jeremy looked over at Aaliss.

"We could if we had control of the vortex Control Center." Aaliss grew silent as she talked to several AIs in the main Control Centers in the Shrieel. Then she turned back toward Jeremy. "There are some inside hatch controls but the Simulins control all the corridors leading to them. There is not going to be enough time to clear the Simulins out before the Eternals arrive."

"Battlecruisers and dreadnaughts are closing on us from their bases inside the Dyson Sphere," reported Kevin.

Jeremy knew most of the dreadnaughts built in this Dyson Sphere were only crewed by Originator AIs and a single military AI. He hesitated for a moment and then made his decision. "Commander Malen, inform Rear Admiral Tolsen she will have command of the Dyson Sphere's dreadnaughts and regular battlecruisers. The enhanced battlecruisers will join our fleet. Rear

Admiral Tolsen will act as a reserve if anything gets past us." Jeremy had no idea what this battle was going to be like. Taking a deep breath, he gazed at the large hatch opening waiting for the first Eternal ships to appear.

Fleet Commander Parnon watched the viewscreen, which was showing a greatly magnified view of the large hatch that led inside the Shrieel. The first two squadrons of Eternal battlecruisers had successfully exited hyperspace near the hatch and launched their attack shuttles before vanishing inside. The attack shuttles were already landing and depositing their loads of warrior robots and Eternal shock troops on the surface.

"Our ground forces are meeting heavy resistance," reported Second Commander Bernon. "The Simulins have some form of robotic drone which is extremely strong and difficult to destroy. There are thousands of them on the surface of the Shrieel."

"Have the next squadron of our battlecruisers target those drones with their energy weapons," ordered Fleet Commander Parnon. "We will thin out their ranks so our warrior robots and shock troops can gain full control. We must find entrances to allow them to enter the Shrieel and take control of the vortex Control Center."

Parnon turned to examine one of the tactical displays. So far, the Shrieel had not been able to bring any of its powerful weapons to bear on his ships. It was only a matter of time before the Shrieel fell to his warrior robots and shock troops. When he reported this victory back to the Council of Eternals, his future as Commander of all Eternal fleets would be assured.

General Wesley was growing deeply concerned. Not only did he have the Simulins and their Conqueror Drones to worry about now the Eternals had arrived also. Reports from one of the military AIs in charge of the Dyson Sphere's defenses indicated heavy fighting was already occurring on the outer hull.

"We may need more troops and combat robots," said General Wesley, turning toward Major Caulder. "We did not plan on facing the Eternals in this battle." They had 2,600 Marines and 30,000 combat robots assigned to this mission. Rear Admiral Barnes had nearly the same assigned to hers.

Brace shook his head. "We're out of luck on the Marines. They would have to come from the Hub and it would take them five days to get here. There are several thousand combat robots in this Dyson Sphere. Should I request they be made available to us?"

General Wesley slowly shook his head. "No, I want two additional squads of Marines and the same number of combat robots assigned to protect all of the six main Dyson Sphere Control Centers as well as the computer core. On the computer core, I want a full platoon plus double that in combat robots. With the Eternals involved, we can't allow them to reach any of those. Deploy heavy weapons with the Marines. Go ahead and contact the Hub and request an additional five thousand Marines and twenty thousand more combat robots. This battle may go on for far longer than we expect."

A concerned look crossed Brace's face. "That will mean pulling the last of our experienced forces from the Hub. Our Marines from the Federation still like a few more weeks before they will be ready to deploy. That's also going to strip most of the available combat robots from the Hub."

"I know," Wesley replied. "This fight is not going to be over in a day or two. From the size of the Eternal fleet that's outside the Dyson Sphere, in all likelihood they're going to be successful in taking the vortex Control Center. We will have to take it back regardless of the casualties. Also, contact General McKinley. Inform him once they have successfully captured the vortex Control Center that Rear Admiral Barnes is assaulting we will need all of his Marines as well as combat robots."

Brace nodded. If General Wesley was calling in so many reinforcements, he must expect this battle to be extremely violent and costly. Brace made his way over to the communications console to begin sending the orders.

-

Captain Werner frowned at hearing his latest orders from General Wesley. It seemed the Eternals were soon going to be involved in this battle. Looking upward, he saw the orbiting fleet was now firing antimatter beams into the masses of Conqueror Drones on the flat metal surface near the vortex crater. This had not been in the plan originally as they had hoped to limit the damage to the massive structure. The fighters and bombers were now concentrating their fire on the Conqueror Drones outside of that area.

"We've secured a number of entrances to the inside corridors," reported Sergeant Hitch. "Should we begin moving inside?"

Captain Werner nodded. "I don't think we dare wait. We can't let the Eternals get too big of a foothold or we will never be able to drive them out. Begin sending the first combat robots and Marine squads in. Also, begin pulling everyone back. We may have Eternal warships coming in through the open hatch any minute." Captain Werner knew with the Eternals involved his casualty estimates had just skyrocketed.

-

High Commander Vetrex stood gazing coldly around him. Their communication attempts to reach other nearby Simulin forces had failed. Communications outside the Great Sphere were being jammed. The unknown aliens were landing some type of combat robot and highly trained soldiers on the surface. It was also obvious the attacking Humans knew of the other aliens as they were now using ship weapons to clear the area around the vortex crater risking damage to the structure.

"Order all of our Conqueror Drones around the vortex crater to withdraw. They are to defend the corridors and compartments leading to this Control Center. Also send reinforcements to block the new aliens from gaining access to any hatches leading inside." Vetrex was not pleased with the steadily worsening situation. He was being forced to defend against two invaders attacking from separate directions. Fortunately he had large numbers of Conqueror Drones as well as Simulin soldiers at his disposal.

"We have erected numerous barricades between this Control Center and all access points. Neither the Humans nor these new aliens will be able to threaten this facility."

High Commander Vetrex did not reply. They were cut off from the empire. The defending Simulin fleets had been destroyed. There was no longer an energy shield over the region. He strongly suspected all that was left was for them was to decide how best to die.

Chapter Nineteen

"Detecting Eternal battlecruisers exiting the hatch," reported Kevin, his eyes showing grave concern.

Jeremy took a deep breath. This was it! "All dreadnaughts and battlecruisers target the Eternals as they emerge. Use of all weapons except missiles is approved." They dared not risk detonating dark matter missiles inside the Dyson Sphere. Even Devastator Three missiles could be dangerous.

Looking at one of the large viewscreens, half a dozen of the four-kilometer battlecruisers of the Eternals appeared. Behind them were even more. They quickly moved upward toward the waiting Originator fleet.

"Locked on target," reported Major Preston. "Firing dark energy cannons."

On the screen, numerous energy beams began impacting the screens of the advancing Eternal vessels.

-

Dark energy beam fire from the dreadnaughts pierced an Eternal ship's energy screen and slammed into the stern of the warship setting off massive explosions and hurling glowing debris into space, which fell back toward the Dyson Sphere. Additional fire from particle beams and antimatter projectors riddled the ship turning it into flaming wreckage. Other Eternal ships were quickly suffering the same fate as they moved upward to engage the Originator fleet.

-

"Fleet has opened fire, and the Eternals are responding," reported Ariel. A moment later Ariel spoke again. "Initial Eternal battlecruisers have been destroyed. More are exiting the hatch. No damage to our fleet as of yet."

"We have reports of intense combat on the outer surface of the Shrieel," added Aaliss. "The Eternals are landing large numbers of their warrior robots as well as shock troops. It's only a matter of time before they gain access."

The *Avenger's* energy screen suddenly erupted with energy.

"Antimatter missiles," reported Kevin, his face turning pale. "Big ones in the one hundred-megaton range."

"Damn, where did they get those," muttered Commander Malen, her eyes wide in shock.

"Ariel, how many defense globes do we have?" Jeremy knew that many of the globes had been taken from the dreadnaughts and sent to the fleet bases to help protect them.

"Not many in our fleet," replied Ariel as she quickly checked. "Fewer than ten thousand. However, the dreadnaughts in Rear Admiral Tolsen's fleet have full complements of the globes. There are over thirty thousand."

"Great!" exclaimed Jeremy. "Have her deploy them. They're to shoot down any Eternal antimatter missile that gets by our fleet. Commander Malen, deploy all of our fleet's defense globes around the vortex crater but out of range of the weapons on the Eternal ships. Their mission is the same, shoot down any Eternal antimatter missiles they detect that comes into range." Jeremy didn't want any stray missiles to strike the Dyson Sphere.

On the viewscreen, several Eternal battlecruisers exploded as they were ripped apart by the massed weapons fire from the dreadnaughts. The stern of another battlecruiser vanished as hundreds of gravitonic beams annihilated it. The rest of the ship soon followed. The space directly in front of the massive tunnel hatch was becoming filled with wreckage as even more Eternal battlecruisers appeared and rose up to join the battle.

The *Avenger* shuddered as two antimatter missiles detonated against her energy screen. The lights in the Command Center flickered and then brightened.

"Those missiles are going to be a problem," said Commander Malen as she began shouting orders for all point defense weapons to target the inbound missiles. All the dreadnaughts had dual power beam turrets for just that purpose.

"Where did they get them?" asked Kevin. "The missiles we encountered before were only ten megatons."

"They built them to counter our dark matter missiles," replied Jeremy as he gripped the armrests of his command chair even tighter. "It's similar to what we did when we developed our Devastator Three missiles."

"More Eternal ships are exiting the tunnel," reported Aaliss. "The fleet inside the Shrieel is growing steadily larger every minute."

Commander Malen turned toward Jeremy. "All ships are launching their defense globes. Power beam turrets have been set to knock down inbound missiles but at the speed they travel I can't guarantee how affective they'll be."

Jeremy nodded. "Every one we knock down is one less that's going to hit our shields or potentially hit the Dyson Sphere."

"We have reports the Eternals are now bombarding the surface of the Shrieel next to the entry hatch," reported Aaliss.

"They're trying to eliminate the Conqueror Drones so their warrior robots and shock troops can gain entry," said Ariel with a deep frown. "This is going to get messy. General Wesley should warn his Marines they may encounter Eternal warrior robots and shock troops near the vortex Control Center."

"How are we going to stop twenty thousand Eternal battlecruisers?" asked Kevin worriedly. "Every minute they're getting more inside the Dyson Sphere. The ones in front are now protecting the ones that are emerging from the hatch. If this keeps up we're going to be outnumbered."

Jeremy didn't reply. He wasn't sure how he was going to destroy or stop this Eternal fleet. This had all the makings of a major disaster.

-

Rear Admiral Massie Tolsen entered the Command Center of the dreadnaught *Dawnstar*. It was a command dreadnaught of 3,600 meters. Being such, it had a large Human and Alton crew. "Report," she ordered as she sat down in the command chair. She took a deep fortifying breath. She wished Race were here to tell her what to do.

"We've launched all of our defense globes to interdict stray Eternal missiles," replied Commander Donovan who was the ship's commanding officer. "Fleet Admiral Strong is requesting we act in a supporting role for now until we're needed. We have three hundred and twelve dreadnaughts and six thousand and forty updated battlecruisers of the old 2,000-meter class."

Massie nodded. Form us up into a disk formation directly behind Fleet Admiral Strong's fleet. Place two thousand of our defense globes between us. They can stop any stray missiles that might get through. How many of the newer defense globes do we have?" Massie was glad she had paid attention to the tactics her brother often used.

"A little over six thousand," reported Captain Stewart Evans from Tactical.

"Place them directly behind our fleet. We will call them forward if the Eternals break through Fleet Admiral Strong's forces. The rest of the globes are to be used to interdict stray Eternal missiles."

Commander Donovan nodded. "Captain Evans, make the necessary adjustments to the globe deployment."

"Fleet is at Condition One and ready for combat," added Tannor. Tannor was an Originator military AI assigned to the *Dawnstar*.

"Communications, contact the battlecarrier *Liberty* and order them to withdraw all fighters and bombers from the surface. They'll be easy targets for the Eternals. Once all the squadrons have landed, the battlecarriers are to retreat behind our fleet formation."

"Message sent," replied Lieutenant Neilson.

Massie took a deep breath. Now all she could do was watch the battle and see where her ships were needed. This was by far the largest fleet she had ever commanded. She just hoped she didn't screw up.

-

Captain Werner was about to enter a hatch leading to the interior of the Dyson Sphere.

"We are a long ways from the vortex Control Center," commented Rakell. He had one of the gold command keys, which should allow them access to all sections of the Dyson Sphere controlled by the Simulins.

A massive explosion seemed to shake the ground around them.

"We need to get inside," said Sergeant Hitch urgently. "The Eternals are starting to target us. If they drop just one of those missiles they're using against our fleet we're all toast."

Werner nodded in agreement. He had already noticed the attacking squadrons of bombers and fighters were gone. "Get everyone inside as soon as possible." General Wesley had already ordered all the shuttles to take off and head to a safer part of the Dyson Sphere effectively stranding the Marines and combat robots. "It's going to be a hell of a lot safer inside than out here." Looking around, he could see pillars of smoke and fire rising into the air. Massive explosions were going off everywhere and the battle above the Dyson Sphere was becoming more intense.

Listening to the command frequency in his combat suit, he could hear of other units meeting heavy resistance inside. Casualties were mounting as the Marines tried to evacuate the surface and move inside the Dyson Sphere. Werner wished Major Wilde were here. She was more experienced in attacking these vortex Control Centers. With a deep sigh, Werner knew this time he was going to be without her suggestions. She was millions of light years away. Once again, he was completely on his own. Taking a deep breath, he stepped through the hatch.

-

General Wesley was in his command shuttle, which had withdrawn to the safety of the orbiting fleet. His shuttle was immediately behind Fleet Admiral Strong's dreadnaughts and battlecruisers.

"We're getting hammered," said Major Caulder as he watched several viewscreens. Eternal energy beams were sweeping across the surface of the Dyson Sphere in the vicinity of the vortex crater indiscriminately wiping our Marines, combat robots, and Conqueror Drones. "We may lose 30 percent of our forces before we can get them safely inside the Dyson Sphere."

"It's only going to get worse," replied General Wesley, his eyes showing the pain of losing such a large part of his attacking force. "Until we clear out the Eternal fleet we can't reinforce our Marines. They're going to be on their own."

Brace stared hard at one of the viewscreens as the ruins of a destroyed Eternal battlecruiser crashed into the surface in a huge ball of fire. He shuddered thinking of how many Marines were probably killed in the blast. A number were still on the surface attempting to make it to one of the hatches that had been opened.

"A number of defense globes have surrounded us," reported the lieutenant, sitting in front of the shuttle's sensor console. The command shuttle was two hundred meters long with an energy shield and light armaments. It had a gravity drive but no hyperspace system. "They're forming into a defensive formation around us."

"We have Marines entering the inside of the Dyson Sphere through fourteen entry hatches," added Captain Turner from Communications.

Brace let out a deep breath. "It's going to take a while still to get all of our Marines and combat robots inside." He didn't add during that time the orbiting Eternal battlecruisers would probably continue targeting them with their energy beams.

General Wesley gazed at a viewscreen showing the ruins of an Eternal warship crashing into the surface where a number of Marines and combat robots were attempting to enter the Dyson Sphere through one of the small entry hatches. A massive explosion covered the area obliterating everything around it. "We're losing too many of our Marines and combat robots."

"Damn, our Marines are going to be cut off from one another," said Brace as he studied a hologram indicating the entry points. None were close to one another. "It's going to take a lot of fighting for any of our units to link up."

General Wesley was silent for a long moment. He knew a lot of the Marines down there fighting. "They're Marines and they're wearing Originator designed combat armor. They'll find a way to survive."

Brace hoped the general was right. This battle had a long ways to go.

Jeremy winced as one of his dreadnaughts blew apart. "How many Eternal ships are currently inside the Dyson Sphere?"

"Nearly four hundred," replied Kevin. "We've destroyed seven hundred and thirty but they keep coming. They're coming through the hatch faster than we can destroy them."

"If we could use our dark matter missiles we could stop them," said Major Preston as he directed the firing of the ship's weapons. "The Eternals are firing off a hell of a lot of their antimatter missiles. So far none have hit the surface."

Looking at a viewscreen, the surface of the Dyson Sphere around the vortex crater was nearly obscured by heavy smoke. A lot of wreckage from destroyed Eternal vessels was continuously raining down on the megastructure. Jeremy was deeply concerned about what this was doing to the ground forces trying to fight their way inside. The Eternals were continuously sweeping the region around the vortex crater with their energy beams. Jeremy greatly feared there were now no surviving Marines or combat robots on the surface. He had no idea how many had made it safely inside.

"This isn't going well," said Kevin, looking over at Jeremy. "We need more ships, combat robots, and Marines."

Jeremy knew Kevin was right. "Aaliss, why aren't the Dyson Sphere's internal weapons firing on the Eternals?"

Aaliss turned toward Jeremy. "They're too low. Once they reach a height of seven hundred kilometers, our weapons system can fire on them."

On one of the viewscreens, several Eternal energy beams penetrated the screen of a nearby battlecruiser. The ship seemed to shudder as several large pieces of the hull were blown away.

Then an Eternal antimatter missile slipped through the weakened screen detonating above Engineering. The ship vanished in a massive fireball.

"We have numerous ships reporting damage," said Lieutenant Lantz. "Some of it is severe."

"Have all ships suffering severe damage to fall back to Rear Admiral Tolsen's formation," ordered Jeremy. "Replace each ship that pulls back with one of her battlecruisers."

"We may need to move her battlecruisers forward," suggested Ariel. "I estimate it would double the firepower we can pour into the emerging Eternal ships."

Jeremy shook his head. "Not yet. We're going to need them but we need to wait until the right moment." Jeremy had a plan in mind for Tolsen's fleet. If it worked, he just might be able to stop this attack by the Eternals.

More Eternal ships continued to exit the large hatch moving to reinforce those already inside. The fighting grew more intense as the Eternals fired their powerful energy beams and the new antimatter missiles in ever-increasing numbers at the defending fleet. Occasionally an Originator dreadnaught or battlecruiser would blow apart as its energy shield was battered down. Other ships were being damaged from energy beams penetrating weakened shields and tearing huge gashes in the ships' hulls.

The Eternals were still losing ships at a faster rate than the Originator fleet. The Eternals were diverting as much power as possible to their energy shields so the ships could survive long enough to give protection to the ones emerging from the massive open hatch. Once enough Eternal vessels were inside the Shrieel, they would surge upward and destroy the Originator fleet.

From the defending fleet, numerous dark energy cannons were drilling through Eternal energy shields and then penetrating deep inside the battlecruisers setting off secondary explosions. It was taking longer to destroy an Eternal vessel as normally when an energy shield began to develop holes in it a dark matter missile would arrive obliterating the warship. That was not happening in this battle. Instead, it was taking multiple hits from energy weapons to destroy the Eternal battlecruisers.

Fleet Commander Parnon listened to the reports coming in. He now had over one thousand battlecruisers intact inside the Shrieel. The inside surface around the vortex crater had been bombarded with energy beams until all fighting ceased. The same had occurred on the outside of the Shrieel. Recent reports confirmed that Eternal shock troops had located six entrance hatches to the Shrieel and successfully blasted them open. Shock troops and warrior robots were pouring inside and encountering heavy resistance. The inside of the Shrieel was crawling with the Simulins' combat robots.

"Our strategy is working," reported Second Commander Bernon. "Once we have enough ships inside we should be able to annihilate the defending fleets."

"We must use caution," warned Fleet Commander Parnon. "The interior of the Shrieel will be protected by powerful defenses. We must secure at least one of the primary Control Centers so we can shut them off."

Second Commander Bernon nodded. "We have special teams of our shock troops prepared to do that. This Shrieel will lead us to total victory over the Originators."

"We are the Eternals," replied Fleet Commander Parnon. "It is our right to rule. The Originators should never have challenged us."

"They are weak," said Second Commander Bernon. "It is only the Humans that have allowed them to have limited victories over our fleets."

Fleet Commander Parnon agreed with Bernon's assessment. "Soon the Humans will be no more. Once we have control of the Shrieels, we will wipe the Humans out so they can never threaten us again."

"In another two hours we will have our entire fleet inside the Shrieel," said Second Commander Bernon. "Shortly after that, victory will be ours."

Captain Werner dropped to the floor of the corridor as several explosive rounds from Simulin troops blew apart two combat robots directly in front of him. Since entering the corridors, they had immediately encountered heavy resistance from both Conqueror Drones and Simulin soldiers. In numerous locations, the corridors were blocked with barricades and heavily armed Simulin soldiers behind them. The Simulins were using both explosive rounds and energy weapons to try to halt the Human advance.

"Communications is getting more difficult with General Wesley the farther inside we go," reported Sergeant Hitch. "It won't be much longer and we won't have any contact at all."

"There is a second Marine unit two kilometers from us," commented Rakell. "I have communication with several of the AIs that are accompanying them. If we can reach them and then take the vortex Control Center, I can use the gold command key to shut the main hatch preventing the Eternals from entering the Shrieel."

Werner stepped back into a side corridor where they would be protected from incoming fire. "Can we reach them?" They were cut off from reinforcements. The only way to increase their numbers was to join up with other units.

Rakell nodded. "There is a side corridor we can take that will get us quite close. The Simulins are bound to be guarding it, but it seems to be our best option. If we agree to try, they will attempt to meet us halfway."

"Let's do it," said Werner. "We don't have the forces with us to reach the vortex Control Center. Not against the resistance we're encountering."

Sergeant Hitch took a deep breath and then spoke. "I would recommend we pull in all the Marines and combat robots we've left behind to secure our rear. We're going to need all of them if we want to survive."

Captain Werner nodded. "Going back to the surface is not a viable option anyway. Go ahead and have them join us and we'll make a concentrated effort to join up with the other unit."

"That will effectively trap us inside," warned Rakell. "If we can't reach the other unit or if they can't reach us we'll be cut off from pulling back and will be surrounded by the Simulins and their drones."

"It's a risk we'll have to take," Werner replied. "Sergeant Hitch, let's get moving."

"I'll inform the other unit's AIs that we're on our way," said Rakell.

"Sergeant Hitch, I want demolition charges set to blow the corridors behind us as we clear them out." Special explosives had been provided by the Originators that could bring the corridors down. "That will buy us some time. The Simulins will have to clear the wreckage before they can attack our rear."

Sergeant Hitch nodded. "I'll take care of it."

"Then let's move out," ordered Captain Werner. "The sooner we reach the Control Center, the sooner this will be over."

Sergeant Hitch hurried away calling out orders over his comm unit to various squads of Marines. The fighting was about to get a lot more intense.

High Commander Vetrex listened to the latest reports coming in from the region of the Great Sphere the Simulins controlled.

"The new aliens have destroyed all of our forces on the surface both inside and outside the Great Sphere," reported Second Commander Trador. "They have attacked the Humans as well annihilating their forces on the inside of the sphere that were engaging ours. We have received reports that a large number of Humans and their combat robots have made it inside and are attempting to fight their way to this Control Center. The new aliens have entered into the sphere from a number of hatches they blew open. They also have some type of combat robot."

"What about the fleet of the Ancients that recently appeared inside the sphere?" asked High Commander Vetrex.

"The new aliens are jumping their ships into the tunnel entrance and are emerging inside the Great Sphere. Their ships are engaging the ships of the Ancients in a great battle. Both sides are losing warships."

This news greatly concerned High Commander Vetrex. The Simulins had no warships that could destroy an Ancient vessel but it appeared these new aliens did.

"Should we close the hatch?" asked Trador. "We still have control over it from here."

High Commander Vetrex shook his head. "No, perhaps the two fleets will destroy each other. We'll let them fight while we focus on keeping possession of this Control Center. The Humans and these new aliens must not reach here."

"They will not," replied Second Commander Trador. "We have emplaced numerous barricades between this Control Center and the advancing Humans and aliens. In several areas they may encounter each other."

"Excellent," replied Vetrex. "Perhaps they will destroy one another as well." Looking around the Control Center, there were a number of Conqueror Drones near the open entry hatch as well as a large number of Simulin soldiers. "Do what you can to lure the two toward one another. Perhaps this fight will be much easier than we expect."

-

Jeremy held onto his command chair tightly as the *Avenger* shook violently. Several red lights flared up on the damage control console.

Jeremy looked quickly around the Command Center to see if everyone was okay.

"We took an energy beam to the bow," reported Commander Malen as she listened to the damage reports. "We have three compartments open to space. Repair robots are enroute. Doctor Rule reports a few broken bones but no serious injuries."

Jeremy looked over at Kevin. "How many Eternal vessels are currently inside the Dyson Sphere?"

"Nearly three thousand," replied Kevin. "We've destroyed about twelve hundred."

"I think that's enough." Jeremy activated the command channel on his comm system so he could speak directly to Rear Admiral Tolsen. "Massie, I need your fleet to join mine. We're going to make a concentrated attack against the Eternal vessels currently inside the Dyson Sphere. I want to destroy this force and then position my dreadnaughts and battlecruisers inside the hatch exit to prevent any more Eternal vessels from emerging. I'm hoping by destroying the ships inside, the rest of the Eternal fleet will give up trying to gain entry. If not I intend to advance through the tunnel and exit outside of the Dyson Sphere. Perhaps I can force the Eternals to exit hyperspace farther from the Dyson Sphere where the surface weapons can be brought into play." Also, once outside, Jeremy's fleet could use its dark matter missiles.

"Ready when you are, Admiral," Massie replied. "What are my orders after your fleet enters the tunnel?"

"Use your fleet and all of the defense globes to block it. Don't let any Eternal vessels through."

"Understood," replied Massie.

"All ships are ready," reported Ariel.

"Commander Malen, take us in," ordered Jeremy as he leaned forward in his command chair. This was not going to be an easy battle.

-

Jeremy's fleet dropped rapidly down toward the Eternal warships followed close behind by Rear Admiral Tolsen's. Weapons fire became more intense but the two Originator fleets heavily outnumbered the Eternals. Massive explosions began lighting up the sky of the Dyson Sphere as ships on both sides were annihilated in massive fireballs of released energy. The Eternals were launching thousands of 100-megaton antimatter missiles, which were knocking down the shields of the inbound

Originator battlecruisers and dreadnaughts. Ship after ship died as antimatter missiles blew them apart.

Jeremy's dreadnaughts were firing their dark energy cannons and every other beam weapon they had. The incoming weapons fire was so heavy numerous Eternal vessels were being riddled by the beams setting off internal explosions causing the ships to tear themselves apart.

The two descending fleets continued to close with the Eternals until they were scant kilometers apart. Flying debris slammed into the energy shields of ships on both sides. Some of the debris was so large it was causing substantial damage. The sky above the Dyson Sphere was now full of falling wreckage and massive explosions. Across the region of the Dyson Sphere around the vortex crater pieces of wreckage plummeted to the ground. Some of the wreckage fell into the crater itself. Dark smoke covered the sky and towering flames hid much of the burning wreckage from view.

-

Jeremy's eyes were glued to the main viewscreens showing the destruction around the *Avenger*. Dreadnaughts and battlecruisers were falling out of the sky wrecked by Eternal weapons fire. However, the Eternals were suffering heavily as the superior numbers of Jeremy and Rear Admiral Tolsen's fleets blew them out of the sky over the Dyson Sphere. On one of the screens, Jeremy watched as the last Eternal battlecruiser plummeted to the ground exploding in a towering pillar of flame.

"Get us inside the tunnel," ordered Jeremy, wanting to prevent any more Eternal ships from exiting. "Get me a status on all fleet ships and the condition of their crews. I want to know the causality figures."

"Jeremy there are more Eternal ships coming down the tunnel," warned Ariel.

Taking a deep breath, Jeremy knew what had to be done. "Commander Malen, advance the fleet. We will destroy the Eternal vessels in the tunnel and then take up a defensive formation just outside the outer hatch. Rear Admiral Tolsen, I am taking my fleet outside. Keep this hatch blocked."

"Yes, Admiral," Massie replied. "We won't let them through."

The battle inside the tunnel was fierce but over quickly as Jeremy's fleet ignored its losses and pushed on through the tunnel to exit into the space beyond. Suddenly the stars were visible.

"We've lost two hundred and twelve dreadnaughts, and nine hundred battlecruisers," reported Commander Malen. "I'm still trying to get a firm number on crew losses."

Jeremy knew they were in trouble. That only left him with an effective force of nearly eight hundred dreadnaughts and eleven hundred of the enhanced battlecruisers. Facing him was a fleet of over fifteen thousand Eternal warships. For a moment he thought about calling Rear Admiral Tolsen's' fleet forward then he tossed that idea aside. She needed to stay where she was blocking the entrance to the interior of the Dyson Sphere.

Fleet Commander Parnon gazed in anger at the large viewscreen showing the emerging Originator fleet. They were blocking the open hatch preventing him from jumping more ships in. It also meant he could not reinforce the Eternal shock troops and warrior robots that had entered the Shrieel. That fleet had to be destroyed and quickly. "Prepare to jump the fleet over the Shrieel. Put us two thousand kilometers above the Originator ships."

"That might put us in range of the Shrieel's weapons," warned Second Commander Bernon. "The blue energy spheres are deadly to our ships."

Parnon gazed at the tactical display, his mind calculating the odds of success. "We jump in and advance. We try to overwhelm the Originator fleet and force our way into the entrance tunnel. If we do this the battle will be ours as well as the Shrieel."

Second Commander Bernon understood. They were the Eternals, and this battle could well decide if the Shrieels could be conquered. "Fleet will jump in two minutes."

"Form up in standard disk formation," ordered Jeremy as he watched the Eternal fleet.

"All offensive weapons on the Shrieel are ready to fire," reported Aaliss. "We just need to keep the Eternals far enough out so the weapons can lock on. If they get within seven hundred kilometers of the surface most of our weapons will not be able to hit them."

Kevin looked over at Jeremy. "Eternal fleet is jumping."

"Our fleet is in formation," reported Ariel. She had been helping the individual ships to maneuver quickly to get in position.

"Stand by to fire," ordered Jeremy. "Use of dark matter missiles is authorized."

Jeremy's eyes were focused on the viewscreens waiting for the first spatial vortexes to form. It would take the Eternals less than a minute to travel from their former location to the Dyson Sphere. Jeremy could sense the tension in the Command Center. They were going to be heavily outnumbered, and this was a battle they could very easily lose.

"Contacts!" yelled Kevin as hyperspace vortexes began to form. There were thousands of them and from each an Eternal battlecruiser appeared.

"Two thousand kilometers," reported Aaliss. "Shrieel weapons are locking on and preparing to fire."

"Eternal fleet is advancing," warned Kevin, looking over at Aaliss. "If the Dyson Sphere's weapons are going to fire it needs to be now."

Suddenly several thousand blue energy spheres appeared striking the advancing Eternal ships. More spheres arrived going through the Eternal's energy screens and striking ship hulls. Dark energy cannons, gravitonic cannons, and ion beams reached out from the surface adding their destructive force to the mix. Eternal battlecruisers were being torn apart under the heavy barrage of the Dyson Sphere's weapons. Brilliant flashes of light indicated the destruction of hundreds of Eternal warships.

"Eternals are at nine hundred kilometers," warned Aaliss. "They'll be out of range of the Shrieel's weapons shortly."

"Fire," ordered Jeremy. He needed to hit them hard while they were still engaged against the Dyson Sphere's weapons.

From all the dreadnaughts and enhanced battlecruisers thousands of dark matter missiles launched. The space in front of the fleet suddenly lit up in monstrous explosions. For a moment all the viewscreens dimmed as the bright light overwhelmed them. Then Eternal ships appeared breaking through the missile barrage and turning their weapons on the Originator fleet.

Antimatter missiles and energy beams slammed into the defending fleet overwhelming energy screens. The top section of an Originator battlecruiser exploded sending debris flying away from the ship. Moments later the warship blew apart. A dreadnaught was hit by over one hundred antimatter missiles. The energy screen collapsed and the ship was disintegrated by the intense heat and energy released by the warheads. All across the Originator disk formation ships were dying.

Looking at a viewscreen, Jeremy could see thousands of Eternal ships dead in space as the deadly blue energy spheres converted them into space dust. Others had been destroyed by the intense weapons fire from the Dyson Sphere and the defending Originator fleet. More were still being destroyed as Jeremy's fleet poured its weapons fire into the advancing Eternal fleet. "How many did we get?"

"Not enough," Ariel answered with a pained look in her eyes. "Twenty-eight hundred were hit by the spheres. Another seven hundred and six were destroyed by the Shrieel's energy weapons. We've taken out another four hundred and fifteen. The rest are still coming toward us."

Just then, the deck heaved under Jeremy and he was nearly thrown from his command chair. Jeremy heard a loud scream and turning his head he saw Commander Malen's body lying on the floor, her head at an odd angle. Several other officers were struggling to stand and get back to their consoles. Alarms were screaming from the damage control console as red lights were rapidly blinking on.

A medical technician rushed to Commander Malen's side and after a moment looked over at Jeremy shaking her head.

Jeremy felt shaken. Kyla had been with him from his first command. She couldn't be gone!

The *Avenger* rocked as another missile detonated against the energy screen.

"We're taking too much damage," Ariel said from Jeremy's side with deep concern showing in her eyes. "We must withdraw back down the tunnel. We can't do any more good here. If we stay, we're all going to die."

Looking at the viewscreens, Jeremy saw his fleet being destroyed around him. He knew if he stayed much longer he would lose the entire fleet. Ariel was right; they needed to withdraw. The battle here was lost. "Pull the fleet back into the tunnel. Aaliss, inform Rear Admiral Tolsen we're coming back and to be prepared for the arrival of a large number of Eternal vessels."

Leaning back in his command chair, Jeremy gazed at the smoke in the Command Center. Several Marines were helping the med tech remove Commander Malen's body. Jeremy felt his heart skip a beat as she was taken for the last time out of the Command Center.

Fleet Commander Parnon felt justified in his decision to jump his entire fleet so close to the Shrieel. He had exposed his fleet to the deadly blue energy spheres but only for a few moments. He had fought his way close enough to the defending Originator fleet that he had nearly destroyed it. The few survivors were retreating back into the tunnel no doubt pulling back to the inside of the Shrieel. He did not intend to give them time to recover. "All ships will advance and enter the tunnel. It is time we end this battle. We are the Eternals and victory shall be ours!"

Chapter Twenty

Rear Admiral Tolsen had been informed of Fleet Admiral Strong's withdrawal. She had already informed her fleet to be ready for the appearance of the retreating ships and to stand by to engage the Eternals. It was all she could do to stop her hands from shaking. She was about to fight a battle that she knew she could not win. She couldn't think of any of the tactics Race had used in the past that would help her in this situation.

"Admiral," said Tannor. "I may have a suggestion. It goes against Fleet Admiral Strong's orders, but I believe it is the only logical solution to stopping the Eternals."

Massie turned toward the military AI. She had been cautioned about the military AIs sometimes being too logical in their assessments of a situation, which often resulted in higher than necessary ship losses. "Go on; I'm listening."

"The Eternals still have enough ships to destroy the rest of Fleet Admiral Strong's ships as well as ours and still have enough left to take over at least the part of the Shrieel around the vortex Control Center. I have spoken to the military AIs in charge of the main Control Centers and they agree with my assessment. As a result we are willing to take a huge risk. We want to set off a series of dark matter missiles in the entry tunnel."

Massie's face turned pale at hearing this. "Won't that risk damaging the Dyson Sphere and even splitting the Dyson Sphere open?"

Tannor nodded. "It's a risk we're willing to take to prevent the Eternals from gaining a foothold inside. If they gain control of a vortex Control Center, it could spell disaster. They could use it to launch invasions of all of the Shrieels sending large fleets through all at once. We're willing to risk major damage to the Shrieel to prevent this."

"Tannor is correct," Lieutenant Neilson reported. "I just received a message from Admiral Kalen that the Originator Council has agreed to allow us to do whatever is necessary to stop the Eternals even if it causes major damage." The message had been relayed through the main communications center in the Dyson Sphere.

Massie took a deep breath. She didn't have time to discuss this with Fleet Admiral Strong. There was too much interference in the tunnel to allow for communication. "Tannor, can you contact Aaliss and have her inform the Fleet Admiral?"

Tannor shook his head. "There is too much interference in the tunnel for even our communications to function. There is still heavy fighting occurring between Fleet Admiral Strong's retreating fleet and the Eternals who are following."

Massie squared her shoulders. "What do we need to do to destroy the Eternals?"

Tannor told her and Massie felt her heart stop. This was madness, but she didn't know what else to do. "Okay. We will implement your plan as soon as Fleet Admiral Strong clears the hatch and his ships can get to safety. What about our own fleet?"

"It needs to be moved away from the hatch. I estimate fifty thousand kilometers to be safe."

"Commander Donovan, issue the orders. The *Dawnstar* and twenty other dreadnaughts will stay here to implement Tannor's attack plan." Massie leaned back in her command chair. She hoped she was doing the right thing. If she wasn't, she was about to kill a lot of people for nothing.

—

General Wesley could not believe what he had just heard. Rear Admiral Tolsen must be insane! She was going to end up killing all of his Marines that were currently trying to attack the vortex Control Center. "Major Caulder. Contact all of our commands and order them to take whatever cover they can."

Brace shook his head. "We can't contact most of them. We only have two units we're still in contact with. I'm afraid most are on their own."

Wesley was silent for a long moment. "Move us away to a safe distance. Let's just hope some of our people survive."

—

Fleet Admiral Strong's fleet was beginning to exit the long tunnel with the Eternals close behind. The tunnel was littered with the wreckage of destroyed ships, both Originator and Eternal.

"Jeremy!" called out Ariel, her eyes showing sudden fear. "We need to get away from the tunnel. The fleet needs to move away at a forty-degree angle so we're not lined up with it. Tannor is saying we need to move away to fifty thousand kilometers and under no circumstances pass in front of the tunnel entrance."

"Ariel, Aaliss, implement that order!" Jeremy knew from the look in Ariel's eyes that he didn't have time to question what was going on. Tannor was the military AI on Rear Admiral Tolsen's ship. He had to trust they knew what they were doing. He leaned back in his command chair feeling apprehensive wondering what Rear admiral Tolsen was going to do.

—

Massie felt shocked as she saw how few ships survived of Fleet Admiral Strong's fleet. Fewer than two hundred vessels exited the tunnel and many of them were heavily damaged. As soon as they were in the clear, they darted away at a forty-degree angle. "Implement the plan," she ordered, looking over at Tannor. Massie knew this order might very well end her career in the fleet.

—

From the *Dawnstar* and the other twenty dreadnaughts with her, one thousand and eight dark matter missiles launched. They were set to detonate at different locations in the long entry tunnel. All the detonations would occur within a microsecond of one another. It only took the missiles a few seconds to reach their detonation points.

The first Eternal battlecruiser was just beginning to emerge when the missiles detonated. The long entry tunnel was lined with the same type of material the outer hull of the Dyson Sphere was covered in. It was nearly impervious to weapons fire and even powerful antimatter warheads could not crack it. The dark matter warheads detonated and the fury of their power was contained and magnified in the tunnel. The energy from the massive blasts had only two ways out. The entry into the Dyson Sphere and the exit on the outer hull. The Eternal ships inside the tunnel were buffeted by the massive blasts, which were greatly amplified and reflected by the walls of the tunnel. Most of the Eternal ships in the tunnel simply ceased to be as the raw energy from the dark matter warheads filled the narrow space. From each end of the tunnel, the energy erupted. Inside the Dyson sphere, a plume of raw energy boiled out reaching over twenty thousand kilometers above the tunnel exit barely missing Rear Admiral Tolsen's dreadnaughts. Outside the Dyson Sphere, it was the same. Many of the Eternal vessels, which were lined up to enter, were blown apart in the fierce eruption of raw energy.

Then what was feared the most happened. A great crack appeared on the surface of the Dyson Sphere, which rapidly spread. More cracks grew and connected. Then in a massive explosion, an area over eighty kilometers across was lifted up and away from the megastructure leaving falling debris in its wake.

-

Inside the Dyson Sphere Jeremy stared in disbelief. There was a hole in the Dyson Sphere reaching out into space. Already Rear Admiral Tolsen's fleet was charging through to engage any Eternal vessels that might have survived. Jeremy slumped back in his command chair. He suspected they had probably just won the battle. He looked over at the empty chair where Commander Malen once sat. The battle had been costly and many had lost their lives. Looking at the hole in the Dyson Sphere, he wondered how he was going to explain this to the Originator Council.

-

Fleet Commander Parnon stared in disbelief at the one functioning viewscreen in his Command Center. Several consoles were on fire and sparks were flying everywhere. Smoke filled the air making it difficult to breathe. On the screen, there was a massive hole in the Shrieel. Most of his fleet was either destroyed or lay in ruins around his flagship. Only a few vessels were reporting as still combat ready. From the huge hole in the Shrieel an Originator fleet was emerging.

"We have lost," said Second Commander Bernon in a calm voice. "Most of our ships are too damaged to fight."

Parnon leaned back in his command chair. His plans to command all the fleets of the Eternals had just gone down in flames. He still had no idea how the Humans had blown up part of the Shrieel destroying most of his fleet.

"Originator vessels are closing," reported the Eternal standing at the barely functioning sensor console. "They are in combat range."

"All ships open fire," ordered Fleet Commander Parnon, knowing he was defeated and could not escape. His last act as Fleet Commander was to send a hyperspace message to the Eternal Council informing them of his defeat.

-

Rear Admiral Tolsen gazed at the wreckage that was once Eternal battlecruisers. She was finding it hard to believe how much damage setting off the dark matter missiles had caused. "Close with what remains of the Eternal fleet and destroy it," she ordered. Once this battle was over, she would accept the consequences for her action.

-

The battle was intense but brief. Only a few hundred Eternal battlecruisers were able to put up a fight. Rear Admiral Tolsen ordered her fleet to fire in groups of twenty, which allowed them to quickly overwhelm the energy shields of the Eternal warships. Dark matter missiles soon made short work of the Eternal survivors leaving glowing wreckage drifting in space.

"That's the last one," Reported Commander Donovan as he turned toward Rear Admiral Tolsen. "Sensors indicate all the Eternal vessels have been destroyed."

Massie nodded. "Scan the surface of the Dyson Sphere. If any Eternal warrior robots or shock troops are detected use our antimatter beams to eliminate them."

As the fleet hovered over the outer hull of the Dyson Sphere, a few antimatter beams flicked out wiping out groups of warrior robots and shock troops detected on the surface. Most had died or been destroyed when the massive hole in the Dyson Sphere blew out.

"A large number have gone inside," reported Tannor. "Many will have been eliminated from the damage the Shrieel has suffered."

Massie looked at a viewscreen showing the huge hole in the hull of the Dyson Sphere her attack had caused. "Can that be repaired?"

"Yes," Tannor answered. "Already calls are being made to other Shrieels as well as the Hub to send construction ships."

"We're going to need to place a fleet out here," said Massie as she gazed at the damage the dark matter warheads had caused. She wondered how many Marines had died as a result. Those closest to the damage would have perished. As large as this hole was, the Eternals could now easily gain access to the Dyson Sphere.

Massie turned toward Commander Donovan. "Place our fleet back in a disk formation and put us directly over the hole we created. We will stay there until ordered otherwise by Fleet Admiral Strong." At the moment her ships were the only ones available to defend the Dyson Sphere. She was determined to remain here until relieved. "Send any ships with major damage to a repair bay."

"I have a message from Fleet Admiral Strong," reported Lieutenant Neilson.

Massie tensed. She expected the Fleet Admiral to relieve her from command for the damage she had caused to the Dyson Sphere. Her command of a large warfleet was going to be short lived. "What is it," she asked, looking down toward the deck expecting the worst. She suspected Fleet Admiral Strong would elevate Commander Donovan to admiral giving him command of the fleet.

"He says you did well and is offering his congratulations in making an important command decision. He says your brother would be proud of you."

Massie' eyes glistened. She now knew why Fleet Admiral Strong's people would follow him through a supernova. "Tell him thank you." Taking a deep breath, Massie leaned back in her chair. Only now did she realize how tense she had been.

-

Captain Werner opened his eyes and shook his head. There had been a monstrous rumbling and then the corridor began to collapse. A beam had struck his helmet knocking him to the floor. Standing up he checked his battlesuit seeing a number of fresh dents but everything else seemed okay. Looking around, the corridor seemed full of smoke and it was covered in debris. "Sergeant Hitch?" he said over the company comm channel.

"Here, a voice called out in between fits of coughing. "I had to dig myself out of a pile of rubble."

All through the corridor, Marines and combat robots began to appear. Glancing at the small HUD unit in his battlesuit, Captain Werner saw a large number of red icons blinking. If he was reading his HUD correctly, he had just lost over twenty of his Marines.

"What happened?" asked Sergeant Hitch as he stumbled over to where Captain Werner was leaning against one of the walls of the corridor. "Did someone drop a bomb on the surface?"

"Something happened to the Shrieel," answered Rakell who appeared through the smoke. "Whatever it was it had to be massive for us to feel it here."

"What about the other Marine unit?" Captain Werner knew they should nearly be to them by now.

"Just up ahead," replied Rakell. "Less than one hundred meters."

Werner nodded. "Sergeant Hitch, we need to get moving. The Simulins could hit us again at any time." Werner hoped the

Simulins had been hit hard by whatever had happened to the Dyson Sphere.

A few minutes later they reached the other Marine unit. It was a full company commanded by Captain Olivia Johnston.

"Do you know what the hell that was that struck us a few minutes ago?" she asked as she reached Captain Werner.

"No," Werner replied. "I lost twenty Marines in whatever that was."

"I lost twelve," Olivia replied. "I still have most of my combat robots though."

Werner looked over at Rakell. "Let's move on toward the Control Center. Our best bet of getting out of this alive and contacting other Marine units is going to be to take control of it."

Olivia nodded. "I agree, let's move out."

Moments later the two companies of Marines and their combat robots were once more moving toward the vortex Control Center.

-

High Commander Vetrex stood up dazed from the shaking felt in the Control Center. Many of the consoles were damaged and no longer functioning. "What happened?"

"I'm getting reports that there's a huge hole in the Great Sphere that extends right up to the vortex crater," reported Second Commander Trador. "Whatever weapons the Humans and the new aliens are using seems to have caused great damage."

"Our soldiers and Conqueror Drones." Vetrex was depending on their numbers to keep the Humans and the new aliens at bay.

Trador shook his head. "We've lost many. The Humans are still coming closer as well as the new aliens. I'm not sure we have enough forces remaining to stop them. Many corridors are blocked and we have no contact with our forces on the other side of the blockages."

High Commander Vetrex took a deep breath. What did it matter anyway? The damage to the vortex Control Center was more than his scientists and technicians could repair. "Pull all of our remaining forces back as close to the Control Center as possible. If we are to die in battle, let it be here on the Great Sphere of the Ancients."

General Wesley gazed in shock at the damage to the Dyson Sphere. A ragged hole over eighty kilometers across was visible and stars could be seen through the far end. The hole extended right up to the edge of the vortex crater. With a heavy heart, he knew many of his Marines would have died as a result of the damage. "She killed them," he muttered, shaking his head in anger. He had trained those Marines for months for this mission and now they were dead.

"She had no choice," Brace said as he gazed at the latest communications from the Dyson Sphere Control Centers. "She also had permission from the Originator Council to do whatever was necessary to destroy that Eternal fleet. If she hadn't blown up that section of the Dyson Sphere, we might have lost control of a major portion of the Dyson Sphere to the Eternals. As much as I hate to admit it, she made the right decision."

Brace looked over at the tactical display. He was relieved to see the green icon of the *Avenger*. He didn't know how he could have returned to the Hub if that ship had failed to make it back.

Jeremy was sitting in the Command Center still trying to recover from the loss of Commander Malen. There were others on board the ship who had been injured and a few others who had died. He didn't have a complete list yet though he would shortly. On the viewscreens, the remnants of his fleet were plainly visible. Many of the dreadnaught and battlecruisers were showing heavy damage to their hulls. Most of the ships would have to spend time in the Dyson Sphere's repair bays before they could make the attempt to return to the Communications and Transport Hub.

"What are we going to do about that hole in the Dyson Sphere?" asked Kevin as he gazed at a viewscreen showing damage. "Seems to me that it's an open invitation to the Eternals."

"I've already sent a message to the Hub. They're going to contact Admiral Tolsen. He'll be bringing his fleet here to defend the Dyson Sphere until repairs are made. In the meantime, we'll place all the defense globes outside at one thousand kilometers. That will force any fleet that jumps in to be in range of the weapons on the Dyson Sphere."

Kevin looked concerned. "Will his fleet be enough?"

"I'm going to leave Rear Admiral Tolsen here as well. We'll reinforce her fleet with enough enhanced battlecruisers to give her ten thousand warships. We'll add a few more dreadnaughts as well."

This seemed to satisfy Kevin as he went back to studying his sensor console.

"Jeremy," said Ariel. "Do you recall the request we received from Major Wilde earlier?"

Jeremy's eyes narrowed. "She wanted to know if it was feasible to capture some Eternals for study." He had forgotten about that with all that was going on.

"Yes," replied Ariel as she pointed to a viewscreen showing the area around the vortex crater. "There are thousands of them getting ready to attack the vortex Control Center. Perhaps we should attempt to capture a few."

Jeremy leaned back in his command chair, his eyes widening at the thought. The entire reasoning behind capturing the Eternals was to see if the Originator scientists from that large stasis facility Major Wilde discovered could shut down the mechanical nanites inside an Eternal. If they could it might change this war to something winnable.

"Lieutenant Lantz, get General Wesley on the comm. I'm about to give him an order he's not going to care for."

-

General Wesley sat down in his command chair a stunned look on his face. "Has everyone gone insane today?" He looked over at Major Caulder. "Fleet Admiral Strong is requesting that I capture some Eternals for him. How the hell am I supposed to do that when I'm completely out of touch with all of our Marine units? I don't even know if what he's asking is possible."

Brace took a deep breath. "General, we have slightly over two thousand combat robots still inside this Dyson Sphere on guard duty as well as the extra Marines we sent to the Control Centers and the primary computer core. We could use them as a Marine force."

General Wesley frowned. "They would need a trained combat officer to lead them and all we have are inside that war zone. The target would have to be the vortex Control Center. That's where we know the Eternals are heading. We have no idea what type of resistance they will face. For all we know everyone we sent into that sector is dead."

Brace shook his head. "Not all combat officers are inside. I'll volunteer to lead them."

Wesley's eyes focused intently on Brace. "Are you certain? This mission will be highly dangerous. We have no idea what the conditions are like inside the combat zone or if any of our Marine units still survive. You may be entirely on your own. It will be days before more reinforcements get here."

"If Fleet Admiral Strong wants those Eternals, I'll get them."

Wesley closed his eyes and then opened them and nodded. "The mission's yours. I'll see what I can do about rounding up some more Marines. Some of our shuttle pilots have combat experience. We might be able to get a platoon or two from them."

Brace nodded. He needed to speak to a few Originator AIs. There were only a couple of ways he was going to be able to get to the Control Center before the Eternals.

Four hours later Brace was clad in an Originator designed battlesuit and was leading a full company of Marines and eighteen hundred combat robots toward one of the entrances that Marines had used earlier to gain entry to the inside of the Dyson Sphere.

Walking beside him was Sergeant Ashley Bryant and Aaliss. Aaliss had volunteered to come with the Marines as she was familiar with what the Fleet Admiral wanted. She was also carrying one of the Originator's gold command keys.

"I've worked in one of the vortex Control Centers at the Communications and Transport Hub," she confided in Brace. "There are several small equipment tunnels that run parallel to some of the main corridors. If we can access one of them it will take us nearly to the Control Center."

"Will the combat robots fit?" asked Brace. This mission would fail without them.

"Barely," replied Aaliss, glancing over at the massive robots. "We'll have to walk in single file."

"At least it's a plan," replied Brace. "Let's do it." Brace didn't even dwell on what Angela would be saying if she knew the danger he was about to put himself in. That command job on the new super exploration dreadnaught was sounding better all the time.

-

Captain Werner took a long deep breath. For hours they had been fighting, pushing back the Simulins and their Conqueror Drones meter by meter down the corridors leading to the vortex Control Center. The corridors behind them were littered with the dead and the torn up bodies of combat robots and Conqueror Drones.

"What's our status?" asked Captain Werner, stopping to take a small sip of water from the canteen he was carrying.

"Not good," replied Sergeant Hitch, sounding out of breath. "Between our company and Captain Johnston's we have thirty-eight who can still fight. We have seventeen wounded who are being helped by the combat robots. As far as the combat robots go, we're down to seventy-eight. Ammunition is becoming scarce also. We're nearly out of explosive rounds as well as armor piercing rounds for our assault rifles. We're still okay with our energy rifles and the combat robots are down to about twenty percent on their ammo."

"Damn," said Werner, feeling worried. "I don't know if that's going to be enough."

"One more corridor," Sergeant Stroud said as he walked up to them. "We have one more long corridor before we reach the vortex Control Center. Captain Johnston sent a couple of combat robots ahead to scout it out. Neither came back. There are at least three massive barricades that are blocking the corridor. It's also full of wall to wall Conqueror Drones."

Captain Werner looked at the two sergeants. "Well we came here to take that Control Center back from the Simulins. Any suggestions?" In this situation Werner was open to ideas.

"Head on charge with the combat robots," said Sergeant Hitch. "It's the only way. They still have enough explosive rounds and power for their energy weapons. They just might be able to make it. We leave our wounded here under the protection of two or three combat robots. Everyone else goes."

Werner looked over at Sergeant Stroud who nodded. "I agree," he said.

Werner looked down at his assault rifle. He had one and a half magazines of armor piercing rounds left. "Let's do it," he ordered as he began walking toward the junction where the next corridor began.

It took a few minutes to get everyone organized and then the combat robots charged around the corner into the corridor firing explosive rounds and their energy cannons. Captain Werner waited a few moments and then followed with the surviving Marines. Instantly he was enveloped in carnage. The corridor was full of smoke. Pieces of Conqueror Drones lay everywhere and even Simulin body parts. It was gruesome and only just beginning. He fired his assault rifle at a Simulin he saw peeking over the nearest barricade seeing him instantly drop from sight.

A loud scream drew Werner's attention. A Conqueror Drone held a Marine in its pinchers pulling him apart. A combat robot leaped forward planting its fist in the center of the carapace of the drone causing it to collapse to the floor and dropping the Marine who lay unmoving. Werner knew with a sick feeling in his gut the Marine was dead. They continued to advance slowly down the corridor. An energy beam struck Werner a glancing blow to the shoulder. His shoulder felt numb but the armor had protected him. It was deeply singed but still intact.

Closer and closer they came to the entrance to the vortex Control Center. Looking around Werner doubted that no more than a dozen combat robots still survived. His Marines were down to less than twenty. Suddenly the hatch to the Control Center slammed shut. Moments later the fighting in the corridor came to a stop. Looking around, Captain Werner saw ten combat robots still standing and only eighteen Marines. Looking at his HUD, he saw that the icon representing Sergeant Hitch was glowing red. He let out a deep breath. Hitch was someone he had come to depend on; he had also become a close friend.

Sergeant Stroud came walking up. "Captain Johnston didn't make it. How are we going to get that hatch open?"

Rakell came forward. He had been back with the wounded. Reaching into his pocket, he took out the small gold globe that was the command key. "This will open the hatch. The question is what's waiting for us on the other side?"

Captain Werner let out a deep sigh. "We don't have what's needed to take the Control Center. If we open the hatch and rush in we'll be wiped out."

"So, what do we do?" asked Sergeant Stroud. "Did we come all of this way for nothing?"

Werner looked up and down the long corridor. Let's set up two barricades in the center of the corridor and wait. We have to hope another Marine unit makes it to us before more Simulins or Conqueror Drones show up."

Sergeant Stroud nodded and immediately began giving orders to the combat robots. The Marines were too worn out be of much help. The wounded were brought forward and after the barricades were set up, everyone took positions waiting for any signs of approaching trouble. They had come so far only to learn they didn't have the forces to finish the mission.

-

For nearly two hours they waited and then a commotion at the far end of the corridor near the junction drew their attention.

"This is it," said Sergeant Stroud as he checked his assault rifle. "I only have half a magazine left, what about you?"

Captain Werner looked down and quickly checked his rifle. "Eight rounds and that's it."

Stroud nodded and aimed his rifle down the corridor.

The noise grew louder and suddenly a metal form appeared around the corner.

"Hold your fire!" yelled Werner excitedly. "It's a combat robot!" Moments later dozens more followed the first.

Major Caulder was surprised to find Marines waiting for them in the corridor leading to the vortex Control Center. After exiting the maintenance tunnel, they had been going down corridors showing evidence of recent heavy fighting and only encountering light resistance. They had found the remains of Marines as well as combat robots strewn throughout the corridors.

Walking up to the first barricade Major Caulder recognized Captain Werner and then he saw Rakell standing beside him.

"I'm not surprised you made it this far," said Brace, reaching over the barricade and shaking Werner's armor covered hand. Captain Werner had been trained by Major Wilde and been responsible for ousting the Simulins out of several other vortex Control Centers in other galaxies. "What's the situation?"

Captain Werner quickly explained what had happened to them and what he thought was still inside the Control Center.

Brace nodded. "I have enough combat robots to take the Control Center. Once that's done we have another mission. He quickly told Werner of Jeremy's orders.

Captain Werner turned pale at hearing they needed to capture some Eternals. "How are we going to do that?" he asked.

"Let's take the Control Center first, and then we'll see about the next part of the mission,' said Brace. "Any suggestions on what we should do?" In this instance Brace was willing to listen to Werner as he had the experience.

High Commander Vetrex waited inside the vortex Control Center behind a final barricade his soldiers and the Conqueror Drones had erected. At any moment he expected the hatch to open and the enemy to appear. He still had thousands of Conqueror Drones scattered throughout the corridors in this section of the Great Sphere. Many were engaged in combat with the strange aliens. Others were engaged against Human forces. All had one goal in mind. Reaching the vortex Control Center.

Suddenly the door swung open and combat robots began swarming inside. Energy beams and explosive rounds began going off everywhere. In mere moments the combat robots overwhelmed the defending Conqueror Drones and killed most of the heavily armed Simulins. Second Commander Trador fell as a combat robot caved in his head with his armored fist. Looking around High Commander Vetrex realized he was alone. Then he did something he had never considered before. He raised his hands and surrendered.

Major Caulder entered the vortex Control Center and stared at something he had never expected to see. A Simulin in the uniform of a High Commander holding his hands up. Shaking his head, he wondered what Jeremy would to with him. As far as he knew they had never captured a Simulin before.

"Sergeant Bryant, assign four guards to watch over our prisoner. I want him alive so our intelligence people can question him."

"Yes, sir,' Bryant replied as she strode off to carry out the order.

"I have communication with General Wesley," reported Rakell. Rakell had inserted the gold command key into the Control Center's main computer. Fortunately the communication console in the center was still functioning.

Brace quickly reported what the current situation was.

"We have more Marines and combat robots coming from the Hub," Wesley said. "You're going to have to stay where you're at for a few days. If the opportunity presents itself, you are to carry out your secondary mission."

"Understood," replied Brace.

A few minutes later Brace took stock of their situation. He had over sixteen hundred functional combat robots and nearly one hundred Marines. He quickly rebuilt some of the Simulins' barricades in the outside corridors and assigned combat robots and a squad of Marines to each one. After inspecting the defenses, Brace was satisfied they had done everything they could. Now they just had to wait.

Hours passed and surprisingly two other Marine units managed to reach the Control Center swelling Braces forces to nearly two thousand four hundred combat robots and one hundred and sixty Marines. What really pleased Brace was what the last group of Marines had brought with them. Eleven wounded Eternals! With the aid of Rakell and Aaliss, he ordered them to be treated for their wounds and bound. He also placed a heavy guard on them including combat robots. Now all he needed to do was wait for the reinforcements to arrive.

Six days later General Wesley watched from his command shuttle as Major Caulder emerged from a hatch to stand once more on the surface of the Dyson Sphere. Reinforcements from the Hub had arrived and several thousand Marines backed by over fifteen thousand combat robots had descended into the corridors surrounding the vortex crater to clean out the last of the Simulins and the Eternals. Other combat robots were enroute from other Dyson Spheres to ensure they had the forces necessary.

What really pleased General Wesley was that they had twenty-nine Eternal captives. Most had been wounded and were captured when they were overrun by Marines and combat robots. The Simulin High Commander would be staying in the Dyson

Sphere under heavy guard. Security would be asking him a lot of questions. So far he had been very cooperative.

General Wesley strongly suspected it would take several weeks to finish sweeping this section of the Dyson sphere for Simulins and Eternals. He planed on staying until the battle was over. With a deep sigh, he knew that many of his Marines had given their lives in the battle. A few more would probably meet their end in combat in the coming days. Overall, General Wesley was proud of his Marines. They had accomplished their missions. The vortex Control Center was now in their hands and they had captured the needed Eternals.

-

Jeremy watched as thousands of Originator warships appeared from the massive intergalactic vortex created by one of the vortex Control Centers. It was Admiral Tolsen's fleet and now Jeremy could relax. With Tolsen's fleet and the reinforcements pouring in from the Hub and the other Dyson Spheres he no longer feared another Eternal attack. Construction ships were also arriving to begin the repair work to the Dyson Sphere. Even though the damage looked severe, Aaliss had assured him a year from now it would be totally repaired.

"How soon before we go home?" asked Kevin.

"Soon," Jeremy responded. "I need to brief Admiral Tolsen and make arrangements to transfer the captured Eternals to a suitable holding site." Jeremy looked at the viewscreen. A dreadnaught floated there with the habitation squares of the Dyson Sphere in the background. A lot of good men and women had lost their lives in the past week. Jeremy knew from inspecting the damage to the *Avenger* just how close his own ship had come to being destroyed. Perhaps it was time for him to quit leading fleets into battle. It was something he was going to discuss with Kelsey when he returned home.

Chapter Twenty-One

The *Avenger* was safely in one of the large repair bays at the Communications and Transport Hub. Most of the crew had already headed home for a few days leave. Jeremy was sitting in his command chair staring at the empty spot where Commander Kyla Malen should be sitting. Her body and several others had been taken to the Dyson Sphere the three Federation races inhabited for a memorial service.

Ariel was standing next to Jeremy respecting his silence.

"I'm getting too old for this," Jeremy said softly. "Maybe it's time someone else took over as Fleet Admiral."

"Fleet Admiral Streth once thought the same," answered Ariel, trying to find the right words. "However, he realized at the time, there was no one else he trusted to do what had to be done. Who else do we have that everyone, including the Originators, would follow?"

Jeremy let out a deep sigh. He knew Ariel was right. There was no one else ready to fill his shoes. Admiral Kalen was an excellent fleet admiral, but a much better administrator. Perhaps Admiral Jackson or Admiral Tolsen in the future could take over. But for now Jeremy would have to continue to hold the weight of overall command on his shoulders.

"Rear Admiral Barnes will be returning in a few more days," added Ariel. "She succeeded in wresting the vortex Control Center away from the Simulins though it suffered heavy damage."

"Not as heavy as the Dyson Sphere we just left." Jeremy could still see the massive hole that Rear Admiral Tolsen had blasted in the Dyson Sphere. In many ways, she reminded Jeremy of her brother.

"Rear Admiral Barnes is sending most of her surviving Marines and combat robots to assist General Wesley in cleaning out the Eternals and Simulins in the Dyson Sphere we left. General Wesley believes with all the reinforcements, the job will be done by the end of the week."

Jeremy nodded as he stood up. "Let's go home. I need to see Kelsey." Kelsey had a way with words that would help Jeremy to put all of this into its proper perspective.

-

On the planet Gardell in the Eternals' home galaxy, the Council of Eternals was meeting.

"Our fleet wiped out!" said Second Leader Queexel, shaking his head in disbelief. "Fleet Commander Parnon dead! We should have taken that Shrieel and the war would soon be over."

"Our scout craft report there's a hole nearly eighty kilometers across in the Shrieel," added Second Leader Nolant. "If we had sent sufficient forces we could have invaded the Shrieel through the hole and taken it over."

Second Leader Fehnral stood up, his eyes cold and calculating. "Perhaps not. Never in the history of the Shrieels has one suffered such damage. These Humans are extremely dangerous and must not be underestimated. They may pose more of a danger to us than the Originators."

First Leader Clondax stood up looking slowly around the large stone table. The others sat down to listen. "The Humans suffered major losses in the battle. Fleet Commander Parnon destroyed a major part of their fleet. Not only that the Shrieel as mentioned earlier is heavily damaged. I propose gathering all of our fleets currently in Originator space into one large fleet and send them to the Shrieel in Galaxy X-938. I will accompany the fleet and will demand the Originators agree to live in one Shrieel and turn all the others over to us. After this most recent battle, they may be willing to negotiate rather than risk other Shrieels suffering similar damage. They must realize if we had another fleet in position, we could have taken the Shrieel."

"What if they refuse?" asked Second Leader Tarmal. "We lost a tremendous number of warrior robots as well as many of our elite shock troops."

First Leader Clondax leaned forward. "Then I will take the entire fleet of over one hundred thousand of our battlecruisers and attack the damaged Shrieel. I firmly believe with the damage the Shrieel has suffered we can easily gain entry. Granted there will be some losses, but the Shrieel will be ours."

The other councilors looked at one another and finally agreed.

"This war needs to end," said Second Leader Fehnral. "We have already committed too many resources to it rather than expanding the empire."

Clondax turned his unwavering eyes toward Fehnral. Fchnral had been openly against this war from the very beginning particularly after he learned that Originators still lived. Once he returned perhaps it would be time to seek a new Second Leader responsible for scientific development. There were several of Fehnral's underlings that would be quite suitable in the position.

"I will send the order to our fleets as well as a message to the Shrieel in Galaxy X-938 that we seek to meet with the Originator leaders to discuss ending this war. We will set the meeting for twenty-six days from now. That will give our fleets time to meet at the designated coordinates." Clondax was confident once the Originators saw the fleet he was bringing and after the damage done to the Shrieel, they would acquiesce to his demands.

—

Later Clondax stood on a balcony overlooking the massive city of the Eternals that governed the empire. It was nearly dark but the city was still busy as the work of running an empire never stopped. The recent battle at the Shrieel where the Simulins controlled a vortex Control Center had stunned him. Fleet Commander Parnon should not have been defeated! He had made a tactical error in committing so many of his ships at once. He should have kept some back in reserve. What did concern Clondax was the growing impudence of these Humans who evidently had unlimited access to Originator technology. That technology was dangerous and should not have been shared with a less intelligent race.

Clondax flexed his hand. With the added strength the mechanical nanites provided he could bend a heavy piece of metal if he so desired. Once he had control of the Shrieels, the rapid expansion of the empire would take place. In another one thousand years, the Eternals would not possess just ten thousand galaxies, it would be one million and sometime in the far future this entire universe would be under Eternal control. The only obstacle to this future were the few Originators who survived and their Human allies. Once the Originators withdrew to one and only one Shrieel, he would eliminate all traces of the Humans. In time, he would be known as the Eternals' greatest leader.

-

Jeremy returned home to be met at the door by Kelsey. She had a sad look in her eyes and Jeremy could tell she had been crying. "Ariel told me about Kyla. I'm so sorry Jeremy. She has been with us for so long it almost feels like we lost a member of the family."

Jeremy took Kelsey in his arms knowing how she felt. He had felt the same way ever since Commander Malen's unfortunate death.

"I was in the Tower when your fleet arrived," confessed Kelsey. "I saw the condition of the *Avenger*. You all could have been killed. I thought you agreed not to lead the fleets anymore but stay here in the Tower?"

Looking down Jeremy nodded. "I did, but this was too important. Once we have enough trained admirals from the Federation, I promise my days of leading fleets into battle like this one will be over. The only fleet I want to command will be the one protecting your new super exploration dreadnaught."

Kelsey nodded. "I'm going to hold you to that promise."

Stepping inside the house, Jeremy looked around. "Where's Ariel?" They had separated at the Tower and Jeremy fully expected her to be here.

"She's in the nursery with Jacob. She thought we could use some time alone."

Even though Jeremy was feeling sad he couldn't help but put forth a weak smile. Ever since he was at the Fleet Academy on the Moon, Ariel had been looking out for him and the others. "Let's go sit down and talk."

Jeremy and Kelsey spoke late into the evening. They spoke of the battle at the Dyson Sphere where Commander Malen died. They talked about their future here on the Dyson Sphere, but most of all they talked about their friends and exploring together on Kelsey's new super exploration dreadnaught. Ariel eventually came out of the nursery informing them that Jacob was sound asleep.

"I will speak to the two of you tomorrow," Ariel said as she left.

Kelsey watched as Ariel went out the door closing it softly behind her. "Sometimes I don't know what we would do without our two overly protective AIs."

Jeremy nodded. He knew that sometimes all five of them took the two for granted.

"What are your plans for tomorrow?"

Jeremy leaned back on the sofa his arm around Kelsey. "I need to meet with the Originator Council as well as Admiral Kalen and Governor Barnes. We need to discuss what is going to happen with those Eternals we captured."

Kelsey sat up, looking concerned. "What did you do with them? You didn't bring them back here did you?"

Jeremy shook his head. "No, we built a facility on an uninhabited moon near one of the fleet bases. "There's a full company of Marines and the same number of combat robots guarding them. A number of Originator research scientists are already there studying the Eternals."

"Do you think they can actually shut them down?"

"I don't know," replied Jeremy, recalling his last conversation with the Originator Council about that possibility. "From what I understand if the mechanical nanites can be neutralized, the Eternals will feel substantially weaker and maybe even confused."

Kelsey nodded as she stood up and pulled Jeremy up with her. "Let's go to bed. You've been gone for a while and I know just what will make you feel better."

"Not tonight," replied Jeremy, running his hand though Kelsey's blonde hair. "I just want a good night's sleep with you beside me."

"I can handle that," Kelsey said in understanding. "We could both use a good night's sleep. Let me go check on Jacob and then I'll join you."

Stretching, Jeremy realized just how tired he was. He had experienced difficulty sleeping ever since Commander Malen's death. The services for her and the others who had died were scheduled for the day after tomorrow. He just hoped with Kelsey at his side he would be able to finally get a full night's sleep and accept the consequences of what had happened at the Dyson Sphere.

–

The next day Jeremy was in the new council chambers in the Tower where the Originator Council met. The council now had five members with the awakening of Councilors Metrecs and Roan.

"I spoke to Reull Alistar earlier today," Councilor Roan said. She looked Jeremy directly in the eyes. "He reports the mechanical nanites in the current Eternals have gone through a number of revisions. However, he is confident he can produce a shutdown procedure for them in a relatively short time. He has nearly his entire research staff with him as well as a few others who came from here. He says Jankel has been particularly useful."

"Jankel's a brilliant research scientist," said Councilor Bartoll. "I'm not surprised Alistar is finding him useful."

"How soon does he think he will be ready to try out the shutdown procedure?" asked Jeremy. They needed something to help keep the Eternals at bay.

Councilor Roan took a deep breath and then answered. "He is already experimenting on the Eternals they have in the facility.

He feels confident, based on their previous research, that he will be successful in just a matter of days."

"It will give us a weapon we can use against them," said Bartoll. "How effective it will be remains to be seen."

"If it works, it will allow us to strike them at what they consider to be their strongest advantage," said Jeremy thoughtfully.

"I spoke to Admiral Kalen earlier," said Bartoll. "It seems our plan to attach tracking devices on the Eternal fleets in our space has been successful. So far six fleets have been identified and are now being followed."

Jeremy looked at the councilors. "We believe there are ten. Once all ten have been identified, we will begin taking offensive measures against them."

"Dazon Fells believes it will be useless," commented Councilor Castille. "He is convinced that for every Eternal fleet we destroy they will just send another."

"Don't forget we have fleets in their space as well," Jeremy reminded the councilor. "If we can force them to commit sufficient ships to protect their galaxies they may not have the warships to send to ours." Jeremy was convinced the Eternals would not continue to allow his fleets to roam their galaxies destroying shipyard after shipyard. At some point in time, they would commit fleets to defend their galaxies.

"We have no choice but to defend the galaxies in our space," said Councilor Bartoll in a guilt-laden voice. "The Eternals are our problem and we have to find a way to deal with them."

"I think we are all in agreement on that," replied Councilor Trallis.

"What progress is being made in locating the rest of the hidden stasis facilities? Jeremy knew Major Wilde was finding more every day.

Councilor Bartoll smiled. "Thanks to Councilors Metrecs and Roan we now know where they all are and even how many Originators are sleeping inside. There was a hidden communications facility here at the Communications and Transport Hub that linked all of them together as well as contained information on their locations. It's how the Defenders of Zorn managed to send the message to all the facilities instructing them not to activate when the cure was found."

"How many are in stasis?" asked Jeremy, feeling curious. Currently, there were around twelve million Originators awake.

"Another seventy to seventy-two million depending on how many stasis chambers have failed," answered Councilor Roan. "We are forming as many teams as we can to hasten the awakening process."

"What about the Defenders of Zorn? Any traces of them?"

"A few Originators that we have awakened were sympathetic in the past toward Zorn's cause," replied Councilor Bartoll. "They have been isolated until we determine if they are a threat. As far as Alborg and Albate, there still has been no trace. We are searching every Shrieel and even the fleet bases. So far there has been nothing."

Jeremy was not pleased to hear this. He understood that due to the massive size of the Dyson Spheres, it would be very easy for someone or even a group of people to stay hidden. "We need to keep looking. I'm afraid we haven't heard the last from those two."

-

Later Jeremy was meeting in his office with Governor Barnes and Admiral Kalen.

"Rear Admiral Marks reports the first group of Federation fleet personnel have completed their classes at the academy," said Admiral Kalen. "That's over 112,000 new fleet personnel we can place on ships. "The Originators built a number of new buildings at the academy just to handle them all."

"Any problems?" Jeremy knew adjusting to life on the Dyson Sphere and the Originators advanced technology might be for a few.

"Thirty-four requested to return to the Federation. They were having a hard time dealing with the Originator AIs."

This didn't surprise Jeremy. Not after the war the Federation had fought against the Hocklyns and the AIs that ruled them.

"We have Originator passenger ships arriving nearly every day from the Federation," continued Admiral Kalen. "Federation fleet personnel as well as Marines. In another month we should have crews available for our dreadnaughts as fast as we're building them. That's a command crew of twelve, a few engineers, and a squad of Marines for each warship."

Jeremy looked over at Governor Barnes. "What about the civilians?"

"Same as the military," replied Barnes. "There are additional passenger ships arriving daily. We have Humans, Altons, and Carethians arriving in large numbers. The Originators are building new cities for the colonists and have arranged for each of them to go through a short indoctrination course on the technology they will be exposed to. The current agreement with the Federation is to allow two million Carethians, six million Altons, and twenty million Humans to come to the Dyson Sphere."

This pleased Jeremy as it would give them a good population base to draw future fleet personnel from. Also the children from the three races would be exposed to Originator technology from a very young age. They would grow up without finding the miraculous technology strange.

"What's Grayseth been up to?" Jeremy tried to keep track of his large Bear friend hoping he was staying out of mischief.

Admiral Kalen smiled. "I've assigned him to a small fleet of dreadnaughts here at the Hub. He's been fighting mock battles with the new Federation recruits. I believe so far he's won 82 percent of the contests. He says it's fine training for the hunt."

Jeremy nodded. Since Marille was expecting their first cubs, Grayseth had been more willing to stay close to the Communications and Transport Hub. "I expect Grayseth will stay close by until after all the new Carethian colonists arrive. He's excited about so many clans coming to the Dyson Sphere to take part in the hunt."

Have you had time to check out Kelsey's new super exploration dreadnaught?"

Jeremy shook his head. "No, I promised her I would wait until it's finished. They're all excited about going out exploring again."

Admiral Kalen looked over at Jeremy. "How do you feel about that?"

"I may be going along with a fleet of dreadnaughts just to make sure they stay safe."

"Who will be the ship's commander?" asked Governor Barnes.

Jeremy grinned. "I can think of only one person I would want in charge of a ship with my family and friends on board."

"My daughter," replied Governor Barnes, nodding his approval. "Have you asked her yet?"

"No, I was going to wait until the ship was finished so she could see what she was getting to command."

"You might as well tell her," Governor Barns said. "The rumors have been flying around for weeks that she is going to get the command."

"Can't keep nothing secret around here," said Jeremy frowning. He had hoped to make this a surprise. "She should be back tomorrow so I'll go ahead and ask her then."

"The new defense stations are coming along nicely," added Admiral Kalen. "I still can't believe how rapidly the Originators can build. In two more weeks we will have twelve hundred of the stations finished. All are equipped with our normal weapons as well as the blue energy spheres and dark energy cannons. I'm pretty confident the Communications and Transport Hub could handle any attack the Eternals might launch against us."

Jeremy was pleased to hear this. "Our biggest advantage at the moment is that the Eternals don't know about the Hub. I want to keep it that way."

The other two men nodded. The Hub was the Originator's biggest secret. The four Dyson Spheres, the massive ship construction yards, the research facilities, and the other structures could carry on the Originators' civilization even if all the others were lost.

The next day Jeremy had just returned from the memorial services honoring those who had died in the battles taking the vortex Control Centers away from the Simulins. He was sitting in his office with Rear Admiral Barnes and Grayseth. Both had attended the memorial.

"I will miss Commander Malen," said Grayseth in his loud booming voice. "She was a great warrior and has now gone on to the Great Hunt. We will talk of her around the fire pits in our dens."

"She would be honored to know that," replied Jeremy.

Kathryn stood and walked over to the large open window looking out over the city. A light breeze was blowing. "We have lost so many over the years. Now we're facing the Eternals and those losses may never end."

"It could for us," said Jeremy, coming over to the window to stand beside her. "Kelsey and the others want you to command their new super exploration dreadnaught as well as the exploration fleet that will be going with it."

Kathryn grinned. "I heard that rumor. Of course I would like to command the ship. A large number of my crew have already signed up to serve on the vessel."

"Kelsey says construction will be finished in another few weeks." Jeremy paused, gazing out at the clouds overhead. It was supposed to rain later in the day. "It will be the most powerful ship the Originators have ever built. Even more powerful than the *Dominator*."

Kathryn laughed. "I bet Kazak won't like hearing that."

"No doubt he'll request the *Dominator* to be upgraded with more weapons," answered Jeremy.

They were interrupted by the sudden appearance of Ariel. She was using one of her holographic figures. "Sorry to interrupt, but we may have a serious problem. I just came from the

Communications Center. We've received a message from the Eternals."

"What! How!" asked Jeremy, his eyes narrowing sharply. The Eternals had never tried to contact them before.

"One of their ships appeared in the outer region of the star system containing the Dyson Sphere in Galaxy X-938. They're requesting a meeting with the Originators and a Human representative to discuss ending the war. If we agree they will pull all of their fleets out of Originator space."

"What's the catch?" asked Jeremy, feeling suspicious.

"All of those fleets will be at the meeting."

Kathryn looked over at Jeremy. "That's over one hundred thousand warships. What are we going to do?"

Jeremy was silent for a long moment and then spoke. "I better speak with Councilor Bartoll and the other council members. Somehow, I don't trust the Eternals to be faithful at this meeting. It may be some type of trick. Why don't you come with me?" Jeremy then turned back toward Ariel. "Contact Admiral Kalen and Governor Barnes, they need to be at this meeting as well."

An hour later they were all assembled in the Originators' council chamber.

"What do you make of this?" asked Governor Barnes, looking over at Councilor Bartoll.

"It worries me," Bartoll admitted. "The Eternals are not known for allowing their rivals to coexist."

"This may be some type of ultimatum they are going to deliver," said Councilor Metrics. "I worry since they are bringing so many ships."

"We must hear what they have to say," said Councilor Castille. "If there is the slightest possibility they are earnest about ending the war, we must listen."

For quite some time the group discussed and argued about what needed to be done. Finally Jeremy stood up and looked intently at Councilor Bartoll. "In the end, this is your decision. I will follow whatever you recommend."

Councilor Bartoll drew in a deep breath. "I think we have to attend the meeting. However, it will not be in the system where the Shrieel resides. We will choose a system a few light years distant to hold the meeting. I want sufficient ships with us so the Eternals cannot attempt to intimidate us with their numbers. We should also make certain the Shrieel is adequately defended."

Jeremy nodded. "I will make the necessary arrangements. We can recall the fleets we currently have attacking Eternal space as well as those we've sent to destroy those Eternal fleets in our space. Rear Admiral Cross will remain at the Dyson Sphere with his fleet to aid in its defense in case this is a trick by the Eternals."

Councilor Bartoll looked around the conference table at the others. "Then we are agreed. In four weeks we will meet the Eternals in Galaxy X-938 to discuss ending this war."

Later Jeremy and Rear Admiral Barnes were back in his office.

"What do you think?" she asked. "I feel very uneasy about this meeting?"

"So do I," replied Jeremy. "But I don't see where we have a choice." There was one thing Jeremy intended to do. He was going to speak to Councilor Roan to push Reull Alistar into finishing his research on shutting down the Eternals' mechanical nanites. He had briefed Kathryn about this earlier. "We may need that mechanical nanite shutdown procedure if this is indeed a trick or a trap of some kind. If it works we just might be able to turn the tables on them."

"We have four weeks to get ready," said Kathryn, folding her arms over her chest. "A lot can happen in that time."

Jeremy nodded. He had a feeling this meeting with the Eternals was not going to go well.

Chapter Twenty-Two

At the secret stasis facility of the Defenders of Zorn, Commander Alvord had just finished informing Councilor Zorn of the planned peace meeting between the Eternals and the Originators.

Zorn stood up and began pacing back in forth deep in thought. He stopped and looked directly at Commander Alvord. "We can't allow this peace conference to occur. This war against the Eternals must continue."

Commander Alvord shook his head. "I don't see how we can stop it. From one of our AIs at the Communications and Transport Hub, there will be over one hundred thousand Eternal vessels there and between thirty to fifty thousand Originator warships. The Originator warships will be commanded by the Humans."

Councilor Zorn sat back down behind his desk. The stasis facility had a number of well equipped offices as well as private living quarters. They weren't luxurious by any means but they were quite comfortable. "These Humans I can live with. They keep defeating the Eternals and inflicting heavy losses on their fleets. We just need to keep them confined to the Communications and Transport Hub. In time, we can provide our own people to defend the other Shrieels."

"What do you recommend?" asked Commander Alvord.

Councilor Zorn's face suddenly lit up as a plan came to mind. "How many warships can we get our hands on?"

"Some," replied Alvord. "We have a number of our AIs working in the shipyards on this Shrieel. We've also embedded some of the people we've sent out into advisory positions at two shipyards. The AIs have no reason to doubt an Originator and have so far followed our orders without question."

"That should work. I have a way to disrupt this peace conference and ensure the war with the Eternals continues until they are defeated. The Eternals are an abomination and must be wiped from this universe."

Commander Alvord waited to hear what Councilor Zorn had decided.

"This is what I want done. We don't have a lot of time so we need to move quickly on this. We must also take care not to be detected." Zorn explained to Commander Alvord what he wanted.

Alvord frowned and then nodded. "It might work. It will be risky but if we succeed, the war will go on."

"Which is what we want," Councilor Zorn replied. "Begin making the arrangements and keep me informed of your progress. I believe Albate will be quite useful in ensuring this plan succeeds."

"He waits to serve," replied Commander Alvord. "As we all do."

-

Two weeks had gone by and Jeremy was at the facility where Reull Alistar was working with the Eternals. Aaliss and Ariel had accompanied him as well as Rear Admiral Barnes.

"What progress have you made?" asked Jeremy. They were standing in a lab where several Eternals were laying upon metal tables unmoving.

"Observe," said Alistar, pointing toward a large viewscreen. On the screen, two Eternals were visible. They were speaking to each other while eating a meal the Originators had provided. Suddenly a glazed look passed over the eyes of both which quickly turned into looks of fear. Both tried to stand only to fall and lay on the floor twitching uncontrollably. After several minutes they managed to stand with a look of confusion on their faces. They tried speaking but only gibberish came out of their mouths. "That's what happens when we shutdown their mechanical nanites."

Rear Admiral Barnes shifted her eyes from the viewscreen to Alistar. "Can we make this into a weapon? Something we can use against their ships?"

"Possibly," answered Alistar. "However to penetrate the energy screens the Eternals use on their battlecruisers will require a tremendous power source. We need to project a signal on an obscure frequency that will order the nanites to shutdown."

"How long were the Eternals you tried this out on affected?" asked Jeremy still looking at the viewscreen. The Eternals seemed to be recovering but were moving very slow, almost sluggishly.

"The confusion wears off in about ten to twelve minutes," replied Alistar. "However, their nanites will stay shutdown permanently. They will require new injections to allow them to operate at their normal level. The Eternals we have experimented on took thirty to thirty-five minutes to realize their nanites were nonfunctional. It took that long for them to be able to control their bodies without depending on the nanites. After several hours they were back to normal but without their nanite enhanced strength. Keep in mind the nanites aid the Eternals to be able to think quicker as well. To them their minds will seem dull, and it will take them longer to resolve problems."

"That could be detrimental to them in a battle," said Rear Admiral Barnes, looking over at Jeremy. "It could give us a decisive advantage."

"How long before they can figure out a countermeasure?" Jeremy could see how disabling the Eternals' mechanical nanites before a battle could seriously hamper how they handled their ships.

Alistar shook his head. "I don't know if they can. We're exploiting a basic weakness in the way the Eternals use the mechanical nanites. The nanites are programmable. Only by reverting to nonprogrammable nanites would they be immune to this weapon."

"The Eternals depend on the nanites to be programmable," explained Aaliss. "It allows them to make changes as they are warranted. Sometimes several times a day. An Eternal has only to think about what he wants changed and the mechanical nanites will make the change if it is in the realm of their programming."

Kathryn shook her head. "These Eternals sound scarier all the time."

"They were an unfortunate error on our part," confessed Alistar. "We should never have allowed the experimentation that was done with the mechanical nanites. At first the nanites were safe and showed great promise but then some of our people took advantage of their programmability to begin changing their bodies and became what we called then, the first Anti-Life."

"How soon can we make this into a weapon?"

"It's ready now," answered Alistar. "I can transfer the information over to Aaliss, and she can take it back with you. My research staff and I would like to continue our work here for the time being. We may never have the opportunity to study Eternals like this again."

"Very well," replied Jeremy. "We need to get back to the Communications and Transport Hub and see if we can find a power source that will allow us to penetrate Eternal energy screens."

Alistar nodded and quickly transferred the information to Aaliss. He also handed over a small computer drive that held a second copy.

Later back on the recently repaired *Avenger*, Jeremy looked over at Kathryn who was standing next to him. "What do you think?"

"If this works as Alistar says it will, we may be able to turn the tables on the Eternals if they are planning something at the peace conference. If we can confuse the Eternals for twenty or thirty minutes, we just might be able to destroy most of their ships if it comes to a battle."

"My thoughts exactly," said Jeremy. "We'll give the peace conference a chance first, but if it is a trick set up by the Eternals, we'll use this new weapon against them."

"I have already sent a message to Clarissa at the Communications and Transport Hub about the need for a major power source for the transmission," said Ariel. "She is going to speak to several of the Originators who have been helping design the power system for the super exploration dreadnaught."

Jeremy nodded. Kelsey had some of the smartest Originators working with her in designing her ship. "Excellent. It will only take us two days to get back. Perhaps by then they'll have a solution." Jeremy hoped so. They needed an ace up their sleeve and at the moment, turning off the Eternals' nanites was the only one they had.

-

First Leader Clondax listened to the latest reports of the fleets that would be available in Galaxy X-938. There would be 114,000 ships from the fleets that were assigned to destroy the Originator fleet bases, and he was bringing another forty thousand from the forces stationed in the home galaxy. The forty thousand would stay just outside of Galaxy X-938 but could be summoned quickly if needed. He was not going to make the same mistake Fleet Commander Parnon made. If this came down to a battle, he intended to wipe out every ship the Originators brought and then proceed to the damaged Shrieel in the Simulins' galaxy and take it over. With the massive hole in its hull, his fleet should be able to destroy the defending fleet and then proceed to conquer the Shrieel.

The Originators had agreed to meet at a small red dwarf star system fourteen light years from the system containing the Shrieel. The two fleets would stay two hundred thousand kilometers apart with three ships from each side meeting in the center. Clondax was curious to see a living Originator to determine how progressed he was with the pathogen. Clondax was still convinced they were dealing with relatively few Originators. In all probability their AIs had awoken them upon learning his people had escaped the trap they had set around the home galaxy so long ago. The few thousand survivors, and Clondax was certain there were no more than that, would be offered to live out their lives in peace in a Shrieel of their choosing. Doubtlessly the disease would make short work of them, and in a few hundred years even that Shrieel would be under Eternal control.

Turning around, First Leader Clondax looked at a large viewscreen with the estimated ship production the Eternals could get from the Shrieels. In time, all of the Shrieels would be heavily populated by Eternals as they took over their rightful heritage. The Shrieels would be turned into massive shipyards building the fleets that would be needed to conquer this universe. The Eternal population would swell as they used the Shrieels as they should have been used long ago. It was only logical that the most advanced and most intelligent race in the universe should rule.

Jeremy was in the council chambers listening to Councilor Bartoll explain his plan for the meeting. "I will be going representing the Originators," he said. "All of the other councilors will remain here in case this is a trap being set by the Eternals."

"I still think one more of us should go," objected Councilor Roan. Alora turned pleading eyes toward Councilor Bartoll. "I would also ask that if you insist on only one of us going that someone else go besides you. You are too valuable to risk."

Councilor Bartoll grinned. "I'm old even by our standards. Besides, Admiral Kalen will be there representing the Humans. Our fleet will be close by. I don't believe there is anything to fear. If it is a trap, my ship will quickly retreat to a position of safety."

"We won't allow anything to happen to Councilor Bartoll's ship," promised Jeremy. "At the first signs of treachery, the fleet will advance to protect the councilor's vessel."

"What of the new weapon?" asked Rear Admiral Barnes, who had been asked by Jeremy to attend the meeting.

"It's ready," answered Councilor Trallis. "We've installed it on four modified heavy dreadnaughts. The dreadnaughts only have a few defensive weapons as we've added two additional antimatter chambers to power the device. There are five antimatter chambers on the ships and four of them will be dedicated to power the nanite shutdown broadcast system.

Several of our scientists who are well versed in energy screens have assured us the transmission will go through the Eternals' screens. Energy screens are not designed to stop such a transmission completely as the frequency is too similar to a communications frequency, which the screens are designed to ignore. It will be the Eternals undoing if they are lying to us."

Councilor Bartoll looked around at his fellow councilors and then at Jeremy, Rear Admiral Barnes, and Admiral Kalen. "I would like to address my fellow councilors and Governor Barnes in private. I have a few things I would like to say to them before we embark on this mission of peace."

Jeremy nodded as they all stood up and left the council chambers. They would be leaving the next day for the rendezvous coordinates. Most of the fleets that had been raiding Eternal space and had been seeking the Eternal fleets in Originator space were already there. Jeremy hoped there were no surprises. They were risking much in the hope the Eternals were serious about seeking peace.

-

The next day Jeremy was standing in his home talking to Kelsey; he had already said his goodbyes to Jacob.

"I'll be back in a few days and hopefully this war with the Eternals will be over, and then we can take your new ship out on her maiden voyage."

Kelsey grinned. "I showed the ship to Rear Admiral Barnes the day before yesterday. Her eyes were glowing as I walked her around. I believe she's going to enjoy commanding this ship. It's so much different than any built before, even the *Distant Horizon*."

"The ship still needs a name."

Kelsey nodded, her eyes twinkling. "I have one. I'll tell you when you come back."

Jeremy leaned forward taking Kelsey in his arms. "I love you," he said softly.

"I love you too," Kelsey replied.

Jeremy gave her one last hug and then stepped back. "I'll be back as soon as I can. Look at it this way; this may be the last time I leave at the head of a massive fleet." Jeremy was taking the Communications and Transport Hub's newly completed Grand Fleet with him. The fleet had ten thousand dreadnaughts and forty thousand of the enhanced battlecruisers. It would put them almost on an even par with what the Eternals were expected to bring.

"Jacob and I will be waiting," Kelsey said as she walked with Jeremy to the door.

—

As Jeremy left, Kelsey let out a deep breath. "You better come back to me. I don't know what I would do if you didn't."

—

Jeremy was once more on board the *Avenger*, perhaps for the last time at the head of a massive fleet. Rear Admiral Barnes and her fleet had already departed through the Accelerator Ring.

"Councilor Bartoll says he's ready," reported Aaliss. She was in contact with several Originator AIs on board the councilor's ship. He was on board a dreadnaught that had been equipped with the most powerful shielding possible.

Taking a deep breath, Jeremy glanced over where Commander Malen should be but her station was empty. He couldn't bring himself to assign a new commanding officer to the *Avenger*, at least not yet. "Aaliss, activate the Accelerator Ring. It's time to go see just what the Eternals want from this peace conference." Jeremy still didn't trust the Eternals' motives. He still suspected there was a hidden agenda they were all missing.

—

In space, the one hundred and ten kilometer in diameter ring activated forming a swirling dark blue vortex. The *Avenger* entered first followed by the rest of the fleet. A few minutes later the ring shut down.

—

On board the *Warrior's Pride*, Grayseth watched as his clan brother left the Communications and Transport Hub. Jeremy had placed Grayseth in charge of the fleet of dreadnaughts and enhanced battlecruisers that were staying behind to defend the Hub.

"They go on the hunt," said Shantor as the Accelerator Ring shut down.

Grayseth nodded. "I fear the Eternals do not want peace only to destroy our warships. Fleet Admiral Strong will not be fooled by their trickery and unhonorable ways. He is our clan brother, and it is not yet time for him to go on the Great Hunt."

"He will return," responded Hawthorn. "He is too great of a warrior to fall in battle."

Grayseth sat down in his command chair. He would wait here until his clan brother returned. It was the way of the hunt and the way it had been for untold generations.

-

It took two days for Jeremy's Grand Fleet to reach the system set for the peace conference. As they approached, the long-range tactical display lit up with red threat icons.

"Detecting one hundred and fourteen thousand Eternal battlecruisers," reported Kevin in a subdued voice. "That's the largest Eternal fleet we've ever faced. A few more than what we expected."

"Only slightly larger than the one we faced at the Lost Originators' star cluster," Ariel said. "And we defeated that one."

"Yes, but look at all the defenses the Lost Originators had around the planet. We have nothing like that here."

"Admiral Jackson?" asked Jeremy. "Admiral Jackson was his most experienced admiral. He was in command of the waiting fleets until Jeremy arrived.

"Detecting thirty-four thousand Originator vessels in the system," reported Kevin. "They're two hundred thousand kilometers from the Eternal fleet."

Jeremy knew as fast as fleets could move that was a very short distance.

"Ariel, as soon as we drop out of hyperspace I want the fleets formed into a disk formation five ships in depth facing the Eternals." If this became a battle, he wanted to be ready.

Several minutes passed and then the fleet began dropping out of hyperspace. Jeremy remained silent as Ariel and the other AIs rapidly formed the fleet into its planned formation.

First Leader Clondax gazed in surprise at the large fleet the Originators had brought to the peace conference.

"Eighty-four thousand Originator vessels detected," reported the Eternal at the sensor console. "They are forming up into a disk formation."

This was far more than expected. "Move us out to the coordinates for the peace conference. It's time I met a real live Originator and Human." He had agreed to go aboard one of the Originators' ships to talk. He would be taking an honor guard of Eternal shock troops as well. If there was a problem, the shock troops could easily overwhelm the crew of the Originator ship and take it over.

Admiral Kalen was in the Command Center of the dreadnaught where the peace talks would be held. All three of the dreadnaughts that would meet the Eternals had been stripped of their dark matter missiles as well as dark energy cannons. If there were any treachery on the part of the Eternals, those two weapons would not fall into their hands. On the viewscreens, he saw the Eternal fleet. It was a solid wall of battlecruisers facing the Originator fleet. If this turned into a battle, he had no idea who would win. It also concerned him as his ship was sitting between the two fleets.

First Leader Clondax stepped off his shuttle with an escort of ten shock troops. Fifteen more would remain inside. The hatch slid shut as soon as he and his escort reached the foot of the ramp.

He was met by twenty armed Human Marines as well as a Human officer. He had been informed earlier that the Marines would be present.

"I am Admiral Kalen and will be representing the Humans in these negotiations," explained Kalen, introducing himself to the Eternal.

Clondax looked around noticing the absence of any Originators though there were several of their AIs present. It was as he suspected. There were few Originators, all possibly extremely weak from the pathogen with possibly very short lifespans still remaining. "Where is the Originator I am supposed to meet? I was expecting him to be here."

"He's waiting in the main conference room," replied Admiral Kalen. "Your escorts will not be allowed to enter the conference room. They can stay here or wait outside the room."

"They will accompany me to the meeting. Two will come inside; the rest will wait outside."

Admiral Kalen hesitated. This did not surprise him. "Very well, but if you're having two armed escorts inside we will have two also. If you will follow me." Kalen turned and began walking toward an open hatch.

Clondax was impressed by the Human. He had shown no fear and had responded to having two shock troops in the conference room by inserting two of his own.

As they made their way through the ship, Clondax could not help but notice how professional the Human Marines were. They reminded him much of his own shock troops. Suddenly his plans of being able to take control of this ship were meeting with doubt. He would have to continue to evaluate the situation as the meeting progressed.

Reaching the corridor where the conference room was Admiral Kalen ordered his Marine escort to come to a stop. He chose two to enter the conference room with him and then opened the door indicating for First Leader Clondax and his two shock troops to enter first.

—

Clondax stepped into the room and stopped in shock. There was an Originator in the room and he appeared perfectly healthy.

There were no signs he was suffering from the life extension pathogen. How was this possible?

"I am First Councilor Bartoll of the Originators," said Bartoll in a calm and measured voice. "I am disappointed to see you feel unsafe in my presence and require armed guards for your protection. I can assure you that no one here will harm you."

Clondax turned back toward his two shock troops and instructed them to go back outside and wait in the corridor. He noticed the two Human Marines did the same.

"Let us sit down and discuss an end to this frightful war," suggested Bartoll. "It has cost many lives and is a strain on resources for both of our civilizations."

"I will remain standing," replied Clondax in a cold and uncompromising voice. "I have come here to offer our terms to allow all Originators currently on the Shrieels to continue to live. You will turn all of your Shrieels over to us but one. You will have sixty days to move all of your people to the Shrieel of your choice where you will be allowed to live out the rest of your lives in peace. You will also turn the Humans over to us. The Humans will either serve us or they will be exterminated."

"And if we refuse?" asked Bartoll as he stood up to face Clondax. "We do not fear the Eternals."

Clondax laughed. It sounded almost inhuman. "We outnumber you by millions to one. How many of you are left, a few thousand?"

"No," answered Bartoll. "There are actually millions of us still surviving and we have a cure for the pathogen. Enough to continue to fight this war if necessary."

First Leader Clondax suddenly felt unsure of himself. Could it be true that there were still millions of Originators? Suddenly he knew what had been inside that star cluster where he had last fought the Humans. It must have been a massive stasis facility! No wonder they had fought so hard to protect the planet. However, this did not change anything.

"I have over one hundred thousand warships with me. I can summon several million more if necessary. You already have one Shrieel that is damaged. Do you want more?"

"Your race is still the same as it was when we imprisoned you in your galaxy," said Bartoll, his face showing his disappointment. "We should have destroyed you then when we had the chance."

"A fatal mistake," replied Clondax coldly. "One we wouldn't have made."

Councilor Bartoll let out a deep breath as he stood to his full height and gazed unafraid into Clondax's eyes. "There is no point in continuing this meeting. We will not agree to any of your terms. This war will continue until we force you back once more into your galaxy. This time you will never escape."

"My fleet will destroy yours!" boasted Clondax. "You will never imprison us again. We are too powerful."

"Perhaps," said Admiral Kalen, glaring at the Eternal. "However, we have defeated you before and we will again. If it is war you want, then it is war you will have. We Humans are not afraid of a fight."

Clondax snarled and turning strode to the hatch, opened it and left.

"Well, that didn't go well," said Bartoll suddenly looking much older. "We better inform Fleet Admiral Strong we may be in for a battle."

"We could still take Clondax into custody," suggested Admiral Kalen.

"No," replied Bartoll, shaking his head. "We will honor our agreement and allow him to return to his ship. As soon as his shuttle departs the flight bay pull all three of our dreadnaughts back behind Fleet Admiral Strong's fleet."

Admiral Kalen nodded. He then turned and headed toward the Command Center. It looked as if there was indeed going to be a major battle.

On board the *Avenger*, everyone was waiting for word of any progress in the peace talks. The fleet was at Condition Two with everyone looking for any signs of possible Eternal treachery.

"Jeremy," called out Kevin from his sensor console. "There is another fleet of Originator ships heading toward us."

Jeremy felt confused. As far as he knew everyone that was supposed to be here was already. "How many?"

"Ten dreadnaughts and one thousand battlecruisers," replied Kevin. "Strange, the battlecruisers are not of the enhanced version."

"I have a communication from the inbound fleet," reported Lieutenant Lantz. "They're from the Dyson Sphere and were sent by Admiral Cross to escort Councilor Bartoll back there if necessary. In case a battle breaks out, they will ensure he gets away safely."

Kevin looked over at Jeremy. "Why would Admiral Cross do that? Did he discover something we don't know about this meeting?"

"I don't know," replied Jeremy, trying to figure out what was going on. "Lieutenant Lantz, inform the commander of that fleet to take up a position directly behind ours. Inform him at the moment that Councilor Bartoll does not need an escort. The peace talks are still ongoing."

Kevin looked back at his sensor console. "At least that's another thousand ships we will have if this peace conference goes south."

"Let's hope that it doesn't," replied Jeremy. It would be nice not to have to worry about war for a while.

A minute later Aaliss spoke with deep concern in her voice. "I just received a message from one of the AIs on board Councilor Bartoll's ship. The peace talks have broken down and the Eternal leader is leaving. These were not peace talks. He delivered an ultimatum which Councilor Bartoll refused to accept. I have a full recording of the meeting if you want to hear it."

Jeremy's face froze. This was what he had been afraid of.

"Jeremy!" called out Ariel with apprehension in her voice. "The fleet from the Dyson Sphere has changed course, it's going to drop out of hyperspace right where the ships attending the peace conference are at."

"What!" Even as Jeremy switched his gaze to the tactical display, the inbound Originator fleet began dropping out of hyperspace and immediately opened fire on the three Originator dreadnaughts and the three Eternal battlecruisers. Dark matter missiles began exploding against the energy screens of all three ships.

"It's the Defenders of Zorn," yelled Aaliss. "Albate is commanding the fleet. They are using dark matter missiles against the ships of the peace conference."

-

Admiral Kalen had just entered the Command Center when the *Intrepid* shook violently and warning alarms began sounding.

"Report!" Surely the Eternals were not attacking. First Leader Clondax's shuttle was still on board.

"We're being attacked by a fleet of Originator ships that just dropped out of hyperspace right on top of us," replied Tanod, who was an Originator military AI. "Aaliss is reporting that it is the Defenders of Zorn!"

"Get us back to the fleet!" ordered Admiral Kalen as the ship shook violently once more. The lights dimmed and several consoles exploded sending bright showers of sparks across the room. Glancing at the damage control console, he saw it lighting up with red lights. Seeing the damage, he knew they would not make it back to the fleet.

"Energy screen is at 12 percent and weakening rapidly," reported Tanod. "It will fail shortly. Our hyperdrive is damaged and our gravity drive is nonfunctional."

Admiral Kalen looked at a flickering viewscreen showing the *Avenger*. He wished he could have talked to Jeremy one last time. In many ways, Jeremy was the son he never had.

-

The Defenders of Zorn focused all of their firepower upon the six ships. In moments screens began to fail. First two of the Eternal vessels were blown apart by dark matter missiles and then one of the Originator dreadnaughts died. The weapons fire increased as hundreds of dark matter warheads detonated. Suddenly the space where the six ships had been looked as if a supernova had erupted. When the brilliance died down all six ships were gone.

Albate grinned. He had succeeded in the first part of his mission. Now for the second. "Advance on the Eternal fleet and open fire," he ordered. He wanted the Eternals to know beyond a shadow of a doubt there could never be peace between the Originators and the Anti-Life.

-

Jeremy leaned back in his command chair refusing to believe what his eyes were showing him. All six ships at the peace conference site were nothing more than flaming wreckage. Their shields had not been able to withstand the multiple explosions of dark matter missiles from the ten dreadnaughts.

"Councilor Bartoll and Admiral Kalen," said Kevin, his eyes showing shock. "They're dead!"

"Eternal fleet is advancing," warned Ariel. "They will be in combat range in twenty seconds. The Defenders of Zorn are already engaging them."

"Place the fleet at Condition One," ordered Jeremy still trying to grasp what had just happened.

"All hands, set Condition One across the fleet," the order went out on the ship-to-ship comm system.

On the *Avenger*, the alarm klaxons began to sound and red lights began to flash. They were going to war!

Chapter Twenty-Three

"What's the status of Defenders of Zorn fleet," demanded Jeremy as he tried to put out of his mind the destruction of the *Intrepid* and the deaths of Councilor Bartoll and Admiral Kalen. The entire fleet was still reeling from what had just transpired.

Kevin changed the view on the main viewscreen, which showed heavy weapons fire between the Defenders of Zorn and the Eternal fleet. "Engaged against the Eternals. They don't stand a chance. Why are they doing this?"

"It does not matter to them," replied Aaliss. "I spoke to Albate briefly a moment ago. He says now there never will be peace. The war will go on until the Eternals are destroyed and wiped from existence." Then she turned and looked worriedly at Jeremy. "He said it is the wish of Councilor Zorn."

Jeremy let out a deep breath. "It is as I feared. Another stasis facility of the Defenders of Zorn does exist, and Commander Alvord and Albate have found and activated it. Councilor Zorn must have been in stasis there as well."

"I don't understand," said Kevin, gazing at the intensifying battle on the viewscreen. "Why are they sacrificing themselves?"

"They are forcing us into a battle," Aaliss answered simply. "They did not know the peace talks had failed. I didn't have time to tell Albate before they attacked the Eternals."

"Hold our position," Jeremy said to Ariel. "Let the Eternals come to us. Aaliss, is there any way to discover where that fleet came from." It was now a high priority that they find the hidden stasis facility and Councilor Zorn before he caused even more trouble. Dealing with the deaths of Councilor Bartoll and Admiral Kalen was going to be bad enough.

Aaliss nodded. "I already know. It is from the Shrieel in Galaxy X-128. I managed to trace the dreadnaughts using the registration numbers on their hulls."

"I want that Shrieel quarantined. No ships in or out. Contact the Communications and Transport Hub and inform them of what has transpired. I want Major Wilde and every available Marine sent to that Dyson Sphere to find Commander Alvord and Councilor Zorn. I want them captured alive if possible. Have Grayseth take his fleet there as well. The new battlestations can defend the Hub if necessary."

"Message sent," replied Aaliss. "The council will be shaken to its core when they hear this was not an actual peace conference and that Lead Councilor Bartoll has been killed."

On the viewscreen, the last dreadnaught of the Defenders of Zorn exploded in a ball of fire. All of their battlecruisers had already been annihilated by the advancing Eternal fleet.

"Albate's ship has been destroyed," confirmed Aaliss. "That's one problem we won't have to deal with."

"Eternals are in combat range," added Kevin. The viewscreens were full of advancing Eternal battlecruisers. The tactical displays were covered in red threat icons.

"All ships fire!" ordered Jeremy over the ship-to-ship comm. "Aaliss are the nanite projectors ready to send the shutdown command?"

"Yes, Admiral."

"Then do so. We can't defeat a fleet of this size with the forces we have here." Jeremy took a deep breath. Now they would find out if the shutdown command for the Eternal mechanical nanites would actually work.

Eternal Fleet Commander Dalon studied the tactical display as his fleet advanced on the waiting Originator fleet. He had already sent a message to the fleet outside the galaxy reporting First Councilor Clondax's death and requesting their support. He was surprised the Originators had attacked sacrificing their own ships to kill the First Councilor. It was a tactic the Eternals might use, but not expected of the Originators. Perhaps these mysterious Humans were behind it.

"We will close with the Originator fleet and destroy it," he ordered. Even with the death of the First Leader, it would still be a great victory for the Eternals if this large fleet of the Originators could be annihilated.

The two fleets began exchanging intense weapons fire. The Eternals were launching thousands of 100-megaton antimatter missiles while the Originators were in turn launching thousands of 400-megaton dark matter missiles. Energy beams, ion beams, antimatter beams, gravitonic beams, and dark energy beams filled the void between the two fleets. Ships began to die in bright flashes of light as shields were quickly overwhelmed.

The front of both fleets looked to be on fire as millions of megatons of raging energy was being released every few seconds.

"Admiral Lankell's flagship has just been destroyed," reported Kevin as the icon representing the powerful heavy dreadnaught flared up and vanished from the tactical display. "It was hit by too many antimatter missiles causing the energy shield to fail. It was sudden; they probably never even knew what happened."

Jeremy winced. He had just lost an admiral. He was deeply afraid he would lose more before this battle was over.

"Firing nanite shutdown projectors," reported Aaliss. "It will take a few minutes to cover the entire Eternal fleet."

Commander Zafron felt rage flow through him like he never imagined possible. He had witnessed the destruction of the *Intrepid* and the deaths of Admiral Kalen and Councilor Bartoll. It was unthinkable that an Originator Councilor had died such a violent death.

"Fire our blue energy spheres at the highest rate possible," ordered Zafron, his voice as cold as ice. "Today we will destroy this Eternal fleet and let them know the price for killing a councilor of the Originators." Zafron knew that Albate had been responsible, but it was the Eternals who had brought everyone to this farce of a peace conference.

Kazak nodded. He had liked Councilor Bartoll. His hands flew over the tactical console as he used his neural link to control the *Dominator's* weapons fire. Hundreds of blue energy spheres exited the ship's launchers as he overrode the safety protocols. He picked out an Eternal battlecruiser and fired the ship's two dark energy cannons watching on a viewscreen above his console as the two beams penetrated the ship's energy screen and cut deep inside. Secondary explosions rattled the Eternal vessel. Several well placed dark matter missiles finished the ship off. The *Dominator* had just become an avenging angel of death.

Rear Admiral Mann had witnessed the destruction of Admiral Lankell's dreadnaught. It had been in the fleet formation next to hers. Without hesitation she took over command of Lankell's fleet adding its ships to her own. "Intensify weapons fire," she ordered. "I want all ships firing in four ship groups." That would better allow them to overwhelm the Eternals' energy shields.

"*Avenger* reports the nanite projectors are broadcasting," reported Commander Sutherland. "We should begin seeing some affects shortly."

"If it works," Hailey replied. She knew if it didn't they were going to lose a major portion of the fleet if not all of it. "Keep pouring our weapons fire into the Eternal fleet." Hailey leaned forward, feeling her pulse race. She didn't know what would happen if they were to lose this battle. On one of the viewscreens, a sudden massive explosion of light marked the destruction of the Eternal battlecruiser her ship had been targeting.

Rear Admiral Barnes took a deep breath as the *Distant Horizon* shook violently. A few red lights blossomed on the damage control console. She couldn't believe Admiral Kalen was gone. She had known him since she was a child. It was difficult to imagine the fleet without him.

"Our fleets are taking a lot of damage," reported Commander Grissim. "We can't take this much longer."

"Nanite shutdown projectors have been activated," reported Clarissa. "I'm scanning the Eternal fleet so see if there are any affects."

Everyone in the Command Center turned toward Clarissa. If they were going to win this battle, the new projectors had to work.

Jeremy winced as more ships of his fleet were destroyed. Brilliant explosions littered space throwing wreckage in all directions. Some ships were being damaged and even a few destroyed as a result of collisions with massive pieces of debris. "The projectors?"

"No affect yet," reported Ariel, sounding disappointed. "The four dreadnaughts equipped with the projectors are boosting the power to the signal."

"It has to work," said Kevin, his eyes focused on his sensors.

"Give it time," answered Jeremy, his hands clenched into fists as he gazed intently at the nearest tactical display. The two fleets were within a few thousand kilometers of each other. Weapons fire was very seldom missing.

"The frequency being produced by the projectors is being varied," added Aaliss. "We should see results shortly."

"We just lost Commander Belson," reported Kevin, his face turning pale. "His ship was hit with over seventy antimatter missiles. It just disintegrated."

Jeremy blinked his eyes. He couldn't afford to keep losing admirals and fleet commanders.

"Jeremy!" called out Kevin. "The weapons fire from several sections of the Eternal fleet has just dropped substantially. It's also becoming erratic."

Jeremy's eyes widened. "All ships," he spoke over the ship-to-ship comm. "Concentrate your weapons fire on the sections of the Eternal fleet that seem to be affected by our new projectors. We must destroy as many of their ships as possible while the

Eternals are suffering from the influence of the nanite shutdown command."

In space, on the Eternal vessels there was pandemonium. Eternals fell to the floor thrashing about as if they couldn't control their bodies. Their eyes glazed over as if their thought processes were frozen. On some ships weapons fire stopped completely. On others, computers took over the ship's weapons sensing the crew had become incapacitated. Weapons fire stopped being coordinated and became more sporadic.

Fleet Commander Dalon was sitting in his command chair when he suddenly felt nauseous and dizzy. He stood up and found he had no control over his legs. He fell to the deck his body twitching uncontrollably. His mind seemed unable to focus. All around him the rest of his crew collapsed as well.

The Originator fleet suddenly shifted it weapons fire to those sections of the Eternal fleet that seemed to be floundering. Eternal battlecruiser after battlecruiser was blown out of space. Very little weapons fire was being returned as computers waited for commands which did not come. After a few moments defensive programs kicked in and the computers took control of firing the weapons. A few energy beams flicked out and then some missiles launched.

The projectors continued to play across the Eternal Fleet. Soon the entire Eternal fleet was demonstrating the affects of the projectors as the Eternals became incapacitated. The battle suddenly shifted heavily in the direction of the Originator fleet as their fire was coordinated and the Eternals was not. The computers on the Eternal vessels were still firing missiles and energy weapons, but they had not been designed to fight a battle. That was the job of the Eternals and not one they trusted to machines. Their computers were also nothing in comparison to an AI. They were programmed with a designated set of parameters they could operate within. Fighting a major battle was not one of them.

"We're destroying four Eternal vessels for every ship we lose," reported Kevin, his eyes showing relief at the sudden turn in the battle. "That rate should increase as almost all of the Eternal fleet is now affected by the projectors. Their weapons fire is becoming very erratic."

Jeremy nodded. "Activate the hyperspace interference fields. I don't want any of their fleet to escape." Jeremy was still furious at the loss of Councilor Bartoll and Admiral Kalen. He was taking out his fury on the Eternal fleet and he intended to destroy it! After the battle, he would turn his attention to the Defenders of Zorn.

-

Fleet Commander Dalon lay unmoving on the floor in the Command Center of his flagship. He was finding it difficult to breathe let alone move. For minutes he had lain in the same spot trying to determine what had happened. His mind seemed sluggish and incapable of making decisions. Finally making a great effort he managed to stand and stumble to his command chair. His legs felt heavy and he could barely raise his arms. It was something he had never experienced before in his long life as an Eternal.

Taking several deep breaths, he gazed at the viewscreens. It was evident whatever had happened had affected the entire fleet. The Originator ships were closing in for the kill.

The hatch to the Command Center suddenly opened and Strold came stumbling in. Strold was responsible for seeing to the health of the Eternals on the ship. "It is our mechanical nanites. Somehow the Originators have found a way to shut them down."

"Our nanites," responded Dalon, forcing the words from his mouth. "How?" Now he knew why he felt so weak and his mind sluggish.

"I don't know. I never thought it could be done."

Other members of the crew were also attempting to stand. Some made it to their consoles others remained on the deck moaning.

Fleet Commander Dalon shifted his eyes to the tactical display. The Originators were decimating his fleet. The computers were fighting back but they had not been programmed for a major fleet engagement like this.

"Can you inject us with new nanites?"

Strold shook his head. "I checked before I came here. All have been neutralized."

Before Fleet Commander Dalon could reply, the ship began to shake violently. Red lights filled the damage control console and then a white light filled the Command Center.

—

"There is a second Eternal fleet inbound," reported Kevin as the long-range sensors picked up the new threat. "Forty thousand detected."

"Two of the ships with the nanite projectors have been destroyed," added Ariel worriedly.

Jeremy looked at the tactical displays. There were still over twenty thousand Eternal ships left though many of them were damaged. "Can we neutralize the nanites on the inbound fleet?"

"Yes," replied Aaliss as she did some quick calculations. "But it will take some time depending on the formation of the fleet once it exits hyperspace."

"How many ships do we have remaining?" Jeremy looked over at Ariel for an answer.

"Over forty-six thousand," she replied. "Many are damaged."

"Correction," said Kevin excitedly. "The Eternal fleet is changing course. They are starting to move away."

Jeremy looked over at Aaliss for an explanation.

"They're confused," she explained. "They must see on their sensors how poorly their ships are doing against us."

"Some of the weapons fire from a few of the Eternal ships is increasing," reported Ariel. "I suspect their crews are starting to recover."

"Then let's end this," said Jeremy, leaning forward in his command chair. "All ships are to close with the Eternals. I don't want a single ship to escape."

For the next twenty minutes the battle raged. As the Eternals managed to regain control of their bodies, the number of Originator vessels being destroyed increased. However, the Eternals could not match the efficiency they once had with their nanites. At the best, the Eternals were losing three ships for every Originator vessel they destroyed.

Jeremy watched a viewscreen as the *Dominator* closed on the last seven surviving Eternal battlecruisers. Blue energy spheres struck the seven ships and a few moments later all that remained was space dust.

"It's over," said Kevin in disbelief. "All 114,000 Eternal vessels have been destroyed!"

"Get me a status on all fleet ships and the condition of their crews." Jeremy knew he had lost over half of his fleet as well as some valuable commanders and admirals. It was the nanite projectors which had been the difference between defeat and victory.

"It will take a while on the casualty figures," Ariel answered. "We lost 42,317 battlecruisers and 6,223 dreadnaughts. We also lost Admirals Akira and Lankell as well as Commander Belson."

Jeremy let out a deep sigh. Commander Belson had impressed him as a military commander. The Originator had been instrumental in saving the sleeping Originators back in the Lost Originator star cluster. "The other Eternal fleet?"

"Still headed away," answered Kevin. "It's almost out of sensor range."

Jeremy nodded. "Let's return to the Dyson Sphere. Many of our ships are going to need to be repaired before we return to the Hub." Looking at the viewscreens, they were full of wreckage from destroyed warships. Some still seemed to be burning. That would stop when their oxygen was depleted.

Before they left Jeremy contacted Rear Admiral Barnes and asked Kathryn to remain at the battle scene with the undamaged vessels from her fleet. She would comb the debris for anything that might be useful as well as destroy any Originator technology that might be in the wreckage. She was also to leave and head for the Dyson Sphere if the other Eternal fleet was detected returning.

"What now?" asked Kevin. "That other fleet is bound to report how strange their ships were behaving in the battle. They were close enough to take some sensor readings."

Jeremy leaned back in his command chair. "I don't know the answer to that. I'm not even sure where we stand with Councilor Bartoll dead. It could change everything at the Communications and Transport Hub."

"The council wouldn't make us leave?" asked Kevin horrified at the thought. "It's our home now."

"It was theirs first," Jeremy reminded Kevin. "Once we get back there will be a lot of decisions to be made. I'm afraid things are going to change again." Jeremy had come to trust Councilor Bartoll and over time, the two had become close friends. He couldn't imagine what it would be like if all the Federation races were forced to leave the Hub.

"Everything will work out," said Ariel, stepping over close to Jeremy. "It always has."

Jeremy did not reply. He wasn't sure what would happen this time.

Epilogue

Jeremy was back at the Communications and Transport Hub waiting nervously for the Originator Council to finish their meeting. He had no idea what was going on as in the last hour Governor Barnes and Grayseth had both been summoned. Neither had come back out. Grayseth had only returned the day before from Galaxy X-128. Admiral Mann had taken his place with her much larger fleet.

"What do you think?" Rear Admiral Barnes asked. She was sitting next to Jeremy anxiously waiting to hear something. The council had interviewed her earlier about the events at the peace conference. "Do you think they'll expel us from the Dyson Sphere?"

Jeremy let out a deep sigh. "I don't know. They were very unhappy about the death of Councilor Bartoll. I can't say I blame them. I promised to keep him safe and failed."

Kathryn looked toward the closed doors. "It was their own people who killed him. The Defenders of Zorn did something none of us could have predicted. How goes Major Wilde's search for their hidden base."

"We may have a lead," Jeremy answered. "We're certain it's one of the facilities listed in the hidden communication center we located here at the Hub. We know the fleet came from Galaxy X-128. According to the records in the communications center, there are seventeen hidden stasis facilities on that Dyson Sphere. Major Wilde has already surrounded all of them and is in the process of seeing what's inside. We should know something shortly."

The door to the Council Chambers suddenly opened and Councilor Roan motioned for the two of them to come inside.

"I guess we're going to find out what they decided," said Kathryn as she followed Jeremy into the large room.

Stepping inside, Jeremy saw Governor Barnes and Grayseth both seated at the conference table. A large chair had been brought in for his Bear friend.

"Have a seat and I will inform you of what we have decided," said Councilor Castille, gesturing for them to sit down.

Jeremy and Kathryn sat down and waited looking expectantly across the table at the four Originators.

"Before Councilor Bartoll left on this peace mission he asked us to promise him to implement certain items if he were not to return," Councilor Castille said with a look of great sadness on her face. "I believe he suspected all along this request for a peace conference was a farce from the Eternals. He also had a strong belief that the future of our race had become intertwined with the three Federation races who had come to live here at the Hub. He wanted to make sure that was not endangered in case he died at the hands of the Eternals."

Jeremy's eyes widened in surprise. He wondered what Councilor Bartoll had arranged.

Councilor Castille looked at Jeremy and then smiled. "The three Federation races will continue to live here at the Communications and Transport Hub. Not only that we will be increasing the size of the council. It will have ten Originators, three Humans including Governor Barnes, two Altons to be named at a later date, and one Carethian." Councilor Castille looked over at Grayseth. "We have already chosen the Carethian Councilor."

Grayseth bared his large incisors in the Bear's form of a grin.

Jeremy felt as if a huge weight had been lifted from his shoulders. Everything would continue with the three Federation races actually having a voice on the council. It was far more than he had ever hoped for.

"By a unanimous vote you will continue to be the head of our fleets and help set our policy in dealing with the Eternals."

Ariel suddenly appeared in the Council Chambers. "I'm sorry to intrude but we just received word from Major Wilde that they've located the hidden stasis facility of the Defenders of Zorn. Her Marines and combat robots are entering the facility now."

Jeremy looked at the four councilors. "What will we do with Zorn if he's captured?"

Councilor Trallis shook his head frowning deeply. "That will pose a problem. Since he is technically a councilor we can't remove him from that position."

"You mean he may end up sitting at this council table?" asked Kathryn in dismay.

"No," Councilor Roan replied. "His actions have resulted in the death of a fellow councilor. As a result, he will be isolated and not allowed contact with other Originators. He will still be a councilor but without any power."

Jeremy looked over at Ariel. "Keep us informed of any developments."

-

On the Dyson Sphere in Galaxy X-128, Major Wilde was descending down a wide well lit tunnel to the hidden stasis facility. A concealed hatch had hidden the tunnel from view.

"We're nearly there," said Sergeant Metz, gripping his assault rifle tightly in his hands. Behind him were two squads of Marines and four squads of combat robots. "We've set charges on the hatch that leads into the facility and will blow it as soon as we arrive. All of the combat robots are armed with stun guns as we want to take anyone inside the facility alive."

Brenda nodded. She had orders from Fleet Admiral Strong to capture both Alvord and Councilor Zorn. They had crimes they needed to answer to.

"Zorn's people will be fanatical," warned Leeda. "We must be on our guard at all times."

-

After several minutes they reached the metal hatch, which was preventing entry to the stasis facility. It had already been wired with explosives.

"We can blow it at any time," said Sergeant Metz as he handed Brenda the detonator.

"Let's do it," she said, making sure everyone was a safe distance away. Pressing the button several loud explosions rang down the long corridor. When the smoke cleared, the metal hatch hung loosely from its hinges. Several combat robots stepped up and easily moved it out of the way.

"Send the combat robots in first," ordered Brenda.

"That won't be necessary, Major Wilde," a voice spoke from inside. Moments later Commander Alvord and his four crewmembers stepped out. "We surrender."

"Where's Councilor Zorn?" asked Breda, peering past Alvord and not seeing anyone else.

Alvord looked at his four crewmembers and then answered. "He went back into stasis to be awakened after the war between the Originators and the Eternals comes to an end. By then our people will recognize him for the leader that he is."

"We'll see," said Brenda as she motioned for her Marines to take Commander Alvord and his crew into custody.

Entering the facility, she found half a dozen stasis chambers in the Control Center. All were occupied. From the descriptions she had been given, she recognized one of them as Councilor Zorn.

"We could end this now," suggested Sergeant Metz. "All we have to do is kill the power trapping them inside."

Brenda took a deep breath. She had instructions to bring Commander Alvord and Councilor Zorn back to the Hub. "No, we'll arrange for transport and take these chambers back with us. What about the others?"

"They're empty," Leeda said as she came back from another hatch that led out of the Control Center. "These six are all that remain."

"How many are missing?"

"Eight hundred," Leeda replied.

Brenda shook her head. Those eight hundred could be anywhere making them nearly impossible to find. Councilor Zorn had been clever. By sending his people out to mix in with the other Originators, they could begin rebuilding his power base. With a deep sigh, Brenda knew what her future job was going to be. It appeared she was doomed to always be looking for missing Originators.

On the planet Gardell, the Eternal Council was once more in session.

"This war cannot go on," said Second Leader Queexel. "This latest battle has cost us over one hundred thousand ships. Not only that, the Originators must have used some unknown weapon to impair the fighting ability of our vessels. The long-range scans from our second fleet indicated many of our vessels behaving erratically. Several of our scientists have claimed the crews must have been knocked out as many of our vessels seemed to be under computer control."

"I said from the very beginning it was a mistake to go to war against the Originators," said Second Leader Fehnral. "This war against the Originators has greatly set back our expansion across this universe."

"What are we to do?" asked Second Leader Barrant.

Fehnral looked slowly around the huge stone table where all the Eternal Councilors stood. "We ask for an armistice. We agree to leave Originator space alone, and they agree to leave our space alone."

"What about the rest of the universe?" asked Second Leader Tarmal. "Who controls it?"

"We fight for it," replied Fehnral, folding his arms across his chest. "The armistice will not extend past our current territories."

"So our empire could still expand," said Second Leader Nolant, looking thoughtful.

Fehnral nodded. "Yes, we can continue to grow our empire. I'm sure the Originators will resist us at every point. It is their way."

"I approve," said Second Leader Tarmal. "The Originators and these Humans will make fine adversaries to train our shock troops against."

The others all voiced their consent as well. An armistice for the immediate future. Perhaps in a few thousand years, they could try once more to conquer Originator space.

A few days later Jeremy was in his office speaking to Councilor Barnes. "I understand Alton Ambassador Tureen is coming to take a spot on the council."

"Yes," replied Barnes. "I can think of no one better to fill one of the two Alton councilor seats." Then a look of seriousness spread across Councilor Barnes' face. "What do you think of this armistice the Eternals are proposing?"

Jeremy frowned. "We leave their space alone and they leave ours alone."

Barnes nodded. "They must be wondering what you did to their fleet to be able to defeat it. Dazon Fells says it makes perfect sense to him. They know we will not break the armistice and it allows them to continue to expand their empire."

"We can't let thousands of other galaxies fall to the Eternals," replied Jeremy. "If we don't resist them, someday this entire universe will swear allegiance to their empire."

"They know that," answered Councilor Barns. "I've seen the document they sent to the Dyson Sphere in Galaxy X-938. Armed combat outside of our two spheres of influence is permitted. They expect us to resist their continued expansion. Fells says the Eternals are looking at the long-term. At some point in time, they may once more try to conquer Originator space but it won't be until their empire is considerably larger. Dazon says we are probably talking about thousands of years in the future."

Jeremy stood up and walked over to the large window gazing out over the city. It was the start of the night cycle and the city was brilliantly lit up. It was an awe inspiring sight seeing the slender towers and narrow walkways all lit up with different colored lights. "So, what are we going to do?"

"The council has decided to continue to build up our fleet and train Federation crews to operate them. Several Originators, including Damold Brim the ship construction expert, are suggesting we build a new and larger battlestation. Something in the range of forty kilometers in diameter. It would be armed with dark energy cannons and the blue energy spheres. These could be deployed to protect any new fleet bases we build in contested galaxies."

"Conflict unending," Jeremy said softly. "This war will never end."

Councilor Barnes seemed startled. "I guess that is true. But at least we will survive. The Communications and Transport Hub is safe and so is the Federation."

Looking out into the distance, Jeremy could see two more cities lit up with lights. These were the new cites for the Human colonists that were starting to arrive. "I thought someday I would see this war end. Then I grew afraid it would become our children's responsibility. Now it seems it will be the responsibility of our future great great grandchildren."

"Maybe," replied Councilor Barnes. "Keep in mind the Originators medical science can greatly extend our lives if we choose to do so. We could still be around in a few thousand years."

A troubled look crossed Jeremy's face. He had no desire to spend several thousand years fighting the Eternals. However, a life that long with Kelsey and the others at his side did sound tempting. It was something he would have to discuss with Kelsey at a later date. For now, it was time to go home and check on his wife and son.

—

Councilor Barnes watched as Jeremy left the Tower to go home. He knew that even though Jeremy might not wish it to be so. He would always have a hand in guiding the Federation races here at the Hub. It was what made him who he was.

Rear Admiral Massie Tolsen was on board the *WarHawk* visiting with her brother. They were both still at the damaged Dyson Sphere.

"This explains what Fleet Admiral Streth prophesized," she said as she read the latest report about the proposed armistice. "He said Jeremy would never win this war."

Race nodded. "Yes, it all makes sense now. This war will continue with neither side ever able to completely defeat the other."

Massie stood up and poured herself a glass of tea. "What about us?"

Race smiled. "We have a job to do. We'll go wherever Jeremy sends us."

Massie nodded. She looked at a viewscreen on the wall in Race's quarters. It showed a view of the interior of the Dyson Sphere. It was so beautiful and awe inspiring. Maybe when she had time, she would do a little exploring. It was something she had always wanted to do.

It was a joyous day for the Special Five. They were all gathered in the massive construction bay that held the recently completed super exploration dreadnaught. The ship was five thousand two hundred meters in length and the most powerful ship the Originators had ever built. It was armed with twenty-four dark energy turrets as well as four primary dark energy cannons on her bow. Other weapons covered the hull adding to the dreadnaughts awesome firepower. In addition, the ship was equipped with the blue energy spheres as well.

Councilor Barns, Rear Admiral Barnes, Ariel, and Clarissa were only a few of the large group that were standing waiting for the name of the ship to be revealed.

"This is exciting," said Katie, elbowing Kevin in the ribs. "It took Kelsey, Angela, and I weeks to find the appropriate name."

"You could have just named it hamburger," suggested Kevin with a sly grin as he stepped back far enough to dodge Katie's elbow.

Kelsey looked around the group of close friends and fellow officers. "This ship is designed for exploration. We will not go out looking for a fight, but if we have to we can defend ourselves. I think everyone here will find the name appropriate." Kelsey nodded toward several AIs who then signaled for the large cover over the ship's name to be dropped.

Jeremy's eyes widened as the name came into view. A tear formed in his eyes as he realized what Kelsey and the others had done.

"I give you the super exploration dreadnaught *New Horizon*," Kelsey said as she gestured toward the ship. "The *New Horizon* was Earth's first interstellar ship. While the ship was destroyed on its maiden voyage, it was where the five of us came together and realized we would never be apart."

"It was the birth of the Special Five," said Ariel. "It was the beginning of what would become the Federation."

Rear Admiral Barnes," said Kelsey, standing formerly in front of Kathryn. "I give you your new ship."

Kathryn stood for several long moments looking at the massive exploration dreadnaught. Then she looked over at Kelsey and the others. "No, it is our ship!"

Everyone started applauding and cheering. For several long minutes there were excited conversations as the gathered officers and friends discussed where the new ship would go first and what it might discover.

"It's a good name," Jeremy said to Kelsey as she came back over to stand next to him.

"It is the right name," Kelsey replied. "If not for the first *New Horizon* we would never have come together as a group."

Jeremy grinned. "Let's go on board and inspect your new ship. I'm sure you have a million things to show me."

"At least," replied Kelsey as she linked her arm in Jeremy's. "You will be going with us on our first exploration mission, won't you?"

"Of course, I wouldn't miss it for anything." Walking arm in arm, they started heading toward the ship followed by the rest of the crowd. This was a day for celebration and the beginning of a new age for the Special Five. The age of exploration.

Ariel and Clarissa followed behind with wide smiles on their faces. For the first time in hundreds of years all five of their friends would be leaving on a ship together. Granted Jeremy would be taking a fleet of dreadnaughts along, but he was expected to spend most of his time on the *New Horizon*.

"We did well," said Clarissa as she watched her smiling and laughing friends. "With everything we've been through, they are still together."

"Of course," replied Ariel with a pleased smile. "After all, they are the Special Five!"

The End

If you enjoyed *The Originator Wars: Conflict Unending* please post a review with some stars. Good reviews encourage an author to write and also help sell books. Reviews can be just a few short sentences, describing what you liked about the book. If you have suggestions, please contact me at my website, link below. Thank you for reading *The Originator Wars: Conflict Unending* and being so supportive.

For updates on current writing projects and future publications, go to my author website. Sign up for future notifications when my new books come out on Amazon.

Website: http://raymondlweil.com/

Follow on Facebook at Raymond L. Weil

Raymond L. Weil

Other Books by Raymond L. Weil
Available on Amazon

Moon Wreck (The Slaver Wars Book 1)
The Slaver Wars: Alien Contact (The Slaver Wars Book 2)
Moon Wreck: Fleet Academy (The Slaver Wars Book 3)
The Slaver Wars: First Strike (The Slaver Wars Book 4)
The Slaver Wars: Retaliation (The Slaver Wars Book 5)
The Slaver Wars: Galactic Conflict (The Slaver Wars Book 6)
The Slaver Wars: Endgame (The Slaver Wars Book 7)
The Slaver Wars: Books 1-3
-
Dragon Dreams
Dragon Dreams: Dragon Wars
Dragon Dreams: Gilmreth the Awakening
Dragon Dreams: Snowden the White Dragon
-
Star One: Tycho City: Survival
Star One: Neutron Star
Star One: Dark Star
Star One
-
Galactic Empire Wars: Destruction (Book 1)
Galactic Empire Wars: Emergence (Book 2)
Galactic Empire Wars: Rebellion (Book 3)
Galactic Empire Wars: The Alliance (Book 4)
Galactic Empire Wars: Insurrection (Book 5)
Galactic Empire Wars: The Beginning (Books 1-3)
-
The Lost Fleet: Galactic Search (Book 1)
The Lost Fleet: Into the Darkness (Book 2)
The Lost Fleet: Oblivion's Light (Book 3)
The Lost Fleet: Genesis (Book 4)
The Lost Fleet: Search for the Originators (Book 5)
-

The Originator Wars: Universe in Danger (Book 1)
The Originator Wars: Search for the Lost (Book 2)
The Originator Wars: Conflict Unending (Book 3)

(All dates are tentative)

Earth Fall: Invasion (Book 1) January 2018

ABOUT THE AUTHOR

I live in Clinton Oklahoma with my wife of 43 years and our cat. I attended college at SWOSU in Weatherford Oklahoma, majoring in Math with minors in Creative Writing and History.

My hobbies include watching soccer, reading, camping, and of course writing. I also enjoy playing with my five grandchildren. I have a very vivid imagination, which sometimes worries my friends. They never know what I'm going to say or what I'm going to do.

I am an avid reader and have a science fiction / fantasy collection of over two thousand paperbacks. I have always enjoyed reading science fiction and fantasy because of the awesome worlds authors create. I can hardly believe I'm now creating those worlds as well.

Made in the USA
Lexington, KY
16 July 2018